The Blacksmith's Bequest

Joss G. Hamilton

DEDICATION

To my beloved wife, whose passion for family history flows like a steady river through our home, weaving together the threads of our heritage with loving care. To my daughters, whose bright curiosity about Scottish graves and colonial hearths kindles the flame of Paterson pride in each new generation.

To my wife's family, whose own stories of connection and belonging have enriched our understanding of what it means to carry forward the wisdom of those who came before us.

To Mick and Betsy Jackes, whose generous sharing of family letters and *Die Mauer* historical notes breathed life into Thomas Staines' hammer and Rivers' preserved wisdom, transforming faded documents into living voices that speak across centuries. To my dear friend Gregory, whose animated conversations about blacksmiths and family legends over pints in Irish pubs first sparked the ember that became this tale. Your storytelling spirit lives in every page.

May this book, born from our pilgrimage to Scotland's ancient soil, carry these precious stories forward to future generations—from Arbuthnott's weathered kirkyard to Glen Lena's aging gates, from shame transformed to love triumphant.

CONTENTS

ACKNOWLEDGMENTS

The Blacksmith's Bequest grew from a pilgrimage to Scotland, where ancient castles and gravestones whispered stories of ancestors whose blood flows strong to this day. This journey to the homeland illuminated not just genealogical connections but the enduring power of family stories to guide and heal across generations.

My deepest gratitude to Mick and Betsy Jackes, whose meticulous research and generous correspondence opened the door to Thomas Staines' extraordinary transformation. Their sharing of family letters, historical documents, and insights from their personal archives provided the foundation upon which Sara Wilson's fictional journey could be built. Without their dedication to preserving family memory, this story could never have been told.

The landscapes that shaped our ancestors also shaped this narrative. Killua Castle's gothic majesty, glimpsed during travels through Westmeath, lent its timeless beauty to scenes of heritage and belonging. The folk ballads heard in Tipperary pubs, with their echoes of masterful storytelling, tuned the rhythm of Thomas's own ballad and the story that unfolded here—proof that some stories demand to be sung as well as spoken.

Special acknowledgment to the digital companions that aided this creative journey: Grok, my faithful travel companion who took notes during the Scotland pilgrimage and helped craft early drafts during holiday moments of inspiration; Claude from Anthropic, whose thoughtful assistance helped weave family history into literary narrative and brought Three Rivers Inn and ancient Scottish gravestones to literary life.

To my wife, daughters, and extended family, your unwavering passion for preserving and sharing family stories provided both inspiration and obligation. You reminded me daily that these tales are not mere entertainment but sacred trust—wisdom earned through sacrifice, preserved through love, transmitted through hope.

To Gregory, whose friendship, encouragement, and deep understanding of what makes stories matter sustained this project from conception to completion. Your influence echoes in every conversation about transformation and redemption.

Finally, to the next generation who will inherit these stories: may you find in Thomas and Catherine's journey the courage to face your own trials with faith, the wisdom to choose love over fear, and the understanding that some legacies are too precious to let fade into forgotten history.

The river flows on, carrying their voices to anyone willing to listen.

1 THE WEIGHT OF LOSS

Glen Lena, Springwood — October 2010

The settlement papers lay scattered across the kitchen table of Glen Lena like fallen leaves, their legal language cold as the Blue Mountains morning that crept through the farmhouse windows. Sara Wilson pressed her palms flat against the worn red gum timber, feeling the grain beneath her fingers—timber that had witnessed four generations of Paterson women, timber that would soon shelter strangers who would never understand the weight of memory it carried in every ring and weathered groove.

The eucalyptus oil that had seeped into the wood over decades released its sharp, medicinal scent as her palms warmed the surface. This was the table where Helena had rolled pastry for Sunday dinners, where Ellen had helped Sara with homework during countless school holidays, where three generations of women had shared secrets and sorrows over cups of tea that grew cold while stories stretched toward evening. Now it bore only the clinical documents that would sever Sara's last physical connection to a century of family history.

At thirty-five, Sara had learned that grief came in waves, but she hadn't expected it to taste like eucalyptus and regret, hadn't anticipated how the sound of a stranger's heels clicking across the verandah boards could feel like violation of sacred ground.

"Five hundred and eighteen thousand," she whispered to the empty kitchen, the number hollow as an echo in a dried well. The figure should have felt like salvation—enough to clear the debts that had accumulated like sediment after Ellen's death eighteen months earlier, enough to start over in Sydney's anonymous embrace. Instead, it felt like selling her bloodline by the pound, trading heritage for mere survival.

The real estate agent's departure had left silence that pressed against Sara's eardrums like deep water. Through the lace curtains—curtains Ellen had sewn by hand in 1965, cream cotton soft as butterfly wings now yellowed by mountain sun—the agent's silver sedan disappeared down the gravel drive that had crunched under four generations of footsteps, bicycle wheels, and the occasional delivery truck bringing supplies to sustain life in this pocket of the Blue Mountains where time moved differently than in the city below.

Ellen's funeral rose unbidden in Sara's memory—the way the chapel had smelled of lilies and grief, how Calvin had stood rigid beside the polished coffin, his carpenter's hands hanging useless at his sides. They hadn't spoken of real things that day, hadn't acknowledged how Ellen's death had left them orbiting each other like distant planets, each trapped in gravitational fields of loss they couldn't bridge. The months since had been careful phone calls and dutiful visits, love preserved in amber but no longer living, breathing, growing between them.

Sara's fingers found Ellen's locket at her throat, the Paterson crest worn smooth by three generations of nervous touching. Her mother had pressed it into her palm the day before she died, her voice paper-thin but fierce: "This stays with you, darling. We're Patersons. We endure."

But what good is enduring, Sara thought, when there's nothing left to endure for?

The phone's shrill ring shattered the kitchen's cathedral silence. Calvin's name appeared on the screen—the first time he'd called since their stilted conversation at Ellen's birthday in March, when they'd managed twenty minutes of careful pleasantries before running out of safe topics. Sara's thumb hovered over the answer button, knowing that conversation would be carved from stone, each word carefully weighed and rationed like wartime provisions.

She let it ring.

The kitchen fell quiet again, save for the grandfather clock's patient tick in the hallway—a clock Rivers Paterson had wound every Sunday morning until her death in 1918, its brass pendulum marking time that connected past to present in steady, reliable rhythm. Four generations of routine, snuffed out by financial necessity and a daughter's inability to hold onto what mattered most.

Glen Lena felt different now that strangers owned it, though the papers wouldn't be filed until Monday. The house seemed to exhale memories through its weatherboard walls—Helena's laughter echoing from the sun-drenched conservatory where she'd cultivated prize-winning roses, Ellen's voice calling from the vegetable garden where she'd taught Sara the difference between weeds and wildflowers, Rivers' presence still lingering in the master bedroom where she'd died peacefully in 1918, surrounded by children who carried her father's story forward into an uncertain future.

How do you explain to new owners that floorboards creak with the weight of whispered confidences? How do you transfer the deed to rooms that hold the accumulated love of a century?

Sara pulled her cardigan tighter against the morning chill and climbed the narrow stairs to the attic, each step a small betrayal of the women who had climbed these same stairs carrying baskets of laundry, boxes of Christmas decorations, and the careful accumulation of a lifetime's worth of things too precious to discard but too fragile for daily use. She'd been putting off this final sweep, knowing that once she'd cleared the last of the family detritus, Glen Lena would truly be lost—not just sold, but emptied of the stories that had made it more than mere shelter.

The attic smelled of lavender sachets and time—Helena's sachets, sewn in 1945 when she'd moved into Glen Lena as Walter's young bride, bringing German recipes and Scottish determination to a house that had been built by love but needed a woman's touch to become truly home. Dust motes danced in the morning light that slanted through the dormer window, and Sara could almost hear her grandmother's voice: *"Stories live in the corners, darling. You just have to know where to look."*

She'd heard that voice often as a child during summer holidays that stretched like golden promises, usually accompanied by the rustle of photograph albums and the sweet-sharp scent of Helena's Victoria sponge cooling on the kitchen windowsill. Helena Jean Paterson had been the family's keeper of stories, her memory a vault of names and dates and small rebellions that stretched back to the Scottish Borders. She'd died when Sara was sixteen, taking most of those stories with her, leaving only fragments that Ellen had tried to preserve through scattered anecdotes and half-remembered genealogical connections.

Stories that would die with this house unless someone claimed responsibility for their preservation.

A tea chest in the corner caught her attention—one she'd somehow missed in previous raids through the accumulated archaeology of family life. The cardboard was soft with age, splitting at the corners like tired skin, but Helena's careful script was still legible across the top: *"R. Paterson - Personal Effects."*

Rivers. The great-grandmother Sara had never met but whose presence haunted every corner of Glen Lena like a benevolent ghost. The woman who'd built this house in 1892 with William's carpentry skills and her own iron determination, who'd raised five children here while preserving her father's memory through stories that transformed shame into pride, exile into opportunity. The woman whose portrait hung in the hallway, her dark eyes serious above a high-necked blouse, her mouth set in a line that suggested she'd seen enough of the world's sorrows to last several lifetimes but had chosen hope anyway.

Sara lifted the chest's flaps with trembling fingers, understanding without words that she was about to encounter something that would change everything she thought she knew about family history, about the weight of inheritance that extended beyond material possessions into the realm of obligation and love.

Inside, wrapped in tissue paper yellow as old bones, lay a collection of items that seemed to pulse with accumulated significance: a hand-stitched sampler reading "Home is Where Love Lives - R.P. 1895," a wooden thimble worn smooth by decades of mending what could be mended, a small leather journal bound with string that had probably once been white but had aged to the color of cream left too long in the sun.

And beneath it all, a tin box no larger than a prayer book, its rust-red surface scratched with initials that made Sara's breath catch in her throat: "T.S."

Thomas Staines—the name whispered in family stories like incantation, Rivers' father who'd drowned in the Bell River the day she was born. The convict blacksmith whose shame had somehow transformed into pride over the generations, whose story had been polished smooth by retelling until it gleamed like something precious rather than shameful.

Inside the tin, five letters lay folded like sleeping birds, their paper translucent with age and handling. The top letter bore an address in careful copperplate that made Sara's throat close with emotion: *"To my daughter, yet to be born."* Below it, a pressed flower—a thistle, its purple petals faded to grey—lay like a bookmark between the pages of the past and whatever revelation awaited in words written by hands that had been dust for nearly sixty years.

Sara sank onto the attic floor, her back against the dormer wall where generations of children had probably sat reading books and dreaming dreams, and unfolded the first letter with surgical care. The ink had faded to sepia, but the words were clear, written in a hand that spoke of limited formal education but unlimited capacity for love:

My dearest child,

I write these words not knowing if I will live to speak them, but knowing that love travels farther than time. You grow in your mother's belly as I write, a hope I may never hold but treasure beyond measure. If you read this, know that your father was a man who fell from grace but climbed toward redemption...

The words blurred as tears tracked down Sara's cheeks. Here was love distilled to its essence, a father's desperate need to be known by the child he might never meet. She thought of Calvin, sealed away in his Gosford workshop with his grief and stubborn pride, his own love locked behind walls that eighteen months of careful distance had only reinforced. When had they stopped talking about anything that mattered? When had duty replaced affection, obligation eclipsed genuine connection?

Outside, a kookaburra's call echoed across the valley, wild and mournful as a song of loss. Sara pressed the letter to her chest and closed her eyes, feeling the weight of four generations settling on her shoulders like a mantle she'd never expected to wear. Ellen had tried to carry these stories forward, but Sara had been too busy with university, then work, then the slow dissolution of her marriage to David to listen with the attention such stories deserved. Now Ellen was gone, Calvin was unreachable behind walls of grief, and Glen Lena was about to belong to strangers who would never understand what they'd inherited.

But Thomas Staines' letters remained. And in them, perhaps, lay the key to understanding what it truly meant to be a Paterson—not just by blood, but by choice, by the deliberate act of carrying love forward through time like an Olympic flame that must never be allowed to die.

Sara looked around the attic one last time, seeing it not as a repository of old things but as a treasure house of stories waiting to be told, wisdom waiting to be claimed by someone brave enough to accept the responsibility that came with such inheritance. The new owners could have the timber and stone, the roses and the rain-stained walls. But they couldn't have this—the accumulation of love and loss that made a house into something more than shelter, that transformed mere dwelling into sanctuary where souls could rest and heal and remember who they were.

She gathered the letters, the tin box, and Rivers' journal into her arms and stood slowly, her decision crystallizing like sugar in cold water. Glen Lena might be lost, but the Paterson legacy didn't have to be. She had a father to reconcile with, a family history to resurrect, and a story to tell that stretched from the convict ships of the 1830s to this moment of grief and possibility in 2010.

The grandfather clock chimed ten as she descended the stairs, its sound no longer mournful but urgent, marking not an ending but a beginning. Calvin might have retreated into silence, but Sara had found her voice in the whisper of old paper and faded ink.

She had work to do.

The kookaburra called again as Sara loaded the last box into her car, its laughter echoing off the mountains like a promise that some stories refuse to die, that love carefully preserved can bridge any distance, that endings are simply beginnings wearing different clothes.

THE BLACKSMITH'S BEQUEST

Three Rivers Inn, Wellington, New South Wales
18th August, 1852

My dearest child,

I write these words not knowing if I will live to speak them, but knowing that love travels farther than time. You grow in your mother's belly as I write, a hope I may never hold but treasure beyond measure. If you read this, know that your father was a man who fell from grace but climbed toward redemption. The Bell River runs high with winter rains outside our inn, its voice a constant reminder of water's power to give life and take it in equal measure. I have learned to listen to such voices in my seventeen years upon this continent, for they speak truths that men in their pride often fail to hear.

You must understand, my precious daughter—for I am certain in my heart that you shall be a daughter, as beautiful and determined as your blessed mother—that I write not from weakness but from the greatest strength I have ever possessed: the knowledge that love requires no promise of return, demands no certainty of survival, asks only that we speak truth across whatever distances may separate us.

I am Thomas Staines, born in the year of our Lord 1806 in England's green counties, where my people worked iron and tilled soil and lived according to principles I thought immutable until pride and desperation conspired to teach me otherwise. Your mother knows some portion of my history—the shame that brought me to these shores in chains, the long years of bondage that were my just punishment for choosing theft over honest poverty, the slow awakening of conscience that finally made me worthy of her love.

The sin that changed my life forever was born in a single moment when pride convinced me that I deserved what another man possessed, when need argued more persuasively than conscience, when the seductive voice of immediate relief drowned out the quieter counsel of long-term wisdom. I took what was not mine—a pony belonging to a farmer who had several, who could afford the loss where I could not afford continued deprivation.

Seven years I served in Sydney's heat, working iron in chains that chafed my wrists but could not prevent me from learning the most important lesson of my life: that a man's worth is not measured by his circumstances but by how he responds to them, not by what he has lost but by what he chooses to preserve, not by the mistakes that brought him low but by the character he builds from the raw materials of humility and hope.

When Governor Gipps granted me my Ticket of Leave in 1843, I walked from Sydney with nothing but the clothes upon my back and the skills in my hands, yet I felt richer than I had ever felt as a free man in England. The pride that had destroyed my former life had been replaced by something far more valuable: the quiet confidence that comes from knowing you have faced your worst self and chosen to become something better.

I met your mother, my beloved Catherine, in Bathurst's market square on a day when spring sunshine seemed to bless every corner of creation with possibilities unlimited. When she smiled at me—a rough ex-convict with calloused hands and a past that shame had marked—I felt for the first time in years that I might be worthy of another person's affection, that love might be possible for a man who had lost everything and slowly, patiently, begun to rebuild his life upon foundations more solid than pride.

We have been wed now these seven years, my darling, and built together this inn that bears your name though you have not yet drawn breath to speak it. Three Rivers Inn stands where the Bell, the Macquarie, and the Cudgegong meet, their waters joining as our lives have joined, flowing together toward destinations we cannot see but trust will prove worthwhile.

If I survive to guide your first steps, teach you to read, help you discover your own gifts and inclinations, I will consider such privilege the greatest blessing of a life that has already received more mercy than any man deserves. If I am called to other service before those opportunities arrive, I will trust that these words carry whatever wisdom my presence might have provided.

Remember that you are beloved—by the mother who carries you with such joy, by the father who writes these words with hands that ache to hold you, by the God who grants second chances to anyone willing to undertake the difficult work of earning them.

Your devoted father, who loves you beyond measure,

Thomas Staines

2 THE FIRST LETTER

Kirribilli Apartment, Sydney — October 2010

Sara Wilson sat at her kitchen table as Sydney Harbor glittered beyond windows that framed the most expensive view in her modest one-bedroom apartment, the tin box open before her like Pandora's container after the lid had been lifted and everything inside released to change the world. The city lights reflected off the water in patterns that shifted with each ferry's wake, but she saw none of it. Her universe had narrowed to the piece of paper trembling in her hands, its edges soft with age and handling, its words written in careful copperplate that belonged to another century entirely.

The grandfather clock she'd inherited from Glen Lena ticked in the corner—the only piece of furniture she'd managed to save from the estate sale—its familiar rhythm now marking time between her old understanding of family history and whatever revelation lay in Thomas Staines' precise script. She'd been staring at the first letter for twenty minutes, reading the same opening lines until they burned themselves into her memory:

My dearest child, I write these words not knowing if I will live to speak them, but knowing that love travels farther than time. You grow in your mother's belly as I write, a hope I may never hold but treasure beyond measure...

The words hit her like physical blows, each sentence reshaping everything she thought she knew about the family stories Helena had whispered during childhood visits to Glen Lena. Thomas Staines—the convict ancestor who'd drowned in a flood—hadn't been some distant, shameful figure whose story was best left buried in the past. He'd been a father writing love letters to his unborn daughter, a man whose words carried such raw emotion that they seemed to pulse with life despite being written more than 150 years ago.

Sara's hands shook as she set the letter down on the kitchen table that bore no resemblance to the worn red gum surface where she'd discovered these treasures hours earlier. This modern apartment with its clean lines and harbor views suddenly felt like a stage set, all surface and no substance, lacking the accumulated weight of memory that had made Glen Lena feel like home even when she'd been forced to sell it.

I need to call Calvin, she thought, reaching for her phone before stopping herself. What would she say? That she'd found letters from a convict great-great-great-grandfather who'd written love letters to his daughter from what sounded like a death bed? That everything they'd been told about Thomas Staines—the family shame, the drowning, the simplified story of colonial hardship—might be fragments of something far more complex and beautiful?

Calvin would listen with the patience he brought to all her enthusiasms, make appropriate sounds of interest, and ask practical questions about provenance and authenticity. But would he understand the way her chest felt like it might explode from the pressure of recognizing something precious that had been waiting in the dark for someone to claim it?

The letter's second sentence made her breath catch: *Know that your father was a man who fell from grace but climbed toward redemption. The Bell River runs high with winter rains outside our inn, its voice a constant reminder of water's power to give life and take it in equal measure...*

Fell from grace. The euphemism her family had always used—"Thomas got into trouble in the old country"—suddenly took on weight and specificity. This wasn't just colonial hardship or bad luck. Thomas Staines had done something that brought him to the attention of the law, something that resulted in transportation to Australia in chains. But the tone of his writing suggested not shame but hard-won wisdom, not bitterness but gratitude for lessons that suffering had taught him.

Sara stood and moved to the windows, looking out at Sydney Harbor where convict ships had once anchored, where thousands of men and women had begun new lives under circumstances that ranged from horrific to miraculous depending on their character and luck. Thomas's ship—whatever vessel had carried him across oceans she could barely imagine—had passed through these same waters, carrying a man who would somehow transform whatever circumstances had brought him here into a love so deep it could reach across centuries to guide a daughter he'd never met.

The city beyond her windows felt different now, charged with historical weight she'd never considered. Every street, every building, every harbor installation existed because people like Thomas had built them—convicts and immigrants and refugees who'd transformed exile into opportunity, who'd created civilization from materials as unpromising as their own broken lives and desperate hopes.

Her laptop sat closed on the counter, and Sara found herself opening it with the unconscious movements of someone whose professional life had trained her to turn confusion into research questions, emotional upheaval into methodical investigation. Her work as a freelance researcher—tracking down documents for legal firms, genealogical societies, and academic institutions—had given her skills that applied perfectly to family history, assuming she could maintain enough emotional distance to treat this as a project rather than personal revelation.

Google: "Thomas Staines convict Australia 1835"

The search returned scattered fragments—genealogical websites that listed him as Rivers Paterson's father, shipping records that mentioned a "T. Staines" aboard HMS *Moffatt* in 1836, brief mentions in colonial history sites that identified him as one of the flood victims at Wellington in 1852. But nothing that captured the voice she'd heard in his letter, nothing that explained how a man who'd "fallen from grace" had become someone capable of writing words that made her throat close with emotion she couldn't name.

Google: "HMS Moffatt convict ship 1836"

More specific results this time—passenger manifests, descriptions of the voyage, historical accounts of transportation that made her stomach turn with their clinical details about overcrowding, disease, and mortality rates that treated human cargo as acceptable losses in the colonial enterprise. She found herself scanning lists of names, looking for Thomas Staines among the hundreds of men whose crimes and sentences were recorded with bureaucratic precision.

"Thomas Staines, age 30, convicted Leicester Assizes, theft of livestock, sentence: transportation for life."

There it was. Not euphemism or family mythology, but official record of whatever had brought him to write letters that carried such emotional weight they seemed to vibrate with accumulated love. Theft of livestock. The crime that had stripped away whatever life he'd built in England and delivered him to circumstances where he'd learned "what prosperity had never taught him."

Sara printed the page and added it to a folder that was already growing thick with preliminary research. Her dining table—a sleek glass surface that had seemed sophisticated when she'd furnished the apartment after her divorce—was now covered with printouts, notebooks, and the fragile letters that had started this obsession. The contrast between Thomas's nineteenth-century handwriting and contemporary laser printing struck her as somehow significant, proof that some things transcended the technologies used to preserve them.

The second letter lay unopened, its seal brittle with age but still intact. Sara found herself reluctant to break it, understanding instinctively that each letter would take her deeper into Thomas's world, further from the safe distance of academic curiosity toward whatever emotional territory awaited someone willing to receive his words with the attention they deserved.

Instead, she reached for Rivers' journal, its leather binding still supple after ninety years of careful preservation. Helena had mentioned this journal during Sara's childhood—"Your great-grandmother Rivers wrote down everything she remembered about her father"—but Sara had assumed it contained the same sanitized family stories she'd heard at holiday dinners, simplified narratives suitable for children who didn't need to know about shame or suffering or the complex process of transformation that had made their family possible.

The journal's first page proved her wrong: *"I write these words to preserve not just my father's memory but the truth of his transformation from convicted thief to beloved father, from man who took what belonged to others to man who gave everything—including life itself—for others' welfare."*

Convicted thief. Rivers had known the truth about Thomas's crime, had understood the magnitude of his transformation from selfishness to sacrifice. The journal promised not just family history but analysis of what that history meant, mature understanding of how one man's journey from shame to honor could guide anyone facing their own choice between despair and redemption.

Sara found herself reading Rivers' careful script with the same intensity she brought to archival research, recognizing in the writing the voice of someone who'd thought deeply about inheritance and obligation, about the difference between preserving family stories and understanding their significance for anyone willing to learn from them.

"He taught me through his letters that redemption is not an event but a process, not something that happens to us but something we choose to make happen through daily decisions to place others' welfare above our own convenience."

The observation made Sara look up from the journal toward the harbor where late-night ferries carried their cargo of workers and tourists and people seeking whatever destinations would provide meaning or comfort or simply the next chapter in lives that required constant navigation between competing demands. How many of them were facing their own choices between selfishness and service, their own opportunities for transformation that required giving up comfort for growth?

Her phone buzzed with a text message: *"Called earlier. Hope you're doing well. Dad."*

Sara stared at the message, feeling the careful distance Calvin maintained even in digital communication. *Hope you're doing well.* Not "I miss you" or "I was thinking about you" or "I need to talk to someone who understands what Ellen's death did to our family." Just polite concern from someone who'd learned that emotional safety required careful rationing of vulnerability.

She thought of Thomas writing to Rivers *"not knowing if I will live to speak them, but knowing that love travels farther than time."* How different those words were from Calvin's careful text, how much more risk they carried, how much more love they demonstrated despite being separated by death and 160 years from their intended recipient.

What if I wrote him a real letter? The thought surprised her with its intensity. Not a text or email or careful phone call, but actual letter on paper, written by hand, carrying the weight of attention that such communication required. Words that couldn't be deleted or edited or sent without conscious decision to risk connection that might not be returned.

But first, she needed to understand what Thomas's letters contained, what wisdom he'd preserved for Rivers that might apply to her own relationship with the father who'd retreated behind walls of grief and pride. The second letter waited, its seal like a promise that more revelations lay ahead for anyone brave enough to break it open.

The harbor sounds provided gentle soundtrack as Sara reached for the letter—ferry horns, gentle lapping of waves against seawalls, the distant hum of traffic crossing the bridge that connected north to south, past to present, isolation to whatever lay beyond the careful distances people maintained to protect themselves from additional loss.

Thomas Staines had written his letters believing he might die before Rivers could read them, understanding that some communications were too important to delay until circumstances felt more favorable. Sara broke the seal and unfolded pages that had waited 160 years for someone ready to receive whatever guidance they contained about transformation, redemption, and the kind of love that proved stronger than death itself.

The letter began: *"My dearest child, I write these words not knowing if I will live to speak them, but knowing that love travels farther than time. You grow in your mother's belly as I write, a hope I may never hold but treasure beyond measure. If you read this, know that your father was a man who fell from grace but climbed toward redemption. The Bell River runs high with winter rains outside our inn, its voice a constant reminder of water's power to give life and take it in equal measure."*

Outside her window, Sydney Harbor stretched toward horizons that had once held impossible promise for people like Thomas, people who'd lost everything they thought they needed and discovered in exile the possibility of becoming someone they'd never imagined possible. Sara settled deeper into her chair and read on, following his voice across oceans and centuries, understanding that she was about to learn something essential about the difference between existing and truly living, between survival and transformation, between the kind of love that protected itself and the kind that risked everything for others' welfare.

The night was no longer young, and she had four more letters waiting to be opened, each one promising to carry her deeper into Thomas's world and closer to understanding what Rivers had learned about redemption, what Helena had preserved about family obligation, what Ellen had tried to pass on before cancer silenced her voice.

Sara read until dawn, Thomas's words teaching her something new about courage, about the kind of transformation that was possible for anyone willing to choose it, about love that could bridge any distance if offered with sufficient faith and patience and willingness to serve purposes larger than individual comfort.

The harbor lightened beyond her windows as she finished the second letter, understanding that her journey into family history had become something far more significant: a map for her own transformation, a guide for healing relationships she'd thought were irreparably damaged, proof that some inheritances were worth more than money or property because they provided wisdom that could reshape everything she thought she knew about love and loss and the courage required to choose connection over safety.

Calvin's text still glowed on her phone screen. Sara picked it up and began typing her response, Thomas's example teaching her that some communications were too important to delay, too precious to reduce to polite pleasantries when honest vulnerability might bridge gaps that careful distance had only widened.

"Dad, I found something at Glen Lena that changes everything I thought I knew about our

family. Can we talk? Really talk? I think you need to hear this story."

She pressed send before courage could desert her, understanding that transformation always began with someone's willingness to risk everything for the chance to create something beautiful from broken materials, to bridge distances that seemed unbridgeable, to prove that love could indeed travel farther than time if offered with sufficient faith and determination.

Outside, Sydney woke to another day of possibility, and Sara Wilson began the work of becoming worthy of the inheritance she'd received, of honoring the sacrifice that had made her existence possible, of proving that Thomas Staines' transformation could still inspire redemption in anyone brave enough to choose it.

Sara's Journal

Kirribilli Apartment, Sydney October 20th, 2010 - 3:47 AM

The Weight of Inheritance

I can't sleep. Thomas's letter lies on my kitchen table like a live thing, his words pulsing with life across 158 years. *"My dearest child, I write these words not knowing if I will live to speak them, but knowing that love travels farther than time."*

How do you process discovering that your family history isn't just names and dates, but actual love made tangible? This isn't genealogy anymore—it's archaeology of the heart, and I'm unprepared for what I'm excavating.

His handwriting is so careful, so deliberate. Each letter formed with the precision of someone who understood words might be all he could leave behind. I keep touching the paper, trying to connect with the hands that held this same page, the heart that bled these words onto paper that somehow survived flood and fire and time itself.

The man who wrote this letter—a convicted thief transported in chains—sounds more like a father than mine ever has. Not because Calvin doesn't love me, but because this Thomas had stripped away every pretense, every social convention, every comfortable distance that keeps us from saying what actually matters.

"If you read this, know that your father was a man who fell from grace but climbed toward redemption."

Redemption. What a loaded word. I've been thinking I inherited failure when Glen Lena slipped through my fingers. But what if I inherited possibility instead? What if the loss of the house was necessary to find these letters, this story, this proof that transformation is possible even when circumstances seem designed to prevent it?

Ellen's locket feels warm against my throat. She would have loved this discovery—not just the family connection, but the story itself. Ellen believed in love that persisted, in the kind of stubborn hope that builds bridges across impossible distances. Thomas's letter proves such love actually exists.

But why does reading about his transformation make me ache for Calvin? We've been so careful with each other since Ellen died, so polite and distant and determined not to cause additional pain. Reading Thomas's raw honesty makes our cautious conversations feel like betrayal of everything love could be if we had the courage to risk it.

"Love travels farther than time."

If that's true, then the distance between Sydney and Gosford is nothing. The silence that's grown between Dad and me since the funeral is nothing. The grief that makes vulnerability feel dangerous is nothing compared to the love that could heal it if we were brave enough to choose connection over safety.

I have four more letters to read. Four more windows into a man who learned to love so completely that death became his final gift to those he cherished. But I suspect this first letter has already changed everything. I can feel something cracking open in my chest—not breaking, but flowering. Like soil that's been frozen too long finally accepting the possibility of spring.

Thomas Staines was transported for theft, but he left behind proof that redemption is possible for anyone willing to choose it. His great-great-great-granddaughter has been transported by grief, but maybe she can learn from his example how to find her way home.

The harbor is beginning to lighten beyond my window. Somewhere in Gosford, Calvin is probably awake too, working in his shop because sleep won't come when the heart is too full or too empty to rest. Maybe it's time to stop protecting our separate griefs and discover what they might become if shared with someone who understands that love is worth whatever risk vulnerability demands.

Thomas wrote to a daughter he might never meet. Maybe I should call a father I've been too afraid to reach.

3 THE CONVICT'S TALE

North Kilworth, Leicestershire — April 1835

The forge breathed like a living thing in the pre-dawn darkness, its coal heart glowing red as a dragon's eye while Thomas Staines worked the bellows with the practiced rhythm that had marked his mornings for fifteen years. At twenty-nine, his hands bore the permanent geography of his trade—black crescents under his nails that no amount of scrubbing could remove, burn scars mapping his forearms like the chronicles of countless small battles with fire and iron, calluses thick as leather from gripping hammer handles that had been shaped by his father's hands and his grandfather's before that.

The village of North Kilworth lay sleeping beyond the forge's circle of light, its thatched cottages and narrow lanes still wrapped in the kind of profound quiet that belonged to rural England before industry discovered the countryside. Here, where the River Avon meandered between water meadows that flooded each winter and dried to gold each summer, time moved according to seasons and harvests rather than the mechanical rhythms that were transforming cities into something Thomas could barely recognize during his rare journeys to Leicester's markets.

But even in this pocket of older time, change pressed against the edges of daily life like flood water testing the boundaries of familiar ground. The economic troubles that had followed Napoleon's final defeat hung over Leicestershire like a permanent storm cloud, making everyone careful, suspicious, desperate in ways that bred both extraordinary generosity and its opposite. Thomas felt the pressure each morning as he lit his forge, understanding that the gap between survival and catastrophe had narrowed to margins that left no room for pride or the comfortable assumptions that had sustained previous generations.

The horseshoe taking shape on his anvil would grace the hoof of Farmer Blackwood's mare—three shillings earned through the marriage of fire, iron, and knowledge passed down from his father before consumption claimed him, and his grandfather before the harvest failures of 1816 broke his spirit along with his back. Three shillings that represented the difference between keeping his forge for another month and joining the ranks of dispossessed craftsmen who wandered the roads seeking work that no longer existed in sufficient quantity to sustain the skills they carried.

Thomas's hammer rang against the steel in steady percussion, each strike calculated to bend metal to his will without shattering it—a lesson that applied to more than blacksmithing in times when pressure could break men as easily as iron if they lacked the wisdom to bend rather than resist forces larger than their individual strength. The work required not just muscle but respect for materials, understanding of how heat and patience could transform raw iron into objects of beauty and utility that would serve their purposes for decades.

The forge itself occupied the ground floor of a stone building that had housed three generations of Staines blacksmiths, its walls blackened by smoke and sparks but solid as the day Thomas's grandfather had fitted each stone with the precision that came from understanding he was creating something meant to outlast his own lifetime. The upstairs rooms had once sheltered a wife and children, but Thomas lived alone now, his bachelor existence shaped more by economic necessity than choice—what woman would marry a man whose prospects had narrowed to three shillings a week and the hope that sufficient work might materialize to justify optimism about the future?

"Early start today, Thomas?"

He turned to find Mrs. Caldwell at the forge door, her market basket and practical dress suggesting a dawn journey to Leicester for supplies her husband's shop couldn't provide. Sarah Caldwell had known him since boyhood, had watched him grow from the scrawny lad who pumped bellows for his father into the broad-shouldered man who now commanded his own anvil with skills that would have been valuable in better times but felt increasingly irrelevant in circumstances that rewarded expedience over craftsmanship.

Her smile held the comfortable warmth of long familiarity, but Thomas caught the shadow of worry that had haunted too many faces in North Kilworth these past months. The village's prosperity had always depended on agriculture and the trades that supported it, but crop failures and falling prices had created a cascade of troubles that touched everyone from landowners to laborers, craftsmen to shopkeepers who extended credit they couldn't afford to neighbors who might never be able to repay it.

"Farmer Blackwood needs his mare shod before the morning plowing," Thomas replied, lifting the horseshoe with his tongs to examine its curve against the light that streamed through windows his mother had cleaned just yesterday, though she would never admit to such charity from someone whose own circumstances left little margin for helping others. "Ground's finally soft enough for the spring sowing, but only if we make the most of these few dry days."

"Aye, we all need to make the most of what little we're given these days," Mrs. Caldwell said, adjusting her shawl against the morning chill that lingered despite the forge's warmth. "My William says trade's been slow this month. Folks mending what they have rather than buying new, making do with tools that should have been replaced years ago."

Thomas nodded, understanding the unspoken questions in her words. How long could a blacksmith survive when farmers couldn't afford to replace worn tools, when the gentry tightened their purses and common folk made do with implements held together by wire and prayer? The economic landscape had shifted beneath their feet like ground made treacherous by hidden springs, making every step forward feel uncertain despite skills that had once guaranteed steady work and reasonable prosperity.

"Work's there for those willing to seek it," Thomas said, the words sounding more confident than he felt. "Always someone needs a shoe fitted, a pot mended, a tool sharpened. Just have to be willing to travel further to find them these days."

Mrs. Caldwell's expression suggested she heard the uncertainty beneath his assurance, the careful optimism of someone trying to convince himself as much as his listener. But she merely nodded and continued toward the village square, leaving Thomas alone with thoughts that circled like water seeking its level, always returning to the mathematics of survival that governed his daily choices with increasing urgency.

The truth was that work had grown scarce as winter wheat in drought years. The rent on his forge—five pounds quarterly to Lord Arbuthnot's estate—loomed like thunder that promised storms whether he was prepared for them or not. His mother's cottage, fifty yards down the lane that connected forge to village proper, needed repairs that required money he didn't possess. The thatched roof leaked rain onto the bed where she slept fitfully through nights made difficult by arthritis that worsened with each damp season.

Mary Staines, at fifty-two, bore her struggles with the quiet dignity Thomas associated with true gentility—the bearing that supported her claims about their Paterson heritage, her insistence that they descended from people who had once held land and position before circumstances and poor choices had reduced their circumstances to the daily struggle for subsistence that marked England's forgotten poor. She never complained about the bucket that caught water from loose thatch, never mentioned the cold that seeped through walls that needed attention he couldn't afford to provide.

Instead, she maintained the small rituals that preserved dignity when prosperity had long since departed: the weekly cleaning that kept their humble quarters spotless, the careful mending that extended the life of clothes worn thin by years of service, the herb garden behind her cottage that provided both medicine and flavoring for meals stretched to cover too many days with too little substance. Her hands, once soft enough to suggest genteel upbringing, now bore calluses from work that gentlewomen weren't supposed to perform, but she approached each task with the grace of someone who understood that character was measured by how one faced adversity rather than how successfully one avoided it.

Thomas had inherited more than blacksmithing skills from his father—he'd inherited the weight of responsibility for his mother's welfare, the knowledge that his choices would determine whether she spent her remaining years in comfort or want. The burden sat heavy on his shoulders each morning as he lit the forge, understanding that his pride and her security were linked in ways that made personal satisfaction secondary to practical necessity.

But it was pride that created the problem, pride that whispered in his ear during the long hours when hammer rang against anvil and sparks flew like prayers seeking heaven. Thomas Staines was a skilled craftsman whose work rivaled anything produced in Leicester's more prosperous shops, whose horseshoes wore evenly and whose tools held their edges through seasons of hard use. Yet he struggled to earn enough for basic necessities while men with less skill but better connections prospered through circumstances that had nothing to do with merit or effort.

The morning progressed in familiar rhythms—the measured breathing of the bellows, the ring of hammer on anvil, the hiss of hot iron meeting the quenching bucket that stood like a baptismal font beside his workstation. Thomas completed Farmer Blackwood's order and began work on a set of nails for the church roof repairs, his hands moving with unconscious competence while his mind wrestled with questions that had no easy answers.

The church commission paid only two shillings but came with the implicit understanding that faithful completion might lead to additional work, recommendations to other parishes facing similar repairs with limited budgets for craftsmen whose skills could ensure that patches lasted long enough to justify their cost. Thomas had accepted the job despite its poor payment because reputation mattered more than immediate profit in communities where word-of-mouth could make or break a craftsman's prospects.

By midday, the forge had grown stifling despite the April breeze that carried the scent of plowed earth and new grass through open doors that framed the village beyond like pictures in a book about rural life that was rapidly becoming historical curiosity rather than living reality. Thomas stripped to his shirt sleeves, his arms gleaming with sweat and the reflected glow of coals that had been his constant companions since boyhood.

The work was honest, the skills inherited from generations of craftsmen who had found dignity in transformation of raw materials into useful objects that served their communities' needs. But honesty, Thomas reflected with growing bitterness, was a luxury that required financial security to maintain. Pride, it seemed, was the privilege of men who could afford their principles without watching their mothers position buckets to catch rainwater while arthritis made every movement a small agony endured without complaint.

His mother appeared in the doorway as the church bells chimed noon, her slight figure silhouetted against spring sunshine that revealed how much weight she'd lost during the winter months when heating their cottage meant choosing between warmth and food. Mary Staines moved carefully these days, arthritis stealing the fluid grace that had once made her the acknowledged beauty of North Kilworth's village dances, but she carried herself with dignity that spoke of inner strength refined rather than broken by trials that would have defeated someone whose character had not been tested and proven worthy of whatever challenges life presented.

"You missed your breakfast again," she said, settling onto the three-legged stool he kept for visitors with movements that spoke of joints that protested such efforts but would not be denied. "A man can't work iron on an empty stomach any more than he can shoe horses with cold metal."

Thomas set down his hammer and accepted the wrapped bread and cheese she produced from her apron pocket, recognizing in the modest meal the sacrifice of someone who had given her own portion to ensure he maintained strength necessary for work that supported them both. The bread was coarse, made from flour that bore the grainy texture of economy rather than preference, but it had been prepared with care that transformed simple ingredients into expression of love that asked nothing in return.

"How are you managing, Mother?" he asked, studying her face for signs of discomfort she would never admit while he had troubles of his own to navigate. "The roof tiles over your bed chamber—they're still loose after last week's storm?"

Mary waved away his concern with the gesture of a woman who had learned to minimize her needs rather than burden others with problems they lacked resources to solve. "I've placed a bucket to catch the drips when the rain comes. It's sufficient until better times arrive."

But Thomas saw the shadows beneath her eyes, the careful way she moved that spoke of nights spent cold and uncomfortable while water found its way through deteriorating thatch that required attention from craftsmen whose services cost more than their combined resources could cover. The cottage that had sheltered three generations of Staines family required repairs that would consume weeks of earnings he couldn't afford to sacrifice without risking the forge that provided their only income.

"The Patersons," he said, settling beside her on a stack of iron bars while they shared the meal that represented both sustenance and communion between two people whose love for each other complicated every decision about money and survival. "Tell me again about the old days, when our people had land and standing, when circumstances didn't force every choice between pride and necessity."

Mary's expression brightened, shadows lifting as she retreated into memories that provided refuge from present difficulties that seemed to multiply like rabbits in spring gardens. Her voice took on the particular cadence reserved for stories that had been polished smooth through countless tellings, narratives that connected their present struggles to heritage that suggested temporary setbacks rather than permanent reduced circumstances.

"Your great-grandfather's brother served Lord Arbuthnot himself," she began, her words painting pictures of comfort and security that felt like fairy tales to someone whose daily reality involved calculating whether three shillings would stretch to cover coal for the forge and food for their table. "Managed the estate accounts and sat at the high table during feast days, where the quality recognized his judgment about matters that affected everyone from tenant farmers to village craftsmen."

She spoke of Paterson men who had been known for their character, their education, their pride in honest dealing that never bent to accommodate expedience or personal advantage. Thomas listened with the part of his attention that wasn't occupied by the bitter irony of hearing about ancestors who had possessed everything he lacked—security, respect, the comfortable assumption that hard work would be rewarded with prosperity sufficient to maintain dignity and provide for family needs without daily anxiety about survival.

"What happened to it all?" he asked, though he'd heard the answer countless times and knew it by heart—the slow erosion that claimed most families who lacked the flexibility to adapt when circumstances shifted beneath their feet like ground made unreliable by hidden springs. "The land, the position, the prosperity that should have been passed down to us?"

"Time," Mary said simply, her tone carrying acceptance that had been earned through decades of facing reality without flinching from its implications. "Poor harvests, unwise investments, the cost of wars that benefited lords but impoverished their servants. Your great-grandfather chose pride over practicality, refused to bend when bending might have preserved what remained. By the time your grandfather inherited, there was little left but stories and the knowledge that we descended from better circumstances."

Thomas chewed the coarse bread thoughtfully, tasting not just the flour that spoke of economy but the accumulated weight of three generations' decline from prosperity to the edge of destitution. Pride, it seemed, had been both their family's greatest asset and its most dangerous liability—the quality that had earned respect and position, but also the flaw that prevented adaptation when adaptation meant survival.

"Pride," he repeated, understanding for the first time how the word contained both blessing and curse, strength and weakness inextricably intertwined. "Seems to me pride has cost our family more than it's preserved over the years."

"Pride rightly directed preserves a man's soul," Mary replied with the firmness of someone who had thought deeply about such matters during long nights when pain prevented sleep and reflection became the only available occupation. "Pride wrongly applied destroys everything it touches. The art lies in learning the difference before circumstances force the lesson upon you."

The wisdom in her words felt heavier than the iron he shaped each day, carrying implications that stretched beyond their immediate circumstances into questions about character and choice that would define whatever future remained available to them. Thomas understood that his mother was offering more than historical explanation—she was providing guidance about the crossroads he approached with each passing day that brought their financial crisis closer to resolution that might require sacrificing everything he believed about honor and dignity.

That evening found Thomas in the Shoulder of Mutton, nursing a pint of ale that cost more than he could afford but provided warmth and companionship he needed against the growing chill of uncertainty that made solitude feel like punishment rather than peace. The inn's main room buzzed with conversation that ranged from crop prospects to the latest political upheavals in London, but Thomas found himself drawn to the corner table where Samuel Dawes held court over a circle of men whose faces bore the particular desperation of those who had exhausted honest options without finding solutions to problems that demanded immediate attention.

Dawes himself was a study in careful presentation—his coat well-tailored despite its age, his boots polished to hide wear that spoke of circumstances reduced but not abandoned to complete neglect. Thomas had known him since boyhood, had watched him evolve from village scapegrace into something more dangerous: a man with schemes for every circumstance and justifications for any action that promised immediate advantage over long-term consequences.

The conversation at Dawes' table carried the particular intensity of desperate men discussing solutions that respectable society would condemn but desperate circumstances made seem reasonable when examined through the lens of immediate necessity. Thomas listened from his position at the bar, understanding that he was hearing about opportunities that pride had previously prevented him from considering but present reality made increasingly difficult to dismiss without examination.

"Thomas Staines!" Dawes called out, noticing his attention and gesturing toward an empty chair with the expansive bonhomie of someone who recognized kindred spirit in another man whose circumstances had narrowed his options to margins that made desperate measures seem less desperate than continued adherence to principles that poverty was rapidly making meaningless. "Come settle a dispute for us. Young Morrison here claims an honest man can prosper in these times through nothing but hard work and patient endurance. I maintain that circumstances require more creative approaches to survival."

Thomas approached the table warily, recognizing the gleam in Dawes' eye that preceded propositions best discussed in shadows where moral clarity became obscured by practical necessity. His mother's words about pride rightly and wrongly directed echoed in his mind as he settled into the offered chair, understanding that he was approaching territory where such distinctions might prove more important than he was prepared to acknowledge.

"Honest work has sustained my family for three generations," he said, settling into the conversation with caution that didn't quite mask his willingness to hear what alternatives might exist for men whose honest work had proved insufficient for survival in times that rewarded expedience over principle. "I see no reason it shouldn't continue to provide what we need."

"Honest work," Dawes repeated, his tone suggesting he found the concept amusing rather than admirable—the innocent optimism of someone who hadn't yet learned that the world had changed while they clung to assumptions that no longer applied to economic realities that cared nothing for tradition or merit. "Tell me, Thomas—how much has your honest work earned this month? Enough to repair your mother's roof? Enough to secure your forge's rent for the coming quarter? Enough to set aside anything for the lean months that stretch between winter's end and harvest time?"

The questions hit their mark with precision of well-aimed arrows, each one striking vulnerabilities that Thomas had tried to shield from public examination through pride that was rapidly becoming luxury he couldn't afford to maintain. Heat rose in his cheeks—partly from shame at having his circumstances dissected for entertainment, partly from anger at the accuracy of observations that reduced his dignity to matters of simple mathematics.

"A man's business is his own," he said stiffly, understanding even as he spoke that the words carried no conviction when spoken by someone whose business was obviously failing to provide even basic necessities for himself and his mother.

"Indeed it is," Dawes agreed, his voice carrying sympathy that might have been genuine or might have been calculation designed to lower defenses that pride insisted on maintaining despite their obvious inadequacy. "And when a man's business fails to provide for his family's needs, when honest work leaves him watching his mother's roof leak while his own security crumbles around him, perhaps it's time to consider whether honesty is a luxury he can afford to maintain."

Morrison, a farm laborer whose face bore the permanent stain of outdoor work and whose circumstances were hardly better than Thomas's own, shifted uncomfortably on his stool. "You're talking about thievery, Dawes. Plain and simple theft dressed up in pretty words that don't change what it is."

"I'm talking about survival," Dawes replied smoothly, his words carrying the seductive logic of desperation refined into philosophy that made wrong seem reasonable when examined from angles that necessity provided. "About recognizing that the world has changed while we've clung to old notions about proper behavior that applied to times when proper behavior was rewarded with proper compensation. The gentry take what they need through law and custom—why shouldn't common men take what they need through wit and courage when law and custom provide no relief for circumstances that honest work cannot remedy?"

Thomas found himself listening despite better judgment that whispered warnings his pride was no longer strong enough to heed, drawn by explanations that made theft sound like practical wisdom rather than moral failure. The ale loosened his tongue and clouded his judgment, making Dawes' arguments seem less like temptation and more like realistic assessment of options available to men whose circumstances had narrowed to margins that made conventional morality feel like luxury only the secure could afford.

"What exactly are you proposing?" Thomas asked, the words feeling strange in his mouth but carrying weight of genuine curiosity about alternatives that pride had previously prevented him from considering seriously.

Dawes leaned forward conspiratorially, his voice dropping to barely above whisper while his eyes gleamed with enthusiasm of someone who had found receptive audience for schemes that required careful presentation to seem reasonable rather than criminal. "Farmer Biggs keeps a pony in the field behind this very inn. Fine animal, worth fifteen pounds at Leicester market, guarded by nothing more than a gate that wouldn't stop a determined child from reaching whatever lay beyond its flimsy protection."

The specific nature of the proposal made Thomas's stomach clench with recognition that they had moved beyond theoretical discussion into actual planning for crimes that would transform him from struggling craftsman into convicted thief if circumstances went wrong. But fifteen pounds represented more money than he could earn in two months of honest work, enough to repair his mother's roof and secure his forge's rent while providing surplus to carry them through lean times that might otherwise force choices between his pride and their survival.

"You're talking about stealing Biggs' pony," Thomas said, needing to hear the words spoken plainly rather than disguised behind euphemisms that made theft sound like reasonable business proposition.

"I'm talking about borrowing against future prosperity," Dawes corrected with smooth facility that suggested long practice in making wrong sound reasonable when examined from proper angles. "Biggs has three ponies and enough wealth to purchase more if needed. You have skills that could transform borrowed capital into legitimate profit through honest work that serves community needs. Who's harmed if a rich man's excess becomes a poor man's salvation when a poor man's need exceeds a rich man's awareness of opportunities for Christian charity?"

The conversation continued around the table while Thomas retreated into thoughts that circled like water seeking level, always returning to mathematics of survival that had brought him to consider actions that would have been unthinkable six months earlier when pride and principle seemed like affordable luxuries rather than dangerous impediments to practical necessity. His mother's face appeared in his mind—the careful way she moved to favor arthritic joints, the bucket positioned to catch water from deteriorating thatch, the pride that refused to admit need even when need was obvious to anyone with eyes to see.

The ale made Dawes' logic seem increasingly persuasive, transforming theft from crime into creative solution to problems that honest work had proved inadequate to address. What good was honesty if it couldn't provide basic security for people who depended on his success? What value had pride if it meant watching his mother suffer while he clung to principles that benefited no one and prevented actions that could alleviate genuine hardship through temporary borrowing from those who possessed surplus beyond their needs?

By closing time, Thomas had agreed to meet Dawes the following evening to discuss details of their proposed venture, understanding that he was crossing an invisible line from consideration into commitment, from theoretical possibility into actual planning for actions that would either solve his problems or destroy whatever remained of his reputation and prospects. As he walked home through North Kilworth's empty streets, starlight providing minimal illumination for progress made unsteady by ale and anxiety, he told himself that he was merely exploring options, gathering information that might prove useful without committing to any particular course of action.

But deep in his heart, Thomas Staines knew he had already made the choice that would define the rest of his life—not the specific decision to steal Farmer Biggs' pony, but the fundamental choice to abandon principles that had sustained his family for generations in favor of expedience that promised immediate relief from circumstances that honest work had proved inadequate to remedy. The transformation from respected craftsman to desperate thief had begun not with criminal action but with mental surrender of beliefs that made such action unthinkable.

The following evening arrived wrapped in clouds that promised rain before morning, darkness that would provide cover for actions that required concealment from honest observation. Thomas spent the day at his forge with unusual intensity, as if honest work might somehow absolve him of dishonest thoughts that had haunted his sleep and made breakfast taste like ashes in his mouth. But with each hammer blow against anvil, each shower of sparks that rose toward chimney like prayers seeking heaven, he found himself thinking about fifteen pounds that Farmer Biggs' pony represented—enough to repair his mother's roof, secure his forge's rent, purchase coal and iron necessary to maintain his trade through lean months that stretched ahead like test of endurance he was no longer certain he possessed strength to complete honestly.

The Shoulder of Mutton felt different when he arrived to meet Dawes, its familiar warmth contaminated by knowledge of what they intended to discuss in whispers that honest men would condemn if overheard. But desperation had refined his hearing to frequencies that detected opportunity in conversations that pride would have dismissed as beneath consideration, making Dawes' schemes seem less like criminal conspiracy and more like practical wisdom adapted to circumstances that conventional morality had never been designed to address.

The plan Dawes outlined over ale and whispered conversation was elegant in its simplicity: wait until Biggs retired for evening made comfortable by drink that ensured sound sleep, remove pony from field protected by gate that existed more for show than security, alter its markings sufficiently to prevent immediate identification, and transport it to Leicester market where no questions would be asked about a working animal offered for sale by apparent farmers whose possession seemed legitimate enough to justify purchase.

"The risk is minimal," Dawes insisted, his voice carrying confidence of someone who had convinced himself that careful planning eliminated danger that might otherwise deter participation. "Biggs drinks heavily of an evening—he'll sleep sound as stone until well past dawn. By the time he discovers his loss, we'll have completed our business in Leicester and returned with enough profit to solve all our immediate problems while providing foundation for honest prosperity that current circumstances make impossible to achieve through conventional means."

Thomas listened with part of his mind that calculated probabilities and weighed advantages against consequences while another part—the part that housed whatever remained of his conscience—remained curiously silent, as if his moral sense recognized that survival sometimes required compromises that peace could not justify but desperation made necessary for preserving what mattered most.

"And if we're discovered?" Thomas asked, understanding that questions about failure needed answers before commitment could become action.

"We won't be," Dawes replied with conviction that brooked no contradiction, the certainty of someone who had never been caught despite previous ventures that success had made seem like vindication of methods that conventional morality condemned. "But if circumstances turn against us, we claim we found the animal wandering loose and were returning it to the proper owner out of community spirit that should be rewarded rather than punished. Who can prove otherwise when our story makes more sense than accusations that paint honest men as criminals?"

The rain began as they left the inn, fat drops that promised to become downpour before night ended, providing both cover for their intended actions and omen that circumstances were aligning to test whether Thomas Staines possessed courage necessary to seize opportunity that might never present itself again. He pulled his coat tighter and followed Dawes through darkened village toward Farmer Biggs' property, his heart hammering against ribs like a caged bird desperate for freedom from circumstances that had made such desperate measures seem reasonable.

With each step toward the field where Biggs' pony grazed in ignorance of the role it would play in Thomas's transformation from respected craftsman to desperate thief, the rational part of his mind offered reasons to abandon madness and return home to an honest forge and clear conscience. But the image of his mother positioning buckets to catch rainwater dripping through the deteriorating roof proved stronger than reason, making fifteen pounds seem like salvation rather than the price of his soul.

Farmer Biggs' pony stood in the field as Dawes had promised, dark silhouette against storm clouds that gathered overhead like judgment waiting to fall upon those who abandoned principles for expedience. The animal seemed to regard their approach with mild curiosity rather than alarm, as if late-night visitors were nothing unusual in its experience of human behavior that ranged from care to exploitation depending on circumstances beyond its understanding or control.

Thomas felt a moment of clarity, a final opportunity to step back from the precipice that yawned before him like opening to hell that would swallow everything he had believed about himself and his place in the world where honor mattered more than immediate comfort. But instead of wisdom, he felt a weight of responsibility for his mother's welfare, knowledge that his choices would determine whether she spent remaining years in dignity or want, understanding that love sometimes demanded actions that contradicted every principle that love itself had taught him to value.

He reached for the gate's simple latch and stepped across a threshold between a man he had been and a man he was about to become, understanding that some choices created consequences that extended far beyond their immediate results into transformation of character that could never be undone regardless of whatever regret or repentance might follow recognition of error that pride and desperation had made seem like wisdom.

The capture proceeded exactly as Dawes had predicted. Pony allowed itself to be led from field without resistance, following docilely as they guided it through the village's sleeping streets toward the road that would take them to Leicester market where fifteen pounds waited to solve problems that honest work had proved inadequate to address. But as they reached village's outskirts, their luck abandoned them with the suddenness of a candle flame extinguished by unexpected wind.

Lantern light blazed from behind them, accompanied by voices that grew louder and more urgent with each passing moment, destroying illusion that their actions could remain secret in a community where everyone knew everyone else's business and unusual activity attracted attention from those whose duty required investigation of circumstances that seemed irregular or suspicious.

"Stop there! Thieves! Stop in the name of the law!"

Thomas turned to see Constable Morrison—same Morrison who had argued for honesty in Shoulder of Mutton—running toward them with two other men, their lanterns casting wild shadows through rain that now fell in earnest, making pursuit and capture seem like a natural conclusion to an evening that had begun with choice between principles and survival. Beside him, Dawes cursed and released his hold on the pony's halter, melting into darkness with practiced ease of someone who had planned for such contingencies and possessed experience necessary for successful escape.

But Thomas stood frozen in the lantern light, still gripping the stolen animal's lead rope as if his hands had forgotten how to release what they had never intended to hold, paralyzed by recognition that he had thrown away everything—reputation, livelihood, his mother's security, his own freedom—for a moment's weakness that pride and desperation had disguised as practical wisdom. The knowledge that he had destroyed his life for fifteen pounds that would now become evidence of a crime rather than solution to problems struck him with physical force that made breathing difficult and thinking impossible.

As constables seized him, their hands rough on arms and shoulders that had never known restraint more severe than social convention, Thomas thought about pride and its consequences, about difference between dignity preserved and dignity destroyed through choices that seemed reasonable until their results revealed the true nature of decisions made in circumstances where fear overcame wisdom. His mother had warned him that pride wrongly applied destroyed everything it touched, but only now—standing in the rain with stolen goods in his hands and a future crumbling around him—did he understand the full weight of her prophecy.

The trial at Northampton proceeded with inexorable logic of justice applied to circumstances that admitted no defense capable of mitigating guilt that evidence made undeniable. Thomas stood in the dock listening to testimony that painted him not as a desperate man driven by circumstances beyond his control, but as a calculating thief who had betrayed trust of a community that had known him since birth for personal gain that revealed character unworthy of mercy or consideration.

The magistrate's words fell like hammer blows against anvil, each sentence shaping his fate with the same precision Thomas had once applied to heated iron that yielded to patient pressure applied with skill and understanding. But there would be no second chances for mistakes made in pursuit of survival that honest work had proved inadequate to provide, no opportunity to reshape decisions that had transformed a respected craftsman into a convicted criminal whose future lay in the hands of a system that valued example over individual circumstance.

"Transportation for life to His Majesty's colony of New South Wales."

The pronouncement echoed through the courthouse with the finality of a church bell tolling for dead, marking the end of Thomas Staines as he had known himself and the beginning of whatever he might become in a distant land that existed more in his imagination than geographical reality. He felt something break inside him—not spirit, which remained stubbornly intact despite circumstances that might have destroyed weaker character, but old understanding of himself as a man whose choices mattered, whose future could be shaped by skill and determination rather than forces beyond his control or comprehension.

In his cell at Northampton Gaol, waiting for transport to ships that would carry him across the world to a land he could not imagine, Thomas began the slow work of reconstructing an identity from the ruins of a former life that pride and desperation had combined to destroy. The man who had stolen Farmer Biggs' pony deserved whatever punishment awaited him in Australian exile, but the man who would emerge from those ruins might yet prove worthy of redemption if willing to undertake patient work of transformation that suffering could provide for those whose character possessed strength to endure trials that would break anyone unprepared for education that only extremity could deliver.

On his final night in England, Thomas carved a Celtic cross from a piece of stone torn from the cell wall, its surface bearing a thistle in memory of Scotland his mother claimed in their heritage despite generations of reduced circumstances that had stripped away everything except stories about better times that might or might not represent historical reality. The work kept his hands busy while his mind grappled with questions that had no easy answers: What legacy could a condemned man leave for children he might never father? How could love survive death of hope? What meaning could be found in circumstances that seemed designed to strip away everything that made a man worth remembering?

The cross, rough-carved but recognizable, would travel with him to whatever fate awaited on the far side of the world that had become his destination through choices that seemed reasonable until their consequences revealed true nature of decisions made when pride and poverty combined to make wrong seem reasonable. Perhaps someday, if God granted him opportunity for redemption through service that transcended personal comfort, he would find answers to questions that tormented sleepless hours in a cell that had become a classroom where pride learned lessons about humility that prosperity could never teach.

But as dawn approached and with it the beginning of a journey into exile that would either destroy or transform him into someone worthy of whatever chances a distant land might offer, Thomas Staines could only hope that love might prove stronger than shame, that distance might heal what proximity had destroyed, and that somewhere in the vast unknown that stretched before him lay the possibility of becoming a man his unborn children might remember with something other than regret for a father whose pride had cost them a heritage that honest work had once provided and criminal folly had stolen forever.

4 QUESTIONS WITHOUT ANSWERS

State Library of NSW, Sydney — October 2010

The State Library of New South Wales rose from Sydney's streets like a temple dedicated to the preservation of memory, its sandstone façade weathered to honey-gold by decades of harbor sun but still commanding the kind of reverence that only institutions devoted to knowledge could inspire. Sara Wilson climbed the broad steps at eight-thirty in the morning, Thomas Staines' first letter carefully tucked in her satchel alongside notebooks, pencils, and the growing sense that her life had divided into two distinct periods: before discovering those letters in Glen Lena's attic, and after.

Three days had passed since her initial reading of Thomas's words to his unborn daughter, three days of sleepless nights and distracted days when ordinary tasks felt meaningless compared to the mystery that had opened before her like a door to rooms she'd never known existed in the house of family history. The brief Google searches she'd conducted from her apartment had only whetted her appetite for the kind of systematic investigation that required access to archives, shipping records, and the accumulated documentation that transformed individual stories into historical narrative.

The Mitchell Library's genealogy section occupied the building's heart like a sanctuary where pilgrims came seeking connection to ancestors whose stories had been preserved in documents that most people never knew existed. Sara had worked in this space before—contracted research for legal firms seeking inheritance documentation, academic institutions requiring historical verification, private clients whose curiosity about family origins had led them to hire professional investigators capable of navigating bureaucratic mazes that guarded Australia's documentary heritage.

But this felt different from any research she'd previously undertaken. Where her professional work had maintained the emotional distance necessary for objective analysis, Thomas's letters had made detachment impossible. Every document she sought carried personal weight that transformed academic exercise into spiritual journey, intellectual curiosity into urgent need to understand who she was and where she'd come from and what obligations such knowledge might create for how she chose to live the years that remained available to her.

"Back again, Sara?" Margaret Chen, the senior librarian whose encyclopedic knowledge of the collection had guided Sara through countless previous research projects, looked up from the circulation desk with a smile that suggested genuine pleasure at seeing a familiar face. "Haven't seen you since the Macarthur estate project last spring. What brings you here this time?"

"Family research," Sara replied, settling her satchel on the desk while understanding that those two words contained multitudes she couldn't yet articulate. "My great-great-great-grandfather, transported as a convict in the 1830s. Thomas Staines, arrived 1836 on HMS *Moffatt*. I'm trying to understand what happened to him after he landed."

Margaret's expression shifted from professional courtesy to personal interest, recognizing in Sara's voice the particular intensity that marked researchers who had moved beyond casual curiosity into the realm of obsession that genealogical investigation could inspire in people whose questions carried emotional weight beyond academic interest. "Convict records can be challenging," she said, pulling out the requisition forms that would provide access to materials held in climate-controlled storage. "But we have excellent shipping manifests from that period, and the New South Wales colonial secretary's correspondence often contains details about individual assignments and movements."

The process of requesting materials felt ritualistic—filling out call slips with careful handwriting, presenting identification that authorized access to documents too fragile for casual handling, settling into chairs designed for long hours of careful study in controlled environments where temperature and humidity were regulated to preserve papers that had survived longer than most of the people who'd created them. Sara found herself surrounded by other researchers whose postures and expressions suggested similar missions: elderly women tracing family trees that stretched back to European villages, middle-aged men seeking military records that might explain gaps in stories passed down through generations, younger researchers whose laptops and digital cameras marked them as members of a generation that expected immediate access to information but still needed to consult original sources for discoveries that hadn't been digitized.

Her first success came within an hour of opening the shipping manifests for 1836, Thomas's name appearing in the clerk's careful copperplate that had recorded the human cargo of HMS *Moffatt* with bureaucratic precision that treated individual tragedies as statistical data: "Thomas Staines, age 30, convicted Leicester Assizes, theft of livestock, sentence: transportation for life."

The entry was brief but devastating in its implications. Not just the confirmation that family stories about Thomas's "troubles" had concealed actual criminal conviction, but the recognition that her ancestor had been thirty years old when he'd made whatever choice had resulted in exile from everything he'd known. Thirty—younger than Sara was now, young enough to have an entire life ahead of him but old enough to understand the magnitude of what he was losing through transportation to a colony that existed at the edge of imagination rather than geographical reality.

"Theft of livestock," she whispered, the words carrying weight of revelation that transformed Thomas from romantic figure of family mythology into a man whose desperation had driven him to actions that nineteenth-century justice considered worthy of permanent exile. The specificity of the charge suggested not casual wrongdoing but calculated crime that had crossed legal boundaries with consequences that extended far beyond immediate punishment into lifelong transformation of identity and prospects.

Sara photographed the page with her phone, understanding that she was documenting not just genealogical discovery but evidence of family story that previous generations had chosen to simplify rather than preserve in its complicated entirety. The truth about Thomas's conviction would need to be balanced against whatever he'd become during his years in Australia, whatever transformation had changed convicted thief into man capable of writing letters that carried such emotional depth they could guide healing across centuries.

"Finding what you need?" The voice belonged to an elderly man at the neighboring table, his own research materials spread around him like archaeological excavation of family history that had clearly consumed months or years of patient investigation. "I'm Robert Hayes—been working on my convict ancestor for three years now. Transportation records can be goldmines if you know how to read between the lines."

Sara introduced herself, grateful for guidance from someone whose experience might help her navigate research territories she'd explored professionally but never with such personal investment. Robert's ancestor had been transported for poaching, a crime that had carried political implications in early nineteenth-century England where game laws protected aristocratic privilege while criminalizing survival strategies that rural poor had practiced for generations.

"Context matters," Robert explained, settling into conversation with enthusiasm of someone who'd learned to appreciate the company of fellow researchers whose obsessions matched his own. "Theft of livestock could mean anything from desperate survival to organized criminal activity. The sentence—transportation for life—suggests serious crime, but economic circumstances of the 1830s made many honest people desperate enough to risk everything for immediate relief."

The observation provided framework for understanding Thomas's conviction that balanced moral judgment against historical context, individual choice against social circumstances that had created conditions where crime might seem like the only available option for people whose honest work had proved insufficient for survival. Sara found herself thinking about the economic pressures that had shaped rural England during the period following Napoleon's defeat, the agricultural depression that had made survival itself an achievement for working people whose skills had lost value in a changing economy.

"The real treasure is usually in the colonial correspondence," Robert continued, gesturing toward call slips that would summon additional materials from storage areas that held generations of official documents. "Once they arrived, convicts were assigned to work details, government projects, private masters who needed labor. The records show where they went, what they did, how they adapted to circumstances that were completely foreign to anything they'd experienced."

Sara spent the remainder of the morning working through colonial secretary's correspondence for the years following 1836, searching for mentions of Thomas Staines among thousands of entries that documented the administrative machinery of convict management. The work required patience and systematic attention that her professional training had developed, but emotional investment made concentration difficult when every reference to convict labor carried personal weight that transformed abstract historical research into intimate investigation of ancestor's daily experience.

The breakthrough came just before lunch break, buried in routine correspondence about work assignments at the Government Forge where skilled blacksmiths were needed to maintain Sydney's expanding infrastructure: "Thomas Staines assigned blacksmith duties Government Forge effective 15 September 1836. Previous experience metalwork. Reliable worker. No disciplinary issues recorded."

The notation was brief but significant in its implications about Thomas's character during early period of his sentence. "Reliable worker. No disciplinary issues." These weren't automatic descriptions applied to all convicts, but specific observations that suggested Thomas had adapted to his circumstances with dignity that earned respect from supervisors whose job required distinguishing between prisoners who could be trusted with greater responsibility and those who required constant surveillance.

"Excellent find," said Patricia Williams, another researcher who had observed Sara's excitement over the document. Patricia specialized in women's convict history, had published articles about female factories and colonial marriage patterns that revealed how transportation had affected families whose stories were often lost in records that focused on male experience." The Government Forge was actually a prestigious assignment for a convict blacksmith. They needed skilled workers for major construction projects—bridges, public buildings, infrastructure that required expertise rather than just manual labor."

The information provided context that began to reshape Sara's understanding of Thomas's convict experience from story of punishment and degradation into narrative of gradual rehabilitation through work that utilized his skills while contributing to the colony's development. The Government Forge wasn't just a prison workshop but an essential facility where Thomas's metalworking abilities would have been valued and developed rather than simply exploited for punishment purposes.

Lunch break provided opportunity to process discoveries while walking through Domain parklands that stretched between library and harbor, city noise replaced by sound of wind through trees that had been planted by convict labor during early decades of colonial settlement. Sara found herself thinking about Thomas walking these same paths—not as tourist or researcher but as prisoner whose movements were restricted yet whose skills were valued enough to provide hope for eventual redemption through patient demonstration of character transformed by circumstances that might have destroyed someone whose spirit had been less resilient.

The afternoon session brought additional discoveries that filled gaps in Thomas's colonial story while raising new questions about his journey from conviction to whatever freedom he'd eventually achieved. His name appeared in work rosters that documented steady employment at Government Forge through 1843, progression from basic blacksmith duties to supervision of younger convicts learning metalworking trades, gradual accumulation of privileges that marked official recognition of rehabilitation demonstrated through consistent excellence in assigned tasks.

"Ticket of Leave granted Thomas Staines, 15 November 1843, conditional on continued good behavior and monthly reporting to appointed magistrate." The document was signed by Governor George Gipps himself, official recognition that Thomas had completed seven years of exemplary service that qualified him for conditional freedom within colonial boundaries.

Sara photographed the Ticket of Leave with hands that trembled slightly from excitement of discovering official confirmation that Thomas's transformation from convicted thief to trusted worker had been documented by authorities who had every reason to be skeptical about convict rehabilitation. Seven years of proving himself worthy of trust, seven years of building reputation that qualified him for privileges that many convicts never achieved regardless of how long they served their sentences.

"That's remarkable," Margaret Chen observed when Sara shared her discoveries during afternoon consultation about additional resources. "Ticket of Leave in seven years suggests exceptional character development. Many convicts served much longer sentences without earning such recognition, especially those transported for serious crimes like livestock theft."

The librarian's expertise provided perspective that made Thomas's achievement seem even more significant—not just personal transformation but official acknowledgment that he'd become someone worth trusting with freedom that could have been revoked at any sign that rehabilitation hadn't been genuine. His Ticket of Leave represented a vote of confidence from colonial administration that had learned to distinguish between prisoners who deserved liberty and those who remained dangers to community security.

The final discovery of the day came in shipping records for 1844, a passenger manifest for a coastal steamer that had carried former convicts from Sydney to inland settlements where opportunities for legitimate employment might provide foundation for building new lives without stigma that attached to convict status in more established communities. Thomas's name appeared among passengers traveling to Bathurst— frontier town beyond Blue Mountains where land was available for men willing to work it, where past mattered less than present willingness to contribute to community development.

"He went to Bathurst," Sara announced to Robert and Patricia, who had become informal research companions during day spent sharing discoveries and frustrations common to genealogical investigation. "Left Sydney in March 1844, just four months after getting his Ticket of Leave. Must have been eager to start over somewhere his convict status wouldn't define how people saw him."

Robert nodded with understanding born from similar discoveries about his own ancestor's post-conviction journey. "Bathurst was a popular destination for ex-convicts during that period. The gold rush hadn't started yet, but there were opportunities for skilled workers willing to help build infrastructure for settlements expanding west of the mountains. Fresh start in a place where character mattered more than past mistakes."

The research day had transformed Thomas from mysterious family figure into a man whose choices could be traced through documentary evidence that revealed character development worthy of admiration rather than shame. From convicted thief to trusted government worker to free settler seeking opportunities in a frontier town—his story emerged as testament to transformation possible for anyone willing to undertake the patient work of earning redemption through consistent demonstration of character refined rather than broken by adversity.

But questions remained that documents couldn't answer, gaps in official record that would require different types of investigation to fill. What had happened to Thomas in Bathurst? How had he met Catherine Krieg, the German immigrant who'd become his wife? When had they built Three Rivers Inn, and what circumstances had led to his death in the 1852 flood that Rivers' birth had somehow survived?

"This is addictive, isn't it?" Patricia observed as they gathered materials at day's end, recognizing in Sara's expression the particular satisfaction that came from successful genealogical hunting combined with hunger for additional discoveries that each answer generated. "You start with a simple question about family history and end up with a research project that could consume years of investigation."

Sara nodded, understanding that she'd crossed the threshold from casual curiosity into committed investigation that would require systematic exploration of archives, local histories, newspaper collections, and whatever other sources might contain traces of Thomas's life after he'd left Sydney for opportunities that the frontier settlement offered to men whose past had prepared them to appreciate second chances that established communities might not provide.

The State Library closed around her like benediction, the reading room emptying of researchers who carried their discoveries home to contemplate during evening hours when excitement of new information combined with anticipation of additional searches that tomorrow might bring. Sara gathered her materials with the reluctance of someone who would have preferred to continue working despite physical exhaustion that came from hours spent hunched over documents, eyes strained from reading handwriting that had faded during decades of storage in archives that preserved but couldn't prevent gradual deterioration that made each page precious and irreplaceable.

The journey home through Sydney streets filled with evening commuters felt like the return from expedition to a foreign country, city noise and traffic creating jarring contrast with peaceful concentration that library research required. Sara found herself thinking about Thomas making a similar journey from Government Forge to whatever accommodation had been provided for convicts whose good behavior earned them privileges that made daily existence bearable rather than merely endurable.

Her apartment, when she finally reached it, felt different than it had that morning—not just a place where she lived but the base of operations for a research project that had become the central focus of her existence in ways she hadn't anticipated when she'd first discovered Thomas's letters. The harbor lights that usually provided entertainment now seemed like connections to the past when sailing ships had carried hopeful immigrants and desperate convicts toward futures that existed more in imagination than certainty.

Sara opened her laptop and began transferring digital photographs of documents into files organized by date and subject, creating a database that would allow systematic analysis of information she'd gathered while providing a framework for additional research that each discovery made necessary. The work felt like archaeology of family history, each document another piece of puzzle that would eventually reveal the complete picture of Thomas's transformation from convicted criminal to man capable of writing letters that carried wisdom earned through trials that had tested but not broken his capacity for love and hope.

But even as she organized evidence of Thomas's documented rehabilitation, Sara found herself thinking about gaps that official records couldn't fill—emotional territory between conviction and redemption where real transformation had occurred through processes that bureaucratic notation could only hint at rather than fully capture. What had Thomas felt during those first months in Sydney, chained to a work gang and sleeping in barracks that reduced individual identity to numbers and assignments? How had he found strength to begin the journey toward character development that would eventually qualify him for freedom and opportunities that many free settlers never achieved?

These were questions that documents alone couldn't answer, mysteries that would require imagination guided by historical understanding to bridge gaps between factual evidence and emotional truth about human experience that statistics could record but not explain. Sara understood that she was beginning a journey into territory where genealogical research became something approaching literature, where family history demanded not just documentation but interpretation that honored both factual accuracy and deeper truths about transformation that made individual stories relevant to anyone facing their own choices between despair and hope.

The night was still young, and she had four more of Thomas's letters waiting to be opened, each one promising to carry her deeper into understanding of a man whose journey from shame to honor provided a template for redemption available to anyone willing to undertake its patient, difficult work. But first, she needed to call Calvin and share discoveries that had transformed their ancestor from family mythology into a documented historical figure whose story deserved preservation and transmission to anyone whose heart was ready to receive its guidance about love that proved stronger than shame, hope that survived even the worst circumstances when approached with sufficient faith and determination.

5 THE VOYAGE

HMS Moffatt, Portsmouth to Sydney Harbor — April to August 1836

The iron cuffs bit into Thomas Staines' wrists as the Northampton gaol's heavy oak door slammed shut behind him for the final time, the echo of the magistrate's gavel still reverberating through his soul like distant thunder that promised storms ahead. March 1836 had surrendered to April's uncertain promise, and with it, any hope that reprieve might arrive through channels he could neither influence nor comprehend. The weight of his conviction—theft of livestock, a crime that reduced a man's entire existence to a single moment of desperate weakness—pressed against his chest like millstone, yet somewhere beneath that crushing burden, an ember of defiance still flickered.

He would not break. Whatever lay ahead in that distant land whose very name sounded like exile made audible, Thomas Staines would endure it with whatever dignity remained to a man who had traded his freedom for a farmer's pony and found the exchange wanting in ways that stretched far beyond simple mathematics of crime and punishment.

The journey from Northampton to Portsmouth passed in a blur of shackles and shame, fellow prisoners chained in wagons that creaked through the English countryside Thomas would never see again. Some wept openly, their tears carving channels through grime that marked them as society's discards, while others maintained grim silence that suggested they had already died to everything that had once given their lives meaning. Thomas found himself cataloguing faces and stories that emerged through whispered conversations during rest stops, understanding that these men would become his community for whatever trials awaited in the antipodean wilderness.

There was young Jamie McBride from County Cork, barely sixteen but already bearing the weathered look of someone who'd learned that survival required compromises that childhood should never have to make. Transported for stealing bread to feed siblings whose parents had died in the fever that swept through their village like God's own judgment on poverty that made children responsible for keeping each other alive. The boy's eyes held a mixture of terror and stubborn hope that made Thomas's throat tighten with recognition of innocence that circumstance was rapidly destroying.

"First time away from home," Jamie whispered during one of their brief stops, his Irish accent thick with homesickness that would have been touching in different circumstances. "Never been further than the next county before this. Me sister Mary made me promise to write when I could, but I don't know how letters find their way across oceans that might as well be to the moon for all I understand about such distances."

Will Patterson—no relation to the Patersons Thomas claimed in his lineage—was a pickpocket from London's East End whose quick hands and quicker wit had finally met their match in a magistrate who believed transportation was kinder than hanging for someone whose crimes had escalated from desperate survival to something approaching

31

professional criminal activity. At twenty-five, he possessed the street wisdom that came from growing up in circumstances where law was an obstacle to be navigated rather than protection to be trusted.

"Trick is not to think about what you're leaving behind," Will advised with cynical philosophy that masked sensitivity he couldn't afford to reveal. "England's done with us, lads. Question now is whether we can do something with Australia that makes the crossing worthwhile instead of just delayed execution in a more exotic location."

Ned Garrison had been a sailor before desperation drove him to theft, his knowledge of ships and weather invaluable as they prepared for a voyage that would test every assumption about endurance and the human capacity for survival in conditions that reduced existence to its most basic elements. He studied HMS *Moffatt* with a professional eye that saw beyond her current conversion to convict transport, recognizing in her lines the naval frigate she'd once been before bureaucratic efficiency transformed warship into floating prison.

"She's sound enough," Ned observed as they were herded aboard, his seaman's expertise providing reassurance that felt precious in circumstances where any comfort was welcome. "Built for service rather than comfort, but that means she'll hold together in weather that might break vessels designed for passenger trade. Captain Morrison's got a reputation for running a tight ship—harsh but fair, they say. Could be worse masters to trust with our lives across oceans that don't care whether we reach the other side or feed the fishes along the way."

Portsmouth Harbor stretched before them like a gateway to purgatory, its waters crowded with vessels of every description: merchant ships fat with cargo bound for distant markets, naval frigates bristling with guns that maintained Britain's dominion over seas she had never seen, and there, riding at anchor like black prophecy against the April sky, HMS *Moffatt*—converted frigate whose gun ports had been sealed and replaced with iron gratings that would provide their only glimpse of sky for the next four months.

The ship squatted in the harbor's grey waters with the malevolent presence of something designed not for exploration or conquest, but for efficient transportation of human misery across distances too vast for imagination to compass. Thomas studied her lines with a craftsman's eye that understood how function shaped form, recognizing in the *Moffatt's* brutal practicality the same logic that governed his forge—every element designed for specific purpose, beauty sacrificed entirely to utility, hope abandoned in favor of grim efficiency.

The boarding process stripped away the last pretense that they remained men rather than cargo. Guards with faces like granite and voices that brooked no dissent herded them up the gangplank in shuffling lines, their chains creating a percussion that spoke of dreams deferred and futures cancelled. Thomas felt his breath catch as he crossed the threshold from dock to deck, from England to whatever lay beyond the horizon, understanding that he was surrendering not just geography but identity that had sustained him through thirty years of believing he understood his place in a world that now seemed determined to prove such understanding had been illusion.

Captain Morrison—a man whose weathered features suggested decades of intimate acquaintance with the sea's more violent moods—surveyed his human cargo with dispassionate assessment of someone evaluating livestock. "Gentlemen," he announced, though his tone suggested the word held more irony than courtesy, "you are no longer citizens of His Majesty's realm. You are convicts bound for New South Wales, and your comfort during this voyage will depend entirely upon your willingness to accept that reality without resistance."

The descent into the ship's belly felt like a journey into the earth's bowels, each step carrying them further from light and air that marked the boundary between civilization and its opposite. The hold where they would spend the next four months had been designed to accommodate cargo, not human beings—vast, low-ceilinged cavern where sixty men would live in conditions that would have been considered cruel for animals, their existence reduced to basic requirements of breathing, eating, and surviving whatever trials the Atlantic and Indian Oceans would present.

The stench hit Thomas first: unwashed bodies layered with fear-sweat and despair, urine-soaked straw that would serve as bedding, metallic tang of chains and sweet-sick smell of men who had already surrendered hope. He pressed hand to mouth, fighting the urge to vomit, and heard laughter behind him—not cruel laughter, but bitter amusement of someone who had witnessed this same reaction countless times.

"First voyage, is it, lad?" The voice belonged to a man whose age was impossible to determine—somewhere between forty and death, his face carved by experiences that had worn away everything soft or optimistic. "Name's Old Tom Sullivan, though the 'Old' came early and the 'Sullivan' might not be the name me mother gave me. Been to Botany Bay twice—once for sheep stealing, once for breaking parole. Both times taught me something useful about survival in circumstances that test everything you think you know about endurance."

Thomas studied the man's face, seeing in its deep lines and knowing eyes accumulated wisdom of someone who had learned life's hardest lessons through direct experience rather than comfortable theory. "Thomas Staines," he replied, extending a hand despite chains that made the gesture awkward. "First time, as you say. Leicestershire blacksmith who thought he understood something about hardship until reality taught him otherwise."

"What brought you here, if you don't mind the asking?" Old Tom settled onto a patch of straw that suggested long familiarity with making best of impossible circumstances. "Always like to know what particular variety of desperation I'm sharing quarters with. Helps me understand who might be worth befriending and who's likely to cause troubles that affect everyone."

"Stole a pony," Thomas said, words still tasting foreign in his mouth despite weeks of imprisonment that should have accustomed him to his new identity as a convicted thief. "Needed money for my mother's roof, couldn't see another way to get it. Pride and poverty make a dangerous combination when man's too stubborn to ask for help that might have been available if he'd swallowed dignity long enough to seek it."

Old Tom nodded with the understanding of someone who had heard similar stories more times than he could count, recognition that most men in their circumstances could tell versions of the same tale—good men who made bad choices when situation left them no good ones, pride that prevented wisdom, desperation that overcame conscience. "Pride before the fall, as Scripture says. Most of us here could tell variations on that theme. Trick now is learning how to be good men again, even when everything around us seems designed to make us worse than we were when we started."

The observation carried weight that would prove prophetic during the months ahead, when circumstances would test every assumption Thomas had held about character, survival, and the possibility that meaning could be found in a situation that appeared designed to strip away everything that made life worth preserving. Old Tom's wisdom, earned through previous transportation and subsequent return to criminal activity that had brought him back to a convict ship, would provide guidance that proved more valuable than any formal education Thomas had received.

As days passed and HMS *Moffatt* fought its way through seas that seemed determined to test every joint and timber in her aging hull, Thomas began to understand the strange fellowship that necessity had forged among convicts. Stripped of former identities, reduced to a common denominator of shared misery, they had created their own society with rules and hierarchies and unexpected moments of grace that revealed humanity's stubborn refusal to surrender dignity even when dignity seemed like a luxury they could no longer afford.

Jamie McBride, the sixteen-year-old bread thief, became something like a younger brother to several older convicts who recognized in his innocence something worth protecting despite circumstances that encouraged every man to focus solely on his own survival. Old Tom took the boy under his protection with fierce gentleness of someone who had learned that kindness was a choice that became more valuable as circumstances made it more difficult to maintain.

"Listen to me, lad," Tom would say during evening hours when the ship's movement gentled enough to allow conversation, his voice carrying authority earned through experience rather than position. "Ocean doesn't care about your crime or your age or your family back home. Ship doesn't care whether you live or die, long as your body doesn't inconvenience other passengers by rotting where it falls. Only thing that matters down here is how we treat each other when nobody's watching except God and our own consciences."

The boy would listen with attention that suggested hunger for guidance from someone who understood how to navigate circumstances that formal education had never prepared him to face. Jamie's questions revealed a mind that remained curious despite conditions that might have reduced a less resilient spirit to mere survival, intelligence that sought understanding even when understanding seemed a pointless luxury in an environment focused entirely on endurance.

"Why do some men go mad while others stay strong?" Jamie asked one evening when a particular violent storm had left everyone exhausted and several convicts babbling incoherently from terror that had overwhelmed their capacity to maintain rational response to circumstances beyond their control.

"Because madness is sometimes easier than facing what we've become," Old Tom replied with honesty that never softened difficult truths for sake of comfort. "Takes courage to look at yourself clearly when looking shows you things you'd rather not see. Some men choose delusion over truth when truth becomes too heavy to carry."

Will Patterson, the London pickpocket, entertained them with stories of his criminal career that were probably half fiction, but fiction delivered with such artistry that truth seemed less important than the momentary escape from present reality that his tales provided. His quick hands, now chained but still clever, could fashion small objects from scraps of rope and metal—toys for Jamie, tools for repairs that made their living space marginally more bearable, art that transformed garbage into objects of beauty that reminded them they remained human despite circumstances designed to reduce them to mere cargo.

"Had a partner once," Will would recount during long hours when the ship's motion prevented sleep and conversation became the only available entertainment. "Mary Flanagan, finest dipper ever worked Covent Garden. Could lift a gentleman's watch while asking directions to the nearest church, smile so sweet he'd thank her for bothering to speak to a working-class lass. Transported year before me for lifting wrong man's purse—turned out to be a magistrate's brother, and family took particular interest in ensuring justice was served with appropriate severity."

His stories revealed the world of London's criminal underclass that none of them had experienced directly, society that operated according to rules that had nothing to do with law or conventional morality but everything to do with survival in circumstances where legal employment provided insufficient income for basic necessities. Will's criminal education had been comprehensive, but his natural intelligence suggested that different circumstances might have produced a respectable tradesman rather than professional thief.

Ned Garrison's maritime knowledge proved invaluable as HMS *Moffatt* encountered storms that made an Atlantic crossing trial by water rather than mere transportation. He could read the sea's moods in ways that seemed almost supernatural, warning them when rough weather approached and teaching them how to brace themselves against the ship's violent motion, how to recognize a difference between ordinary discomfort and genuine danger that might require preparation for survival in circumstances where the ship herself might not prove adequate protection against the ocean's fury.

"Storm coming from southwest," Ned would announce after studying the sky through a grating that provided their only visual connection to a world beyond their floating prison. "Big one, by look of clouds. Ship'll ride it fine if Captain Morrison knows his business, but we'll be climbing walls for the next day or two. Best secure anything loose and prepare stomachs for motion that'll test whether you've got sea legs or just land-based courage that don't translate to circumstances where solid ground becomes a memory rather than reality."

But it was during the darkest hours of their passage, when sickness claimed men faster than their bodies could be committed to the deep, that Thomas discovered most profound transformation of his voyage toward whatever fate awaited in the antipodean wilderness. Watching Jamie burn with a fever that left him delirious and calling for a mother whose comfort existed only in memory, seeing Will's quick hands grow still as illness sapped strength that had sustained him through London's meanest streets, Thomas felt something crack open in his chest—not spirit breaking, but something hard and protective around his heart finally giving way.

The Celtic cross he had carved during the final night in Northampton Gaol, hidden beneath his shirt and pressed close to skin that bore permanent stains of blacksmith trade, became anchor during endless hours when the ship pitched and rolled through seas that seemed determined to test every man's will to survive whatever trials ocean and distance might present. Fashioned from a piece of stone torn from the cell wall, its surface bore a thistle that represented his mother's stories of their Scottish heritage—stories that had seemed like harmless mythology when life was secure, but now felt like the only connection remaining to anything that transcended their present suffering.

The cross provided comfort during moments when despair threatened to overwhelm whatever reserves of strength remained after weeks of deprivation, physical discomfort, and psychological pressure that reduced an existence to basic requirements of breathing, eating, and maintaining sufficient hope to justify continued struggle against circumstances that suggested surrender might be a wiser choice than persistence.

But more than a personal talisman, the cross became a symbol that connected him to purposes larger than individual survival. When fever claimed men whose names he'd learned during weeks of shared misery, Thomas would hold their hands during the final hours, offering what comfort he could to people whose deaths would be noted only as a reduction in the ship's human cargo rather than loss of irreplaceable individuals whose stories deserved preservation rather than bureaucratic notation.

"Tell me about home," dying men would whisper, their voices carrying need for connection to places and people that had given their lives meaning before crime and transportation reduced them to numbers in colonial administrative records. Thomas would share stories of North Kilworth—its forge and fields, its seasonal rhythms and village characters—creating verbal bridges between approaching death and memories that provided whatever peace might be available to souls departing life in circumstances that bore no resemblance to anything they had imagined possible during years when a future seemed predictable rather than terrifying.

These deathbed conversations taught Thomas lessons about dignity that no formal education could have provided. He learned that men facing their final moments revealed truth about character that prosperity and comfort often concealed, that courage and cowardice, generosity and selfishness, wisdom and folly became clearly visible when stripped of social conventions that normally obscured their operation.

"You've got a gift for this," Old Tom observed after Thomas had comforted another dying convict, his voice carrying respect that felt precious in circumstances where respect was a scarce commodity. "Not everyone can sit with death without fear making them useless to a person who needs human contact more than medicine or hope of recovery. Takes a particular kind of strength to offer comfort when you can't offer cure."

The observation suggested that Thomas possessed qualities he hadn't recognized in himself before transportation forced their development through circumstances that revealed capacities that peaceful existence had never required him to discover. His blacksmith hands, trained for precision work with heated metal, proved gentle enough to provide comfort during final hours, strong enough to offer support when dying men needed an anchor to keep them steady during transition from life to whatever awaited beyond breathing.

The transformation was occurring not through conscious decision but through accumulated choices made in circumstances where a character revealed itself through actions rather than intentions, where what man did mattered more than what he claimed to believe or feel. Thomas was learning to find meaning in service that served no purpose except alleviating the suffering of people whose welfare had become more important to him than his own comfort or convenience.

When storms came in June, as they rounded Africa's treacherous cape where Atlantic and Indian Oceans met in battles that had been raging since the world was young, HMS *Moffatt* became the testing ground for everything Thomas had learned about courage, community, and possibility that love could survive circumstances designed to destroy everything except the most basic survival instincts.

The hold became a madhouse during these passages—men flung against bulkheads with force enough to break bones, air thick with vomit and terror as the ship climbed mountainous swells only to plunge into valleys deep enough to hide cathedrals. Thomas found himself praying with an intensity he had never experienced, not for deliverance from circumstances but for strength to meet whatever trials awaited them with something approaching grace rather than mere endurance.

It was during worst of these storms, when water poured through the sealed gun ports and it seemed certain that *Moffatt* would join countless vessels that had found final rest in these violent waters, that Thomas experienced what he would later recognize as a pivotal moment of his spiritual transformation. Jamie, delirious with fever and terror, called out for mother with such desperate longing that every man in the hold felt a sound like a physical blow to whatever remained of their capacity for hope.

Without conscious thought, Thomas began to sing—not one of ribald songs that sometimes provided momentary distraction from their misery, but a hymn his mother had taught him during childhood, a song about finding peace in midst of trials, about discovering that love could survive any storm if held with sufficient faith and determination.

His voice, rough from years of breathing forge smoke and untrained in formal music, nevertheless carried something that reached beyond a mere melody—quality of hope that seemed almost impossible in their circumstances yet somehow absolutely necessary for maintaining sanity in a situation that tested every assumption about meaning and purpose. One by one, other voices joined his: Old Tom's wavering bass, Will's surprisingly pure tenor, Ned's sea-weathered baritone, until the entire hold resonated with sound that transformed their shared suffering into something approaching worship.

When the storm finally passed and *Moffatt* limped into calmer waters under skies that seemed impossibly blue after days of grey violence, Thomas found that something fundamental had shifted within him. The man who had stolen Farmer Biggs' pony from motives of pride and desperation had died somewhere in that storm's fury, replaced by someone who understood that survival meant more than simply drawing breath—it meant choosing, again and again, to preserve whatever capacity for love and service remained after circumstances had stripped away everything that seemed essential.

6 CALVIN'S SILENCE

Gosford Workshop, NSW — October 2010

Calvin Wilson stood at his workbench in the dawn light that filtered through windows he'd cleaned just yesterday, though the glass already bore the fine coating of sawdust that marked his workshop as a place where beautiful things emerged from patient labor rather than pristine showrooms. His hands—seventy-five years old but still steady, still sure of their purpose—moved across the surface of red cedar that would become a jewelry box for Mrs. Chen next door, whose husband had died three months ago and who needed something beautiful to hold the wedding ring she could no longer bear to wear but couldn't bring herself to put away.

The wood grain spoke to him in patterns that had taken fifty years of careful attention to learn to read. Cedar from the north coast, probably harvested decades ago and seasoned until its character had been refined by time and patience into something worthy of preserving precious things. His fingers traced the natural whorls and knots, understanding how the piece wanted to be shaped, where the hinges would sit most naturally, how the internal compartments could follow the wood's own logic rather than imposing arbitrary geometry upon it.

This was how Calvin had always processed the world—through his hands, through the patient transformation of raw materials into objects that served purposes beyond mere utility. Ellen had understood this about him from the beginning of their marriage forty-three years ago, had learned to read his moods in the projects that emerged from his workshop. When he was happy, he made toys for neighborhood children. When he was worried, he built furniture that would outlast whatever troubles had prompted its creation. When he was grieving...

When he was grieving, he made boxes. Small containers designed to hold things too precious to leave exposed to ordinary light and air, compartments that protected what couldn't be replaced if lost or damaged.

The jewelry box for Mrs. Chen was the third he'd completed since Ellen's death eighteen months ago. Each one had taught him something different about loss and preservation, about the human need to create sanctuary for memories that felt too fragile to survive without careful tending. But this one carried additional weight because Mrs. Chen reminded him of Sara—proud, independent, trying to navigate grief alone rather than risk the vulnerability that asking for help required.

His phone lay silent on the workbench beside tools he'd inherited from his own father, arranged with the precision that came from decades of knowing exactly where everything belonged. He'd called Sara yesterday evening, listening to the ring echo in her Kirribilli apartment while imagining her staring at the screen, deciding whether their careful relationship could bear the weight of actual conversation about anything that mattered.

She'd let it go to voicemail, as he'd known she would. As he'd been secretly relieved she would, if he was honest with himself about his own capacity for the kind of honest communication their relationship needed but neither knew how to initiate.

What would I say anyway? Calvin thought, his plane taking a gossamer shaving from the cedar's surface. *That I miss her mother so much I can barely breathe some mornings? That I don't know how to be Sara's father without Ellen there to translate my silences into words she could understand? That every conversation feels like walking through a minefield where one wrong word might destroy what little connection we have left?*

The workshop smelled of linseed oil and cedar shavings, familiar scents that connected him to his father's workspace and his grandfather's before that—generations of Wilson men who'd understood that some truths could only be expressed through the patient application of skill to materials that rewarded honesty with beauty. But unlike his ancestors, who'd lived in communities where everyone knew their neighbors' stories and grief was shared rather than privatized, Calvin found himself isolated by circumstances that felt too large for his vocabulary to encompass.

Ellen's death hadn't just taken his wife; it had taken the translator who'd helped him communicate with a daughter whose inner world remained mysterious despite thirty-five years of loving her as best he knew how. Ellen had been the bridge between his silences and Sara's need for words, his practical expressions of care and her hunger for emotional connection that felt safe enough to trust.

The jewelry box was taking shape under his hands, its corners joined with the kind of precision that would make it last for generations while maintaining the organic flow that honored the wood's natural character. Calvin had learned decades ago that the best furniture emerged from collaboration between craftsman and material, human intention guided by respect for what the wood itself wanted to become.

Like relationships, he thought, then pushed the analogy away before it could lead him toward territories his mind wasn't equipped to navigate without Ellen's help.

Through the workshop windows, Brisbane Water sparkled in the morning sun, its surface broken by the wakes of early commuter ferries carrying people toward Sydney's towers and traffic and all the complexities of contemporary life that felt increasingly foreign to Calvin's sensibilities. He'd built this workshop forty years ago, when Gosford was still a sleepy regional town rather than a commuter suburb, when the pace of life allowed for the kind of patient craftsmanship that couldn't be rushed without sacrificing quality.

The town had changed around him, but the workshop remained a pocket of older time where hours were measured by the rhythm of hand tools rather than digital clocks, where progress was visible in shavings accumulating on the floor rather than numbers flickering on screens. Ellen had understood the sanctuary this space provided, had brought him tea in the afternoons when complex projects required sustained attention, had learned not to interrupt when he was working through problems that required his hands and eyes and the accumulated wisdom of decades spent learning how to make beautiful things from ordinary materials.

Now the tea grew cold on the windowsill, brewed by habit each morning but forgotten as he lost himself in work that provided the only reliable escape from thoughts that circled like vultures around the crater Ellen's death had left in his understanding of who he was and how he was supposed to navigate the years that remained.

Calvin set down his plane and picked up sandpaper, beginning the patient process of smoothing the cedar's surface to silk. This was meditative work that required attention without demanding conscious thought, allowing his mind to drift toward the phone call he'd made yesterday and the text he'd sent afterward—careful words that conveyed concern without risking the kind of emotional exposure that might drive Sara even further into the independence that protected her but also isolated her from the support she might need.

"Called earlier. Hope you're doing well. Dad."

The message had taken him twenty minutes to compose, each word weighed against the possibility that too much feeling might overwhelm Sara's careful boundaries while too little might confirm her suspicion that his silence represented indifference rather than inadequacy. How do you tell your daughter that you think about her constantly but don't know how to bridge the gap between thought and action, between love felt and love expressed in ways she could recognize and trust?

Ellen had been the one who remembered birthdays and anniversaries, who called Sara just to check in, who maintained the emotional infrastructure that kept their small family connected across the distances that geography and personality had imposed. Calvin's contributions had been practical—the bookshelf he'd built for Sara's first apartment, the kitchen table that had followed her through three moves, the jewelry box he'd made for her wedding to David that now probably held memories she'd rather forget.

Objects last longer than relationships, he thought, then immediately felt guilty for the cynicism that grief had made easier to access than hope.

The sandpaper whispered against cedar grain, each stroke revealing new depths in the wood's color and character. Calvin had learned to find peace in this repetitive motion, the way it anchored him to immediate physical reality when thoughts threatened to carry him toward territories too painful for sustained exploration. Ellen had teased him about this habit—"You sand things smooth when your heart feels rough, don't you, love?"—but she'd said it with the affection of someone who understood that everyone processed difficult emotions differently.

Her voice was becoming harder to recall with precision, despite the forty-three years they'd shared. Calvin found himself working harder to remember the exact cadence of her laughter, the particular way she hummed while cooking Sunday dinner, the dozen small gestures that had constituted the language of their marriage. Grief, he was learning, was a thief that stole not just future possibilities but the clarity of past experiences, making even precious memories feel unreliable.

The workshop door opened with its familiar creak, and Calvin looked up to see Tom Morrison—his neighbor for twenty years, fellow craftsman, and one of the few people who understood that some forms of support required no words at all. Tom carried two cups of coffee and the morning newspaper, his daily ritual of checking on Calvin without making it feel like charity or obligation.

"Morning, Cal," Tom said, setting one cup on the workbench beside tools that bore the patina of decades of careful use. "Saw your light on early again. This for Mrs. Chen?"

Calvin nodded, accepting the coffee with gratitude that went beyond caffeine. Tom's presence never required conversation about feelings or healing or any of the topics well-meaning people seemed to think widowers needed to discuss. Instead, they talked about wood grain and joint techniques and the small practical challenges that could be solved through skill and patience rather than emotional archaeology.

"She's having a rough time," Calvin said, running his thumb along the jewelry box's edge to check for smoothness. "Forty-seven years married. Don't know how you rebuild a life after that long with someone."

Tom settled onto the stool Calvin kept for visitors, understanding that Calvin was talking about himself as much as Mrs. Chen. "Maybe you don't rebuild. Maybe you just keep building, one day at a time, using whatever materials are available."

The observation hit closer to home than Calvin was prepared to acknowledge directly. Instead, he picked up his sandpaper again, letting the rhythm of smoothing wood provide counterpoint to thoughts that felt too large for the workshop's comfortable confines.

"Sara's been on my mind," Calvin said after several minutes of companionable silence. "Don't know how to reach her. Ellen always knew what to say, when to push and when to wait. I just make things with my hands and hope somehow that translates to caring."

Tom studied the jewelry box with the appreciation of someone who understood the skill required to make something so deceptively simple. "Maybe that's exactly what she needs right now. Someone who shows love through making things last, creating something beautiful when everything else feels broken."

Calvin's phone buzzed against the workbench, startling him from the peaceful focus that Tom's presence had restored. Sara's name appeared on the screen with a text message that made his chest tighten with emotions too complex for easy identification.

"Dad, I found something at Glen Lena that changes everything I thought I knew about our family. Can we talk? Really talk? I think you need to hear this story."

He stared at the message, feeling the workshop's familiar sanctuary suddenly charged with possibility and risk. This wasn't the careful communication they'd maintained since Ellen's funeral—polite updates and obligatory check-ins that preserved connection without demanding vulnerability. This was Sara reaching across the silence that had protected them both, asking for the kind of conversation that might heal what grief had damaged or reveal how irreparable the damage actually was.

"Good news?" Tom asked, reading something in Calvin's expression that suggested significance beyond ordinary daily concerns.

"Don't know yet," Calvin replied, his thumb hovering over the keyboard while he tried to compose a response that would match Sara's courage without overwhelming it. "She wants to talk. Really talk, she says. About family history."

"Then you better talk," Tom said simply. "Whatever she found, it's important enough to risk reaching out. Don't make her regret taking that chance."

Calvin typed slowly, each word chosen with the same care he brought to selecting wood for projects that needed to last: *"Come for dinner Sunday. I'll cook that fish you used to like. Bring whatever you found. I'm ready to listen."*

He pressed send before doubt could interfere, understanding that some bridges required leaping before you could be certain they would hold your weight. Outside the workshop windows, Brisbane Water caught the morning light like scattered coins, and Calvin felt something shift in his chest—not healing exactly, but the possibility of healing, the recognition that love might prove stronger than loss if given the chance to rebuild itself from materials that grief had left scattered but not destroyed.

The jewelry box waited under his hands, its cedar surface smooth as silk now, ready for the delicate work of cutting compartments that would hold Mrs. Chen's treasures safely while allowing easy access when she needed to touch what couldn't be replaced. Calvin picked up his marking gauge, understanding that the most important work—on wood and relationships both—required patience and precision and the faith that beautiful things could emerge from the most unlikely circumstances if approached with sufficient care and courage.

Tom finished his coffee and stood to leave, understanding that Calvin needed time to process whatever change Sara's message represented. "See you tomorrow," he said, pausing at the door. "And Cal? Ellen would be proud of you for taking this chance."

Calvin nodded, not trusting his voice to respond without revealing emotions too raw for casual conversation. But as Tom's footsteps faded across the gravel yard, Calvin felt his isolation begin to crack like ice in spring sunshine. Sara was coming home. They were going to talk—really talk—about family history that apparently mattered enough to bridge the silence that had protected them both from additional loss.

He returned to his work with renewed focus, understanding that he had four days to prepare for a conversation that might restore what grief had damaged or confirm that some things couldn't be repaired no matter how much skill and patience were applied to their reconstruction. But either way, the work was worth doing. Love, like fine craftsmanship, required willingness to risk failure for the chance to create something beautiful enough to last.

The jewelry box took shape under his hands, each cut and joint a small act of faith that precision and patience could transform raw materials into objects worthy of holding what people treasured most. And perhaps, Calvin thought as cedar shavings accumulated around his feet like prayers made visible, relationships followed similar principles—requiring the same attention to grain and character, the same respect for natural patterns, the same willingness to let the materials guide the process rather than imposing arbitrary designs upon them.

Sunday would come, and with it the chance to discover whether forty-three years of marriage had taught him enough about love to help rebuild a connection with the daughter who carried Ellen's curiosity and his own stubborn determination to make beautiful things from whatever circumstances provided for their construction.

The morning light strengthened beyond the workshop windows, and Calvin Wilson worked on, his hands steady and sure, preparing for the most important conversation of his life with the same careful attention he brought to creating objects meant to preserve what couldn't be replaced if lost or damaged.

7 CHAINS AND CHOICES

Sydney, New South Wales - August 1836 to November 1843

The Sydney sun fell upon Thomas Staines' shoulders like a blacksmith's hammer forged from fire itself, each ray carrying heat that penetrated to his bones and reminded him that he was no longer in England's temperate embrace. Hyde Park Barracks rose before the newly landed convicts like a monument to ordered misery—three stories of golden sandstone that might have seemed beautiful in other circumstances, but here served as visible proof that even exile could be made systematic, efficient, and utterly without hope of appeal.

The August morning air shimmered with heat that made breathing feel like swallowing flame, and Thomas felt sweat already beginning to trace familiar patterns down his back despite the early hour. Four months aboard the *Moffatt* had prepared him for many hardships, but nothing could have readied him for this furnace climate that seemed designed to test whether men might literally melt under sufficient pressure.

"Form lines, you scum!" Sergeant Morrison's voice cut through the harbor morning like a cat-o'-nine-tails applied to flesh—not merely loud, but designed to strip away whatever dignity the voyage might have left intact. "His Majesty's colony has work for willing hands and harder work for unwilling ones. You'll learn the difference quick enough."

Thomas shuffled forward with his fellow passengers, their leg irons creating a percussion that spoke of dreams deferred and freedoms cancelled. The chains that bound them were heavier than those they'd worn aboard ship, their weight a constant reminder that Sydney might offer different varieties of suffering but no reduction in its intensity. Around him, men who had survived the crossing now faced the reality that their ordeal had been merely preparation for trials that would test everything the voyage had failed to break.

The barracks' interior offered no relief from the heat—if anything, the sandstone walls seemed to concentrate the sun's assault, creating chambers that felt like ovens designed for slow cooking. The building itself was a masterpiece of institutional efficiency, designed to house eight hundred souls with the same attention to human comfort that might be given to storing grain or coal. Three floors of dormitories stretched above a ground level that contained the administrative offices where convict fates were decided by men who had never worn chains themselves.

Thomas found himself assigned to Dormitory C on the second floor, a vast chamber that housed sixty men in space that might have been adequate for thirty, their hammocks strung so close together that privacy became a concept as foreign as the landscape visible through barred windows. The room's high ceiling, designed to aid ventilation in the oppressive heat, also created an echo that turned every snore, cough, and whispered prayer into a symphony of human misery that provided soundtrack for sleepless nights.

The daily routine began at five o'clock with the sound of a bell that shattered whatever peace the pre-dawn hours might have offered. Roll call followed immediately—six hundred names shouted into the morning heat, responses that confirmed another night had passed without successful escape attempts. The men stood in formation in the central courtyard, their convict uniforms of coarse grey wool already damp with perspiration despite the early hour, while guards with muskets counted and recounted to ensure that His Majesty's property remained properly accounted for.

Breakfast consisted of porridge that tasted like paste mixed with disappointment, accompanied by bread that seemed designed to test whether human teeth were capable of chewing substances that approached the hardness of wood. The meal was consumed standing in the courtyard, metal bowls held in hands that bore the calluses and scars that marked different trades—carpenters, tailors, farm laborers, and men like Thomas whose blacksmith skills would soon be put to colonial use.

The work assignment that would define the next seven years of his life arrived with bureaucratic efficiency: "Staines, T. - Blacksmith. Government Forge, Macquarie Street. Report to Supervisor Walsh, dawn tomorrow." Thomas read the orders with something approaching relief—at least his skills would be employed, even if the circumstances were far removed from his North Kilworth workshop where he had been master of his own domain.

The march to work sites proceeded through Sydney's growing streets, past free settlers whose expressions ranged from pity to disgust to the careful indifference of people who had learned not to see what might disturb their sense of their own security. The convict gangs moved in formation, their leg irons creating rhythm that spoke of reduced humanity, while guards on horseback provided supervision that was equal parts protection and threat—protecting the community from the convicts, protecting the convicts from the community, and threatening both with consequences should either forget their proper place in the colonial hierarchy.

The Government Forge proved to be a cruel parody of everything Thomas had loved about his trade. Where his English workshop had been a place of creation—horseshoes that carried men safely across difficult terrain, tools that helped other craftsmen ply their trades, gates and hinges that protected what families held dear—this colonial furnace served primarily to create the implements of bondage. Chains for convicts, leg irons for punishment cells, bars for windows that would never open to let in anything as dangerous as hope.

Supervisor Walsh proved to be a man carved from the same unforgiving stone as the colony itself—fair in his way, but with fairness measured by colonial standards where survival trumped sentiment and efficiency mattered more than comfort. He was perhaps forty years old, weathered by decades of Australian sun, with hands that bore the scars of someone who had worked his way up from manual labor to administrative authority through competence rather than birth or education.

"You know your trade, Staines," Walsh observed after watching Thomas work for a week, his assessment delivered with the clinical precision of someone who had learned to evaluate men as tools rather than individuals. "Question is whether you'll use that knowledge to make yourself valuable or waste it nursing grievances about circumstances you can't change."

The message was clear: adaptation meant survival, while resistance promised only additional suffering. Thomas chose adaptation, throwing himself into his work with an intensity that surprised both supervisors and fellow convicts. The forge became his refuge, the only place where the skills that defined him could find expression, even if that expression now served purposes that would have horrified his former self.

The work itself was both familiar and alien—familiar in the basic techniques of heating and shaping metal, alien in its purposes and the conditions under which it was performed. The Government Forge operated from dawn to dusk six days a week, its fires never allowed to die completely lest the time required to reheat them reduce overall productivity. Thomas found himself assigned initially to the most basic tasks—maintaining the fires, sorting scrap metal, preparing materials for the skilled tradesman who shaped them into finished products.

But Walsh was a man who recognized competence when he saw it, and Thomas's years of experience quickly became apparent in the quality of his work and his understanding of metallurgy that exceeded what might be expected from someone whose education had been limited to practical apprenticeship. Within a month, he had been promoted to working the bellows for the master smith, and within three months, he was trusted with his own anvil and the responsibility for training newer arrivals whose blacksmith skills were less developed.

The irony was not lost on him: Thomas Staines, who had been brought to this place by chains, now spent his days forging the very instruments that would bind other men to similar fates. Each link he welded, every shackle he shaped, felt like a small betrayal of the pride he had once taken in his craft. Yet the work was honest, if brutal, and honesty had become a precious commodity in his reduced circumstances.

The daily rhythm of convict life ground on with merciless regularity, but within that routine, Thomas began to discover possibilities for small satisfactions that made endurance not just possible but occasionally meaningful. His growing reputation for quality work earned him privileges that other convicts envied—better food rations for skilled workers, permission to remain at the forge after official hours to complete projects that required extra attention, and gradually, the kind of trust that allowed him to work with minimal supervision.

Walsh's management style was pragmatic rather than cruel. He understood that skilled workers produced better results when treated with something approaching respect, and he had learned to distinguish between the convicts who could be trusted with responsibility and those who required constant surveillance. Thomas fell clearly into the former category, his work ethic and technical competence earning him a place among the handful of prisoners whose skills made them valuable assets rather than mere burdens to be endured.

"Good work on the prison hinges, Staines," Walsh said one afternoon, examining a set of door hardware that Thomas had crafted with particular care. "Hardware like this should last twenty years if properly maintained. Shows you understand the difference between adequate work and proper craftsmanship."

The compliment was earned rather than offered from mere politeness, and Thomas felt the deep satisfaction that came from recognition of his skills. But more than personal satisfaction, he felt the growing awareness that excellence in his trade could provide something beyond mere survival—it could provide purpose, meaning, even a form of dignity that chains could not entirely strip away.

His relationship with fellow convicts at the forge developed along lines that had little to do with the crimes that had brought them to Sydney and everything to do with their willingness to work together toward common goals. Old Tom Sullivan, his mentor from the *Moffatt*, had been assigned to road construction work that was gradually destroying his health, but other men at the forge proved capable of friendship that transcended their circumstances.

Billy Henderson, a Londoner transported for burglary, possessed an intuitive understanding of metallurgy that complemented Thomas's more formal training. Their collaboration on complex projects created partnership that made difficult work more manageable while producing results that impressed even Walsh's critical standards.

James MacReady, a Scotsman whose theft of sheep had earned him fourteen years of bondage, brought humor and storytelling skills that made the long hours pass more quickly while maintaining morale among workers whose spirits might otherwise have been crushed by the repetitive nature of their labor.

But it was during the evening hours, when official work ended and convicts were left to find whatever meaning they could in their reduced circumstances, that Thomas discovered the most profound transformations of his Australian exile. The barracks after dark became a different world—one where men who had been stripped of their former identities struggled to create new versions of themselves from whatever materials remained after the Crown had claimed everything else.

The dormitory that housed sixty souls in space designed for half that number might have been expected to become a breeding ground for violence and despair. Instead, Thomas found that shared hardship had created its own forms of community, its own systems of mutual support that helped men survive trials that might have destroyed them individually. Those with reading skills taught those without. Men with musical ability provided entertainment that transformed grey evenings into something approaching celebration. Those with particular trades shared knowledge that might help others find better work assignments or avoid the brutal punishments that awaited those who failed to meet official expectations.

Thomas's blacksmith skills made him valuable not just to the colonial administration but to his fellow convicts, many of whom needed small repairs to personal possessions that represented their only connection to lives they had left behind. A broken watch chain, a damaged tool, a piece of jewelry that carried memories of loved ones—these items might have been worthless in monetary terms, but they possessed emotional significance that made their repair acts of genuine service rather than mere technical exercise.

The work was performed in secret, after lights-out when guards were less vigilant, using tools improvised from materials that would not be missed from official inventory. Thomas found himself working by candlelight on projects that served no purpose except preserving other men's connections to whatever had made their former lives meaningful. The satisfaction that came from such work was different from anything he had experienced during his years as a village blacksmith—deeper, more personal, connected to service rather than profit.

These activities were strictly forbidden, carrying penalties that could add years to existing sentences or result in punishments that might permanently damage health or spirit. But Thomas gradually understood that the risk was worthwhile, not just for the practical benefits it provided to other convicts but for what it taught him about the difference between existing and truly living, between surviving hardship and being transformed by it.

Governor George Gipps' annual inspection of the Government Forge arrived in March 1838, accompanied by the kind of preparation that suggested careers might depend upon the impression created during the few hours of official scrutiny. Walsh spent weeks ensuring that every aspect of the operation met standards that exceeded normal requirements, while convicts found themselves subjected to additional grooming and instruction designed to present the most favorable possible impression of colonial efficiency.

On the morning of the inspection, Thomas prepared his work station with unusual care, ensuring that every tool was properly arranged, every surface cleaned, every project organized to demonstrate both competence and pride in craft. When the Governor arrived—a man whose bearing suggested he was accustomed to command but not necessarily comfortable with the human consequences of the power he wielded—

Thomas continued his work without obvious attention-seeking, allowing his skills to speak for themselves.

The Governor studied the specialized chains Thomas had created for use in the colony's expanding mining operations, hardware that demonstrated both technical proficiency and artistic sensibility unusual in convict work. "This man's work shows both skill and care," Gipps observed to Walsh, his tone suggesting genuine appreciation rather than mere official politeness. "Unusual to find such combination of qualities in a convict assignment."

"Thomas Staines, Your Excellency," Walsh replied, his own pride in supervising quality work evident in his voice. "Transported for theft, but has proven himself entirely reliable. No disciplinary issues, consistent output, shows positive influence on other convicts assigned to his supervision."

The brief interview that followed became one of the defining moments of Thomas's transformation from bitter convict to man capable of redemption. When asked about his crime, he answered with honesty that reflected genuine understanding rather than calculated performance: "I stole because I believed poverty justified taking what belonged to another man. I was wrong. Poverty might explain my choice, but it doesn't excuse it. A man is responsible for his actions regardless of his circumstances."

Governor Gipps' approval was evident in his manner as much as his words: "Continue your excellent work, Staines. The colony benefits from men who understand that redemption must be earned rather than simply claimed."

The remaining years of Thomas's sentence passed with increasing hope rather than mere endurance. His reputation for excellence spread beyond the Government Forge to other areas of colonial administration, creating opportunities for expanded responsibilities that gradually prepared him for eventual freedom. He supervised younger convicts learning blacksmith skills, consulted on engineering problems that required metalworking expertise, and even created decorative items for colonial officials whose appreciation for craftsmanship transcended their awareness of his convict status.

More importantly, he developed relationships with free settlers whose respect for his work led to conversations about life beyond the barracks walls. These men—farmers who needed tools repaired, merchants who required specialized metalwork, even clergy who appreciated his ability to create religious items that combined functionality with beauty—gradually began to see him not as convict 537 but as Thomas Staines, skilled craftsman whose past mistakes had been balanced by years of reliable service.

When his Ticket of Leave finally arrived in November 1843—seven years to the month after his landing at Sydney Cove—Thomas stood in the Government Forge holding the document that restored his freedom of movement within the colony and felt not triumph but profound gratitude. Not for his circumstances, which remained difficult, but for having survived them with his capacity for hope intact, his skills refined rather than diminished, his character strengthened rather than broken by trials that might have destroyed someone whose spirit had not been prepared through suffering to receive whatever wisdom hardship could provide.

His fellow convicts gathered that evening to mark his departure from the barracks where he had lived for seven years—not with celebration, which would have attracted unwanted official attention, but with the quiet recognition of men who understood that one among them had successfully navigated the passage from bondage to freedom through patient commitment to becoming worthy of the second chance that colonial society might offer to those who proved themselves capable of redemption.

As he prepared to leave Sydney for the frontier town that represented his chance to build a new life from the raw materials of exile and hard-won wisdom, Thomas felt the weight of the Celtic cross against his chest and understood that his real journey was just beginning. The man who walked away from Hyde Park Barracks bore little resemblance to the proud blacksmith who had stolen a pony from desperation and self-righteousness.

This new Thomas Staines carried in his heart the accumulated wisdom of seven years spent learning that dignity came not from circumstances but from choices, that love could survive any hardship if it was willing to transform itself from possession into service, that redemption was always possible for men willing to accept responsibility for their failures while working patiently to become worthy of forgiveness.

8 THE SECOND LETTER

Kirribilli Apartment, Sydney - March 2011

Sara Wilson sat at her kitchen table with the second letter spread before her like a map to territory she wasn't certain she was ready to explore. The harbor lights beyond her window created patterns that shifted with the evening breeze, but her attention remained fixed on Thomas Staines' careful handwriting, words written from Three Rivers Inn in August 1852 as flood waters began their assault on everything he and Catherine had built together.

Two weeks had passed since she'd discovered the tin box in Glen Lena's attic, two weeks of carrying these letters like sacred texts while trying to understand what they demanded from her own life. The first letter had shattered her understanding of what family legacy meant—not just bloodlines and property, but wisdom earned through suffering and transmitted through love that transcended death itself. Now the second letter waited, promising deeper revelations about transformation and the courage required to choose hope over despair.

She lifted the paper with hands that trembled slightly, understanding that she was about to encounter Thomas's voice at the moment when his understanding of redemption was being tested by circumstances that threatened everything his seven years of patient rebuilding had accomplished. The water stains on the edges spoke of composition during crisis, words written while flood waters rose around the inn that represented his life's greatest achievement.

"My Most Precious Daughter," the letter began, *" The Bell River rises with each hour that passes, its waters now lapping at our inn's foundation stones as I write by candlelight in what may be our final night of safety. Your mother sleeps fitfully above, her body heavy with carrying you toward a world that grows more uncertain with each rumble of thunder through our valley."*

Sara read the opening passage aloud, her voice carrying across the apartment to where Calvin dozed in his chair, having driven down from Gosford that afternoon with fish fresh from Brisbane Water and the comfortable silence that had developed between them during these weeks of shared discovery. He stirred at the sound of Thomas's words, his eyes opening to find her studying the letter with the kind of intensity that suggested she was receiving instruction rather than merely reading family history.

"The second letter?" Calvin asked, understanding immediately what held her attention so completely.

"Written as the flood began," Sara replied, already sensing that this letter would reveal different aspects of Thomas's transformation—not just his understanding of individual redemption but his grasp of what it meant to build something lasting with another person, to create love that could survive whatever trials the future might present.

As she continued reading, Thomas's voice carried her back to 1852, to Three Rivers Inn during those final hours before the Bell River claimed everything except the love that had made the building meaningful. His words painted pictures of domestic happiness that seemed almost impossible for someone whose journey had begun in Northampton Gaol—mornings spent watching Catherine move through their kitchen with the efficiency of someone who had found her calling, evenings when travelers gathered in their common room to share stories that connected strangers through recognition of shared humanity.

"Your mother possesses wisdom I am still learning," Thomas wrote, *"the knowledge that true strength lies not in demanding that the world conform to our expectations but in adapting ourselves to meet whatever challenges life presents while maintaining the essential goodness that makes us worthy of love and respect."*

The observation struck Sara with particular force, its relevance to her own circumstances impossible to ignore. She had been demanding that grief conform to her expectations—that it follow predictable patterns, respect reasonable timelines, leave her relationship with Calvin essentially unchanged except for the absence of Ellen's mediating presence. Thomas's words suggested different possibilities: that strength might come from adapting to loss rather than resisting it, from finding new ways to connect rather than accepting separation as inevitable.

But it was Thomas's description of watching Catherine prepare for their child's arrival that made Sara understand why Rivers had preserved these letters with such care. His words captured not just personal happiness but universal truth about love that serves rather than demands, that builds rather than consumes, that finds in another person's welfare its own deepest satisfaction:

"Watching her sew tiny garments with hands that have never known idleness, singing lullabies in the German tongue that carries her father's memory, planning for a future that includes another person to love and protect and guide toward whatever destiny awaits—I am overwhelmed by gratitude for blessings I could never have imagined when I stole Farmer Biggs' pony in what seems like another man's lifetime."

Sara set the letter down, understanding that she was witnessing love in its purest form—not the desperate need that masqueraded as affection, but the genuine care that placed another person's happiness above personal comfort. This was the love she wanted to offer Calvin, the love she hoped to receive, the kind of connection that made any loss worthwhile because of the meaning such love created.

The afternoon had grown late while she read, harbor sounds providing gentle soundtrack for her growing understanding of what Thomas's transformation meant for anyone willing to learn from his example. Calvin had joined her at the table, his carpenter's hands gentle on pages that carried weight far beyond their physical substance, his presence providing comfort that made the difficult passages easier to bear.

"He learned something most of us never figure out," Calvin said quietly, his voice carrying the particular wisdom that came from seventy-five years of observing how people chose to love or fail to love those who mattered most. "That happiness isn't something you find or receive—it's something you create by choosing to serve someone else's welfare even when it costs you personally."

The observation resonated with everything Sara had been feeling since discovering these letters, everything she had been avoiding since Ellen's death created the chasm between them that they had been afraid to bridge. She thought about the careful distance they had maintained, each protecting their own pain while trying not to cause additional hurt to someone they loved but didn't quite know how to reach anymore.

What would it mean to love Calvin the way Thomas had learned to love Catherine? Not safe love that avoided difficult conversations, but transformative love that risked rejection for the chance to create something beautiful from the materials grief had left them. Not careful relationship that prevented additional loss, but honest connection that made whatever loss came feel worthwhile because of the meaning such love created.

The phone sat beside her elbow, its silent presence both invitation and challenge. She had thought about calling Calvin dozens of times during these past weeks, but always found excuses to postpone conversations that might demand more vulnerability than she felt ready to offer. Now, with Thomas's words fresh in her mind and Calvin's physical presence providing courage she didn't usually possess, she understood that some risks were worth taking.

"Dad," she said, her voice carrying the tentative quality that marked important conversations, "I need to tell you something. These letters, Thomas's story—it's changing how I see everything. How I understand what love means, what family means, what we owe to each other."

Calvin's attention sharpened, his craftsman's focus directed toward words that might require the same precision he brought to measuring twice before cutting, to ensuring that joints fit properly before permanent assembly. "Tell me," he said simply.

The words came slowly at first, then with increasing confidence as Sara found herself explaining not just what Thomas's letters contained but what they had taught her about transformation and redemption and the courage required to choose hope over resignation. She spoke about his journey from convicted thief to devoted husband, about Catherine's bravery in crossing oceans to find better life, about their gradual understanding that two broken people could create something beautiful together if willing to serve each other's welfare rather than demand personal satisfaction.

But more than historical narrative, Sara found herself speaking about present possibilities—about her own need for transformation, her own choice between emotional exile and vulnerable love, her own understanding that some connections were worth risking everything to preserve. She talked about the months since Ellen's death when they had circled each other like careful strangers, both wanting connection but afraid that intimacy might lead to additional loss.

"I've been playing it safe," she admitted, the words carrying weight that made speaking them difficult but necessary. "Keeping enough distance to protect against losing you too, but that distance has been keeping us from the kind of relationship Ellen would have wanted us to have."

Calvin's eyes filled with tears that spoke of recognition rather than sadness, understanding that her words named truths he had been feeling but hadn't known how to express. "I've been doing the same thing," he said quietly. "Hiding in my workshop, staying busy with projects that don't require risking my heart again, telling myself that careful friendship was better than the kind of love that makes loss devastating."

The conversation that followed lasted until harbor lights began to twinkle beyond the window, covering ground they hadn't touched since Ellen's funeral—their shared grief and individual struggles with loss, their mutual fear of causing additional pain to someone they loved but didn't know how to reach, their recognition that careful distance had protected them from vulnerability but also prevented the kind of healing that required honest connection.

As they talked, Sara found herself understanding what Thomas's letters had been trying to teach her about love that served rather than demanded, that built rather than protected, that risked everything for the chance to create meaning that survived whatever circumstances might impose. This was the sacred obligation Rivers had written about—not just preserving family stories but proving them through personal choice, demonstrating their continued power to inspire transformation in anyone willing to follow their example.

The phone call she had been avoiding for weeks became unnecessary when love found expression through direct conversation rather than electronic mediation. Calvin's presence in her apartment, his willingness to stay for dinner and evening conversation, his gradual opening to emotions he had been protecting since Ellen's death—these developments represented progress toward the kind of connection Thomas and Catherine had built through patience and mutual commitment to each other's welfare.

Later that evening, as Calvin prepared to drive back to Gosford, Sara felt compelled to make one attempt at the phone call she had been contemplating. Not to her father, who was standing in her doorway ready to leave, but to herself—a practice run for the kind of vulnerable honesty that real connection required.

She dialed Calvin's mobile number while he stood watching, understanding that this was symbolic gesture rather than practical communication but needing to demonstrate her willingness to risk rejection, to reach across whatever distance might separate them, to choose connection over the safety of emotional isolation.

The phone rang once before Calvin answered, his voice carrying amusement that made the gesture feel like beginning rather than ending, promise rather than mere sentiment. "Yes, love?"

"I wanted to tell you while I still had courage," Sara said, her words carrying across the few feet between them while somehow bridging the months of careful distance that had kept them from this kind of honesty. "I love you, Dad. Not just because you're family, but because you're someone I genuinely like and respect and want in my life. Ellen's death doesn't change that—it just makes it more precious."

Calvin ended the call and crossed the room to embrace her with the kind of physical affection they hadn't shared since the funeral, his carpenter's arms strong around her shoulders while she felt the accumulated tension of months finally beginning to dissolve. "I love you too," he said simply. "Always have, always will. Just needed to remember that love meant choosing connection rather than protecting against loss."

As he drove away through Sydney streets that carried him back to his Gosford workshop where he created beautiful things from raw materials, Sara understood that something fundamental had shifted between them. Not completion of healing—that would require time and continued effort—but beginning of repair work that honored both Ellen's memory and their own need for relationship that could survive whatever trials the future might present.

The second letter lay on her kitchen table, Thomas's words about transformative love providing guidance for anyone willing to learn that happiness came not from receiving but from giving, not from demanding but from serving, not from protecting but from risking everything for the chance to create meaning that survived whatever circumstances might destroy its physical manifestations.

Outside her window, harbor water flowed toward destinations unknown but somehow essential, carrying with it the accumulated stories of everyone who had ever loved deeply enough to risk everything for others' welfare. Sara felt herself becoming part of that eternal flow, understanding that the sacred obligation Rivers had identified began with the relationships closest to home, with proving that love could indeed bridge any gap if approached with sufficient courage and faith.

Thomas's journey from individual shame to shared redemption was becoming her template for choosing connection over isolation, hope over the comfortable numbness of limited expectations. The letters had more to teach her, but already they had provided foundation for understanding that transformation was possible for anyone willing to choose service over selfishness, vulnerability over safety, love over fear.

The phone sat silent beside Thomas's words, no longer representing communication postponed but connection achieved through different means—direct conversation, honest emotion, the kind of presence that electronic mediation could supplement but never replace. Sara had learned something Thomas understood completely: that the greatest gifts came through giving rather than receiving, that love multiplied when shared rather than diminishing when offered freely, that redemption remained available to anyone brave enough to choose it.

THE BLACKSMITH'S BEQUEST

Three Rivers Inn, Wellington, New South Wales
22nd August, 1852

My Most Precious Daughter,

The Bell River rises with each hour that passes, its waters now lapping at our inn's foundation stones as I write by candlelight in what may be our final night of safety. Your mother sleeps fitfully above, her body heavy with carrying you toward a world that grows more uncertain with each rumble of thunder through our valley.

Four days have passed since I wrote my first letter to you, my darling child—four days that have transformed the crude hope of a newly-freed convict into the seasoned love of a man who has learned to build happiness from materials that once seemed fit only for despair. If my previous words spoke of transformation through suffering, let these speak of the far more difficult art of discovering joy without forgetting the pain that purchased it.

You grow stronger each day within your mother's womb—I feel your movements when I place my hand upon her swelling belly, tiny pressures that speak of life insisting upon itself despite the chaos surrounding us. Catherine maintains you will arrive in September, when winter's fury has passed and spring begins to warm this valley we call home. I pray God grants her prophecy truth, for I would meet you in sunshine rather than storm.

But if the Almighty's plans differ—if these rising waters demand payment that includes my own life—then know I face such fate with gratitude rather than bitterness, for I have been granted nine years in this colony to discover what true wealth means, to transform the shameful legacy of a convicted thief into the respectable foundation of a man who learned to love without counting the cost.

When I walked from Sydney's Hyde Park Barracks in November 1843, clutching my Ticket of Leave like a sacred text, I believed freedom meant the absence of chains, the restoration of choices stripped away by conviction and transportation. How simple that understanding seems now, how pathetically incomplete.

True freedom, my beloved daughter, proves far more complex and infinitely more valuable than mere absence of external constraint. It is the capacity to choose service over selfishness, humility over pride, love over fear—especially when such choices require sacrificing immediate comfort for long-term meaning. The man who left Sydney possessed liberty of movement but remained chained to patterns of thinking that had brought him to ruin. The man who writes to you tonight has learned to forge different chains—bonds of affection and responsibility that strengthen rather than constrain, that connect rather than isolate.

The journey from Sydney to Bathurst—two hundred miles through country that seemed designed to test whether human determination could overcome geographic indifference— became my education in this higher form of freedom. Walking alone through landscape bearing no resemblance to England's gentle countryside, carrying everything I owned in a swag lighter than the chains I had worn for seven years, I discovered that solitude could serve as teacher if approached with proper humility.

The eucalyptus forests spoke in voices I had never heard—not familiar rustling of English oak and ash, but something alien yet oddly comforting, as if the land itself offered welcome to anyone willing to accept it on its own terms. Each encounter taught me the difference between earning respect and demanding it, between deserving trust and claiming it as right, between building community and merely occupying space near others.

By the time I reached Bathurst in March 1844, I had become someone my former self would scarcely recognize—not broken by experiences but refined by them, not bitter over what I had lost but grateful for what I had discovered, not focused on what I deserved but committed to earning whatever happiness might yet be possible through patient commitment to principles that suffering had taught me were more valuable than any material possession.

It was in Bathurst's market square, on a morning when spring sunshine seemed to bless every corner of creation, that I first saw your blessed mother. She stood behind a stall laden with bread of her own baking, her auburn hair catching light that seemed to emanate from beyond the merely physical, her voice carrying melodies that spoke of homeland and exile and the particular courage required to build new lives from fragments of old dreams.

Catherine Krieg—for that was her name before she became Catherine Staines and made my own name something worthy of pride—had crossed oceans that dwarfed even my own transportation, leaving behind family and culture and everything familiar to seek something better in a land that existed more in hope than certainty. When she smiled at my fumbling attempts to purchase bread with coins earned through honest labor, I felt for the first time in years that I might be worthy of another person's affection.

Our courtship taught me that love could indeed survive any hardship if it was willing to transform itself from possession into partnership, from demand into offering, from taking into giving. Catherine's own story—her father's death in Württemberg, her mother's struggle to maintain their modest bakery, her eventual decision to seek opportunity in a colony that promised fresh starts—had prepared her to appreciate qualities that more fortunate women might have overlooked.

When we wed in Kelso's stone church on a September morning in 1845—exactly seven years from the month you will make your entrance into this world—I felt I was not merely gaining a wife but recovering a part of myself I had thought permanently lost to the shame of conviction and transportation.

The years we have spent building Three Rivers Inn from nothing but determination and shared vision have been the happiest of my life. Our inn stands where three rivers meet, their waters joining as our lives have joined, flowing together toward destinations we cannot see but trust will prove worthwhile. Your mother's strength sustains everything we have built—her German recipes, her songs that turn our common room into something approaching a cathedral, her business sense that has allowed us to prosper where others have failed.

Yet tonight, as waters rise and threaten everything we have labored to create, I am reminded that happiness remains subject to forces beyond our control. The Bell River that has provided life for our crops now threatens to claim our inn and perhaps our lives as payment for believing we could build permanent security in a world where nothing remains unchanged except the certainty of change itself.

Should morning find me called to other service while you and your mother remain to carry forward what we have built together, I will trust that these letters provide whatever guidance a father's presence might have offered, that love proves strong enough to bridge any distance if held with sufficient faith.

Learn from my mistakes, my darling child, but do not let knowledge of them prevent you from taking risks that might lead to happiness. I stole because I was too proud to accept charity, too frightened to trust that honest work would provide what I needed, too impatient to wait for solutions requiring time rather than immediate action. But neither should you let caution prevent you from loving deeply, working passionately, hoping boldly for possibilities that cannot be guaranteed but remain worth pursuing.

Your mother and I hope to give you confidence to face whatever trials life presents with the knowledge that you are loved without reservation, supported without condition, valued not for what you might accomplish but for who you are in the deepest places of your heart where accomplishments matter less than character.

Remember me not as the proud young blacksmith who stole from desperation, but as the man who learned through your mother's love that service to others provides the only foundation upon which lasting happiness can be built. Most of all, remember that you are beloved—by the mother who carries you with such joy, by the father who writes these words with hands that ache to hold you, by the God who grants second chances to anyone willing to undertake the difficult work of earning them.

Your devoted father, who loves you beyond all earthly measure,

Thomas Staines

Journal Entries
State Library of NSW
December 15th, 2010 –Evening

The Architecture of Connection

Three months of research have transformed my understanding of what inheritance actually means. I thought I was looking for family history, but I've been discovering something far more precious: proof that connection transcends every limitation—death, distance, time itself.

The marriage certificate I found today made Thomas and Catherine's love real in ways their letters couldn't quite achieve alone. "Rivers Staines, née Staines, born 1852, Wellington, New South Wales. Father: Thomas Staines, deceased. Occupation: Blacksmith." Such simple words to contain such an extraordinary transformation.

But it's Catherine's story that's been haunting me as I trace these connections. Nineteen years old, crossing oceans alone to find opportunities her homeland couldn't provide. The courage that must have required—leaving everything familiar for the promise of something better, trusting that the unknown held more possibility than the known offered security.

I keep thinking about the parallel. Catherine left Germany because staying meant accepting limitations that didn't match her capacity for growth. I've been staying in grief because leaving it means accepting possibilities that might lead to additional loss. But Catherine's example suggests that love willing to risk everything gains the power to heal anything.

State Library Reading Room
December 22nd, 2010

Found the shipping records for Catherine's voyage on the Friedeburg. She traveled with forty-three other women, most listed as "seeking domestic employment." But Catherine's entry includes a notation I haven't seen on others: "Skilled in domestic arts, including baking and preserving. Literate."

Even then, she was someone who brought value wherever she went. Not just seeking opportunity, but carrying skills that would enrich whatever community received her. It makes me think about what I bring to relationships, what skills I offer for building connection rather than just maintaining comfortable distance.

Gosford Train Platform *January 8th, 2011*
Called Calvin this morning. Actually called, stayed on the line, had a real conversation instead of exchanging careful pleasantries. Told him about Catherine's courage and Thomas's transformation, about the research that's been teaching me what family connection actually means when it's based on shared purpose rather than mere biological accident.

"I'd like to see these letters," he said, and something in his voice suggested he meant more than casual curiosity. "Been thinking about your mum's stories, about the family she was always trying to help us understand better. Seems like these letters might be the missing pieces she was looking for."

The train is pulling into Gosford now. In twenty minutes, I'll be sharing Thomas's words with the person who needs them most—the father I've been too afraid to love completely because complete love makes complete loss possible. But Thomas's example suggests that love which protects itself from risk is love that dies with its possessor, while love willing to give everything becomes immortal.

Calvin's Workshop
January 8th, 2011 – Late evening

Dad's hands shook when he held Thomas's letters. Actually shook, like autumn leaves in a harbor wind. We sat in his workshop surrounded by the smell of cedar shavings and machine oil, and I watched my seventy-five-year-old father cry over words written by a man he'd never met but whose example illuminated everything he'd been trying to tell me about love and loss and the courage required to choose connection over safety.

"Your mother would have loved this," he said, voice thick with emotion that had been carefully contained for months. "She always said the best stories were the ones that taught you how to love better, how to be braver than your fears suggested was possible."

We talked until the harbor lights were reflecting off workshop windows, sharing discoveries that felt like archaeology of the heart. Calvin showed me the cedar box he'd been making for Thomas's letters—intricate thistle carvings that connected our Australian present to Scottish heritage that had shaped our capacity for both endurance and transformation.

But it was when he read Thomas's second letter aloud that something fundamental shifted between us. The description of learning humility through chains that became liberation, of discovering that true freedom meant choosing responsibilities that aligned with values rather than escaping external constraint—Calvin understood immediately what Thomas's transformation meant for our own relationship.

"Been hiding in my workshop since your mum died," he admitted, fingers tracing the carved thistles with the same precision Thomas had applied to his Celtic cross. "Thought keeping busy with beautiful things would be enough, that creating something lasting would fill the hole her absence left. But reading this—understanding how this man learned to love without reservation—makes me realize I've been building walls instead of bridges."

The sacred obligation Rivers wrote about isn't abstract duty—it's immediate opportunity. The chance to honor Thomas's sacrifice by choosing our own transformation, our own willingness to risk the vulnerability that real love always demands. Dad and I are planning the Scotland trip together now, understanding that heritage isn't just about bloodlines but about choosing to continue the story in ways that honor what previous generations built through their courage and sacrifice.

Thomas wrote letters to ensure his love survived death. Rivers preserved them to guide future generations. Now it's our turn to prove that their example still has power to heal, still can inspire the kind of vulnerable love that makes any loss worthwhile because of the meaning such connection creates.

The research continues, but the real discovery is complete: family isn't just what you inherit, but what you choose to build from the materials love provides when you're brave enough to use them.

9 THE GOVERNMENT FORGE

Sydney, New South Wales - March 1838 to November 1843

The Government Forge had become more than a workplace for Thomas Staines by his second year of bondage—it had evolved into the proving ground where his transformation from bitter convict to skilled craftsman could be measured in the quality of iron shaped by hands that had learned to find dignity in honest labor regardless of the circumstances that compelled it. The building itself stood on Macquarie Street like a monument to colonial pragmatism, its sandstone walls thick enough to contain the furnace heat that made Sydney's summer climate feel mild by comparison, its tall windows designed to catch whatever breeze might provide relief from the perpetual fire that kept the forges burning six days a week.

By March 1838, eighteen months after his arrival at Sydney Cove, Thomas had established himself as one of the forge's most reliable workers—not through dramatic gestures or obvious attempts to curry favor, but through the steady accumulation of small excellences that marked the difference between adequate work and genuine craftsmanship. Supervisor Walsh had noticed, as had the free workers whose cooperation was essential for maintaining the complex operations that supplied metalwork for the colony's expanding infrastructure.

The morning routine began before dawn with the lighting of fires that had been banked overnight to preserve coals too precious to waste through complete extinction. Thomas arrived each day as the first grey light touched Sydney Harbor, joining the handful of workers whose dedication to their craft transcended the legal obligations that brought them to the forge. In the pre-dawn darkness, with only the glow of carefully tended embers to provide illumination, he found a peace that the daylight hours rarely offered—solitude that allowed him to prepare both his tools and his spirit for the challenges that each day would bring.

"Early again, Staines," observed Patrick McNeal, a free settler whose metalworking skills had earned him supervisory responsibilities over the convict workers assigned to specialized projects. McNeal was perhaps thirty-five, weathered by colonial sun but possessed of the kind of steady competence that made him valuable to colonial administrators who needed results more than ceremony. "You know Walsh doesn't require you here until sunrise."

"Tools work better when they're properly prepared," Thomas replied, checking the temper of iron bars that would be shaped into hinges for the new courthouse being constructed on King Street. "Metal has moods like people—treat it with respect, and it responds accordingly."

The observation was practical rather than philosophical, but McNeal had learned to recognize the difference between convicts who approached their work as necessary burden and those who found in it something approaching calling. Thomas fell clearly into the latter category, his attention to detail and commitment to excellence marking him as someone whose character had been refined rather than broken by the circumstances that brought him to Sydney.

As the forge came alive with the sounds of hammers and bellows, Thomas found himself increasingly assigned to projects that required both technical skill and artistic sensibility. The colonial government needed utilitarian metalwork—chains and hinges and bars that would serve functional purposes for decades—but it also required decorative elements that would transform necessary buildings into structures worthy of representing British civilization in this distant outpost of the empire.

The courthouse hinges he crafted that morning were examples of such work—functional hardware that would support heavy doors for generations, but shaped with scrollwork that transformed mere utility into something approaching art. Each piece required hours of patient work, heating and hammering and filing until the iron surrendered its rough origins and emerged as something that could grace a building designed to last centuries.

"Beautiful work, Thomas," said James Whitmore, the master smith whose approval was worth more than official recognition from administrators who understood policy better than craftsmanship. Whitmore was a free man, skilled enough to command good wages in the colonial economy, but generous enough to treat convict workers as fellow craftsmen rather than mere tools to be utilized until they broke. "Hinges like those should outlast the building they're meant to serve."

The compliment was earned through months of patient effort to prove that his convict status didn't diminish his capacity for excellence, that chains around his ankles couldn't prevent his hands from creating work that honored both his trade and the materials that shaped it. But more than personal satisfaction, Thomas felt the growing recognition that quality work could provide something beyond mere survival—it could provide purpose, dignity, even a form of redemption that external circumstances couldn't entirely prevent.

The diversity of workers at the Government Forge reflected Sydney's character as a community where free settlers, emancipated convicts, and current prisoners labored side by side on projects that served the colony's expanding needs. This mixing of social classes would have been impossible in England, where birth and circumstances determined not just opportunities but the very people with whom one might associate. But colonial necessity created its own hierarchies based more on competence than breeding, more on reliability than social position.

Billy Henderson had arrived on the same ship as Thomas but possessed skills in metallurgy that complemented formal training with intuitive understanding of how different metals behaved under heat and pressure. His father had been a London silversmith before drinking destroyed both his business and his family, leaving Billy with knowledge of fine metalwork but circumstances that led inevitably to the theft that earned him transportation. Together, Thomas and Billy collaborated on projects that neither could have completed alone—Thomas providing systematic technique while Billy contributed the kind of artistic vision that transformed functional objects into things of beauty.

"Look at this bronze work for the Governor's residence," Billy said one afternoon, displaying a door handle whose surface bore intricate patterns that caught and reflected light like captured sunshine. "Takes three different alloys to get metal that responds properly to chasing, but the effect—" He rotated the piece slowly, showing how the patterns seemed to move as light played across its surface. "Makes the extra work worthwhile."

James MacReady brought different strengths to their informal partnership—physical power that made the heaviest work manageable, and storytelling abilities that transformed long hours of repetitive labor into something approaching entertainment. MacReady's sheep stealing had earned him fourteen years of bondage, but his Highland background included traditions of oral narrative that made him valuable for maintaining morale among workers whose spirits might otherwise have been crushed by the institutional nature of their circumstances.

During the midday break when official work paused for meals that barely qualified as adequate nutrition, MacReady would regale his listeners with tales that ranged from Scottish folklore to contemporary adventures of convicts who had successfully completed their sentences and built respectable lives in the colony. These stories served purposes beyond mere entertainment—they provided hope for men who might otherwise have despaired of ever reclaiming social standing, examples of transformation that proved redemption remained possible for anyone willing to undertake its patient work.

"Tell us about Stewart again," Billy would request during particularly difficult weeks when the work seemed endless and the heat made every breath an effort. "The one who opened the inn in Parramatta."

MacReady would settle into the storytelling rhythm that had been passed down through generations of Highland tradition, his voice carrying the particular cadence that made even familiar tales feel immediate and compelling. "Robert Stewart, transported in '25 for poaching deer that belonged to Lord Pemberton's estate. Served his seven years working government road gangs, learned discipline and patience and the value of honest work performed without complaint."

The story would unfold with details that varied slightly with each telling but maintained essential truth about transformation being possible for anyone willing to choose it consistently. Stewart's progression from bitter convict to respected innkeeper provided a template that other men could follow—not dramatic conversion but gradual accumulation of small choices that eventually created character worthy of society's trust and respect.

"Got his ticket of leave in '32, worked as free laborer for two years to save enough capital for land purchase in Parramatta. Married Sarah McKenzie, widow woman with three children who saw past his convict origins to recognize the man he'd become through patient effort. Built the Crown and Anchor Inn through honest work and fair dealing, now employs six people and serves the best meals between Sydney and the Blue Mountains."

Such stories mattered because they proved that the future remained open to possibility rather than predetermined by past mistakes. Thomas found himself listening with particular attention to accounts of men who had rebuilt their lives through competence and character rather than connections or inherited advantages. These examples suggested that his own transformation might lead somewhere beyond mere survival, that the skills and reputation he was building could provide foundation for meaningful life once his sentence was complete.

But it was the small acts of kindness, performed without expectation of recognition or reward, that truly marked Thomas's evolution from self-centered pride to something approaching wisdom about what made life worth living. These gestures began modestly—sharing food rations with newer arrivals whose systems hadn't yet adapted to the inadequate nutrition that marked convict existence, teaching younger workers techniques that would help them avoid accidents that could result in permanent injury or extended sentences.

The forge's apprentices were particularly vulnerable to exploitation by workers whose own suffering had made them callous to others' pain. Thomas found himself serving as informal protector for boys whose youth and inexperience made them targets for abuse that colonial authorities either couldn't prevent or chose to ignore. David Morrison, barely sixteen and transported for stealing bread to feed his starving siblings, possessed intelligence and willingness to learn that reminded Thomas of his own apprenticeship years before pride and desperation led him astray.

"Metal's like people, David," Thomas explained during one of their informal lessons, heating iron to the precise temperature that would allow shaping without brittleness. "Treat it roughly when it's not ready, and you'll destroy what you're trying to create. But apply heat and pressure gradually, with patience and respect for its nature, and you can transform it into something beautiful and useful."

The lesson applied to more than metallurgy, as both teacher and student understood. David's transportation had been trauma that could either destroy his faith in justice and human decency or refine his character through understanding that some experiences, however painful, could prepare him for achievements that would have been impossible without such harsh schooling.

Thomas's reputation for fair dealing and technical excellence gradually extended beyond the Government Forge to Sydney's broader community of free settlers who required metalwork that combined functionality with the kind of reliability that made colonial existence more manageable. Farmers needed tools that could withstand conditions that would destroy inferior implements. Merchants required specialized hardware for buildings designed to last generations in climate that tested everything European construction techniques could devise.

These private commissions were officially forbidden—convict labor belonged entirely to the Crown during assigned hours, and unauthorized work could result in punishments that added years to existing sentences. But Walsh had learned to recognize the difference between activities that undermined official purposes and those that enhanced the skills his workers brought to government projects. Quality private work made men better craftsmen, and better craftsmen produced superior results for colonial administration.

"Staines," Walsh said quietly one afternoon when official work had ended and other convicts had returned to barracks routine, "Mrs. Patterson needs hinges for her store building on George Street. Complex work that requires someone who understands both function and appearance. Interested?"

The offer represented trust that extended far beyond normal supervisor-convict relationships. Private work meant working alone, unsupervised, with access to tools and materials that could theoretically be stolen or misused. More importantly, it meant interaction with free citizens who would judge Thomas not by his convict status but by the quality of work he produced and the character he displayed during their business dealings.

"Appreciate the opportunity," Thomas replied, understanding that acceptance meant accepting responsibility for proving that such trust was justified. "When would she need the work completed?"

"No particular hurry, but she wants quality that will last twenty years without maintenance. Willing to pay accordingly for craftsmanship that meets her standards." Walsh's expression suggested that he understood the significance of what he was offering. "Your work's been noticed by people whose opinions matter in this community. Opportunity to build reputation that could serve you well once your sentence is complete."

The Patterson commission marked the beginning of Thomas's gradual integration into Sydney's economy as skilled tradesman rather than mere convict laborer. Mrs. Eleanor Patterson proved to be a woman whose German heritage had taught her to value craftsmanship over expedience, quality over economy when the difference meant decades of reliable service versus frequent replacement of inferior work.

"My father was a cabinetmaker in Hamburg," she explained during their initial consultation, her accent lending musical quality to English that had been learned through necessity rather than birth. "He taught me to recognize work performed with pride versus work performed merely to satisfy immediate requirements. I require the former, whatever the cost difference might be."

The hinges Thomas created for Patterson's store demonstrated everything he had learned about transforming raw materials into objects that served both practical and aesthetic purposes. Each piece was shaped with attention to detail that exceeded functional requirements, surfaces finished to standards that would prevent rust while displaying the kind of visual appeal that marked superior craftsmanship. The scrollwork incorporated motifs that complemented the building's architecture while remaining subtle enough to enhance rather than dominate the overall design.

More importantly, the project required interaction with Mrs. Patterson that tested Thomas's capacity for conducting business relationships based on mutual respect rather than the submission that marked his dealings with colonial authorities. She evaluated his work with the critical eye of someone who understood quality, offering suggestions that improved the final result while acknowledging the expertise he brought to technical challenges she couldn't solve herself.

"Beautiful work, Mr. Staines," she said upon completion, her use of formal address marking recognition that their relationship transcended his convict status. "Hinges like these should serve my grandchildren when they inherit this building. That represents value beyond mere monetary consideration."

The payment she offered exceeded what he had expected, but more valuable than coins was the recommendation she provided to other free settlers whose projects required metalwork that combined reliability with aesthetic appeal. Word spread through Sydney's community of merchants and professionals that convict 537 could be trusted with complex work, that his character matched his technical skills, that he represented the kind of redemptive possibility that made transportation more than mere punishment.

By 1841, three years before his ticket of leave would restore freedom of movement within the colony, Thomas had established himself as one of Sydney's most sought-after metalworkers for projects that required both skill and artistic sensibility. The irony was not lost on him that his convict status, which might have been expected to limit his opportunities, had instead provided the kind of intensive training and reputation-building that would have taken decades to achieve through normal apprenticeship and gradual advancement.

The colonial government's policy of assigning skilled convicts to work that utilized their abilities had created situations where men like Thomas could demonstrate competence and character under circumstances that revealed their true nature. Unlike free workers who might change employers or relocate when difficulties arose, convicts were required to prove themselves consistently over years of constant observation by supervisors who had learned to distinguish between those who could be trusted with responsibility and those who required perpetual surveillance.

This extended evaluation period worked to Thomas's advantage, allowing him to build reputation based on sustained excellence rather than momentary impressions. Each project completed to client satisfaction, each deadline met despite challenging circumstances, each interaction conducted with professionalism that transcended his legal status—all contributed to accumulating evidence that his transformation from bitter convict to reliable craftsman represented genuine character development rather than calculated performance designed to manipulate official opinions.

The relationships Thomas developed with fellow workers at the Government Forge provided another form of education in the collaborative skills that colonial success required. Unlike the hierarchical structures that dominated English society, where birth and breeding determined social position regardless of individual merit, Sydney's circumstances demanded cooperation between people whose diverse backgrounds might have prevented association under different conditions.

Working alongside free settlers like McNeal and Whitmore taught Thomas about the attitudes and expectations that characterized successful colonists—pragmatism over prejudice, competence over breeding, reliability over charm. These men had risked everything to seek opportunity in a land that offered no guarantees except the chance to succeed or fail based on individual effort rather than inherited advantage.

Their acceptance of Thomas as a fellow craftsman rather than mere convict laborer provided glimpses of the social position he might achieve once legal restrictions were removed. But more than future possibilities, their respect for his current work offered daily confirmation that redemption remained available to anyone willing to earn it through patient demonstration of character that transcended past mistakes.

The convict workers with whom Thomas shared daily labor provided different but equally valuable lessons about survival and transformation under circumstances that tested every assumption about human nature. Some, like Billy Henderson and James MacReady, had channeled their circumstances into opportunities for personal growth that prepared them for meaningful freedom once their sentences were complete. Others had allowed bitterness and resentment to poison their spirits, creating cycles of punishment and resistance that ensured perpetual bondage regardless of legal status.

Observing these different responses to similar circumstances taught Thomas about the choices that determined whether hardship became a stepping stone or stumbling block, whether suffering refined character or destroyed it. The difference seemed to lie not in the severity of trials faced but in the willingness to accept responsibility for one's response to those trials, to choose service over selfishness even when selfishness seemed justified by harsh treatment.

This understanding became particularly important during Thomas's final year of bondage, when anticipation of approaching freedom created temptations to reduce effort or take shortcuts that might jeopardize the reputation he had spent six years building. Other convicts facing similar situations sometimes succumbed to the belief that their remaining obligations to the Crown were mere formalities to be endured with minimum effort rather than opportunities to demonstrate continued commitment to the principles that had guided their transformation.

Thomas chose differently, understanding that character revealed itself most clearly during periods when external oversight was reduced and personal choice became the primary determinant of behavior. His final year at the Government Forge saw some of his finest work—decorative ironwork for St. James' Church that would grace the building for generations, hardware for the new General Hospital that combined functionality with aesthetic appeal that honored both colonial aspirations and the skills of craftsmen who created it.

When Governor Gipps announced his intention to conduct a final inspection of the Government Forge operations before Thomas's scheduled release, the event felt less like examination than celebration of transformation successfully completed. The Governor's assessment of Thomas's work and character would influence not just his immediate prospects for freedom but his long-term opportunities for establishing himself as independent tradesman in colonial society.

"Mr. Staines," the Governor said, using formal address that acknowledged Thomas's approaching transition from convict to free man, "your work during seven years of bondage has been exemplary. More than that, your conduct has demonstrated that transportation can serve redemptive purposes when approached with proper attitude and commitment to personal improvement."

The words carried weight beyond their immediate meaning, representing official recognition that Thomas's transformation had been genuine rather than merely calculated performance designed to manipulate administrative decisions. This assessment would follow him into freedom, providing foundation for reputation that could support whatever ambitions his liberty might allow him to pursue.

As November 1843 approached and with it the end of his sentence, Thomas found himself reflecting on the seven years that had transformed him from bitter convict into skilled craftsman whose work was valued by free citizens and whose character had earned respect from supervisors and colleagues alike. The Government Forge had provided more than employment—it had offered laboratory for testing whether redemption was possible for someone whose pride and desperation had led to choices that seemed to preclude any meaningful future.

The answer, proven through daily choices to serve others' welfare while rebuilding his own character, was that transformation remained available to anyone willing to undertake its patient work. The metal he had shaped with hammer and fire was no more malleable than the human spirit when subjected to proper pressure applied with sufficient skill and determination.

On his final day at the Government Forge, Thomas completed a set of decorative brackets for the new courthouse steps—ironwork that would welcome generations of citizens seeking justice in a society that offered second chances to those who proved themselves worthy of redemption. The symbolism was not lost on him: his last official act as convict was creating something that would serve the community's pursuit of fairness and order, values he had violated through theft but had learned to honor through service.

The ticket of leave that would restore his freedom of movement within the colony lay waiting in Walsh's office, but Thomas felt no impatience to claim it. The document represented not escape from bondage but graduation from intensive education in character development that had prepared him for challenges and opportunities that lay ahead. He had entered the Government Forge as a broken man whose pride had led to destruction. He would leave as a craftsman whose skills were valued, whose character was respected, and whose future remained open to possibilities that seemed impossible seven years earlier.

10 PIECES OF THE PAST

State Library of NSW, Sydney — November 2010

Three weeks had passed since Sara Wilson's first expedition into the State Library's genealogical archives, three weeks during which Thomas Staines had transformed from mysterious family figure into obsession that colored every waking hour and haunted dreams filled with convict ships and colonial sunshine. Her Kirribilli apartment had become base camp for a research expedition that sprawled across every available surface—photocopied documents arranged in chronological order, genealogical charts that traced bloodlines back through centuries of Scottish parishes, notebooks filled with questions that each discovery generated faster than answers could be found.

The library had become her second home, its reading rooms as familiar as her own kitchen, its staff greeting her with the particular warmth reserved for researchers whose dedication bordered on the heroic. Margaret Chen, the senior librarian whose encyclopedic knowledge had guided Sara through countless previous investigations, now saved particularly promising call slips for her arrival each morning, understanding that Sara's quest had moved beyond casual family history into territory where academic rigor met personal revelation.

"You're becoming something of a legend among the other researchers," Margaret observed as Sara settled into her usual chair, materials spread around her like an archaeological excavation of family memory. "Mrs. Patterson was asking yesterday whether you'd found the secret to convict research success. She's been hunting her ancestor for five years without the kind of breakthrough you achieved in your first week."

Sara felt heat rise in her cheeks, recognition that her success stemmed not from superior research skills but from emotional investment that made every document feel precious rather than merely informative. Thomas's letters had provided framework for understanding that transformed bureaucratic records into intimate details of human experience, criminal justice statistics into evidence of individual transformation that defied easy categorization.

"Just persistent," Sara replied, though she knew persistence alone couldn't explain the way information seemed to arrange itself into patterns that revealed rather than concealed the story she sought. "And lucky enough to have an ancestor who left clear tracks through the official records."

But luck felt insufficient to describe the discovery that awaited her in materials Margaret had requisitioned from storage areas that held generations of colonial correspondence, shipping manifests, and administrative documents that documented Australia's convict period with precision that made individual stories recoverable for anyone willing to undertake the patient work of connecting scattered references into coherent narrative.

Today's focus was Catarina Krieg, the German immigrant who had become Catherine Staines and given birth to Rivers on the night Thomas died saving his neighbors from flood waters that claimed Three Rivers Inn. Sara had found fragments of Catherine's story—passenger manifest that documented her 1843 arrival from Hamburg, marriage certificate that recorded her union with Thomas in 1845—but the woman herself remained elusive, her voice filtered through official documents that recorded facts without capturing character. Catherine wasn't her real name, it was Catarina, and she had assumed a different name some time before meeting and marrying Thomas.

The breakthrough came in correspondence between colonial immigration officials and German consular representatives, files that documented the assisted passage scheme that had brought thousands of German immigrants to Australia during the 1840s. Catherine's name appeared in a report that made Sara's breath catch: "Catarina Krieg, age 19, skilled baker, traveling alone following death of parents in Württemberg. Exceptional references for character and industry. Recommended for placement with German families in Bathurst district where her skills would serve community needs."

Traveling alone following death of parents. The phrase carried weight of grief that connected Catherine's journey to Sara's own experience of loss, recognition that emigration had often been chosen by people whose circumstances left them little alternative to starting over in places that existed more in hope than geographical certainty. Catherine had been nineteen when she crossed oceans to build a new life from whatever materials courage and skill could provide—younger than Sara had been when she married David, younger than she'd been when she thought she understood anything about resilience or the capacity for transformation that desperate circumstances could reveal.

"Margaret," Sara called across the reading room, her voice carrying excitement that made other researchers look up from their own investigations. "Could you help me access the Hamburg passenger records for 1843? I think I've found something that explains why my ancestor Catherine left Germany."

The Hamburg records, when they arrived from storage, painted a picture of economic and social upheaval that had driven thousands of Germans to seek opportunities in colonies that promised land and work for anyone willing to undertake the risks that emigration required. Catherine's father, Johann Krieg, had been master baker whose death in 1842 had left his family facing poverty that made survival in Württemberg impossible without male support that traditional society considered essential for women's security.

"Johann Krieg, master baker, died 15 October 1842 of consumption. Widow Margaret Krieg and daughter Catarina left without means of support following dissolution of bakery business. Daughter possesses exceptional skills in bread-making and pastry preparation, excellent character references from parish officials."

The notation continued with details that transformed Catherine from historical figure into woman whose choices could be understood through the lens of economic necessity and personal courage: *"Margaret Krieg died 3 February 1843, leaving daughter Catarina orphaned at age 18. Parish officials recommend assisted passage to Australian colonies where her skills would provide opportunities for self-sufficiency not available to unmarried women in current economic circumstances."*

Sara stared at the documents, understanding that she was reading about trauma that paralleled her own experience of loss, recognition that Ellen's death had left her facing choices about how to rebuild life from fragments that grief had scattered. Catherine's orphanhood had led to emigration that seemed impossibly brave; Sara's loss had led to isolation that felt protective but ultimately inadequate for building anything meaningful from the raw materials of survival.

The German consular correspondence provided additional details that brought Catherine's personality into focus through official observations that captured character as well as circumstances: *"Miss Krieg demonstrates remarkable composure for young woman facing such dramatic change in circumstances. Her baking skills rival those of professional establishments, and her character references suggest reliability and industry that would benefit any community fortunate enough to receive her services."*

But it was the final notation that made Sara's throat close with emotion: *"Miss Krieg requests permission to carry her father's recipe collection and baking implements to Australian settlement, stating these represent her only inheritance and connection to family traditions she hopes to preserve in a new country. Such dedication to familial memory suggests character worthy of colonial investment."*

Her father's recipes. Catherine had carried her heritage across oceans in the form of knowledge that could create sustenance and comfort for anyone willing to appreciate the difference between mere bread and food prepared with love that honored traditions while adapting to new circumstances. The recipes that had made Three Rivers Inn famous throughout the Bathurst district had traveled from German bakeries to Australian frontier through woman whose courage had preserved cultural wisdom while embracing opportunities that a homeland couldn't provide.

Sara photocopied the documents with hands that trembled slightly from recognition that she was documenting not just genealogical discovery but evidence of resilience that had shaped her own capacity for facing loss and choosing hope over despair. Catherine's story provided template for transformation that honored past while embracing future, preserving what mattered most while releasing what no longer served purposes that new circumstances required.

The morning session had revealed Catherine's character in ways that official marriage records couldn't capture, but questions remained about how she had met Thomas, what had attracted a German baker's daughter to an ex-convict blacksmith whose reputation would have been known throughout the small frontier community. The social dynamics of colonial Bathurst, where conventional barriers between classes and backgrounds had been softened by shared challenges of frontier existence, would have created opportunities for connections that European society might have prevented through rigid adherence to social conventions.

Lunch break provided an opportunity to process discoveries while walking through the Domain parklands that stretched between library and harbor, city noise replaced by sound of wind through trees that had witnessed more than a century of researchers seeking connections to ancestors whose stories had been preserved in documents that transformed individual lives into historical narrative. Sara found herself thinking about Catherine walking unfamiliar streets of Bathurst, carrying recipes and skills that would eventually sustain the inn that became a community gathering place where former convicts and free settlers discovered common ground.

The afternoon session brought focus to shipping records that documented passenger movements between Sydney and inland settlements, manifests that tracked the gradual expansion of European settlement into territories that had been Aboriginal land for thousands of years before colonization imposed new arrangements on the ancient landscape. Sara was searching for evidence of Catherine's journey from Sydney to Bathurst, the specific voyage that had carried her toward the encounter with Thomas that would transform both their lives.

The discovery came in routine correspondence about passenger accommodations on coastal steamers that connected Sydney to river ports where smaller vessels could navigate inland waterways toward settlements that depended on such connections for supplies and communication with colonial administration. Catherine's name appeared in the manifest for SS *Sophia*, departed Sydney 15 December 1843, destination Bathurst via river transport that would carry passengers through landscape that few Europeans had seen until gold discoveries brought thousands seeking fortune that most would never find.

"Miss Catarina Krieg, passenger to Bathurst, traveling alone, luggage includes baking equipment and personal effects. Destination: German community settlement, letter of introduction from Hamburg consular office."

But more significant than Catherine's individual journey was the passenger manifest that documented the diverse population seeking opportunities in frontier districts where conventional social arrangements had been modified by practical necessities of colonial existence. The *Sophia* had carried former convicts whose tickets of leave allowed inland travel, free immigrants seeking land grants that urban employment couldn't provide, merchants establishing businesses in growing towns that served agricultural districts expanding beyond the Blue Mountains.

Thomas could have been on this same ship, Sara realized, cross-referencing dates with chronology she had established for his release from government service and journey to Bathurst. His ticket of leave had been granted November 1843, timing that would have allowed departure for the frontier settlement during the same period when Catherine was making her own journey toward opportunities that Bathurst's German community provided for skilled craftspeople whose abilities could serve diverse population's needs.

The possibility that they had met during the voyage rather than after arrival added a romantic dimension to the story that official records couldn't document but circumstances made plausible. Colonial passenger manifests rarely noted relationships that developed during travel, but shared journey through landscape that challenged every assumption about comfort and convenience might have created bonds between people whose backgrounds would have prevented such connections in more conventional circumstances.

Sara spent the remaining afternoon hours searching for additional references to either Thomas or Catherine in correspondence about Bathurst's development during 1844, documents that might provide evidence of their meeting and eventual marriage that transformed both their individual struggles into a shared success story. The search yielded fragments—mentions of a German baking establishment that provided bread for the growing community, references to a reliable blacksmith whose services supported agricultural expansion—but nothing that definitively connected their stories until the marriage certificate that documented their union in September 1845.

But fragments were sufficient to construct a narrative framework that honored both documented facts and emotional truth about two people whose individual journeys from loss to hope had intersected in ways that created something beautiful from broken materials that neither could have repaired alone. Thomas's transformation from convicted thief to trusted craftsman, Catherine's courage in crossing oceans to preserve family traditions while embracing new opportunities—their stories had converged in a frontier town where past mattered less than present willingness to contribute to community development.

The library closed around Sara like a blessing, the reading room emptying of researchers who carried their discoveries home to contemplate during evening hours when excitement of new information combined with anticipation of additional searches that tomorrow might bring. But unlike her usual reluctance to end productive research sessions, tonight Sara felt urgency about sharing discoveries that had transformed Catherine from historical figure into a woman whose courage and character had shaped every subsequent generation of their family.

Calvin needed to hear this story. Not just because genealogical discovery added details to family history they both valued, but because Catherine's example provided guidance for anyone facing their own choices about how to honor heritage while embracing change, how to preserve what mattered most while releasing what no longer served purposes that new circumstances required. Ellen's death had left both of them struggling with questions about continuity and adaptation that Catherine's story addressed through lived example rather than theoretical advice.

The evening journey home through Sydney streets filled with commuters felt like a return from expedition to a foreign country where past and present occupied the same landscape, where individual stories connected to larger patterns of human movement and adaptation that had shaped a continent whose contemporary prosperity rested on foundations built by people whose names appeared in archival documents rather than history textbooks. Sara found herself thinking about Catherine walking unfamiliar streets toward an uncertain future, carrying recipes that would eventually feed travelers from around the world who found sustenance and community at Three Rivers Inn.

Her apartment, when she finally reached it, felt like base camp for an expedition that was approaching its most important discovery—not additional facts about family history, but understanding of how past wisdom could guide present choices about love and loss and the courage required to choose hope over fear when circumstances demanded such choosing. The harbor lights that usually provided entertainment now seemed like connections to ships that had carried hopeful immigrants and desperate convicts toward futures that existed more in imagination than certainty.

Sara spread her day's discoveries across the kitchen table that had become command center for research that was transforming casual curiosity into committed investigation of family legacy that deserved preservation and transmission to anyone whose heart was ready to receive its guidance about resilience and redemption. But documentation alone felt insufficient for honoring what she had learned about Catherine's character and Thomas's transformation. The story demanded sharing with someone who could appreciate its significance for understanding how people facing impossible circumstances could create meaning through choices that served others' welfare rather than advanced personal comfort.

Her phone lay beside photocopied documents that testified to courage and character that had shaped her own capacity for facing loss and choosing hope despite circumstances that suggested despair might be a more reasonable response to grief that seemed too heavy for individual hearts to carry. Calvin's number appeared on screen with a familiar mixture of anticipation and anxiety that marked their relationship since Ellen's death had made communication feel dangerous because honesty might reveal pain that careful distance had been designed to protect.

But Catherine's example suggested different possibilities—that isolation, however protective, prevented the kind of connection that could transform individual struggle into shared strength, that love required vulnerability that made additional loss possible but also made meaning available to anyone brave enough to choose relationship over safety. Thomas and Catherine had found each other through circumstances that might have defeated people whose character had not been refined by trials that revealed strength rather than weakness.

Sara dialed Calvin's number before courage could desert her, understanding that some communications were too important to postpone until circumstances felt more favorable for conversations that might heal what grief had damaged or reveal how deep the damage actually extended. The phone rang twice before his voice answered with a familiar mixture of hope and caution that had marked their interactions since Ellen's funeral made them both careful about expectations that might not be fulfilled.

"Sara? Everything all right?" Calvin's voice carried immediate concern that suggested he had been waiting for calls that might bring news about crises rather than discoveries, understanding that their careful relationship had been built around avoiding topics that might disturb peace purchased through emotional distance.

"Dad, I found something amazing today," Sara said, her voice carrying excitement that made careful conversation impossible. "About Catherine—Thomas's wife. Her whole story, why she came to Australia, how she met him. It changes everything I thought I knew about courage and starting over when everything familiar has been lost."

The pause that followed felt like eternity, but it wasn't empty silence—it was the sound of someone gathering strength to receive information that might require emotional investment he wasn't certain he possessed resources to sustain. When Calvin spoke again, his voice carried a different quality, warmth that hadn't been present during months of careful conversations that preserved connection without demanding vulnerability.

"Tell me," he said simply, those two words carrying invitation that felt like a gift offered without conditions or expectations about what response might be appropriate or safe.

Sara found herself speaking for twenty minutes without interruption, sharing Catherine's story with enthusiasm that made past feel present, historical figures feel like people whose choices could guide contemporary decisions about love and loss and the courage required to choose hope when circumstances suggested that despair might be a more realistic response to trials that tested everything she thought she knew about resilience and faith.

Calvin listened with attention that felt like a blessing, occasionally asking questions that suggested genuine interest rather than polite acknowledgment of obsession he couldn't share but was willing to tolerate for sake of maintaining relationship that both valued despite uncertainty about how to navigate grief that had made communication feel dangerous. His questions revealed understanding of emotional weight that genealogical discovery carried when approached as guidance for living rather than merely academic exercise in historical research.

"She was nineteen," Calvin repeated when Sara finished describing Catherine's journey from orphaned baker's daughter to frontier innkeeper whose recipes had preserved German traditions while serving diverse community needs. "Same age as your cousin Emma, facing circumstances that would challenge someone twice her age with twice her experience. Makes you think about what we're capable of when necessity strips away everything except what really matters."

The observation carried weight that connected Catherine's nineteenth-century courage to their own twenty-first-century choices about how to face loss and build meaning from whatever materials grief had left available for construction of lives worth preserving. Calvin's voice held recognition that Catherine's story wasn't just family history but an instruction manual for anyone seeking guidance about how to honor heritage while embracing change, how to preserve what mattered most while releasing what no longer served purposes that new circumstances required.

"I keep thinking about Ellen," Sara said, understanding that some conversations required honesty that made additional pain possible but also made healing available to people brave enough to choose relationship over protection. "How she would have loved this story, how excited she would have been to learn about Catherine's recipes and Thomas's letters. But also how she would have understood what their example means for us—how to face loss without giving up on the possibility that beautiful things can still be built from broken materials."

Calvin's response came after pause that felt like prayer, words chosen with care that suggested understanding of weight they carried for rebuilding relationship that grief had damaged but might yet be restored through shared recognition of what their ancestors' love had made possible. "Your mother always said the best stories were the ones that taught you something essential about yourself, about the people whose love made your existence possible. She would have seen Catherine and Thomas as teachers rather than just relatives, guides for anyone willing to learn what they discovered about transformation and hope."

The conversation continued for another hour, past transitioning from historical discussion into personal territory they had avoided since Ellen's funeral made communication feel too dangerous for hearts already carrying more pain than seemed bearable. But Catherine's example provided a bridge between individual grief and shared understanding that loss could become foundation rather than barrier, common experience that deepened rather than divided their appreciation of what family meant when approached as a source of wisdom rather than mere biological connection.

When they finally ended the call, Sara felt something had shifted between them—not healing exactly, but recognition that healing was possible if approached with patience and willingness to risk vulnerability that might not be returned but offered the only path toward connection that honored Ellen's memory while creating space for a relationship that could survive whatever trials the future presented.

Calvin was coming for dinner Sunday. They would continue sharing discoveries that transformed family history from casual curiosity into a guide for living, but more importantly, they would continue rebuilding a relationship that grief had damaged but Catherine and Thomas's example suggested could be restored through choices that served love rather than fear, hope rather than the comfortable numbness of limited expectations.

Outside her window, Sydney Harbor stretched toward horizons that had once held impossible promise for people like Catherine, people who had lost everything they thought they needed and discovered in exile the possibility of becoming someone they had never imagined possible. Sara settled into her chair with Thomas's letters and Catherine's immigration records spread around her like a map for a journey that was just beginning, understanding that research had become more than genealogical investigation—it had become pilgrimage toward understanding of what inheritance really meant when received with hearts ready to be changed by wisdom that proved love could travel farther than time if preserved with sufficient care and transmitted with adequate courage.

The night was young, and she had stories to tell, connections to explore, a relationship to rebuild with a father whose grief had taught him about isolation while Catherine's example promised to teach them both about courage required to choose hope over fear, love over safety, connection over the careful distance that protected against additional loss but also prevented the kind of meaning that made loss worthwhile.

11 THE TICKET OF LEAVE

Government Forge, Sydney - November 1843

The morning of Governor Gipps' final inspection arrived with the kind of crystalline clarity that made Sydney Harbor look like polished silver, its surface broken only by the gentle wake of early fishing boats whose crews understood that the best catches came to those willing to rise before the city stirred to life. Thomas Staines stood at his anvil in the Government Forge, putting finishing touches on a set of communion rail brackets for St. Andrew's Cathedral, his movements precise and unhurried despite knowing that this day would determine not just his immediate freedom but his long-term prospects for establishing himself as an independent tradesman in colonial society.

Seven years of bondage had taught him that character revealed itself most clearly under observation, that the difference between performed compliance and genuine transformation became apparent to anyone skilled in reading human nature. Governor Gipps possessed such skills, honed through decades of evaluating men whose futures depended upon his assessment of their readiness for the responsibilities that freedom entailed.

Supervisor Walsh moved through the forge with unusual attention to details that normally required no special consideration—tools properly arranged, work surfaces cleaned to standards that exceeded daily requirements, projects organized to demonstrate both productivity and artistic sensibility that marked superior craftsmanship. The inspection would cover not just Thomas's individual performance but the entire operation's success in transforming convict labor into valuable colonial resource.

"Nervous, Staines?" Walsh asked, though his tone suggested he already knew the answer. Seven years of working together had created relationship based on mutual respect rather than mere supervisory necessity, understanding that transcended the legal distinctions between free overseer and bonded worker.

"Eager," Thomas replied, testing the weight of a bracket whose balance would determine how gracefully it supported the carved woodwork that would complete the cathedral's interior design. "Seven years of preparation should be sufficient for any examination worth passing."

The observation reflected confidence earned through consistent excellence rather than bravado designed to mask uncertainty. Thomas understood that his transformation from bitter convict to skilled craftsman was complete not because external authorities declared it so, but because he had become someone capable of contributing to community welfare while finding personal satisfaction in service that served purposes larger than individual advancement.

When Governor Gipps arrived at mid-morning, his entourage included Colonial Secretary Edward Deas Thomson and Superintendent of Convicts Frederick Augustus Hely—men whose administrative responsibilities required them to distinguish between prisoners who could be safely released and those who remained threats to colonial stability. Their presence transformed routine inspection into formal evaluation that would influence not just Thomas's immediate prospects but policies governing convict rehabilitation throughout New South Wales.

"Your Excellency," Walsh said, his voice carrying the particular formality reserved for occasions when individual performance reflected broader institutional success, "may I present Thomas Staines, completing seven years of assigned service with exemplary conduct and superior craftsmanship that has enhanced this facility's reputation throughout the colony."

Governor Gipps studied Thomas with attention that seemed to penetrate surface appearances to evaluate character and motivation that determined whether freedom would be used constructively or squandered through return to criminal behavior. His assessment would be based not just on work quality but on evidence of genuine transformation that prepared convicts for productive citizenship rather than mere compliance with legal requirements.

"Mr. Staines," the Governor said, his use of formal address acknowledging the approaching transition from convict to free man, "I have reviewed reports of your conduct and performance during seven years of bondage. Supervisor Walsh speaks highly of your technical skills and character development. Tell me, in your own words, how transportation has affected your understanding of responsibility and citizenship."

The question demanded honest self-assessment rather than calculated response designed to produce favorable administrative decision. Thomas understood that his answer would reveal whether years of hardship had produced genuine wisdom or merely sophisticated ability to manipulate official opinions through carefully crafted performances.

"Transportation stripped away everything I thought defined me, Your Excellency," Thomas replied, his voice carrying conviction earned through painful experience rather than theoretical understanding. "Pride, possessions, social position—all removed by consequences of my own poor choices. What remained was opportunity to discover who I might become when external supports were eliminated and character became the only foundation for building meaningful existence."

He paused, recognizing that the Governor's attention suggested genuine interest in understanding rather than mere fulfillment of administrative obligations. "Seven years of forced labor taught me that dignity comes not from circumstances but from how we respond to circumstances, that redemption must be earned through consistent demonstration of values rather than claimed through words or intentions."

Governor Gipps nodded, his expression suggesting that Thomas's response aligned with official hopes about transportation's rehabilitative potential. "And what do you intend to do with the freedom that will be restored to you?"

"Serve the community that has given me opportunity for redemption, Your Excellency. Use the skills refined through colonial service to contribute to society's welfare while building life worthy of the second chance I have been granted." Thomas gestured toward the communion rail brackets that represented his final project as assigned convict. "Beautiful things require patient work and respect for materials. The same principles apply to building character and earning trust that freedom requires."

The Governor examined the brackets with attention that revealed genuine appreciation for craftsmanship that exceeded functional requirements. The ironwork demonstrated not just technical competence but artistic sensibility that transformed necessary hardware into objects that enhanced their surroundings while serving practical purposes.

"Exceptional work," Governor Gipps observed, running his fingers along scrollwork that would grace the cathedral for generations. "This represents the kind of contribution that justifies our confidence in transportation's capacity to transform destructive impulses into productive capabilities."

Superintendent Hely stepped forward with documents that would formalize Thomas's transition from convict to conditionally free resident of New South Wales. "The ticket of leave grants freedom of movement within the colony and permission to seek employment according to your skills and character. Violation of its terms will result in immediate return to bondage with additional penalties appropriate to the nature of your transgression."

Thomas accepted the documents with hands that trembled slightly—not from fear but from recognition that he was receiving more than legal freedom. These papers represented official acknowledgment that his transformation had been genuine, that seven years of patient effort had successfully rebuilt character from foundations more solid than the pride that had led to his original downfall.

"I understand the responsibility that accompanies this privilege," Thomas replied, studying language that defined both opportunities and obligations that would shape his life as a conditionally free man. "The Crown's confidence will not be betrayed through poor choices or failure to honor the principles that redemption requires."

Colonial Secretary Thomson consulted notes that summarized Thomas's record during seven years of assigned service—work evaluations, conduct reports, assessments from supervisors who had observed his daily behavior under circumstances that revealed true character rather than mere public presentation.

"Your case will be studied as an example of successful rehabilitation," Thomson said, his administrative perspective focused on broader implications of individual transformation. "Transportation serves multiple purposes—punishment for criminal behavior, removal of threats to social order, and opportunity for character reformation that benefits both individuals and colonial society. Your record suggests that these objectives can be achieved when proper principles guide both official policy and personal choices."

The formal inspection concluded with Governor Gipps' final assessment, delivered with authority that carried implications extending far beyond Thomas's individual circumstances. "Mr. Staines, your conduct during seven years of bondage has demonstrated that redemption remains possible for any man willing to undertake its patient work. You have earned freedom through consistent demonstration of character that serves community welfare while rebuilding personal dignity from foundations stronger than those destroyed by original criminal behavior."

He paused, allowing the weight of official recognition to settle before delivering final guidance that would influence Thomas's approach to the challenges and opportunities that lay ahead. "Use your freedom wisely. Remember that liberty is not license but responsibility to continue serving purposes larger than individual satisfaction. The colony benefits from citizens who understand that true success comes from contributing to others' welfare rather than merely advancing personal interests."

As the official party departed, leaving behind an atmosphere charged with significance that transcended routine administrative procedure, Thomas remained at his anvil completing final details on work that would mark his transition from convict labor to independent craftsman. The brackets he shaped with patient attention to detail represented not just functional hardware but symbols of transformation that had required seven years of consistent effort to achieve.

Walsh approached with expression that combined professional satisfaction with personal pleasure at witnessing successful completion of process that had occupied seven years of careful supervision and gradual trust-building. "Well done, Thomas. Your conduct has reflected credit on this facility and demonstrated what's possible when men choose redemption over resentment."

"Couldn't have achieved it without guidance from supervisors who understood the difference between punishment and rehabilitation," Thomas replied, recognizing that his transformation had been collaborative effort rather than individual achievement. "You gave me opportunity to prove myself worthy of trust rather than simply enduring my sentence."

The conversation was interrupted by approach of James Whitmore, the master smith whose approval had been more valuable than official recognition throughout Thomas's years at the Government Forge. Whitmore carried himself with dignity that came from knowing his skills were essential to colonial progress, but also with humility that acknowledged the circumstances that had brought talented men like Thomas within reach of his instruction.

"Heard the Governor's assessment," Whitmore said, his weathered face creased by smile that suggested genuine pleasure at Thomas's success. "Couldn't ask for better recommendation for a man seeking to establish himself as an independent tradesman. Your work's spoken for itself these past years—now it'll speak for your character in the broader community."

The master smith extended his hand with a gesture that marked transition from a supervisor-subordinate relationship to association between equals in the brotherhood of skilled craftsmen. "You'll be missed here, but the colony needs men of your abilities working where they can do most good. Build something worthy of the skills you've developed."

As evening approached and Thomas prepared to spend his final night in Hyde Park Barracks before beginning life as a conditionally free man, he reflected on the seven years that had transformed him from bitter convict into someone capable of contributing to community welfare while finding personal satisfaction in service that transcended individual advancement.

The ticket of leave that restored his freedom of movement within the colony represented more than a legal document—it was certification that his character had been rebuilt from foundations more solid than the pride and desperation that had led to his original downfall. Tomorrow would bring challenges and opportunities that would test whether his transformation could survive the pressures of independence, but tonight he felt prepared for whatever trials and possibilities lay ahead.

The communion rail brackets that marked his final project as assigned convict would grace St. Andrew's Cathedral for generations, silent testimony to redemption achieved through patient work and character rebuilt through consistent choices to serve others' welfare rather than merely endure punishment. Like the metalwork he had shaped with hammer and fire, his spirit had been refined rather than broken by trials that revealed strength rather than weakness, wisdom rather than bitterness.

Seven years of bondage were ending, but the real work—proving himself worthy of the freedom he had earned—was just beginning.

12 THE JOURNEY WEST

Sydney to Bathurst - November 1843 to March 1844

The road that led west from Sydney stretched before Thomas Staines like a promise written in red dust and possibility, each mile carrying him further from the man he had been and closer to whoever he might become when nothing from his past could dictate the limits of his future. November 1843 had blessed New South Wales with the kind of weather that made even hardship seem bearable—clear skies that stretched to horizons unmarked by anything except the Blue Mountains rising like ancient promises in the distance, temperatures that warmed without oppressing, winds that carried scents of eucalyptus and new growth rather than the institutional odors that had marked seven years of confined existence.

His possessions fit easily into the swag that rested across his shoulders with less weight than the chains he had worn during bondage, but infinitely more meaning. Two shirts of good cloth, spare trousers that marked him as working man rather than vagrant, tools of his trade that represented both identity and livelihood, letters of reference from Walsh and Whitmore that testified to character and competence earned through years of patient demonstration. But most precious of all was the Celtic cross he had carved aboard the *Moffatt* eight years earlier, its stone surface bearing the accumulated marks of transformation—thistle for heritage that connected him to Scotland's stubborn beauty, additional details added during quiet hours when memory and hope had shaped rough material into artifact that spoke of love transcending every limitation circumstance could impose.

The journey itself would take months rather than weeks, not because distance demanded such duration but because Thomas had learned the difference between traveling and wandering, between movement with purpose and mere restless displacement. He carried with him not just geographical destination but spiritual intention—to discover what freedom meant when earned rather than inherited, to test whether seven years of forced rehabilitation had prepared him for choices that would define the remainder of his existence.

Sydney's boundaries dissolved gradually rather than suddenly, urban order giving way to rural patterns that spoke of settlement pushing steadily westward against a landscape that had been shaped by forces older than human intention. The road itself bore witness to colonial determination—cut through forest and carved around obstacles that would have deterred less committed efforts, maintained by convict labor that included men whose circumstances paralleled Thomas's own recent bondage. Each mile marker represented not just distance traveled but progress achieved through patience and persistence that characterized both individual and collective success in circumstances that demanded adaptation rather than submission.

The first night's camp was made beside a creek whose clear water spoke of origins in mountains still days ahead, its gentle sound providing a soundtrack for reflections that had been impossible during years when privacy was luxury rather than necessity. Thomas built his fire with attention to detail that prison routine had made automatic, but this flame served his own purposes rather than official requirements, warming food he had chosen rather than rations assigned by institutional necessity.

Sitting beside water that flowed toward Sydney Harbor where his transformation had begun, Thomas felt the weight of choice settling upon his shoulders like a garment that required conscious decision to wear properly. Freedom was proving more complex than mere absence of chains—it was responsibility to determine direction when no external authority provided guidance, to choose wisely when poor decisions would affect only himself rather than attracting punishment that might be shared with others.

The second day brought an encounter with William Morrison, a free settler whose farm lay perhaps twenty miles west of Sydney, struggling with a wagon wheel that had cracked under load too heavy for its construction. Morrison was perhaps forty years old, weathered by colonial experience but possessed of optimism that suggested success rather than mere survival in circumstances that had defeated less determined spirits.

"Heading west?" Morrison asked as Thomas approached, his greeting carrying the particular warmth that marked people who understood value of human contact in a country where isolation was constant threat rather than occasional inconvenience.

"Bathurst," Thomas replied, already calculating what would be required to repair a wheel that represented difference between successful harvest delivery and crop lost to weather that waited for no man's convenience. "Looks like you could use assistance before continuing your journey."

The repair required most of the afternoon—careful work that tested skills refined at the Government Forge but applied now for purposes that served individual need rather than colonial administration. Thomas shaped iron bands that would reinforce the damaged timber, using portable tools to achieve results that approached workshop quality despite primitive conditions. The work was performed without expectation of payment beyond gratitude, but Morrison's appreciation suggested recognition that extended beyond mere mechanical assistance.

"Haven't seen work like that since leaving Yorkshire," Morrison observed, examining repairs that should serve reliably for years rather than merely addressing immediate crisis. "You've got trade that's valuable anywhere men need things built or mended properly."

The conversation that developed while tools were cleaned and materials properly stored revealed Morrison's own journey from English tenant farming to colonial landowner, transformation achieved through willingness to risk everything for opportunities that existed nowhere except places where traditional limitations didn't apply. His success represented what might be possible for anyone willing to work patiently toward goals that required adaptation rather than mere persistence.

"Country rewards men who understand that security comes from what you build rather than what you inherit," Morrison said, his philosophy shaped by experience rather than theory. "Birth and breeding matter less here than competence and character, willingness to help neighbors and honor obligations without constant supervision."

As evening approached, Morrison invited Thomas to share a meal and shelter that revealed colonial hospitality at its most genuine—generosity offered not from obligation but from recognition that isolation was the enemy that could be defeated only through mutual support among people whose circumstances required cooperation rather than competition.

The farmhouse itself spoke of prosperity achieved through patient effort rather than inherited advantage—solid construction that would shelter generations, furnishings that combined functionality with comfort that marked homes rather than mere shelters, evidence throughout of lives built deliberately rather than simply endured. Morrison's wife Sarah welcomed Thomas with a warmth that suggested previous experience offering hospitality to travelers whose circumstances might be difficult but whose character had proven worthy of trust.

"William says you're heading for Bathurst," Sarah observed during the meal that transformed simple ingredients into a feast through attention to detail that made sharing food into celebration rather than mere nutrition. "Long journey for a man traveling alone. You've family waiting there?"

"No family," Thomas replied, understanding that honesty served better than elaborate explanations that might reveal more about his convict past than wisdom recommended. "Seeking opportunity to establish myself as an independent tradesman where skills might be valued and character can be proven through reliable service."

The answer satisfied curiosity without providing details that might create complications, while establishing his status as a free man seeking legitimate employment rather than vagrant whose presence might threaten community security. Sarah's nod suggested acceptance that required no additional justification, recognition that colonial society included many whose origins were less important than their intentions.

The evening passed in conversation that ranged from practical advice about traveling through country that could challenge unprepared travelers to philosophical discussion about what made life meaningful in circumstances that offered freedom to succeed or fail based entirely on individual choices. Morrison's experience spanning both English tenancy and colonial ownership provided perspective on different forms of security—inherited versus earned, traditional versus innovative, dependent versus independent.

"Biggest adjustment wasn't climate or crops," Morrison reflected, his insight shaped by a decade of comparing two entirely different approaches to organizing existence. "Was learning to think like an owner rather than tenant, to plan for generations rather than just seasons, to understand that success here depends on serving community needs rather than merely satisfying landlord requirements."

Thomas absorbed the lesson with attention that recognized its relevance to his own transition from convict status to independent craftsman. The skills he had developed during bondage were transferable, but the mindset required for success as a free man demanded a different understanding of relationship between individual welfare and community prosperity.

Morning brought departure accompanied by Morrison's letter of introduction to contacts in Bathurst who might provide employment or guidance for skilled tradesman seeking to establish himself in the frontier community. But more valuable than specific recommendations was example the Morrison represented—proof that transformation was possible for anyone willing to work patiently toward goals that required character as much as competence.

"Country ahead will test everything you think you know about endurance," Morrison warned, his advice delivered with concern for a fellow traveler rather than mere politeness. "Not just physical challenges—though those are real enough—but questions about who you want to become when nobody's watching to ensure you make proper choices."

The third day's travel carried Thomas into landscape that began reflecting proximity to Blue Mountains, terrain that spoke of geological forces that had shaped a continent before human presence added its own layer of meaning to ancient patterns. The road itself required more attention than the previous day's easier passage—steeper grades that tested both physical conditioning and determination, surfaces that demanded careful foot placement lest misstep result in injury that could end a journey before destination was reached.

But the increasing difficulty was matched by increasing beauty that made hardship feel like privilege rather than burden. Views that opened unexpectedly around bends in the road revealed vistas that spoke of the country's true scale, distances that reduced human concerns to proper proportion while suggesting possibilities that existed beyond immediate experience. Thomas found himself stopping frequently not from fatigue but from desire to absorb scenery that made every step feel like pilgrimage to sacred destinations.

The fourth night's camp brought encounter with an Aboriginal family whose presence reminded Thomas that this land had been home to others long before European settlement imposed its own patterns of meaning and possession. The family—man, woman, and two children—observed his fire from a distance that suggested caution rather than hostility, their attention focused on determining whether his presence represented threat or opportunity for peaceful interaction.

Thomas approached slowly, hands visible and movements deliberate, understanding that successful communication would require respect for customs he didn't fully understand but could attempt to honor through attention to their responses to his gestures. The man was perhaps thirty years old, possessed of dignity that spoke of knowledge systems entirely different from European understanding but equally valid for navigating challenges that this country presented to anyone seeking to thrive rather than merely survive.

"Traveling to the mountains?" the man asked in English that carried an accent unfamiliar to Thomas but clear enough to permit conversation that might benefit both parties.

"Bathurst," Thomas replied, offering information that established his destination without suggesting intentions that might threaten territorial claims he didn't fully understand. "Learning about country, meeting people, discovering what opportunities might exist for a man with blacksmith skills."

The conversation that developed revealed perspective on colonial settlement that differed dramatically from official government accounts or settler narratives Thomas had heard during his years in Sydney. From Aboriginal viewpoint, European presence represented change that created both opportunities and challenges, disruption of traditional patterns balanced by access to tools and techniques that could enhance rather than replace indigenous knowledge.

"Country teaches patience," the man observed, his philosophy shaped by generations of understanding that predated written records but contained wisdom accumulated through direct experience of landscape and climate that demanded adaptation rather than conquest. "Take what land offers, give back what land requires, understand that survival comes from cooperation rather than competition."

The lesson resonated with everything Thomas had learned about redemption requiring service to purposes larger than individual advancement, about character being revealed through choices made when external oversight was absent. Aboriginal understanding of relationship between human welfare and environmental stewardship provided a different perspective on the same principles that had guided his transformation from selfish criminal to a man capable of contributing to community prosperity.

Morning brought a gift that marked the Aboriginal family's assessment of Thomas's character—a piece of carved wood whose intricate patterns spoke of artistic traditions that transformed functional objects into items of beauty that transcended mere utility. The carving was small enough to carry easily but complex enough to provide contemplation for years of careful study, its meanings probably deeper than surface appearance suggested but immediately recognizable as expression of excellence applied to materials that deserved respect.

"For journey," the man explained, his generosity offered without expectation of reciprocal exchange but with understanding that meaningful gifts created connections that transcended immediate circumstances. "Remember that country gives to those who give to country, that wisdom comes from listening rather than demanding answers."

Thomas accepted the carving with gratitude that went beyond politeness to recognition that he had received instruction from teachers whose knowledge systems differed from but complemented everything his European background had provided. The Aboriginal perspective on relationship between individual welfare and collective prosperity aligned with lessons learned during his convict years about service being foundation for redemption.

The fifth day brought approach to Penrith, settlement that marked transition from coastal plains to mountain foothills, final outpost of familiar territory before the journey entered landscape that would test every assumption about what constituted adequate preparation for challenges ahead. The town itself was small but substantial, buildings constructed with attention to permanence that suggested confidence in future growth despite current limitations imposed by distance from Sydney's markets and services.

Here Thomas encountered Mrs. Clara McKenzie, widow whose husband's death had left her struggling to maintain a farm that provided the only security available for herself and three children whose futures depended entirely on her ability to manage responsibilities that would have challenged a man with full partnership to share burdens. Her wagon wheel had cracked under strain of carrying supplies from town, leaving her stranded with winter approaching and no means of completing repairs that required both skill and tools she didn't possess.

The repair required a full day's careful work—not just an immediate fix but reinforcement that would serve reliably for years rather than merely addressing present crisis. Thomas shaped new iron bands that would distribute stress more effectively than original construction, using techniques refined through government forge experience but applied now for purposes that served genuine need rather than institutional requirements.

Mrs. McKenzie's gratitude was evident not just in words but in invitation to share an evening meal with a family whose circumstances had been improved through his intervention. The children—two girls and boy ranging from perhaps eight to fourteen years—studied him with curiosity that reflected limited experience with strangers whose presence might represent either opportunity or threat to their carefully maintained security.

"Haven't seen work like that in years," Mrs. McKenzie observed, examining repairs that demonstrated craftsmanship exceeding functional requirements. "My late husband used to say you could tell a man's character by watching him work—patience you showed, care you took with details that won't be visible once the wheel's back in use."

The observation provided opportunity for Thomas to explain his background without revealing the convict origins that might create complications. "Trained as a blacksmith, spent years learning that proper work requires respect for materials and attention to purposes that tools will serve long after craftsman has moved on to other projects."

During evening conversation, Mrs. McKenzie revealed her own story of adaptation to circumstances that had required developing capabilities she never expected to need. Widowhood in a colonial setting demanded skills that English society would have assigned exclusively to male responsibilities—business decisions, negotiations with suppliers, agricultural planning that determined whether a family prospered or merely survived.

"Hardest part wasn't learning new skills," she reflected, her insight shaped by two years of managing challenges that would have overwhelmed someone whose character hadn't been strengthened by trials that revealed capacity rather than simply testing endurance. "Was learning to trust my own judgment when nobody else was available to provide guidance, to understand that mistakes were education rather than disasters if approached with proper attitude."

Her children contributed their own perspectives on colonial life that differed significantly from adult concerns—excitement about exploration and discovery balanced by awareness that security required constant attention to details that European upbringing hadn't emphasized. They spoke of Aboriginal neighbors whose knowledge proved invaluable for understanding seasonal patterns and resource availability that books couldn't teach, of learning to read landscape and weather in ways that European education had never addressed.

The evening's entertainment included stories that connected their present circumstances to heritage that stretched back through generations of people who had chosen adventure over security, opportunity over certainty, hope over resignation to limitations that circumstances might seem to impose. Mrs. McKenzie's family had left Ireland during difficulties that made emigration seem preferable to remaining in a homeland that couldn't provide adequate opportunities for prosperity.

"Father used to say that courage wasn't absence of fear but willingness to act despite uncertainty," the eldest daughter recalled, her memory preserving wisdom that had guided family decisions to risk everything for possibilities that existed only in distant land that promised nothing except chance to succeed or fail based on individual effort rather than inherited circumstances.

Thomas found himself sharing his own story—carefully edited to emphasize transformation and redemption without revealing specific details about convict origins that might create unnecessary complications. He spoke of learning that character was revealed through response to hardship, that redemption required patient work to rebuild reputation through consistent demonstration of values rather than mere claims about reformed intentions.

The conversation continued until late evening, ranging from practical advice about traveling through mountain country that could challenge unprepared travelers to philosophical discussion about what made life meaningful when traditional social structures provided less guidance than personal choices about how to respond to circumstances that offered both opportunity and risk.

Morning brought departure accompanied by Mrs. McKenzie's blessing and letter of introduction to contacts in regions ahead who might provide assistance to a traveler whose character had been proven through generous service performed without expectation of reward. But more valuable than specific recommendations was confirmation that his transformation had been genuine enough to inspire trust from people whose own survival depended on accurate assessment of character.

"You'll be welcomed wherever men value honest work and reliable character," Mrs. McKenzie said, her assessment carrying weight of someone whose circumstances required practical evaluation rather than sentimental generosity. "Country ahead needs people who understand that community prosperity comes from individual contributions rather than competitive advantage."

The sixth through tenth days carried Thomas through landscape that gradually revealed Blue Mountains' true character—not a single range but a complex system of ridges and valleys that had been carved by forces operating over geological time scales that reduced human concerns to appropriate proportion. The road itself became testament to colonial determination, engineering achievement that required moving enormous quantities of earth and stone to create passage that would serve transportation needs for generations.

Each night's camp provided opportunity for reflection that had been impossible during years when privacy was luxury rather than necessity. Thomas found himself reviewing not just immediate experiences but an entire journey from proud blacksmith through convict bondage to the present moment when a future remained open to possibilities that depended entirely on choices he would make without external coercion or guidance.

The transformation felt complete in ways that went beyond mere legal status—he had become someone capable of serving others' welfare while finding personal satisfaction in work that honored both his trade and the community that provided opportunities for meaningful contribution. But completion of one phase simply prepared him for challenges that lay ahead, tests that would determine whether reformation achieved under forced circumstances could survive pressures of independence.

On the eleventh day, the approach to Bathurst revealed a settlement that embodied colonial aspirations at their most ambitious—substantial buildings that suggested confidence in permanent prosperity, streets laid out with geometric precision that imposed European order on a landscape that had never required such organization, evidence throughout of community that had moved beyond mere survival to begin creating culture that honored both practical necessities and higher aspirations that made life worth preserving.

The sight of his destination filled Thomas with emotions that ranged from gratitude for having survived a journey that tested everything seven years of bondage had taught him about endurance, to anticipation of opportunities that awaited someone whose skills were valued and whose character had been proven through patient demonstration of reliability. But strongest of all was the sense of homecoming to a place he had never seen before—recognition that Bathurst represented not just a geographical destination but spiritual arrival at circumstances where redemption could be proven through service that benefited others while providing personal fulfillment.

As he walked through streets where his future would be determined by choices he made without reference to past mistakes that had been redeemed through patient work, Thomas felt the weight of the Celtic cross against his chest and understood that his real journey was just beginning. The man who entered Bathurst bore little resemblance to the bitter convict who had carved that cross during a voyage that brought him to a colony where punishment became opportunity for transformation.

This new Thomas Staines carried skills refined through hardship, character strengthened through trials that revealed wisdom rather than weakness, and most importantly, understanding that redemption was ongoing process rather than single achievement—commitment to serve purposes larger than individual advancement while finding in that service the satisfaction that made freedom precious rather than merely pleasant.

The road behind him stretched back toward Sydney and seven years of bondage that had prepared him for this moment. The road ahead led toward possibilities that existed nowhere except in places where character mattered more than ancestry, where future could be shaped by individual choices rather than inherited limitations, where love might yet be possible for a man who had learned to give before expecting to receive.

13 FAMILY THREADS

Calvin's Workshop, Gosford — December 2010

The December morning hung heavy with humidity that promised storms before evening, but inside Calvin Wilson's workshop the air moved with gentle efficiency through windows positioned to catch sea breezes that had cooled sawdust and soothed craftsmen for forty years of careful creation. Sara stood in the doorway, breathing in scents that belonged to her childhood—linseed oil and cedar shavings, the metallic tang of well-maintained tools, and underneath it all the particular fragrance of patience applied to materials that rewarded honest work with beauty that would outlast the hands that shaped it.

"Come in, love," Calvin said, looking up from the workbench where he was assembling what appeared to be a document storage box, its corners joined with the precision that marked everything he created. "Been working on something I thought you might find useful for all those papers you've been collecting about Thomas and Catherine."

Three weeks had passed since their phone conversation about Catherine Krieg's immigration records, three weeks of tentative messages and careful exchanges that felt like two people learning to trust that shared interest in family history might provide a bridge across grief that had made communication feel dangerous since Ellen's funeral. This was the first time Sara had visited Calvin's workshop since her mother's death, the first time she'd stood in the space that had always been his sanctuary when the complexities of family life required retreat into work that made sense through its predictable response to skill and attention.

The workshop felt different now—not physically, for everything remained exactly as she remembered, but emotionally charged with awareness that this space had sustained Calvin through months of grief she'd barely begun to understand. Where she'd found refuge in genealogical research and the anonymous bustle of Sydney's streets, he'd found comfort in familiar rhythms of measuring, cutting, joining materials that yielded to patient pressure applied with accumulated wisdom of five decades spent learning how to make beautiful things from ordinary wood.

"It's beautiful," Sara said, running her fingers along the box's edge where Calvin had carved a subtle thistle pattern that echoed the symbols Thomas had inscribed on his Celtic cross during the darkest period of his exile. "You've been thinking about their story too."

Calvin nodded, his carpenter's hands gentle on the piece that had clearly occupied many hours of careful attention to details that served function while honoring heritage that connected them to ancestors whose courage had made their own existence possible. "Couldn't stop thinking about Catherine carrying her father's recipes across oceans, Thomas carving that cross in his prison cell. Made me want to create something that would protect what they left behind, keep their documents safe for whoever comes after us."

The observation carried weight that went beyond practical consideration of document preservation into recognition that family stories required active stewardship from each generation, that inheritance meant responsibility for maintaining whatever wisdom previous struggles had accumulated for guidance of those who would face their own trials with whatever strength such examples could provide. Calvin had been thinking not just about their family history but about his own role in preserving and transmitting wisdom that Ellen's death had made seem precious rather than merely interesting.

"Have you been working on this since our phone call?" Sara asked, settling onto the stool where she'd sat during childhood visits when Calvin's workshop had seemed like a magic kingdom where scraps of wood transformed into toys and furniture through processes that appeared miraculous to young eyes that couldn't distinguish between skill and sorcery.

"Started the day after," Calvin admitted, his voice carrying the shy pride that marked craftsmen revealing work they'd undertaken from love rather than commission. "Ellen always said the best way to process difficult emotions was to make something useful with your hands, something that would outlast whatever troubles had prompted its creation. Been thinking about that advice quite a bit lately."

The mention of Ellen's name hung in the air between them like a blessing rather than wound, the first time either had spoken of her with warmth instead of careful neutrality that had characterized their interactions since grief made her memory feel too precious for casual conversation. Sara felt something loosen in her chest, recognition that Calvin's grief had taken a different form than her own but carried equal weight of loss that isolation had only intensified.

"I miss her," Sara said simply, the words feeling both inadequate and necessary for acknowledging what they'd both been carrying alone when sharing might have made the burden bearable rather than overwhelming. "Miss her voice on the phone when I'd call with research discoveries, miss the way she'd get excited about family stories and ask questions that made me think about them differently."

Calvin set down his sandpaper and looked directly at her for the first time since she'd arrived, his seventy-six-year-old face bearing lines that eighteen months of grief had deepened but not broken. "I miss her every morning when I make tea for two people and remember I'm only making it for one. Miss the way she'd bring me lunch when I was working on complicated projects, miss having someone to share discoveries with who understood why such things mattered."

The acknowledgment of mutual loss created space for conversation they'd been avoiding since Ellen's funeral, when shared grief had felt too dangerous to examine directly because honesty might reveal pain that careful distance had been designed to protect. But Thomas and Catherine's example had taught them something about courage required to choose relationship over safety, to risk vulnerability that might not be returned but offered the only path toward connection that honored Ellen's memory while creating possibilities for healing.

"Show me what you've found," Calvin said, gesturing toward the satchel where Sara carried the accumulated documentation of weeks spent transforming casual curiosity into systematic investigation. "All of it. I want to understand not just what you've discovered but how you've been making sense of it, what patterns you've been seeing that connect their story to ours."

Sara unpacked materials that had become precious beyond their genealogical value—photocopied shipping manifests, marriage certificates, colonial correspondence that documented Thomas's transformation from convicted thief to trusted craftsman, Catherine's journey from orphaned baker's daughter to frontier innkeeper whose recipes had preserved German traditions while serving diverse community needs. But more than individual documents, she'd begun creating a visual timeline that connected scattered references into coherent narrative about two people whose love had transformed individual struggle into shared strength.

Calvin studied each document with attention he brought to furniture plans, reading not just information but implications about character and circumstances that had shaped choices documented in bureaucratic language that couldn't capture emotional weight of decisions made when survival required adaptation to circumstances that formal education had never prepared them to navigate.

"Look at the timing," Sara said, spreading documents across his workbench in chronological order that revealed a pattern of convergence between their ancestors' separate journeys toward intersection that had changed both their lives. "Thomas gets his Ticket of Leave in November 1843, departs Sydney for Bathurst in March 1844. Catherine arrives from Hamburg in October 1843, travels to Bathurst in December. They're both making their way toward same frontier town during the same period, both seeking opportunities that established communities couldn't provide."

Calvin traced the timeline with a finger that bore calluses from decades of honest work, understanding a pattern that suggested not coincidence but natural convergence of people whose circumstances had prepared them to appreciate qualities that prosperity might have concealed but hardship had revealed. "Two people who'd learned that starting over required courage to leave everything familiar, faith that better circumstances were possible if approached with proper attitude and willingness to work for them."

The observation connected their ancestors' nineteenth-century choices to decisions that faced anyone whose circumstances required adaptation rather than mere endurance, change rather than simple persistence with arrangements that no longer served purposes that new realities demanded. Sara found herself thinking about her own choices since Ellen's death—the isolation that had protected against additional loss but also prevented the kind of connection that could transform grief into wisdom, individual pain into shared understanding.

"There's something else," Sara said, reaching into her satchel for folder that contained the most recent discoveries, documents that had been waiting for a proper moment to share with someone who could appreciate their significance for understanding not just family history but contemporary choices about how to honor heritage while embracing change. "I found correspondence about their wedding, details about how the community responded to a marriage between ex-convict and German immigrant."

The wedding documents, when Calvin examined them, revealed social dynamics of a frontier community where conventional barriers between classes and backgrounds had been modified by practical necessities of colonial existence that valued character over circumstances, contribution over origin stories that mattered less than the present willingness to serve community needs through whatever skills and strengths individual experience had developed.

"Witnesses included both German immigrants and former convicts," Sara explained, pointing to names that appeared on the marriage certificate and supporting documents. "The local magistrate wrote that their union represented 'happy convergence of industry and character that will benefit the entire district through combination of complementary skills and shared commitment to community welfare.'"

Calvin smiled, the first genuine expression of happiness Sara had seen since Ellen's funeral, recognition that their ancestors' love story provided evidence that transformation was possible when approached through partnership rather than individual effort, shared purpose rather than isolated struggle. "Sounds like Thomas had earned respect that made his convict past irrelevant to people who knew his character, and Catherine had proven herself valuable enough that her foreign birth didn't matter to a community that needed her skills."

The documents painted a picture of wedding celebration that had brought together a diverse population of frontier settlement where past mattered less than present contribution, where individual stories of hardship and adaptation had created bonds stronger than conventional social arrangements that might have prevented such unions in more established communities. Thomas and Catherine's marriage had been celebrated not just as personal happiness but as community achievement that demonstrated possibilities for redemption and integration that frontier existence made available to anyone willing to embrace them.

"Ellen would have loved this," Calvin said, his voice carrying gratitude rather than pain as he spoke his wife's name in context of discovery rather than loss. "She always believed the best love stories were the ones that proved two people could become more together than either could achieve alone, that real partnership multiplied individual strengths rather than simply combining them."

The reference to Ellen felt natural rather than forced, recognition that her wisdom about love and family could guide understanding of ancestors whose example provided a template for building relationships that honored past while creating space for growth and change. Sara felt encouraged to share an observation that had been forming during weeks of research, understanding about inheritance that extended beyond material possessions into the realm of responsibility and wisdom.

"I think that's what we're supposed to learn from their story," Sara said, organizing documents into patterns that revealed rather than concealed connections between nineteenth-century transformation and contemporary choices about grief and healing. "Not just facts about where we came from, but guidance about how to face our own trials with the kind of courage that creates something beautiful from broken materials."

Calvin stood and moved to the window that overlooked Brisbane Water, his seventy-six-year-old frame still solid from decades of physical work but carrying weight of grief that isolation had intensified rather than healed. "Been thinking about that quite a bit lately," he said, his voice carrying admission that felt like a gift offered without expectation of return. "About how Ellen's death left me feeling like everything meaningful had been taken away, but Thomas and Catherine's story suggests different possibilities."

The acknowledgment invited deeper conversation than they'd attempted since Ellen's funeral, recognition that grief had isolated them from each other precisely when connection might have provided comfort that individual struggle couldn't achieve. Sara joined him at the window, understanding that some conversations required shared focus on the external landscape while internal territories were being explored with caution that prevented overwhelming emotions that careful distance had been designed to protect.

"Different possibilities?" Sara asked, though she suspected she understood what Calvin meant, having reached similar conclusions during her own wrestling with questions about how to honor Ellen's memory while building meaning from circumstances that grief had made seem empty of purpose or hope.

"That loss doesn't have to be ending," Calvin said, his words chosen with precision that marked conversations about territory too important for casual language. "That people who love us don't disappear when they die—they become part of whatever we choose to build with the time that remains available to us. Thomas carried his mother's memory from England to Australia, Catherine preserved her father's recipes, Rivers maintained Thomas's story for her children. Each generation found ways to honor what came before while creating something new."

The observation provided framework for understanding inheritance that transcended material possessions or even historical information, suggesting that love itself could be preserved and transmitted through choices that served others' welfare rather than simply advanced personal comfort. Ellen's love had shaped their capacity for facing loss and choosing hope, but only if they were willing to risk the vulnerability that relationship required.

"I've been thinking about writing their complete story," Sara said, sharing an idea that had been forming during weeks of research but hadn't been articulated until this moment when Calvin's workshop provided safe space for discussing possibilities that felt too ambitious for casual conversation. "Not just preserving the documents we've found, but creating something that honors their transformation while making their example available to anyone who needs guidance about redemption and love."

Calvin turned from the window to study Sara's face with attention he brought to complex projects that required understanding not just what needed to be built but why such building mattered enough to justify effort and patience that excellence demanded. "You mean a book? About Thomas and Catherine?"

"A novel," Sara clarified, understanding that fiction might capture emotional truth about transformation and love in ways that historical documentation alone couldn't achieve. "Based on everything we've discovered but focused on the human story rather than just genealogical facts. Their journey from individual brokenness to shared healing, from shame to honor, from isolation to community. The kind of story that proves redemption is possible for anyone willing to undertake its patient work."

The idea felt both impossibly ambitious and absolutely necessary, recognition that Thomas and Catherine's wisdom deserved preservation in a form that could reach hearts ready to receive guidance about courage and transformation and the difference between existing and truly living. Calvin's workshop, surrounded by evidence of patient craftsmanship applied to materials that rewarded honest work with beauty, seemed like an appropriate place for discussing the project that would require similar dedication to honoring traditions while creating something new.

"Ellen always said you had a gift for writing," Calvin observed, his voice carrying memory of conversations Sara had forgotten but he had preserved because they demonstrated Ellen's faith in possibilities that grief had made seem unrealistic rather than simply challenging. "Said you could make family stories feel like they were happening to people you could meet tomorrow rather than relatives who died before you were born."

The encouragement felt like a blessing from sources both living and departed, recognition that the project which had seemed like a personal obsession might actually serve purposes larger than individual satisfaction. Calvin's workshop held evidence that beautiful things could be created through patience and skill applied to ordinary materials, that inheritance meant responsibility for preserving and transmitting whatever wisdom previous generations had accumulated for guidance of those who would face their own trials.

"Would you help me?" Sara asked, understanding that some projects required partnership rather than individual effort, shared commitment to honoring heritage while creating something that served contemporary needs for guidance about love and loss and the courage required to choose hope when circumstances suggested despair might be a more reasonable response.

Calvin's answer came without hesitation, his voice carrying conviction that made doubt impossible. "Of course. Ellen would want us working together on something that honors their memory while bringing us closer to each other. She always believed the best projects were collaborative efforts that strengthened relationships while creating something neither person could achieve alone."

The afternoon dissolved into shared work that felt like prayer made visible—Calvin teaching Sara traditional joinery techniques while she organized documents in chronological order that revealed a pattern of transformation and love that had shaped their family's character across generations. The document box took shape under their combined attention, its corners joined with precision that would ensure centuries of protection for papers that documented wisdom earned through trials that had tested but not broken the human capacity for redemption.

"This one's special," Calvin said, indicating a compartment he'd designed specifically for Thomas's letters, a space that would protect the original documents while allowing easy access when their guidance was needed for navigating circumstances that required wisdom about love and sacrifice and the difference between surviving and truly living. "Letters like those deserve special protection. They're not just family history—they're an instruction manual for anyone seeking guidance about transformation."

As evening approached and the workshop filled with golden light that made ordinary tools seem sacred, Sara and Calvin found themselves surrounded by the evidence of an afternoon spent rebuilding a relationship that grief had damaged but shared purpose had begun to heal. The document box stood complete except for final sanding that would smooth rough edges, its compartments designed to hold not just papers but legacy that connected them to ancestors whose love had made their own existence possible.

"Thank you," Sara said, understanding that her gratitude applied to more than carpentry instruction or document organization, encompassing Calvin's willingness to risk emotional investment in a project that might not succeed but offered opportunity for connection that honored Ellen's memory while creating space for relationship that could survive whatever trials the future presented.

"Thank your ancestors," Calvin replied, his voice carrying warmth that hadn't been present during months of careful conversation that preserved connection without demanding vulnerability. "They're the ones who showed us that love can survive any circumstances if approached with sufficient courage and determination to serve purposes larger than individual comfort."

The drive back to Sydney took Sara through familiar landscape that felt different after an afternoon spent rediscovering a relationship with a father whose grief had taught him about isolation while Thomas and Catherine's example promised to teach them both about the courage required to choose hope over fear, connection over safety, love over the careful distance that protected against additional loss but also prevented the meaning that made loss worthwhile.

Calvin had promised to visit her apartment the following weekend, bringing tools necessary for building a proper display case for family documents that deserved presentation worthy of the wisdom they contained. But more than practical assistance, he was offering partnership in a project that would honor their inheritance while creating something that served contemporary needs for guidance about transformation and love.

The document box, when completed, would hold more than papers—it would contain evidence of an afternoon when grief began its transformation into gratitude, isolation into partnership, careful distance into willingness to risk vulnerability that relationships required. Thomas and Catherine had found each other across impossible circumstances and chosen to build something beautiful together. Their descendants were finally learning to follow their example, choosing love over fear, hope over despair, connection over the safety that preserved nothing because it attempted to protect everything.

Ellen's voice seemed to whisper through the coastal wind that carried Sara home to an apartment where novels waited to be written, relationships rebuilt, wisdom preserved for anyone whose heart was ready to receive guidance about love that proved stronger than death when transmitted through stories that honored past while serving present needs for hope and healing.

14 CATHERINE'S MARKET

Bathurst, New South Wales - March 1844

The Bathurst market square pulsed with the particular energy of frontier commerce on Saturday morning, a weekly transformation that turned the town's central space into a crossroads where the colony's diverse population converged to trade goods, share news, and maintain the social connections that made survival possible in circumstances that demanded cooperation rather than mere individual effort. Thomas Staines stood at the square's eastern edge, his swag light on his shoulders after four months of westward travel but his heart heavy with the accumulated weight of seven years' transformation from prideful blacksmith to something he was still learning to define.

The market itself reflected Bathurst's character as a community that had moved beyond mere survival to begin creating prosperity that honored both practical necessities and higher aspirations. Stalls arranged in rough geometric patterns offered everything from fresh produce grown in soil that had been coaxed to European productivity, to manufactured goods that had traveled impossible distances to reach customers who valued quality over mere convenience. The sounds—voices calling prices in accents that spoke of origins spanning half the globe, wheels of carts creaking under loads that represented weeks of careful preparation, livestock protesting their temporary confinement while awaiting purchase by farmers who understood their value—created a symphony that celebrated human determination to build meaningful lives from whatever materials circumstances provided.

But it was the sight that stopped Thomas mid-stride and changed the entire trajectory of his carefully planned approach to building a new life in this frontier town that made his breath catch and his understanding of possibility expand beyond anything seven years of patient transformation had prepared him to imagine. Behind a modest stall laden with bread that gleamed golden in the morning sunshine stood a woman whose presence seemed to emanate light that had nothing to do with mere reflection of Australian sun.

Catherine Krieg moved with unconscious grace that spoke of someone who had learned to find beauty in necessary tasks, her auburn hair catching highlights that shifted from copper to gold as she bent over her wares, her voice carrying melodies that spoke of a distant homeland and hard-won wisdom. She was explaining something to a customer in English that bore the musical accent of German heritage, each word carefully chosen but delivered with confidence that suggested years of patient practice in making herself understood in a language that had not shaped her childhood dreams but had become essential for survival in circumstances that demanded constant adaptation.

Thomas studied her with attention that went beyond mere aesthetic appreciation to recognition of character that seemed to complement his own understanding of what it meant to rebuild life from materials that had been broken by circumstances beyond individual control. Her hands as she wrapped bread in clean cloth spoke of skills refined through necessity, efficiency that honored both the food she had created and the customers who would be sustained by her labor. The care she took to ensure each purchase represented fair value for payment offered suggested business practices based on service rather than mere profit, commitment to community welfare that transcended immediate personal advantage.

But it was her smile—warm and genuine rather than calculated for commercial purposes—that made Thomas understand he was witnessing something rare and precious in colonial society where hardship often wore away the softer qualities that made human interaction meaningful rather than merely functional. Catherine Krieg possessed something that seven years of convict bondage had taught him to recognize and value: the capacity to find joy in circumstances that might have defeated someone whose character had not been refined through trials that revealed strength rather than destroying it.

As Thomas approached her stall, he found himself thinking about the journey that had brought this German woman to Bathurst's market square, circumstances that must have required courage comparable to his own transportation but chosen rather than imposed, voluntary exile that spoke of character willing to risk everything for opportunities that existed nowhere except places where traditional limitations didn't apply.

Catherine's story, Catarina was actually her second name yet she chose to go by Catherine once she migrated to Australia, as it would emerge through weeks of careful conversation, began in Asperg, a small town in Württemberg where her father Johann Krieg had an established bakery that served local community with bread whose quality reflected generations of knowledge about transforming simple ingredients into sustenance that nourished both body and spirit. The Krieg family had prospered modestly for twenty years, their reputation built on reliability and excellence that made their shop essential to daily life in a community that valued traditional craftsmanship over industrial efficiency.

But Johann's death from consumption in 1841 had destroyed more than family stability—it had eliminated the economic foundation that supported Catherine, her mother Christina, and younger brother Wilhelm in circumstances that offered few opportunities for women to maintain independent businesses. Württemberg's laws prohibited female ownership of commercial enterprises, while social customs that might have provided informal support were strained by economic difficulties that made survival challenging even for established families with male leadership.

The decision to seek opportunity in Australia had emerged not from adventure but from careful analysis of alternatives that offered little hope for maintaining dignity while ensuring survival. Anna Krieg's health had been undermined by grief that made her unable to adapt to circumstances that demanded energy she no longer possessed, while Wilhelm's youth made him unsuitable for assuming responsibilities that required both physical strength and business experience he couldn't acquire without resources the family no longer commanded.

Catherine's choice to emigrate had been motivated by recognition that her father's training in baking arts represented portable wealth that could serve her well in colonial society that valued practical skills over social connections, competence over breeding, willingness to work over inherited advantage. The recipes and techniques Johann had taught her during childhood spent helping in the family bakery provided foundation for independence that would have been impossible to achieve in a homeland where women's capabilities were constrained by legal and social limitations that colonial circumstances might not impose.

The journey itself had required two years of preparation—selling family possessions to purchase passage money, learning basic English from a local pastor who understood the value of education for emigrants seeking success in British territories, developing physical and emotional strength necessary for crossing oceans to destinations that existed more in hope than certainty. Catherine had worked as a domestic servant for wealthy Asperg families, saving every pfennig while absorbing lessons about household management and business practices that would serve her well in circumstances where such knowledge could mean the difference between prosperity and mere survival.

The voyage aboard the *Friedeburg* in October 1843 had tested everything Catherine thought she understood about endurance, community, and the courage required to build meaningful life from broken materials. Four months at sea with 200 other emigrants had created its own society with customs and hierarchies that bore little resemblance to European patterns, circumstances where character revealed itself through response to hardship rather than adherence to inherited social positions.

Catherine had emerged from that crossing with an understanding that paralleled Thomas's own education in what made life worth preserving—knowledge that dignity came not from circumstances but from choices, that redemption required service to purposes larger than individual advancement, that love was something practiced rather than merely felt. The women she had traveled with included some whose circumstances were desperate, others whose situations offered hope, all united by a willingness to risk everything for possibilities that existed nowhere except places where a future could be shaped by individual effort rather than predetermined by birth and breeding.

Her arrival in Sydney had been followed by months of work as a domestic servant for colonial families who valued her skills while providing opportunity to perfect English language abilities and understand social customs that governed interactions in society that combined British legal structures with frontier pragmatism. But Catherine's goal had always been independence that could be achieved only through establishing a business that utilized her father's training while serving community needs that colonial circumstances had created.

Bathurst had attracted her attention through reports that reached Sydney about opportunities in frontier towns where traditional services were scarce and skilled practitioners could build substantial businesses if willing to adapt European techniques to Australian conditions. The town's position as a regional center for expanding agricultural development meant a steady population of farmers, merchants, and professional men who valued quality food preparation but lacked access to traditional bakery services that required both skill and commitment to excellence that commercial enterprises in larger cities might not maintain.

The stall where Thomas first encountered Catherine represented eighteen months of patient effort to establish a reputation for reliability and quality that made her bread essential to daily life in a community that had learned to value practical excellence over mere convenience. Her success had been built on understanding that colonial society rewarded service that enhanced others' welfare rather than mere commercial transactions that benefited only sellers, an approach to business that honored both her father's memory and her own commitment to contributing to community prosperity rather than simply extracting profit from others' needs.

"Fresh bread, sir?" Catherine asked as Thomas approached, her voice carrying a musical quality that would haunt his dreams for weeks afterward while he struggled to understand what her presence meant for possibilities he had not dared to imagine during seven years of patient preparation for freedom. "Baked this morning from flour I ground myself, with yeast my mother taught me to cultivate before I left the old country."

The bread itself was a revelation that spoke of traditions that stretched back through generations of knowledge about transforming basic ingredients into sustenance that nourished more than mere physical hunger. The loaves displayed on her wooden counter represented varieties that reflected different purposes—dense rye that would last for days without spoiling, wheaten bread whose lighter texture provided luxury that marked special occasions, sweet pastries that transformed simple ingredients into a celebration of human capacity to create beauty from ordinary materials.

But it was the woman herself who commanded Thomas's attention, a presence that suggested character refined through trials that paralleled his own journey from circumstances that might have destroyed someone whose spirit had not been prepared to receive whatever wisdom hardship could provide. Catherine Krieg possessed something that seven years of convict bondage had taught him to recognize immediately: the quiet strength that came from choosing service over selfishness, hope over resignation, love over fear.

"I'm no sir," Thomas replied, his voice rougher than he would have preferred, marked by years of command-following rather than confident conversation he wished he could offer someone whose attention he wanted to earn rather than simply claim. "Just a traveling smith looking for honest work and wondering if your bread tastes as good as it looks."

Catherine's laugh was like music made from ordinary sound, carrying notes of genuine amusement rather than polite acknowledgment that marked most commercial interactions. "Only one way to discover that, I think. But first, tell me—what brings a traveling smith to Bathurst? We have Mr. Henderson for horseshoes and wagon repairs, and he's served the district well for many years."

The question was fair, delivered without suspicion but with practical curiosity that characterized someone who understood how small communities functioned, where new arrivals needed to justify their presence through contribution rather than mere intention. Thomas recognized this as his first test—not just of his skills or credentials, but of his willingness to be honest about circumstances that might not recommend him to the respect of law-abiding citizens.

Around them, the market square continued its weekly transformation into the social center that connected Bathurst's diverse population through commercial activities that served purposes beyond mere exchange of goods for money. Thomas observed the careful choreography of frontier commerce—Aboriginal workers whose knowledge of local conditions made European agricultural success possible, Chinese immigrants whose industriousness had earned them acceptance despite cultural differences that might have created barriers in more established communities, Irish refugees whose flight from famine had brought valuable skills along with a desperate determination to succeed in circumstances that offered what the homeland could not provide.

Free settlers moved among the stalls with confidence that spoke of success achieved through adaptation rather than mere persistence, their purchases reflecting prosperity that had been earned through willingness to serve community needs while building personal security. Emancipated convicts conducted business with dignity that marked successful completion of transformation from bondage to citizenship, their acceptance by the broader community proving that redemption was possible for anyone willing to undertake its patient work.

But it was the women who commanded particular attention—not just because colonial society included fewer females than males, creating social dynamics that differed significantly from European patterns, but because their presence represented courage that often exceeded that displayed by men whose circumstances might have been easier to navigate. Women like Catherine had chosen voluntary exile for opportunities that existed nowhere else, risks that required character strong enough to survive whatever trials awaited in destinations that promised nothing except chance to succeed or fail based on individual merit.

Mrs. Eleanor Patterson, the German widow whose similar background had created a natural alliance with Catherine, approached the bread stall with a smile that spoke of friendship based on shared heritage and mutual respect for qualities that transcended immediate circumstances. "Guten Morgen, Catherine. The usual order for the hotel, plus extra sweet rolls if you have them. Travelers are commenting favorably on the quality that exceeds anything they've encountered since leaving Sydney."

The interaction provided a glimpse into Catherine's integration into Bathurst's commercial network, relationships that had been built through consistent demonstration of reliability and excellence that made her services essential to businesses whose success depended on satisfying customers who valued quality over mere convenience. Her bread supplied not just individual families but establishments that served the broader community—hotels, restaurants, boarding houses that fed travelers whose experiences in Bathurst would influence the town's reputation throughout the colony.

"Certainly, Mrs. Patterson," Catherine replied, her English now carrying only a slight accent that marked foreign birth without impeding communication that served both business purposes and social connection. "Mr. Thompson mentioned that mining engineers from Sydney particularly appreciated the rye bread—reminds them of European quality they haven't found elsewhere in colonial settlements."

Thomas listened to the exchange with attention that revealed Catherine's sophisticated understanding of market dynamics that went beyond simple supply and demand to encompass reputation management and customer relationships that sustained businesses through economic fluctuations that could destroy enterprises based solely on immediate profit margins. Her success represented more than individual achievement—it demonstrated possibilities available to anyone willing to serve community welfare while building personal prosperity through honest work that honored both tradition and innovation.

As Mrs. Patterson completed her purchases and moved on to other vendors, Catherine's attention returned to Thomas with curiosity that suggested genuine interest rather than mere commercial politeness. "You mentioned traveling from Sydney? Long journey for a man seeking work in a territory where established tradesmen already serve local needs."

"Came from Sydney with my Ticket of Leave," Thomas said simply, understanding that honesty offered the only foundation upon which anything lasting could be built, regardless of immediate consequences that truth might create. "Served seven years for theft, learned my trade working the government forge, thought perhaps there might be opportunity in country like this for a man willing to work hard and prove himself worthy of trust."

He watched Catherine's face carefully, prepared for withdrawal that such honesty usually provoked from people who had never faced circumstances desperate enough to make crime seem a rational alternative to continued suffering. Instead, her expression deepened with something that might have been understanding, as if his admission had revealed character rather than disqualified him from consideration for whatever possibilities their conversation might explore.

The market square around them continued its weekly celebration of colonial commerce and community connection, sounds and sights that spoke of a society that had moved beyond mere survival to begin creating prosperity that honored both practical necessities and higher aspirations. But for Thomas, the world had narrowed to a single point of connection with a woman whose presence suggested possibilities he had not dared to imagine during years of patient preparation for freedom whose full meaning was only now beginning to reveal itself.

15 THE RESEARCHER'S TRAIL

Various Archives and Sara's Apartment, Sydney — January 2011

The New Year had arrived with the kind of crisp clarity that made even ambitious resolutions seem achievable, and Sara Wilson had resolution that consumed every spare moment: tracking the Nicol family connections that would complete the genealogical puzzle stretching from nineteenth-century Australian colonies back through centuries of Scottish parish records to whatever heritage had shaped Thomas Staines' understanding of identity and belonging. Her Christmas holidays had been spent not with friends or relaxation, but hunched over laptop and documents, following paper trails that wound through archives scattered across Sydney and correspondence that bridged oceans to reach repositories in Scotland where ancient records waited for researchers patient enough to navigate bureaucratic procedures that protected precious documents from casual handling.

The breakthrough had come through William Paterson's marriage certificate, where his mother's name appeared with tantalizing specificity: "Margaret Fleming, née Paterson, daughter of Janet Paterson and Robert Fleming of Arbuthnott Parish, Kincardineshire." That single notation redirected months of Nicol-line assumptions. The Nicol connection, Sara realised, was collateral — through an earlier Fleming marriage that linked the Patersons by kinship, not direct descent.

January's first week found her at the Genealogical Society of New South Wales, their Chippendale headquarters housing collections that complemented the State Library's official records with donated materials from families who understood that preserving heritage required active effort from each generation. The society's librarian, Dorothy Matthews, had become an invaluable guide through Scottish records that early immigrants had carried to Australia, understanding that colonial families often preserved documentation that might have been lost in a homeland where official repositories faced centuries of war, fire, and neglect.

"Kincardineshire records are particularly well-preserved," Dorothy explained as they navigated shelves that held transcribed parish registers, cemetery records, and family histories compiled by descendants whose curiosity about heritage had driven systematic preservation efforts. "The Church of Scotland maintained meticulous records, and many families emigrated with copies of baptismal certificates, marriage lines, and other documents that prove invaluable for researchers trying to connect colonial generations to their Scottish origins."

Sara had requested everything related to Arbuthnott Parish, understanding that a systematic approach required examining all available materials rather than hoping for lucky discoveries that might never materialize. The parish records, when they arrived, painted a picture of a rural Scottish community where the same families had lived for centuries, their names appearing in baptismal registers, marriage records, and burial notifications that documented the cycle of life in an agricultural society where seasons determined rhythm of existence more than human ambition or political upheaval.

The Nicol family appeared consistently throughout eighteenth-century Arbuthnott records — and while Sara now understood they connected to her line through the Flemings rather than by direct descent, their proximity in parish life remained essential for reconstructing the web of kinship that bound the Patersons, Flemings, and Stewarts together. Their entries suggesting solid yeoman farmers whose children married within established community networks that preserved both property and bloodlines through careful attention to family connections that served economic as well as social purposes.

Genealogy, Sara reflected, was as much about correction as discovery. Each false start sharpened the truth, reminding her that family history rarely ran in straight lines. Sometimes the most important findings came not from confirming what she hoped to prove, but from realising where the path had quietly turned another way.

Margaret Nicol's baptism was recorded in 1820, daughter of John Fleming and Jane Fleming, née Nicol—notation that made Sara's pulse quicken with recognition that the Stewart surname had appeared in family tradition as a possible connection to nobility.

"The Stewart line could be significant," Dorothy observed when Sara pointed out the connection. "That name appears frequently in medieval Scottish records, often associated with royal bloodlines and noble families that held extensive lands before political upheavals redistributed property and titles. Family tradition claiming descent from Lady Agnes Schelis might have more foundation than most such stories, which are often wishful thinking rather than documented fact."

Dorothy traced the Fleming–Paterson line further and found that, through marriage alliances, it converged with the old Stewart families of Kincardineshire — the same circles in which Lady Agnes Schelis had lived and married. The Stewart connection, it seemed, was by alliance rather than blood, but no less woven into the family's sense of inherited character and place.

The possibility that their family tree might include genuine nobility felt simultaneously thrilling and overwhelming, understanding that such connections required verification through sources that extended beyond parish records into medieval documents housed in repositories that protected materials too precious and fragile for ordinary research access. But Sara had learned enough about genealogical investigation to understand that extraordinary claims required extraordinary evidence, that family traditions needed documentation that could withstand scholarly scrutiny rather than simply romantic speculation about heritage that might exist more in imagination than historical reality.

The afternoon session brought focus to correspondence that would extend her research beyond Australian repositories into Scottish archives where original documents might provide evidence that colonial transcriptions could only hint at rather than definitively establish. Sara composed letters to the National Records of Scotland, Aberdeenshire Archives, and local historical societies whose volunteers often possessed intimate knowledge of family histories that official records documented only partially.

"Dear Sir/Madam, I am writing from Sydney, Australia to request assistance with genealogical research into the Nicol family of Arbuthnott Parish, Kincardineshire. I am particularly interested in Margaret Nicol, born 1820, daughter of Robert Nicol and Agnes Nicol née Stewart, who married William Paterson in approximately 1845 before emigration to Australia..."

Each letter required careful crafting that balanced specificity about information sought with acknowledgment of staff limitations and institutional priorities that made volunteer assistance precious rather than automatic. Sara had learned through professional experience that successful international genealogical research depended upon building relationships with archivists and volunteers who possessed knowledge that no amount of independent investigation could duplicate, understanding that courtesy and patience often proved more valuable than credentials or payment when seeking access to materials that institutions guarded carefully.

The week continued with visits to archives she'd never explored despite years of genealogical work, understanding that systematic investigation required casting wider nets than casual research typically attempted. The Australian Catholic University's archives held immigration records that focused on assisted passages that had brought thousands of European settlers to colonies that promised opportunities for anyone willing to undertake risks that emigration required. The University of Sydney's Fisher Library contained Scottish historical collections donated by immigrants who understood that preserving heritage meant maintaining connections to cultural traditions that colonial circumstances might otherwise have allowed to fade into memory.

Each repository demanded different research strategies, navigation of unique cataloging systems, adaptation to institutional cultures that reflected the personalities and priorities of librarians who had shaped collections according to their own understanding of what materials deserved preservation and how researchers should access them. Sara found herself developing expertise in institutional diplomacy, learning to present her research interests in ways that aligned with each archive's mission while maintaining focus on questions that drove her investigation.

The breakthrough came not from official archives but from unexpected correspondence that arrived at her apartment on a Thursday evening when January heat had made research travel impossible and she was working through accumulated photocopies that covered her dining table like archaeological excavation of family memory. The letter bore return address of the Kincardineshire Family History Society, response to an inquiry she'd sent three weeks earlier and forgotten amid the flood of information that each successful discovery generated.

"Dear Ms. Wilson, Your inquiry about the Nicol family of Arbuthnott Parish has been forwarded to me as current keeper of our memorial inscription records. I believe I can provide information that will be of considerable interest to your research. Margaret Fleming of Arbuthnott Parish — wife of William Paterson — is indeed recorded in our parish cemetery records. Her headstone bears a carved thistle emblem, and date of 1692 rather than 1820 as suggested in your letter. Adjacent memorials record members of the Stewart family, through whom the Paterson-Fleming line connects indirectly to Lady Agnes Schelis ..."

Sara read the letter three times before its significance fully registered. Margaret Nicol 1692, not 1820—a century earlier than the Margaret she'd been researching, suggesting that the family connection extended much deeper into Scottish history than colonial records had indicated. The carved thistle emblem provided direct link to symbols that Thomas had inscribed on his Celtic cross, proof that family traditions about Scottish heritage contained more historical accuracy than she'd dared to hope.

"...The inscription is weathered but legible, and our volunteer photographer has created detailed images of all seventeenth-century memorial stones that show family symbols and heraldic devices. Margaret Nicol's stone includes not only the thistle but Celtic knotwork patterns that suggest family connections to traditions predating written parish records. More significantly, our medieval manuscript collection includes references to the Nicol family in documents dating to the fifteenth century, with possible connections to the Stewart royal line through Lady Agnes Schelis..."

The letter continued with details that transformed casual genealogical curiosity into serious historical investigation requiring access to materials that existed in only a few repositories worldwide. Lady Agnes Schelis appeared in medieval Scottish records as minor nobility whose death in 1460 had been documented in royal chronicles that mentioned her marriage connections to families whose surnames included both Stewart and Nicol, suggesting that family tradition about noble heritage might have foundation in documented historical fact rather than romantic speculation.

Sara's hands trembled as she set down the letter, understanding that she was holding evidence of heritage that connected her Australian present to Scottish medieval nobility, bloodlines that stretched across centuries of political upheaval, religious persecution, and social transformation that had reduced noble families to common farmers whose descendants eventually sought opportunities in colonial territories that promised fresh starts for anyone brave enough to cross oceans in pursuit of better circumstances.

The implications extended beyond personal satisfaction about family heritage into recognition that Thomas Staines' transformation from convicted thief to community hero might have been supported by genetic inheritance that predisposed him toward leadership and resilience, character traits that had survived centuries of reduced circumstances to emerge when Australian exile created opportunities for redemption that a homeland had never provided. Noble blood didn't excuse his crime or diminish his achievement, but it might explain the strength that had enabled transformation that lesser character might not have accomplished.

Evening brought frantic activity as Sara composed responses to Scottish correspondents, expressing gratitude for information received while requesting access to additional materials that might document the medieval connections that transformed family tree from genealogical curiosity into historical treasure requiring careful preservation and scholarly verification. Her apartment filled with the sounds of printer and scanner working overtime to create copies of documents that would need professional analysis to determine authenticity and significance.

But beyond documentation and verification, Sara found herself thinking about responsibility that such heritage created for contemporary choices about how to honor inheritance that transcended material possessions or social status. Noble blood meant nothing without noble character, medieval heritage carried no weight without contemporary wisdom that transformed past achievements into present guidance for anyone seeking to understand what it meant to build lives worthy of preservation.

Calvin needed to hear this discovery, but not through a hurried phone call that might diminish significance of information that deserved careful presentation and thoughtful discussion about implications for understanding their family's character and their own responsibility for preserving and transmitting wisdom that had survived centuries of trials. Instead, Sara scheduled dinner at her apartment for Saturday evening, planning to share discoveries in context that honored both historical importance and emotional weight of learning that their heritage included connections to Scottish nobility whose story had become part of their own identity.

The week's final research session took place at the Mitchell Library, where Sara worked through Scottish historical collections that might provide context for medieval connections that personal correspondence had revealed. The Stewart royal line was well-documented in Scottish history, their political and military achievements recorded in chronicles that painted a picture of family that had shaped national identity through centuries of warfare, diplomacy, and cultural development that had made Scotland distinct from the larger English kingdom that eventually absorbed it through political union that preserved local identity while creating broader British identity.

Lady Agnes Schelis appeared in these historical records as a minor figure whose importance lay not in individual achievement but in marriage connections that had linked noble families during a period when such alliances determined inheritance of land, titles, and political influence that shaped regional development for generations. Her death in 1460 had occurred during Scotland's most turbulent medieval period, when warfare between noble families had created constant flux in property ownership and family fortunes that could be lost or gained through single battles or political decisions.

But medieval records also suggested that Lady Agnes had been known for character that transcended social position, reputation for wisdom and compassion that had made her memory worthy of preservation in chronicles that typically focused on military achievement and political maneuvering rather than personal virtue. The observation connected her to family tradition that valued character over circumstances, service over self-advancement, qualities that had emerged in Thomas Staines' transformation and Calvin's workshop philosophy that honored craftsmanship as expression of moral commitment rather than mere economic activity.

Friday evening brought completion of a research summary that Sara had been preparing for Calvin, a document that organized scattered discoveries into coherent narrative about family heritage that stretched from contemporary Australia back through centuries of Scottish history to medieval nobility whose character had shaped regional development through choices that served community welfare rather than advanced personal ambition. The summary required careful balance between historical accuracy and emotional truth about inheritance that transcended genealogical curiosity to provide guidance for contemporary choices about how to honor heritage while serving present needs for wisdom and hope.

"Our family tree extends from Thomas and Catherine's nineteenth-century transformation back through the Paterson and Fleming families of Kincardineshire — where Margaret's thistle-carved stone stands beside Stewart memorials that trace to Lady Agnes Schelis of 1460, of medieval Scottish nobility whose character was preserved in royal chronicles that suggest she embodied qualities of wisdom and service that have characterized our family across five centuries of adaptation to changing circumstances..."

The documentation felt like a treasure map that revealed not just geographical origins but spiritual inheritance that connected them to people who had chosen character over comfort, service over selfishness, hope over fear when facing circumstances that tested everything they believed about meaning and purpose. Thomas's transformation hadn't occurred in a vacuum but drew upon heritage that predisposed him toward redemption, while their own choices about grief and healing continued family tradition of choosing love over fear when circumstances demanded courage that drew upon resources deeper than individual strength.

Saturday's dinner would mark the transition from individual research into a shared project that honored past while serving present needs for connection and healing. The document box Calvin had built waited in her apartment, ready to hold original documents that proved their heritage extended beyond material circumstances into a realm of character and wisdom that made noble blood meaningful only when accompanied by noble choices about how to serve purposes larger than individual satisfaction.

Outside her window, Sydney Harbor sparkled with lights that had guided ships from around the world, carrying hopeful immigrants and desperate convicts toward futures that existed more in imagination than certainty. Soon, she and Calvin would follow a similar path back to Scotland, not as emigrants seeking opportunities but as descendants returning to honor heritage that had shaped their capacity for transformation and love, proving that some journeys completed circles that had been centuries in the making.

The research trail had led from Thomas's letters through Catherine's immigration records to medieval Scottish nobility whose blood had carried forward character traits that enabled redemption and transformation when circumstances demanded such choices. Now it was time to share discoveries with Calvin, to plan pilgrimage that would complete genealogical investigation by standing on ground their ancestors had called home before exile scattered their bloodline across oceans and continents but never diminished its capacity for producing people who chose hope over fear, love over isolation, service over selfishness when facing trials that revealed character refined rather than broken by circumstances that would have defeated anyone whose heritage had not prepared them for transformation that seemed impossible until attempted with sufficient faith and determination.

16 BUILDING LOVE

Bathurst, New South Wales - April 1844 to September 1845

The courtship of Thomas Staines and Catherine Krieg unfolded with the measured pace that characterized all meaningful construction in colonial society—careful foundation work that tested materials and methods before attempting structures that would need to endure whatever trials the future might present. Their relationship developed through accumulated small encounters rather than dramatic gestures, daily interactions that revealed character through response to ordinary circumstances rather than extraordinary events that might produce behavior unrepresentative of true nature.

Thomas had found employment with Samuel Henderson, Bathurst's established blacksmith, whose initial suspicion of convict competition gradually transformed into appreciation for skills that exceeded his own capacity and work ethic that freed him to focus on business aspects of maintaining a frontier smithy. Henderson was a fair man, weathered by twenty years of colonial experience but possessed of practical wisdom that recognized value regardless of its origins, competence regardless of circumstances that had developed it.

"You've got trade knowledge that goes beyond what most men learn through ordinary apprenticeship," Henderson observed after watching Thomas work for two weeks, his assessment delivered with grudging respect that marked successful completion of a probationary period. "Question is whether you'll use those skills to build a reputation that serves this community or waste them nursing grievances about circumstances you can't change."

The message was familiar—adaptation meant survival, while resistance promised continued hardship—but Thomas had already chosen his path during seven years of bondage that had taught him the difference between enduring punishment and transforming it into preparation for meaningful freedom. Henderson's smithy became not just a workplace but laboratory for testing whether redemption achieved under forced circumstances could survive pressures of independence.

The work itself differed significantly from Government Forge assignments that had served institutional rather than individual needs. Colonial blacksmithing required versatility that went beyond specialized production to encompass everything from horseshoes and wagon repairs to household hardware and agricultural implements. Each project demanded understanding of customer requirements that extended beyond immediate function to encompass durability expectations, aesthetic preferences, and economic constraints that shaped rural life.

But it was the daily visits to Catherine's market stall that provided the real education Thomas needed for understanding what kind of life might be possible in Bathurst for a man whose past had prepared him to appreciate present happiness without taking it for granted. Their conversations, conducted within sight of community members whose acceptance would determine his long-term prospects, revealed layers of experience and character that made each encounter feel like discovery rather than mere social obligation.

Catherine's story emerged gradually, revealed through casual observations that painted a picture of courage rivaling his own journey from disgrace to respectability. Her father's death in Württemberg had eliminated not just an emotional anchor but economic foundation that supported family whose survival depended entirely on business that laws and customs prevented women from inheriting or maintaining independently.

"Mother tried to continue father's work," Catherine explained during one of their afternoon conversations, her hands busy with kneading dough for the next day's baking while her voice carried memories that had been transformed from sharp pain into manageable sadness through years of patient acceptance. "But guild regulations required male ownership of a commercial bakery, and customers gradually transferred loyalty to establishments that could guarantee continued service without uncertainty about legal complications."

The injustice of such circumstances resonated with Thomas's own experience of being denied opportunities through prejudice rather than lack of ability, though his exile had been forced by legal conviction while hers had been chosen through recognition that remaining meant accepting limitations that would prevent her from using gifts that deserved expression in circumstances that appreciated excellence regardless of its source.

"So you came to Australia," Thomas said, understanding that her journey had required different kinds of courage than his own but perhaps no less determination to build something meaningful from whatever materials circumstances provided.

"So I came to Australia," Catherine agreed, her smile carrying pride in achievement that had been earned through risks that might easily have led to disaster rather than success. "Passage money earned through selling everything my family had accumulated over three generations, a voyage completed with women whose reasons for crossing oceans were as varied as their destinations once they reached colonial shores."

Her accommodation to Australian circumstances had required adaptations that paralleled Thomas's own struggle to discover identity that could encompass both criminal past and reformed present. The bread-baking skills that had been restricted in Germany found eager market in a frontier town where anything that improved daily existence was valued according to utility rather than gender of whoever provided it.

But more than commercial success, Catherine had discovered in Bathurst the same possibility for reinvention that drew Thomas beyond Sydney's familiar constraints. Here, her accent marked her as exotic rather than foreign, her skills were appreciated rather than restricted, her ambitions could find expression in circumstances that rewarded excellence without regard for social conventions that might have prevented such opportunities in more established communities.

Their courtship proceeded with formal propriety that frontier society demanded, but with feelings that transcended any conventions about appropriate timing or expression. Thomas understood that Catherine represented not just personal happiness but completion of his transformation from convicted thief to a man worthy of building a family, a business, a legacy that could survive whatever trials the future might present.

The proposal, when it finally came after six months of careful conversation and gradual recognition of mutual affection, took place not in a romantic setting designed to overwhelm practical considerations with emotional appeal, but in Bathurst's market square where their relationship had begun, surrounded by daily commerce that represented their shared commitment to building useful lives through honest work and community service.

"Catherine Krieg," Thomas said, his voice carrying formal dignity appropriate to a moment that would determine trajectory of both their futures, "I am not the man I was when I first arrived in this colony. Seven years of bondage taught me lessons about character that I could have learned no other way. Six months of knowing you have taught me about love that serves rather than demands, that builds rather than consumes, that offers partnership rather than claims ownership."

He paused, understanding that what he said next would either complete his transformation from criminal exile to respectable citizen or mark him as someone whose presumption exceeded his worthiness for the kind of happiness he was asking her to share.

"I have little to offer except hands willing to work, skills that can serve our community's needs, and a heart that has learned to find meaning in service to purposes larger than personal satisfaction. If you would consent to be my wife, I pledge to spend whatever years God grants us building something together that would honor both your courage in crossing oceans to find better life and my determination to prove that redemption is possible for any man willing to undertake its difficult work."

Catherine's response was immediate, delivered with the same directness that had marked their entire relationship. "Thomas Staines, I did not cross the world to accept limitations imposed by other people's understanding of what should be possible. I came here to discover what I might build with someone whose character had been tested by circumstances that revealed strength rather than weakness, wisdom rather than bitterness, love rather than selfishness. Yes, I will marry you, and together we will create something that honors both our journeys toward this moment."

Their engagement was announced at Bathurst's Catholic church on a Sunday morning when spring sunshine seemed to bless every corner of creation with unlimited possibilities, marking not just a union of two individuals but a community's acceptance of Thomas as someone whose past had prepared him for a useful future rather than marking him as permanently unworthy of trust and respect.

Father Matthews, whose pastoral duties included evaluating the character of parishioners seeking his blessing for significant life decisions, had spent weeks in conversation with both Thomas and Catherine, exploring motivations and expectations that would determine whether their marriage served God's purposes or merely satisfied personal desires that might prove inadequate foundation for lifelong commitment.

"Marriage represents more than a legal contract," Father Matthews explained during their final consultation, his guidance shaped by twenty years of observing which unions produced lasting happiness and which dissolved under pressures that stronger foundations might have withstood. "It requires shared vision of what you hope to accomplish together, complementary strengths that create partnership stronger than either individual could achieve alone, commitment to serving purposes larger than personal satisfaction."

Thomas found himself explaining not just his feelings for Catherine but his understanding of what their union could accomplish for Bathurst's continued development as a community that combined individual prosperity with collective welfare. "We've discussed establishing an inn that would serve travelers while providing a gathering place for neighbors, a business that would utilize both my construction skills and Catherine's hospitality abilities to create something valuable for the entire district."

The inn concept had emerged through months of observation and conversation about Bathurst's needs and opportunities. The town's position as a regional center for expanding agricultural development created a steady flow of travelers requiring accommodation that combined comfort with reliability, while local residents needed a venue for social gatherings that built community connections essential for mutual support during difficulties that isolated families might not survive alone.

"Three Rivers Inn," Catherine added, her voice carrying excitement that spoke of a shared vision rather than mere acceptance of Thomas's proposal. "Named for the confluence where Bell, Macquarie, and Cudgegong meet, symbolizing how separate streams become something larger and more powerful through union."

The site they had chosen stood on elevated ground overlooking the river junction that provided both practical advantages and symbolic significance for an establishment that would serve as a meeting place for people whose diverse backgrounds might otherwise prevent meaningful interaction. The location offered protection from flooding while providing access to water transportation that connected Bathurst to Sydney markets, scenic beauty that would attract travelers seeking respite from journey's hardships, and proximity to the town center that made services easily accessible to local residents.

Construction began in January 1845, immediately following their wedding ceremony that brought together Bathurst's diverse population in celebration that transcended differences in origin, circumstance, or social position. The building itself was designed to accommodate multiple functions—guest rooms that could house families or individual travelers, a common room large enough for community gatherings, kitchen facilities that would allow Catherine to expand her baking operations while providing meals that combined German traditions with colonial ingredients.

Thomas's construction skills, refined through government forge experience and months of frontier problem-solving, found the ultimate expression in creating a structure that would shelter not just their own family but provide refuge for anyone whose journeys brought them to this intersection of geography and hope. The building's design incorporated lessons learned through seven years of observing what made colonial architecture successful—local materials that connected structure to landscape, elevated foundation that would survive seasonal flooding, flexible interior spaces that could adapt to changing needs as business grew and evolved.

The community's response to their project revealed colonial society's capacity for embracing innovation when it served collective welfare rather than merely individual advancement. Neighbors contributed labor during barn-raising weekends that transformed construction from private undertaking into social events that strengthened connections between families whose cooperation was essential for survival in circumstances that tested individual capabilities.

William Morrison, the farmer whose wagon Thomas had repaired during his westward journey, arrived with sons and tools for foundation work that required coordinated effort exceeding what two people could accomplish alone. "Heard you were building something special," Morrison said, his greeting carrying warmth that marked successful transition from stranger to accepted community member. "Figure we owe you assistance after that wheel repair that saved our harvest delivery."

The work proceeded with efficiency that reflected colonial experience in cooperative building projects where individual expertise contributed to collective achievements that benefited an entire community. Thomas directed structural elements that required a blacksmith knowledge of load distribution and joint construction, while Catherine coordinated domestic arrangements that would transform the building from mere shelter into a home that welcomed travelers while serving local needs.

But it was the evenings, when official work ended and participants shared meals prepared by Catherine from ingredients contributed by various families, that revealed social dynamics that made their project successful. These gatherings created opportunities for conversation that connected people whose backgrounds might otherwise have prevented meaningful interaction—free settlers and emancipated convicts, English immigrants and German refugees, established families and recent arrivals seeking their own places in a community that judged contributions rather than origins.

"Haven't tasted bread like this since leaving Hamburg," declared Wilhelm Brennan, whose own German heritage created natural sympathy for Catherine's efforts to maintain cultural traditions while adapting to colonial circumstances. "Makes a man remember why food matters for more than just nutrition—connects us to homeland and family even when distance makes physical return impossible."

These informal endorsements from community members whose opinions influenced local business patterns provided confirmation that Three Rivers Inn would succeed not just as a commercial venture but as an institution that enhanced Bathurst's character as a place where a diverse population could discover common ground despite differences that might have created barriers elsewhere.

The construction phase also revealed Thomas's evolution from skilled individual craftsman to project coordinator whose responsibilities extended beyond technical execution to include leadership that inspired others to contribute their best efforts toward shared goals. His experience managing convict workers at Government Forge had taught him about motivating people whose circumstances might discourage excellence, while his recent months of independence had developed confidence necessary for making decisions that affected other people's welfare.

"Thomas has a gift for seeing how different pieces fit together," observed Samuel Henderson, whose initial skepticism about employing an ex-convict had been replaced by recognition that Thomas's background had prepared him for challenges that ordinary experience might not have addressed. "Not just construction elements—people's abilities, community needs, business opportunities that others might overlook."

The inn's design incorporated features that reflected both practical necessities and aesthetic considerations that would make Three Rivers a destination rather than mere accommodation. The common room's fireplace was large enough to warm the entire space during winter months while providing a focal point for social gatherings that would define the establishment's character as a meeting place rather than a simple lodging house. The kitchen facilities included a brick oven that would allow Catherine to expand bread production while preparing meals that combined German techniques with colonial ingredients to create cuisine that honored tradition while embracing innovation.

By June 1845, Three Rivers Inn had progressed from foundation to fully enclosed structure whose completion attracted attention from throughout central New South Wales. Travelers who had heard descriptions of the establishment under construction began planning routes that would include overnight stays to experience hospitality that promised to exceed anything previously available in the district. Local residents made reservations for family celebrations that required venues larger than domestic spaces could accommodate.

But the inn's success was measured in more than commercial terms—it represented proof that two people willing to combine individual strengths could create something that enhanced an entire community's prosperity while providing personal fulfillment that neither could have achieved alone. Thomas's construction expertise and Catherine's hospitality skills had merged to produce a business model that served multiple constituencies while maintaining profitability necessary for long-term sustainability.

The grand opening in September 1845 brought visitors from Sydney and surrounding districts to witness what had been accomplished through a partnership that honored both individual heritage and shared vision of what was possible when love focused on service rather than mere personal satisfaction. Governor Gipps himself attended the celebration that included traditional German music performed by immigrants who had followed Catherine's example in seeking colonial opportunities, English folk songs that connected established settlers to homeland traditions, and Aboriginal ceremonies that acknowledged the land's deeper history while blessing new enterprises built upon its ancient foundation.

"Three Rivers Inn represents the finest example of what our colony can achieve when individual enterprise serves community welfare," Governor Gipps declared during remarks that provided official recognition of Thomas's successful transformation from convicted criminal to respected businessman whose character had earned trust from citizens and government alike. "Mr. and Mrs. Staines have created an establishment that honors both their separate heritage and their shared commitment to building prosperity that includes rather than excludes, that welcomes rather than restricts, that demonstrates redemption's possibility for any individual willing to undertake its patient work."

The Governor's endorsement carried implications extending far beyond immediate commercial benefits—it represented official acknowledgment that transportation could achieve rehabilitative purposes when properly administered and received, that colonial society benefited from policies that offered genuine second chances to those who proved themselves worthy of trust and responsibility.

As evening approached and the celebration continued with music and dancing that brought together Bathurst's diverse population in recognition of what had been accomplished through a vision that transcended individual circumstances, Thomas and Catherine found themselves standing on the inn's veranda overlooking the river confluence that had inspired their establishment's name. The water below reflected lights from windows where travelers would soon find rest, neighbors would gather for fellowship, and community would discover that some dreams were large enough to include everyone willing to contribute to their realization.

"We built something beautiful," Catherine said, her voice carrying satisfaction that came from seeing years of planning and work transformed into reality that exceeded their original expectations. "Not just for us, but for everyone who needs proof that new beginnings are possible when approached with proper faith and determination."

Thomas nodded, understanding that their inn represented more than a successful business venture—it was monument to transformation that had been achieved through patient work, visible proof that redemption was available to anyone willing to choose service over selfishness, love over fear, hope over resignation to limitations that circumstances might seem to impose.

The stars appearing in the darkening sky above the river valley where they had chosen to build their future looked down on an establishment that would serve travelers for generations, providing rest for weary journeys while offering proof that some loves were strong enough to create lasting value from materials as simple as individual determination and shared commitment to purposes larger than personal advancement.

Three Rivers Inn stood ready to welcome whatever challenges and opportunities the future might present, its foundation solid as the character that had built it, its promise as enduring as the love that had made its construction possible.

17 CALVIN'S STORY

Sara's Apartment, Kirribilli — January 2011

The January evening settled over Sydney Harbor like a blessing, the city's heat giving way to harbor breezes that carried the promise of cooler hours ahead while Calvin Wilson arranged old photograph albums across Sara's dining table with the careful precision he brought to furniture assembly. At seventy-six, his movements had acquired the deliberate quality that came from understanding that some tasks couldn't be rushed without sacrificing the attention they deserved, and tonight's conversation about family memory demanded the kind of patience that grief had been teaching him through eighteen months of learning to navigate loss that changed everything while leaving daily routines deceptively unchanged.

"Found these in Ellen's craft room last week," Calvin said, his voice carrying the mixture of pain and gratitude that marked his occasional references to his wife's presence throughout their Gosford home. "She'd been organizing family photos before she got sick, trying to create some kind of record for you that would preserve stories I'm not very good at telling. Always said I knew more family history than I realized, but needed someone to ask the right questions before the memories would surface."

Sara watched her father's hands—carpenter's hands that bore seventy-six years of honest work but remained gentle enough to handle photographs that had become precious beyond their original intentions—as he opened albums that chronicled not just individual events but the accumulation of love that had sustained forty-three years of marriage through circumstances that had tested their understanding of commitment and partnership. Ellen's organizational skills were evident in the careful documentation: dates written in her neat handwriting, locations identified, people named with relationships explained for descendants who might otherwise wonder about faces that had once been familiar but would become strangers without such preservation efforts.

"She knew," Calvin continued, settling into the chair Sara had positioned to catch harbor breezes while providing clear view of materials that would guide their evening's journey through Wilson family history that had received less attention than the dramatic convict narrative that Thomas Staines' letters had provided." Knew that her illness meant time was limited for passing on stories that die with the people who carry them if they're not shared while sharing is still possible. Made me promise to tell you about my father's family, about the Wilson heritage that brought different strengths to whatever we became through marriage and children."

The first album opened to wedding photographs from 1967, black and white images that captured not just ceremony but the joy of two people whose individual struggles had prepared them to appreciate partnership that multiplied strengths while compensating for weaknesses through cooperation rather than competition. Ellen at twenty-three, radiant in a dress she'd sewn herself because ready-made gowns couldn't match her vision of what such occasions required. Calvin at twenty-six, solid and serious but with a smile that suggested happiness too deep for casual expression, understanding that he'd found someone whose love would provide foundation for building whatever life their combined efforts could create.

"Look at her," Calvin said, his finger tracing Ellen's face in a photograph that had captured something essential about character that transcended physical beauty into the realm of spirit that made ordinary moments feel sacred through attention and care that transformed daily existence into ongoing celebration. "Twenty-three years old and already understanding more about love than most people learn in lifetimes. Could see past my shyness to whatever was worth preserving, help me become someone I didn't know I could be."

Sara studied her parents' wedding photographs with new appreciation for love that had shaped her entire existence without her fully recognizing its daily operation through countless small choices that served partnership rather than individual convenience. The ceremony had taken place at St. Stephen's Catholic Church in Sydney, same church where Rivers Paterson had been baptized in 1852 and later married Walter in 1880, continuing family tradition of marking significant moments in sacred spaces that connected personal celebrations to community identity and spiritual understanding that transcended immediate circumstances.

"Tell me about before," Sara said, understanding that some conversations required invitation rather than assumption that privacy could be breached without permission. "About how you met her, what your life was like before marriage made you part of each other's stories."

Calvin turned pages until he found photographs from an earlier period, black and white images that documented his bachelor existence in Gosford where carpentry work had provided a livelihood but not the kind of meaning that a relationship would eventually create through shared purposes that gave individual efforts significance beyond immediate practical results. His workshop appeared in several photographs, recognizable despite four decades of accumulated tools and projects, its essential character unchanged from an early period when it had been refuge rather than sanctuary, a place to work rather than space for processing emotions too complex for casual conversation.

"Was working for Harrison Construction then," Calvin said, his voice carrying the memory of a period when his skills had served other people's visions rather than his own creative impulses that marriage would eventually encourage through Ellen's faith in possibilities he hadn't recognized in himself. "Good steady work, building houses for families that were starting to spread beyond Sydney into suburbs that promised a better life for people willing to commute farther for more space and cleaner air. But nothing that felt like it belonged to me until Ellen showed me what it meant to create things that would outlast the circumstances that prompted their making."

The photographs revealed a young man whose competence was evident but whose potential remained undeveloped until partnership provided both challenge and support necessary for growth that required risks he might not have taken without someone whose faith made courage seem reasonable rather than reckless. Calvin at twenty-four, serious and capable but somehow incomplete, lacking the settled confidence that marriage would develop through years of building something together that neither could have achieved alone.

"How did you meet her?" Sara asked, settling deeper into a conversation that felt like exploration of territory she'd never thought to examine despite living her entire life within a landscape that her parents' love had created. "Ellen always said it was a romantic story, but she never gave me details about how romance actually worked when people had to build relationships through circumstances that didn't include all the technologies that make modern dating so complicated."

Calvin's smile carried a memory that had retained emotional warmth despite eighteen months of grief that had made most memories feel dangerous because a happiness past made current loss more difficult to bear. "Church social dance, winter of 1966. I was twenty-five and convinced I was too old to meet anyone worth marrying, too set in bachelor ways to adjust to partnership that would require sharing space and decisions with someone whose needs might conflict with routines I'd developed for managing life that made sense when nobody else's welfare had to be considered."

The story emerged gradually, Ellen's organizational skills evident in photographs that documented their courtship through images that captured not just events but emotional progression from cautious attraction to committed love that would sustain them through four decades of circumstances that tested every assumption they'd held about marriage and family and the work required to build relationships that served both individual growth and shared purposes.

Ellen had been working as a seamstress for a department store that served Sydney's expanding middle class, her skills with fabric and design providing independence that was unusual for women of her generation who were expected to move from paternal protection to marital dependency without periods of autonomous existence that might develop character and confidence necessary for true partnership rather than mere traditional arrangement. Her apartment in Paddington, small but carefully furnished with pieces she'd selected and arranged according to her own aesthetic sense, had impressed Calvin as evidence of someone who understood the difference between house and home, between mere shelter and space that reflected personality and values.

"She was different," Calvin said, his voice carrying wonder that eighteen months of grief hadn't diminished, recognition that Ellen's character had transcended conventional expectations about women's roles and capabilities in ways that had made their marriage more interesting and satisfying than relationships that followed predictable patterns without room for individual growth or shared discovery. "Not just beautiful, though she was that, but independent in ways that made me want to become worthy of partnership rather than simply seeking someone to take care of domestic responsibilities I didn't want to handle myself."

Their courtship had proceeded through activities that reflected both practical considerations and genuine compatibility: church functions that provided supervised social interaction, family dinners that allowed evaluation of character through observation of behavior in domestic settings, shared interests in craftsmanship and design that suggested they might build something beautiful together if individual skills could be combined through cooperation rather than competition.

"Your grandmother approved of her immediately," Calvin continued, reaching for photographs that showed Ellen with Mary Wilson, Calvin's mother whose Norwegian heritage had shaped family traditions that Calvin had inherited without fully understanding their significance until Ellen's curiosity prompted exploration of genealogical connections that extended beyond immediate family into cultural identity that transcended individual circumstances." Said Ellen had the kind of practical wisdom that made good wives and mothers, but also the creative spirit that would keep marriage interesting through decades when many couples ran out of things to talk about."

The mention of Norwegian heritage surprised Sara, who had focused so intensely on the Scottish connections through Thomas and Catherine that she'd never explored Calvin's paternal ancestry beyond the Wilson surname that could have originated in any number of geographical locations. Calvin noticed her expression and reached for a different album that contained photographs of his parents and grandparents, faces that bore Scandinavian features that became more obvious once identified as such.

"Wilson's not always Scottish," Calvin explained, opening an album to photographs that revealed family gatherings where traditional Norwegian foods and customs had been preserved through immigration that had brought his great-grandparents to Australia during the 1870s when economic opportunities in colonial territories attracted Scandinavian emigrants seeking alternatives to homeland limitations. "My great-grandfather Erik Wilhelmsen changed his surname to Wilson when he arrived in Sydney, but the family kept Norwegian traditions alive through recipes and stories and Christmas celebrations that mixed Lutheran customs with Anglican practices in ways that created something uniquely Australian."

The photographs revealed family celebrations that had maintained cultural identity while adapting to Australian circumstances that required integration with the broader community rather than isolation within ethnic enclaves that might have preserved traditions at the cost of limiting opportunities for advancement and acceptance. Calvin's grandfather Magnus Wilson appeared in several images as a solid, bearded man whose Norwegian features were unmistakable despite Australian clothing and English surname that concealed heritage from casual observation.

"Magnus was a ship's carpenter before he came to Australia," Calvin said, pointing to a photograph that showed his grandfather with tools that resembled those still hanging in Calvin's workshop, evidence of craft traditions that had traveled across oceans and generations to shape understanding of work as an expression of character rather than mere economic necessity. "Built boats in Bergen before emigrating with skills that served him well in Sydney where harbor activities required craftsmen who understood how to work with wood that would be subjected to salt water and weather that tested every joint and connection."

The Norwegian connection explained aspects of Calvin's approach to craftsmanship that Sara had observed but never understood as cultural inheritance rather than individual preference. His attention to joinery that prioritized longevity over appearance, his respect for materials that demanded patience rather than forcing, his understanding of seasonal rhythms that affected wood behavior—all reflected Scandinavian traditions that had been preserved through immigration and adaptation while maintaining essential character that distinguished such work from other cultural approaches to similar challenges.

"Ellen was fascinated by the Norwegian stories," Calvin continued, his voice carrying warmth that speaking of his wife's interests could still generate despite grief that had made most memories feel dangerous because happiness past emphasized loss present." Spent hours getting my grandmother to tell stories about Bergen and the sailing ships that brought emigrants to Australia, about traditional woodworking techniques and holiday customs that connected our family to heritage that went back to Viking times."

The album included photographs of holiday celebrations that Ellen had organized to honor Norwegian traditions while creating new family customs that served contemporary circumstances. Christmas preparations that included traditional Scandinavian baking alongside Australian holiday foods, decorations that combined Viking symbols with Christian imagery, gift-giving patterns that emphasized handmade items that demonstrated love through time and attention rather than commercial purchase that required only money rather than personal investment.

"She made me proud of a heritage I'd taken for granted," Calvin said, his hands gentle on photographs that captured Ellen's enthusiasm for family traditions that she'd adopted and enhanced through her own creative interpretation of cultural practices that immigration had modified but not eliminated. "Helped me understand that being Australian didn't mean abandoning what came before, that family identity could include multiple layers of heritage that enriched rather than confused understanding of who we were and where we belonged."

Sara found herself looking at her father with new appreciation for the complexity of identity that extended beyond immediate family into cultural heritage that had shaped a character in ways she'd never considered. The Norwegian connection provided context for understanding Calvin's approach to craftsmanship and his response to family crisis that emphasized quiet endurance rather than dramatic emotional expression, patience rather than urgency, building rather than talking as preferred method for processing difficult circumstances.

"Did Ellen research the Norwegian connections the way I've been researching Thomas and Catherine?" Sara asked, understanding that her own genealogical obsession might have precedent in family tradition rather than representing unprecedented departure from normal interests in family history.

Calvin nodded, reaching for a folder that Ellen had organized before her illness made such projects impossible to continue. "Found ship manifests that brought Erik Wilhelmsen to Australia in 1873, traced family back to Bergen where church records documented generations of ship builders and carpenters whose skills had served Norwegian maritime traditions for centuries. Even found connections to medieval craftsmen who had built stave churches that still stand today, evidence that our family's woodworking abilities have deeper roots than just individual talent or modern training."

The folder contained Ellen's careful notes about Norwegian family history, her handwriting familiar from years of household organization but applied here to genealogical investigation that revealed a systematic approach to research that paralleled Sara's own methods while focusing on different cultural heritage that had shaped different aspects of family character. Ellen had traced Wilson ancestry back through Bergen church records to medieval craftsmen whose cathedral work had survived centuries of political upheaval and religious transformation, proving that some skills transcended immediate circumstances to serve purposes that outlasted individual lives.

"She wanted to visit Norway," Calvin said, his voice carrying regret that plans interrupted by illness would never be completed, understanding that some journeys became impossible when postponed too long rather than undertaken while opportunity still existed. "Had started planning a trip that would take us to Bergen and surrounding areas where our ancestors had lived and worked, churches they had built and ships they had crafted. Said it would complete our understanding of heritage that immigration had preserved but distance had made abstract rather than immediately real."

The observation connected Calvin's loss to Sara's own sense that family history required physical pilgrimage to ancestral ground where stories had taken root in soil and stone that still held the memory of people whose blood shaped contemporary character through inheritance that transcended geographical separation. Ellen's death had prevented one journey while inspiring another, her organizational skills providing foundation for research that would continue through Sara's Scottish investigation even though Norwegian exploration might require a different approach.

"We could still go," Sara said, the words emerging without conscious planning but carrying conviction that surprised her with its intensity. "To Norway, I mean. After Scotland. Make the journey Ellen planned as a way of honoring her research while completing our understanding of heritage that includes both Scottish resilience and Norwegian craftsmanship."

Calvin's expression shifted from grief to possibility, recognition that travel could serve purposes beyond tourism when approached as pilgrimage that honored family memory while creating new experiences that proved life could continue growing even after devastating loss had made growth seem impossible. "She would have liked that," he said, his voice carrying the first genuine enthusiasm Sara had heard since Ellen's funeral. "Would have approved of using her research to build something together rather than just preserving it as a memorial to projects that circumstances prevented her from completing."

The evening progressed through albums that documented Calvin and Ellen's marriage as it developed from hopeful beginning through decades of shared challenges that had tested their understanding of commitment while strengthening bonds that proved capable of supporting whatever trials life presented. Sara watched her parents' story unfold through photographs that captured not just events but emotional evolution from individual people to a partnership that had created home where love expressed itself through daily choices that served each other's welfare rather than advanced personal convenience.

"She was proud of you," Calvin said as they reached albums that documented Sara's childhood and adolescence, photographs that revealed Ellen's attention to preserving memories that would become precious when time made them irreplaceable. "Proud of your curiosity about family history, your skill with research, your determination to understand connections that other people might have taken for granted. Always said you'd inherited the best qualities from both sides of the family—Scottish persistence and Norwegian patience, Thomas's capacity for transformation and Erik's understanding of craftsmanship as an expression of character."

The observation provided a framework for understanding identity that included multiple sources of strength rather than a single family tradition, recognition that contemporary character drew upon heritage that extended across continents and cultures to create resources that could serve whatever challenges circumstances might present. Sara felt herself connected not just to Thomas and Catherine's transformation but to Norwegian craftsmen whose patience had created beauty that survived centuries, to Ellen's organizational skills that had preserved family memory, to Calvin's quiet strength that had sustained love through every trial that four decades of marriage had presented.

"Tell me about when I was born," Sara said, understanding that some conversations provided opportunities for healing that formal therapy couldn't achieve, recognition that shared memory could transform grief into gratitude when approached with sufficient care and attention to emotional truth that connected past happiness to present possibility for rebuilding a relationship that honored what had been lost while creating space for what might yet be possible.

Calvin's smile carried a memory that felt like sunrise after a long darkness, warmth that hadn't been present in his voice since Ellen's death had made most references to family happiness feel dangerous because joy past emphasized sorrow present. "Ellen was so excited she couldn't sleep for weeks before you arrived, had everything organized with the precision she brought to major projects. Hospital bag packed two months early, nursery arranged and rearranged until every detail met her standards for welcoming someone she'd been waiting her entire life to meet."

The story that followed revealed Calvin's wonder at fatherhood, his careful attention to responsibilities that required learning skills no previous experience had taught him, Ellen's natural competence with motherhood that had made their partnership even stronger through shared dedication to raising a daughter who would understand love through consistent demonstration rather than mere verbal declaration. Sara found herself seeing her childhood through a lens that emphasized not her parents' limitations but their dedication to creating circumstances where love could flourish through daily choices that served her welfare while strengthening a marriage that proved capable of supporting whatever additional responsibilities family life required.

"She documented everything," Calvin said, showing photographs that proved Ellen's commitment to preserving childhood memories that would become treasures when time made them irreplaceable. "First steps, first words, school events, birthday parties—everything organized and labeled so you'd understand when you were older how much joy your existence brought to people who'd been waiting to love someone the way we loved you."

As midnight approached and the harbor lights reflected off water that connected all rivers to the sea, father and daughter sat surrounded by evidence of love that had created the foundation for whatever relationship they chose to build from materials that grief had left scattered but not destroyed. Calvin's story had revealed heritage that included not just dramatic convict transformation but patient Norwegian craftsmanship, not just individual achievement but partnership that had sustained love through every trial that four decades of marriage had presented.

Ellen's presence filled the apartment not as absence to be mourned but as a foundation to be honored through choices that served love rather than fear, connection rather than isolation, hope rather than the comfortable numbness of grief that preserved nothing because it protected everything from risk that relationship required. Calvin and Sara were learning to carry Ellen's memory forward through continued growth rather than static preservation, understanding that the best memorial to love was love itself, expressed through relationships that honored past while serving present needs for healing and hope.

18 THREE RIVERS INN

Wellington, New South Wales - September 1845 to August 1852

Three Rivers Inn had become more than a successful business by the winter of 1847—it had evolved into the beating heart of a community that stretched from Bathurst's established boundaries to the scattered homesteads that dotted the Bell River valley like seeds of civilization taking root in soil that had known only Aboriginal presence for countless generations before European ambition reshaped the landscape according to dreams imported from distant shores. Thomas and Catherine Staines had created something that transcended mere commercial enterprise: a gathering place where the colony's diverse population could discover common ground despite differences that might have prevented meaningful connection in more rigid societies.

The inn's success was measured not just in ledger books that recorded steady profitability, but in testimonials from travelers whose journeys had been transformed by hospitality that honored both practical needs and deeper human requirements for rest, fellowship, and renewal that made continued travel possible. The guest register bore signatures from Sydney merchants seeking new markets in expanding agricultural districts, government officials whose duties required them to inspect colonial development beyond established urban centers, immigrant families whose westward movement represented faith in possibilities that existed nowhere except places where a future could be shaped by individual effort rather than predetermined by inherited circumstances.

But it was the inn's role in the daily life of local residents that truly marked its importance to community that had grown around the river confluence where three waterways joined their separate histories into shared destination. The common room that Thomas had designed with help from neighbors whose barn-raising assistance had made construction possible served multiple functions that reflected colonial society's need for gathering spaces large enough to accommodate celebrations, meetings, and informal socializing that maintained connections essential for survival in circumstances where isolation was a constant threat.

Sunday afternoons brought families from homesteads within twenty miles to share meals that combined Catherine's German culinary traditions with ingredients that colonial conditions provided, creating cuisine that honored old-world knowledge while embracing new-world possibilities. The Morrisons arrived regularly from their expanded farm that now included additional acreage purchased with profits from crops that Thomas's wagon repair had helped deliver to market successfully. Their children had grown from shy observers into confident participants in community gatherings that provided education in social skills that frontier existence might not otherwise have offered.

"Mrs. Staines' sauerbraten reminds me why I left Yorkshire," William Morrison declared during one such gathering, his appreciation for Catherine's cooking extending

115

beyond mere gustatory pleasure to recognition that food could connect people to heritage while building new traditions appropriate to circumstances that required adaptation rather than mere preservation of European customs. "Takes ingredients we can produce here and transforms them into something that honors both where we came from and where we're going."

Catherine's kitchen had become legendary throughout the district, not just for quality of meals she prepared but for her willingness to share techniques with other women whose own efforts to adapt European recipes to Australian ingredients had met with limited success. These informal cooking lessons, conducted during afternoon visits that combined practical instruction with social connection, created networks of mutual support that helped families maintain cultural traditions while developing innovations that served colonial needs.

"Secret is understanding that ingredients want to become something beautiful," Catherine explained to Sarah McKenzie, the widow whose broken wagon wheel had provided Thomas's first opportunity to demonstrate character through service during his westward journey. "German recipes teach patience and respect for natural processes, but Australian conditions require modifications that honor both tradition and local circumstances."

The bread that had first attracted Thomas's attention in Bathurst market had expanded into a comprehensive bakery operation that supplied not just Three Rivers Inn but hotels, restaurants, and private families throughout central New South Wales. Catherine's reputation for excellence had spread through testimonials from satisfied customers whose recommendations carried weight with people who valued quality over mere convenience, craftsmanship over mass production, reliability over dramatic innovation that might prove inadequate when tested by real-world conditions.

But beyond commercial success, Catherine's work represented something more precious: proof that skills developed in one context could find meaningful expression in circumstances that differed dramatically from original circumstances. Her father's training in the Württemberg bakery had prepared her for success in a colonial environment that appreciated competence regardless of its origins, excellence regardless of gender of whoever provided it, innovation that honored tradition while serving current needs.

Thomas's contributions to the inn operations extended far beyond construction and maintenance that kept physical plant functioning despite challenges that frontier conditions imposed on any establishment that aspired to permanence. His blacksmith skills, refined through the government forge experience and adapted to meet diverse colonial needs, made Three Rivers Inn self-sufficient in ways that reduced operating costs while ensuring that mechanical problems could be addressed immediately rather than requiring time-consuming trips to Sydney for repairs that local expertise could accomplish more efficiently.

The stable complex that housed guests' horses had been designed with attention to details that reflected Thomas's understanding of what travelers required for continuing their journeys with confidence that their animals had received proper care. Each stall provided adequate space for rest and feeding, while exercise areas allowed horses to recover from travel stresses that could affect their performance during subsequent stages of long-distance journeys. The forge facilities that Thomas had built for his own use also served travelers whose equipment required repairs that might otherwise have forced dangerous delays in a territory where assistance was scarce.

"Haven't seen smithwork of this quality since leaving Scotland," declared Malcolm Fraser, a sheep farmer whose expansion into wool production for export markets required equipment that could withstand conditions that would destroy inferior tools.

"These shears you've modified should serve my operation for many seasons without requiring replacement, while the original design would have failed within the first season."

Such endorsements from customers whose expertise qualified them to evaluate technical competence created a reputation that extended Three Rivers Inn's influence far beyond hospitality services to encompass a position as a regional center for specialized trades that supported agricultural and commercial development throughout central New South Wales. Thomas's shop became the destination for farmers, merchants, and government officials whose projects required metalwork that combined functionality with reliability that justified investment in quality rather than mere economy.

The inn's guest accommodations reflected Catherine's understanding of what made temporary shelter feel like temporary home—attention to cleanliness that transformed necessity into comfort, furnishings that provided genuine rest rather than mere protection from weather, personal touches that reminded travelers they were valued guests rather than sources of revenue to be extracted efficiently. Each room contained handmade quilts whose patterns reflected both German artistic traditions and colonial materials, furniture that Thomas had crafted specifically for inn use, and small amenities that demonstrated consideration for guests' needs that extended beyond basic survival requirements.

But it was the common room that truly distinguished Three Rivers Inn from mere accommodation to an institution that served a community's social and cultural needs. The space that Thomas had designed for multiple functions hosted everything from wedding celebrations that brought together extended families scattered across vast distances, to business meetings where farmers and merchants negotiated contracts that shaped regional economic development, to educational gatherings where children from isolated homesteads could receive instruction that individual families might not have been able to provide independently.

Winter evenings brought storytelling sessions that preserved oral traditions while creating new narratives appropriate to colonial circumstances. James MacReady, the Highland Scot whose transportation for sheep stealing had ended with emancipation and successful establishment as the district's most reliable shepherd, entertained listeners with tales that ranged from traditional Celtic folklore to contemporary adventures of ex-convicts who had rebuilt their lives through character and competence rather than connections or inherited advantage.

"Tell us about the flood of '44," young David Morrison would request during particularly cold nights when the wind through eucalyptus forests created sounds that reminded everyone of a landscape's capacity for both beauty and danger. "The one where Aboriginal knowledge saved Henley's farm when European methods would have failed."

MacReady would settle into a storytelling rhythm that had been passed down through generations of Highland tradition, his voice carrying a particular cadence that made even familiar tales feel immediate and compelling. The stories served purposes beyond mere entertainment—they provided instruction in colonial survival, examples of successful adaptation to circumstances that required innovation rather than mere persistence, proof that cooperation between different cultural traditions could produce results that individual knowledge systems might not have achieved alone.

These gatherings created bonds that transcended differences in origin, circumstance, or social position that might have prevented meaningful interaction in more stratified societies. Ex-convicts whose transformation had earned community acceptance sat beside free settlers whose voluntary immigration had required different kinds of courage, while Aboriginal workers whose traditional knowledge made European agricultural success possible participated as valued contributors rather than mere observers of colonial social life.

The inn's role as a regional communication center reflected colonial society's dependence on personal networks for information that more established communities might have received through newspapers, government announcements, or commercial correspondence. Travelers brought news from Sydney about political developments that affected colonial policy, market conditions that influenced agricultural planning, and social changes that shaped opportunities for advancement or warned of challenges that required preparation.

"Governor's announcing new land grants for qualified settlers," reported Edward Thompson, a government surveyor whose mapping work took him throughout central New South Wales. "Emphasis on agricultural development that serves both individual prosperity and colonial food security. Preference given to applicants who demonstrate community contribution rather than mere financial capability."

Such announcements were discussed during evening conversations that allowed local residents to evaluate opportunities while considering implications for regional development that affected everyone's long-term prospects. These informal conferences often produced collaborative ventures that individual families might not have attempted independently—joint livestock purchases that reduced individual risk while improving breeding stock, cooperative marketing arrangements that increased bargaining power with Sydney merchants, shared labor agreements that allowed completion of projects that required more workers than individual homesteads could provide.

Thomas found himself serving not just as innkeeper but as informal mediator for disputes that required someone whose own experience of redemption qualified him to understand that most conflicts arose from fear rather than malice, that patience and willingness to listen could resolve difficulties that seemed impossible when approached with pride or prejudice. His reputation for fairness, established through years of consistent demonstration of character that transcended his convict origins, made him valuable for addressing tensions that might otherwise have escalated into feuds that damaged an entire community.

The most challenging mediation involved a boundary dispute between Heinrich Brennan, the German immigrant whose farming methods had produced exceptional crops but required irrigation that affected water rights, and Patrick O'Brien, the Irish refugee whose sheep operation depended on the stream access that Brennan's diversions had reduced. Both men possessed legitimate claims and reasonable grievances, but resolution required an understanding that went beyond legal technicalities to encompass community welfare that depended on cooperation rather than competition.

"Problem isn't water rights," Thomas observed during a three-day conference that brought both families together with neighbors whose own interests were affected by whatever settlement was reached. "Problem is the assumption that success requires someone else to fail, that prosperity is a finite resource rather than something that can be increased through collaboration."

The solution that emerged from patient discussion honored both families' needs while creating a partnership that enhanced regional agricultural development. Brennan's irrigation techniques, adapted to include seasonal accommodation of O'Brien's livestock requirements, increased both crop yields and pasture productivity while demonstrating that innovation could serve multiple purposes when approached with proper attitude and willingness to consider others' welfare.

Catherine's pregnancy, announced in spring of 1851, transformed Three Rivers Inn from a successful business into a symbol of hope for the future that would inherit whatever prosperity and wisdom the current generation could accumulate through patient work and mutual cooperation. The anticipation of new life growing within the walls that had sheltered so many travelers and neighbors created an atmosphere of celebration that extended far beyond immediate family to encompass the community that had invested emotional as well as economic support in the inn's success.

"The child will be born into circumstances that few previous generations could have imagined," reflected Father Matthews during a blessing ceremony that acknowledged both personal significance of the expected birth and a broader meaning for community that had been shaped by Thomas and Catherine's example of transformation achieved through love and service. "An heir to heritage that combines German traditions with Australian possibilities, convict redemption with colonial opportunity, individual achievement with community contribution."

The preparations for Rivers' arrival included modifications to inn operations that would accommodate family needs while maintaining service standards that had established Three Rivers' reputation throughout New South Wales. Thomas designed and built nursery furniture that reflected both practical necessities and artistic sensibilities that transformed functional objects into family heirlooms that could serve multiple generations. Catherine planned menu modifications that would provide proper nutrition for a nursing mother while maintaining the cuisine quality that attracted travelers from considerable distances.

But it was the community's response to news of an expected birth that truly revealed how completely Thomas and Catherine had been accepted as essential elements of regional social fabric. Neighbors organized volunteer schedules that would ensure inn operations continued smoothly during Catherine's recovery period, while also providing assistance with childcare that would allow gradual return to full responsibilities without compromising either family welfare or business commitments.

Mrs. Eleanor Patterson, whose own German heritage had created a natural friendship with Catherine, took charge of coordinating domestic support that reflected a colonial women's understanding of mutual dependence that made survival possible in circumstances where isolation could prove fatal. "Community takes care of its own," she declared with authority that came from twenty years of frontier experience. "Catherine's work has fed half the district—our turn to ensure she receives whatever assistance new motherhood requires."

The summer of 1852 brought record rainfall that created both agricultural prosperity and growing concern about river levels that seemed to be approaching dangerous thresholds. Thomas's experience with flood management during his years at Government Forge provided expertise that became increasingly valuable as community leaders evaluated preparations that might be necessary if water levels continued rising beyond normal seasonal variations.

"Rivers behave differently here than in England," Thomas explained during a town meeting that brought together property owners whose interests would be affected by potential flooding. "Sudden rises, massive volume increases, rapid changes that require advance planning rather than reactive response when crisis has already developed."

The flood preparations that occupied much of July and August 1852 created a strange mixture of anxiety and excitement as residents balanced concern about potential damage against appreciation for water that would ensure agricultural prosperity for years to come. The inn's elevated position provided safety for guests and operations while also serving as a coordination center for community response to whatever challenges rising waters might present.

But beneath practical preparations lay the deeper awareness that Three Rivers Inn had become more than a commercial establishment—it had evolved into a symbol of what was possible when individual transformation served community welfare, when love found expression through service that honored both heritage and innovation, when redemption proved strong enough to create lasting value from materials as simple as determination and faith.

As August progressed and Catherine's pregnancy approached full term, Thomas found himself reflecting on seven years that had transformed him from bitter convict into a man worthy of being trusted with responsibilities that affected other people's welfare. The inn that bore witness to their happiness represented more than a successful business venture—it was a monument to love that had proven capable of building something beautiful from circumstances that might have defeated people whose character had not been refined through trials that revealed strength rather than weakness.

The river confluence that had inspired their establishment's name flowed past their windows each morning and evening, carrying water from mountains to plains and onward to harbors much like Sydney Harbor where Thomas's own transformation had begun. The sight reminded him daily that some currents were strong enough to carry dreams across any distance, that patient work could shape even the hardest materials into forms that served purposes larger than individual satisfaction, that love carefully tended could survive whatever trials the future might present.

Three Rivers Inn stood ready to welcome whatever challenges and opportunities lay ahead, its foundation as solid as the character that had built it, its promise as enduring as the commitment that made continued growth possible. Within its walls, a new generation was preparing to enter a world that would inherit whatever wisdom the current generation could accumulate through service that honored both individual achievement and community welfare.

The flood waters that would soon test everything they had built together could claim timber and stone, but they could never destroy what Thomas and Catherine had learned about love that multiplied when shared rather than diminished when given freely, service that created rather than consumed, hope that grew stronger under pressure rather than surrendering to circumstances that might seem overwhelming to anyone who had not learned the secret of finding meaning in purposes larger than personal preservation.

19 THE THIRD LETTER

Kirribilli Apartment, Sydney - April 2011

The third letter lay unopened on Sara Wilson's kitchen table like a door to territory she wasn't certain she was ready to explore, though three weeks of carrying Thomas Staines' words had already transformed her understanding of what family legacy meant beyond mere genealogical curiosity. The harbor evening light filtered through her apartment windows with the kind of golden quality that made even difficult conversations feel possible, while Calvin's presence in her living room—his overnight bag suggesting this visit might extend beyond their usual careful afternoon encounters—provided courage she hadn't possessed since Ellen's death created the careful distance they had been afraid to bridge.

The phone conversation two nights earlier had changed everything between them, not through dramatic revelation but through the simple acknowledgment that grief had made them strangers to each other when they might have been allies in preserving what Ellen's love had taught them both about family connections that transcended individual loss. Calvin's willingness to drive down from Gosford with fish fresh from Brisbane Water and stories about the garden gate he was building in Ellen's memory suggested readiness for deeper conversation than they had managed since the funeral that had marked the beginning of their mutual retreat into protective isolation.

"This one feels different," Sara said, her fingers tracing the envelope that bore Thomas's careful script and the water stains that spoke of composition during crisis that would test everything his transformation had prepared him to offer. "The paper's heavier, the ink darker. Like he knew this letter needed to survive whatever happened to the others."

Calvin looked up from the genealogical charts they had been studying together, his carpenter's attention focused on details that might reveal information about their family's journey from Scottish soil to Australian shores. The weeks of research had expanded their understanding far beyond the initial discovery in Glen Lena's attic, creating a timeline that connected their present circumstances to heritage that stretched back through centuries of people who had chosen persistence over surrender, hope over resignation to limitations that circumstances might seem to impose.

"Date on the envelope?" Calvin asked, understanding that chronology mattered for placing Thomas's words within context of events that had shaped colonial Australia during the 1850s.

"August 22nd, 1852," Sara replied, noting how Thomas's handwriting remained steady despite circumstances that must have tested his composure. "Just days before the flood that claimed Three Rivers Inn and his life. Catherine was eight months pregnant with Rivers, their business was thriving, everything they'd built together was about to be destroyed by waters that recognized no human claim to permanence or security."

The weight of that knowledge settled between them like blessing and burden combined—blessing because it connected them to love that had proven strong enough to

121

transcend death itself, burden because it demanded they prove worthy of inheritance that had been purchased at such enormous cost. Calvin's presence in her apartment, his willingness to stay overnight for the first time since Ellen's funeral, represented progress toward the kind of vulnerable honesty that real healing required.

"Should we read it together?" Calvin suggested, his voice carrying the particular gentleness that marked conversations when people understood they were approaching territory that might change everything they thought they knew about possibilities available to anyone willing to choose transformation over resignation.

Sara nodded, understanding that Thomas's third letter belonged to both of them—not just as genealogical curiosity but as instruction about love that served rather than demanded, that built rather than protected, that risked everything for the chance to create meaning that survived whatever circumstances might destroy its physical manifestations. She unfolded the pages with care that honored both their antiquity and their emotional weight, feeling the texture of paper that had absorbed hope and determination in equal measure.

The letter's opening words struck her like a physical blow: *"My Most Precious Daughter, The Bell River has risen higher than any man can remember, its waters now lapping at our inn's foundation stones as I write these words by candlelight in what may be our final hours of safety, yet I have never felt more blessed or more determined to ensure that love finds ways to transcend whatever limitations mortality might attempt to impose."*

Calvin's hand found hers across the table as she read aloud, their fingers intertwining like Celtic knots Thomas had carved into his cross, like family stories that connected past to present through accumulated wisdom about what made life worth preserving. The letter continued with Thomas's reflection on seven years of marriage to Catherine, their gradual understanding that two broken people could create something beautiful together if willing to serve each other's welfare rather than demand personal satisfaction.

But it was Thomas's description of preparing for their child's arrival that made Sara understand why Rivers had preserved these letters with such devotion: *"Your mother sleeps fitfully above, her body heavy with the burden of carrying you toward a world that grows more uncertain with each rumble of thunder that echoes through our valley. Each day brings new evidence of the miracle growing within your mother's body—tiny movements that speak of life insisting upon itself despite circumstances that seem designed to test whether hope can survive whatever trials the future might present."*

"He's describing Rivers' birth preparation," Sara said, her voice thick with emotion that made speaking difficult but necessary. "The love that was strong enough to write letters to a child he might never meet, detailed enough to guide her entire life, patient enough to believe that such investment would somehow reach its intended recipient despite circumstances that seemed designed to prevent any transmission."

"I have carved additional details into the Celtic cross that has accompanied me since my darkest hours, adding symbols that represent our love and our faith that you will inherit more than mere material possessions."

Calvin squeezed her hand, understanding settling between them like recognition that they were witnessing something rare and precious—not just family history but an instruction manual for anyone willing to learn what Thomas had discovered about the difference between existing and truly living, between surviving hardship and transforming it into wisdom that could serve others facing their own trials.

The letter continued with Thomas's analysis of what their life at Three Rivers Inn had taught him about community and service, about building something that enhanced others' welfare while providing personal fulfillment that selfish pursuits could never achieve. His words painted pictures of evening gatherings where neighbors shared stories that connected them across differences that might otherwise have prevented meaningful friendship, of travelers who found in their hospitality proof that kindness existed even in circumstances that might have been expected to breed only suspicion and self-protection.

But it was Thomas's sudden shift to practical matters that made Sara realize this letter served different purposes than his previous correspondence: *"I have enclosed with this letter documents that establish your legal inheritance of properties and investments that your mother and I have accumulated through seven years of patient work. But more precious than material assets are the connections we have built within this community—relationships that will provide support and guidance long after our own voices have been silenced."*

"Legal documents," Calvin observed, his practical mind immediately grasping implications that Sara's emotional focus had temporarily overlooked. "He's not just writing letters—he's ensuring Rivers would inherit everything they'd built together, both material and social capital that would support her after his death."

The realization transformed their understanding of Thomas's letters from sentimental family preservation to comprehensive estate planning that demonstrated sophisticated understanding of what children needed for successful navigation of colonial society. His love had found expression not just through emotional declaration but through practical provision that would serve Rivers' welfare throughout her life.

Sara turned the page to find Thomas's most detailed description yet of his transformation from convicted thief to respected community member, his analysis of choices that had led from shame to honor through patient commitment to serving others' welfare: *"Redemption proved possible not through dramatic gesture but through accumulated small choices to place community needs above personal convenience, to find satisfaction in others' success rather than demanding recognition for individual achievements, to understand that the greatest wealth comes from what we give rather than what we receive."*

The wisdom felt directly applicable to their own circumstances—two people whose grief had created distance that love might yet bridge if approached with sufficient courage and commitment to vulnerable honesty. Calvin's presence in her apartment, his willingness to extend their usual brief visits into an overnight stay that suggested real comfort with intimacy they had been avoiding, provided evidence that transformation remained possible even for relationships damaged by loss and pride and mutual fear of causing additional pain.

"I've been thinking about Scotland," Calvin said suddenly, his words seeming to emerge from contemplation that had been building during their weeks of shared discovery. "About the trip we discussed, visiting the places that shaped our ancestors before transportation brought them to Australian soil."

Sara felt her heart lift with excitement that had been growing since their phone conversation two nights earlier, understanding that such a journey would represent more than genealogical tourism—it would be a pilgrimage to sources of character that had enabled people like Thomas and Catherine to build meaningful lives from circumstances that might have defeated anyone whose spirit had not been refined through trials that revealed strength rather than weakness.

"The research is almost complete here," Sara replied, gesturing toward the charts and documents that covered her table like evidence of detective work that had revealed family secrets spanning centuries and continents. "Margaret Nicol's grave in Arbuthnott churchyard, the Paterson family holdings in Kincardineshire, the departure ports where our people began journeys that led to this moment when we're rediscovering what they sacrificed to give us."

The conversation that followed lasted until harbor lights began to twinkle beyond her windows, covering practical aspects of international travel while exploring deeper significance of visiting places where their bloodline had taken root before emigration scattered families across oceans that seemed impossible to cross. Calvin's carpenter knowledge of construction and measurement provided practical framework for understanding how Scottish heritage had shaped colonial architecture, while Sara's research skills had identified specific locations that could be visited to verify connections that family stories suggested but documentation needed to confirm.

"Spring would be perfect timing," Calvin said, his enthusiasm building as planning transformed abstract possibility into concrete intention. "April or May, when Scottish weather becomes tolerable and we'd have time to prepare properly for travel that requires more than casual tourist arrangements."

Sara opened her laptop and began searching flight schedules and accommodation options, understanding that this trip would serve multiple purposes beyond mere heritage exploration. It would be an opportunity to prove that their relationship had healed sufficiently to support shared adventure, a test of whether they could travel together without falling back into careful distance that protected against intimacy but also prevented genuine connection, a demonstration that Thomas's example of vulnerable love could inspire contemporary application of principles he had proven through sacrifice that claimed his life but preserved his legacy.

"Edinburgh first," Sara said, noting flight options that would carry them from Sydney's harbor to Scotland's ancient capital in less time than Thomas's convict voyage had required. "Then north through Kincardineshire to find the actual graves, the parishes where marriages were recorded, the estates where our people worked before economic necessity forced emigration that seemed like catastrophe but became opportunity for building better lives in circumstances that rewarded character rather than breeding."

Calvin nodded, his understanding of how journeys required both destination and purpose making him valuable planning partner for an expedition that would combine historical research with emotional exploration of what heritage meant for people whose present circumstances had been shaped by ancestors' courage in leaving familiar surroundings to seek opportunities that existed nowhere except places where future could be determined by individual effort rather than inherited limitations.

The evening's planning session revealed how completely their relationship had been restored through shared discovery of Thomas's story, their mutual recognition that his transformation provided a template for anyone facing their own choice between resignation and renewal, isolation and connection, fear and the kind of love that proved strong enough to bridge any gap if approached with sufficient faith and determination.

"We should visit Wellington too," Sara suggested, her research having identified locations throughout Australia where their family story had unfolded. "The Bell River valley where Thomas made his final sacrifice, the site where Three Rivers Inn stood before flood waters claimed everything except the love that had made it meaningful, the memorial that still honors his memory more than 150 years after his death."

The scope of their projected journey expanded as enthusiasm overcame practical considerations about time and expense, their shared excitement about connecting present circumstances to historical foundations that had shaped their understanding of what family meant beyond mere biological connection. This would be a comprehensive exploration of heritage that stretched from medieval Scotland to contemporary Australia, proof that some stories were powerful enough to inspire pilgrimage across whatever distances their transmission required.

Calvin's suggestion that they document their travels for future generations transformed simple heritage tourism into an active preservation project that would honor Thomas and Catherine's memory while providing a resource for descendants who might need similar guidance about transformation and redemption and the courage required to choose hope over despair. Sara's writing abilities and Calvin's practical documentation skills would combine to create a record that served both family history and broader illustration of how individual stories could illuminate universal truths about love and sacrifice and the possibility of building meaningful lives from broken materials.

"A photo journal with historical context," Calvin proposed, his vision encompassing both immediate documentation and long-term preservation that would make their discoveries available to anyone seeking evidence that redemption remained possible for people willing to undertake its patient work. "Your writing paired with a visual record of places that shaped our ancestors, creating something that honors their memory while inspiring others who need proof that transformation is available to anyone brave enough to choose it."

The planning session concluded with reservation confirmations for flights that would carry them to Scotland in late April, when spring weather would make travel pleasant while providing optimal conditions for photography that would serve both personal remembrance and educational purposes. Their excitement about shared adventure felt like the completion of a healing process that had begun with the discovery of Thomas's letters and continued through patient rebuilding of trust that grief had damaged but love had proven strong enough to restore.

As Calvin prepared for his first overnight stay in her apartment since Ellen's funeral, Sara understood that their Scotland trip would represent more than heritage exploration—it would be a celebration of the relationship that had survived loss and distance and mutual fear of vulnerability that real intimacy required. Thomas's example of love that served rather than demanded, that built rather than protected, that risked everything for others' welfare had provided guidance for their own choice to bridge gaps that seemed unbridgeable through accumulated small choices to place connection above safety.

The third letter lay completed on her table, its wisdom absorbed into an understanding that would guide not just their Scottish pilgrimage but their ongoing commitment to proving worthy of inheritance that had been purchased through sacrifice that claimed Thomas's life but preserved his legacy for anyone willing to receive it with proper reverence and determination to carry it forward through choices that honored his memory while serving present needs.

Scotland waited across oceans that no longer seemed impossible to cross, its ancient churchyards holding stones that marked where their people had lived and died before emigration scattered families across distances that love had proven capable of bridging. In six weeks, they would stand together in Arbuthnott parish where Margaret Nicol's grave bore thistle symbols identical to those Thomas had carved into his Celtic cross, physical proof of connections that transcended individual lifetimes to create a heritage that survived whatever trials the centuries might present.

The harbor lights beyond her window reflected off water that flowed toward the same sea that had carried their ancestors to Australian shores, connecting past to present through currents that recognized no boundaries except those imposed by human limitation and fear. Sara felt herself becoming part of that eternal flow, understanding that the sacred obligation Rivers had identified was not burden but privilege—opportunity to carry forward wisdom that had been earned through suffering and preserved through love that refused to be silenced by death or distance or the passage of time that measured mortal existence but could not diminish spiritual inheritance that passed from generation to generation through anyone willing to receive it with gratitude and commitment to transmission.

The journey to Scotland would begin their active demonstration that Thomas's transformation could still inspire contemporary application of principles he had proven through choices that transformed convicted thief into community hero, individual shame into shared redemption, personal failure into family legend that continued teaching anyone willing to learn what love could accomplish when willing to transcend every limitation mortality could impose.

Three Rivers Inn, Wellington, New South Wales
22nd August, 1852

My Most Precious Daughter,

The Bell River has risen higher than any man can remember, its waters now lapping at our inn's foundation stones as I write these words by candlelight in what may be our final hours of safety, yet I have never felt more blessed or more determined to ensure that love finds ways to transcend whatever limitations mortality might attempt to impose.

Your mother sleeps fitfully above, her body heavy with the burden of carrying you toward a world that grows more uncertain with each rumble of thunder that echoes through our valley. Each day brings new evidence of the miracle growing within your mother's body—tiny movements that speak of life insisting upon itself despite circumstances that seem designed to test whether hope can survive whatever trials the future might present.

Seventeen years have passed since that April morning when constables seized me with stolen property in my hands and my future crumbling around me. Seventeen years of learning that redemption must be earned rather than simply claimed, that character is revealed through choices made when external oversight is absent, that the greatest wealth comes from what we give rather than what we receive.

The community that has gathered within our walls tonight—neighbors whose own homes have been claimed by waters that show no discrimination between worthy and unworthy—represents everything I have learned about the difference between existing and truly living. Mrs. Morrison tends her frightened children with courage that honors her late husband's memory. Old Mrs. Hennessy clutches photographs that connect her to family scattered across the colony. Young Jamie O'Brien sits beside his mother with eyes that reflect trust in adult competence, faith that someone will find solutions to problems that exceed a child's capacity to understand.

Their presence here makes our inn more than shelter—it transforms our sanctuary into proof that some purposes are worth preserving regardless of cost, that community creates value that transcends individual property, that love multiplies when shared rather than diminishing when given freely.

I think often of the Celtic cross I carved aboard the convict ship that brought me to these shores, its stone surface bearing symbols that connected me to heritage I had dishonored through crime but might yet honor through choices that served purposes larger than personal advancement. The thistle at its center represents Scotland I shall never see again, but also the thorny beauty that can emerge from harsh circumstances when approached with patience and faith. I have carved additional details into the Celtic cross that has accompanied me since my darkest hours, adding symbols that represent our love and our faith that you will inherit more than mere material possessions.

You will inherit this cross, my darling child, along with whatever other legacy our love has created through eight years of building something worthy of preservation. But more precious than any material artifact is the knowledge that your father learned to transform shame into honor, exile into opportunity, chains into liberation through consistent commitment to becoming worthy of the love he received. I have enclosed with this letter documents that establish your legal inheritance of properties and investments that your mother and I have accumulated through seven years of patient work. But more precious than material assets are the connections we have built within this community—relationships that will provide support and guidance long after our own voices have been silenced.

The water continues to rise, and I can hear the sound of structural timbers shifting under pressures they were never designed to bear. Our refuge may not survive the night, but the love that built it will endure to build again, the community that has been shaped by our example will survive whatever destruction claims physical structures, and you will inherit wisdom that has been earned through trials that revealed strength rather than weakness.

If these rising waters claim my life before I can hold you in my arms, know that I face such fate with gratitude that overwhelms any regret about opportunities that will be lost, experiences we will not share, guidance I will not be able to provide during years when you most need a father's wisdom and protection.

Remember me not as the proud young blacksmith who stole from desperation, but as the man who learned through your mother's love that service to others provides the only foundation upon which lasting satisfaction can be built, that love multiplies when shared rather than diminishing when given away, that courage is required not for dramatic gestures but for daily choice to place others' welfare above our own convenience. Redemption proved possible not through dramatic gesture but through accumulated small choices to place community needs above personal convenience, to find satisfaction in others' success rather than demanding recognition for individual achievements, to understand that the greatest wealth comes from what we give rather than what we receive.

The greatest gift I can leave you is not property or position but the knowledge that transformation is always possible for anyone willing to undertake its patient work, that love can triumph over any adversity, that even the worst mistakes can become preparation for the most meaningful achievements if approached with sufficient faith and patience.

Your devoted father, whose love for you makes even death seem small compared to the privilege of having lived and loved so well,

Thomas Staines

Sara's Journal
Kirribilli Apartment March 15th, 2011 – Morning

The Cartography of Home
The Scotland trip is booked. Edinburgh to Arbuthnott, following the thread that connects our Australian present to Scottish past, but really following something deeper—the understanding that home isn't a place you inherit but a story you choose to continue.

Calvin and I spent yesterday afternoon planning the route, spreading maps across my kitchen table like archaeologists plotting excavation sites. But we weren't just planning geography; we were designing pilgrimage, choosing to trace the bloodlines that had shaped our capacity for both endurance and transformation.

"Think Helena would approve?" I asked as we marked Kincardineshire on the detailed map.

"Think she'd pack our bags herself if she could," Calvin replied, his smile carrying the warmth that had been absent for too many months. "Your grandmother always said that some journeys were necessary even when their destinations remained unclear, that understanding where you came from was prerequisite for knowing where you belonged."

The healing between us feels complete now, but not in ways that erase the grief or pretend Ellen's absence doesn't matter. Instead, we've learned what Thomas discovered during his years of exile—that love becomes stronger when tested by loss, more precious when its fragility is acknowledged, more capable of creating meaning when it's willing to serve purposes larger than personal comfort.

Manly Beach
March 18th, 2011 – Sunset

Walked the beach today thinking about Catherine's courage in crossing oceans to find opportunities her homeland couldn't provide. The waves rolling in felt like time itself, carrying stories from distant shores to this Australian present where their echoes still shape lives they never could have imagined touching.

What kind of faith does it take to leave everything familiar for the promise of something better? Catherine had no guarantee that Australia would welcome her skills, that she'd find community to replace what she'd abandoned, that the risks she was taking would prove worthwhile. But she came anyway, trusting that the unknown held more possibility than the known offered security.

I've been thinking about my own crossings—not geographic but emotional. The journey from safety to vulnerability, from protection to connection, from the comfortable isolation grief provided to the dangerous intimacy that real healing requires. Thomas's letters have been my passport for this crossing, proof that transformation is possible even when circumstances seem designed to prevent it.

Dad texted this afternoon: *"Finished the cedar box. Thistles came out better than expected. Think our ancestors would approve."* The image he sent shows craftsmanship that speaks of love made tangible, heritage honored through hands that understand the difference between creating something functional and creating something that will endure.

State Library Reading Room
March 22nd, 2011

Found the final pieces today—parish records from Arbuthnott that confirm Margaret Nicol's burial in 1692, the thistle-carved headstone that's been weathering Scottish storms for over three centuries. The symbolism feels prophetic: beauty that emerges from harsh circumstances, strength that grows more resilient under pressure, identity that transcends individual limitation.

The librarian, Mrs. Chen, commented on my dedication to this research. "Must be some story," she said, watching me photograph documents with the reverence usually reserved for sacred texts.

"It is," I replied, understanding that she was witnessing more than genealogical curiosity. "It's the story of people who refused to let their worst moments define their ultimate legacy, who chose transformation over resignation, who proved that love could triumph over any adversity if approached with sufficient faith and patience."

Mrs. Chen nodded with the wisdom of someone who had seen countless researchers discover that family history was really spiritual archaeology, that tracing bloodlines meant excavating the accumulated courage and wisdom that made present happiness possible.

The Scotland trip represents completion of this phase—not ending the research but shifting from discovery to pilgrimage, from understanding to honoring, from preserving memory to celebrating legacy that continues shaping lives across centuries and continents.

Calvin's Workshop, Gosford
March 25th, 2011 – Evening

Dad presented the finished cedar box tonight with a ceremony appropriate to housing Thomas's letters. The thistle carvings are exquisite—each thorn and petal rendered with precision that speaks of love applied to material craftsmanship, beauty created through patience and skill applied to raw materials that seemed unlikely to yield anything precious.

"For keeping the important things safe," he said, settling the letters into their new home with hands that had learned the weight of what they were preserving. "But also for remembering that some gifts become more valuable when they're shared rather than hoarded."

We're leaving for Scotland in six weeks. The anticipation feels like standing at the edge of revelation, understanding that we're about to complete something that began when Thomas carved his Celtic cross aboard the *Moffatt* in 1836, continued when Rivers preserved his memory at Glen Lena, and culminated when grief brought us to the edge of losing each other before his example taught us how to choose connection over safety.

But beyond the Scotland pilgrimage, I'm beginning to understand another calling—one that Rivers identified in her journal as "sacred obligation." Preserving Thomas's story isn't enough. It needs to be shared, transmitted, used to guide and heal and inspire anyone whose heart is ready to receive proof that transformation is always possible.

I've been thinking about writing their complete story—not just family history but literature that captures the universal truth of what they discovered about love and loss and redemption. Thomas and Catherine's journey from individual brokenness to shared healing provides a template that works as well in 2011 as it did in 1852, because the human heart's capacity for transformation doesn't change even when circumstances do. The sacred obligation Rivers wrote about isn't just about preserving family memory—it's about proving that memory still has power to inspire actual change, genuine healing, real transformation in anyone willing to learn from examples of love that chose service over selfishness, hope over despair, connection over the safety that isolation promises but never truly provides.

Scotland will be a pilgrimage to honor the past. But returning to write their story will be an offering to the future—proof that some loves are indeed strong enough to bridge any distance, heal any wound, transform any life that's ready to receive their patient, persistent, ultimately triumphant guidance.

20 RIVERS ON THE WAY

Three Rivers Inn, Wellington - July to August 1852

The Bell River ran higher than anyone could remember as July surrendered to August, its normally gentle voice transformed into something approaching a growl that carried undertones of power barely contained within banks that had channeled its flow for countless seasons before European settlement imposed new patterns of meaning upon a landscape shaped by forces older than human memory. Catherine Staines moved through Three Rivers Inn with the careful grace of a woman eight months pregnant, her body heavy with the child who would inherit whatever legacy she and Thomas could preserve from circumstances that seemed increasingly determined to test every assumption about security and permanence.

The inn's common room had become an informal headquarters for community discussions about flood preparations that occupied every conversation between neighbors whose homesteads stretched along river valleys that provided both agricultural prosperity and growing concern about water levels that continued rising beyond normal seasonal variations. Thomas found himself serving not just as innkeeper but as coordinator for collective response to challenges that required cooperation rather than individual effort, his experience with flood management during government forge years providing expertise that became increasingly valuable as community leaders evaluated what measures might be necessary if water levels continued their relentless advance.

"River's carrying more volume than I've seen in twenty years," observed William Morrison during one of the evening gatherings that brought together property owners whose interests would be affected by potential flooding. Morrison's farm lay upstream from the inn, his elevated position providing a vantage point for observing water levels that had already begun encroaching on pastures that normally remained well above flood stage throughout winter months. "Snowmelt from the mountains, combined with rainfall that's been heavier than usual, creating conditions that could overwhelm any defenses we might attempt to construct."

The assembled farmers and townspeople represented a cross-section of colonial society that had grown around the river confluence where Three Rivers Inn provided a focal point for the community that included free settlers whose success had been earned through adaptation to circumstances that demanded innovation rather than mere persistence, emancipated convicts whose transformation had qualified them for acceptance based on character rather than origins, and immigrant families whose diverse backgrounds had created a cultural richness that enhanced rather than complicated social dynamics.

Heinrich Brennan, the German farmer whose irrigation techniques had revolutionized agricultural productivity throughout the district, brought maps that detailed water flow patterns based on observations accumulated during fifteen years of studying seasonal variations that affected crop planning and livestock management. "Traditional European flood control relies on engineering solutions that may not be appropriate for Australian conditions," Brennan explained, his accent lending gravity to an analysis that reflected both theoretical knowledge and practical experience. "River systems here behave differently—sudden rises, massive volume increases, rapid changes that require advance planning rather than reactive response when crisis has already developed."

The technical discussions that followed revealed the community's sophisticated understanding of challenges that required balancing individual property protection with collective welfare that made survival possible in circumstances where isolation could prove fatal. Each family's preparations would affect neighbors whose own security depended on a coordinated response that honored both personal interests and broader considerations about what served the entire district's long-term prosperity.

Patrick O'Brien, the Irish sheep farmer whose partnership with Brennan had created innovative agricultural practices that increased productivity while protecting environmental resources, contributed a perspective shaped by experience with flooding that had devastated his homeland during years when inadequate preparation had transformed natural challenges into human disasters. "Key is understanding that water will go where water wants to go," O'Brien reflected, his philosophy shaped by hard-won wisdom about working with natural forces rather than attempting to dominate them through engineering that ignored environmental realities." Question becomes whether we can direct that movement in ways that minimize damage while maximizing benefits that flooding can provide for future agricultural prosperity."

Catherine's pregnancy had become a community celebration that transcended individual family joy to encompass collective anticipation of new life that would inherit whatever prosperity and wisdom the current generation could accumulate through patient work and mutual cooperation. The women of the district had organized a support network that would ensure both medical assistance during delivery and domestic help during the recovery period, their coordination reflecting colonial society's understanding that survival depended on relationships that extended beyond immediate family to include neighbors whose welfare was interconnected with one's own success.

Mrs. Eleanor Patterson, whose German heritage had created a natural friendship with Catherine while her experience as the district's unofficial midwife provided medical expertise that could mean the difference between successful delivery and complications that frontier conditions might not be able to address adequately, visited Three Rivers Inn daily to monitor Catherine's condition while coordinating preparations that would be necessary when labor began.

"Child's positioned properly, heartbeat strong, mother's health excellent despite circumstances that would challenge anyone carrying such a burden during crisis that tests an entire community's resources," Mrs. Patterson reported during an evening consultation that included Thomas and several neighboring women whose own experiences with frontier childbirth qualified them to assist with a delivery that might occur during emergency conditions. "Primary concern is ensuring that flooding doesn't prevent access to assistance that complex deliveries sometimes require."

The contingency planning that emerged from these discussions reflected the community's commitment to protecting its most vulnerable members while maintaining preparations for challenges that could affect everyone's survival. Alternative transportation routes had been identified in case rising waters made normal travel impossible, emergency supplies had been positioned at strategic locations that would remain accessible regardless of flood conditions, and communication systems had been established that would allow coordination of assistance even if circumstances prevented normal social interaction.

Sarah McKenzie, the widow whose broken wagon wheel had provided Thomas's first opportunity to demonstrate character through service during his westward journey seven years earlier, had become Catherine's closest friend among the district's established families. Her own experience raising children in frontier conditions provided practical wisdom about managing domestic responsibilities while adapting to circumstances that could change rapidly without warning.

"Important thing is remembering that babies arrive according to their own schedule rather than our convenience," Sara observed during an afternoon visit that combined social support with practical assistance in preparing nursery facilities that would accommodate the newborn while maintaining inn operations that supported community needs. "Baby will come when Baby is ready, flood or no flood, and our job is ensuring that arrival happens in circumstances that honor both child's importance and mother's welfare."

The nursery that Thomas had constructed in anticipation of their child's arrival reflected both practical necessities and emotional significance that transformed functional furniture into family heirlooms that could serve multiple generations. The crib he had crafted from local timber bore carved decorations that incorporated Celtic symbols connecting their child to heritage that stretched back through Scottish bloodlines, while German motifs honored Catherine's cultural traditions that would shape their child's understanding of what it meant to belong to a family whose stories transcended individual circumstances.

But it was the community's response to Catherine's approaching delivery that truly revealed how completely Thomas and Catherine had been integrated into the social fabric that measured worth through contribution rather than origin, character rather than breeding, service rather than mere presence. Neighbors competed to offer assistance that ranged from practical help with inn operations to emotional support that acknowledged the anxiety that naturally accompanied a first pregnancy in circumstances where medical assistance was limited and complications could prove dangerous.

The Aboriginal workers whose traditional knowledge made European agricultural success possible contributed their own understanding of childbirth practices that had sustained their communities for countless generations before colonial contact introduced different approaches to managing delivery that might benefit from indigenous wisdom about working with natural processes rather than attempting to control them through techniques that ignored environmental factors.

"Baby knows how to be born," explained Mary, an Aboriginal woman whose bilingual abilities had made her a valuable interpreter between different cultural approaches to managing pregnancy and childbirth. "Mother's job is listening to what her body teaches, trusting processes that worked before doctors existed to complicate what should be natural cooperation between woman and child who both want safe arrival."

These cross-cultural consultations created educational opportunities that enhanced colonial society's understanding of child-rearing practices while demonstrating that cooperation between different knowledge systems could produce results that individual traditions might not achieve independently. Catherine's pregnancy had become a symbol of community's capacity for embracing innovation when it served collective welfare rather than merely individual preference.

The flood preparations that dominated community attention throughout July had required coordinating individual property protection with collective infrastructure that served broader district needs. Thomas's blacksmith skills had been essential for creating specialized hardware that secured buildings and equipment against water damage while maintaining functionality that would be necessary for recovery operations once flooding receded.

But the technical challenges were exceeded by social complexities that arose when individual security conflicted with community welfare, when family protection required choices that might disadvantage neighbors whose own survival depended on a cooperative response to crisis that affected everyone's long-term prospects. The evening discussions at Three Rivers Inn had become essential forums for addressing these tensions through conversation that honored both personal interests and collective responsibility.

"Morrison's upstream diversions will reduce flood impact on his property while increasing downstream flow that affects everyone below his position," observed James Whitmore, the master smith whose technical expertise qualified him to evaluate engineering proposals that required understanding both immediate effects and long-term consequences. "Question becomes whether such individual protection serves or undermines community welfare that depends on shared responsibility for managing challenges that exceed any family's independent capacity."

The resolution of such conflicts required leadership that could balance competing interests while maintaining social cohesion that made collective action possible. Thomas found himself serving in this role despite his convict background that might have disqualified him from such responsibility in more traditional societies, his reputation for fairness and practical wisdom having earned trust that transcended legal distinctions between different categories of colonial citizenship.

As August progressed and Catherine's pregnancy approached full term, the confluence of personal anticipation and community crisis created an atmosphere of heightened awareness that made every decision feel weighted with significance that extended beyond immediate circumstances. The child who would soon arrive would inherit whatever prosperity and wisdom the current generation could preserve through choices that honored both individual welfare and collective responsibility.

The river continued its relentless rise, each day bringing water levels closer to thresholds that would transform inconvenience into genuine crisis requiring evacuation of lower-lying properties and the coordination of emergency response that tested every assumption about community preparedness. The sound of flowing water had become a constant presence that reminded everyone of nature's power to reshape human plans according to forces that recognized no distinctions between worthy and unworthy, prepared and unprepared, beloved and forgotten.

Yet within Three Rivers Inn, surrounded by neighbors whose friendship had been earned through years of reliable service and mutual support, Catherine awaited their child's arrival with a confidence that reflected both personal faith and community commitment to protecting those whose circumstances made them most vulnerable to challenges that individual effort could not overcome. Rivers would be born into world that had been shaped by people who understood that some things were worth preserving regardless of cost, that love could create value that survived whatever destruction circumstances might impose upon its physical manifestations.

The flood was coming, but so was new life that would carry forward whatever lessons the current generation could teach about transformation and redemption and the courage required to build meaningful existence from materials that seemed inadequate for creating anything beautiful or lasting. The bell tower that marked Three Rivers Inn's position at the confluence where separate waterways joined their individual histories into shared destination would soon be tested by waters that recognized no human claim to permanence, but the love that had built the inn and prepared for the child would prove stronger than any force that threatened to destroy what patience and faith had created through service to purposes larger than individual advancement.

21 THE RISING WATERS

Three Rivers Inn, Wellington - August 26th, 1852

The sound that woke Thomas Staines from his restless vigil beside Catherine was not the gradual creaking of settling timber that had provided background symphony throughout the night, but the sharp crack of something fundamental giving way—the specific sound of structural failure that his blacksmith's ear recognized with the same certainty that others might identify a familiar voice calling their name. He rose from the chair where he had been watching his wife sleep fitfully, her eight-month pregnancy making rest difficult even under normal circumstances, and moved to the window that framed a view of the Bell River valley transformed beyond recognition.

Where Three Rivers Inn had once commanded a pastoral vista of rolling hills dotted with homesteads that spoke of careful cultivation and patient prosperity, nothing remained but an inland sea that stretched to horizons blurred by rain and mist. The water had risen twenty feet above its normal course during the night, carrying with it the accumulated debris of a winter that had tested every structure, every assumption about safety, every human attempt to impose permanence upon a landscape governed by forces that operated according to logic older than civilization itself.

The inn itself stood like an island in the midst of destruction, its elevated position providing temporary safety while water lapped at foundation stones that Thomas had placed with such care seven years earlier, never imagining they would need to withstand assault from currents that treated massive timber and carefully mortared stone like kindling scattered by irresistible force. Through the pre-dawn darkness, he could see lights from neighboring homesteads that had achieved sufficient elevation to remain above the flood, their windows gleaming like stars reflected in water that had transformed familiar territory into an alien seascape.

But it was the sound of voices—human cries carrying across the water that muffled and distorted them until they seemed like ghostly echoes of lives being overwhelmed by circumstances beyond any individual's capacity to control—that made Thomas understand this was no ordinary flood but a catastrophic event that would test everything the community had built together, every relationship that had been forged through years of mutual support and shared commitment to collective welfare.

"Thomas?" Catherine's voice carried across their bedroom with the particular quality that marked someone surfacing from sleep that had been more struggle than rest. "What is it? The baby's been restless all night, moving like she knows something's happening that requires preparation."

He turned from the window to find his wife sitting up in bed, her hands cradling the swell of their unborn child with a protective instinct that spoke of maternal wisdom that transcended rational understanding. In the candlelight that had burned throughout the night, Catherine's face showed the strain of pregnancy combined with a growing awareness that their carefully planned future was being tested by forces that recognized no human claim to security or permanence.

"The flood," Thomas replied simply, understanding that euphemism served no purpose when circumstances demanded an honest assessment of dangers that would require all their combined strength to survive. "Worse than anyone predicted. Water's reached our foundation level and still rising."

Catherine's response was immediate and practical, shaped by seven years of frontier life that had taught her to meet crises with action rather than panic, adaptation rather than despair. "How long before we need to evacuate to higher ground?"

The question forced Thomas to confront calculations he had been avoiding throughout the night, mathematical realities that suggested their options were narrowing faster than he had wanted to acknowledge. The inn's main floor stood perhaps six feet above current water level, but the river's continued rise showed no signs of slowing, while structural sounds that had been awakening him suggested the building itself might not survive pressures that exceeded its capacity to resist forces that had been building throughout the wettest winter in colonial memory.

"Depends on how much higher the water rises," Thomas replied, his honesty tempered by recognition that Catherine's condition required hope as much as truth, confidence as much as preparation for possibilities they both preferred not to contemplate. "Inn was built to withstand ordinary flooding, but this—" He gestured toward the window where dawn was beginning to reveal the full scope of devastation that had occurred while they slept. "This is beyond anything we planned for."

The conversation was interrupted by sounds from below—voices calling out in distress, feet splashing through water that had somehow found its way inside their sanctuary, evidence that their temporary safety was becoming increasingly temporary with each hour that passed. Thomas pulled on his clothes with movements that reflected urgency tempered by recognition that panic would serve no useful purpose when circumstances demanded clear thinking and coordinated action.

Descending to the inn's common room, Thomas found chaos that spoke of a community in crisis responding according to character that trials had either strengthened or revealed as inadequate for challenges that exceeded ordinary human capacity to endure. The Morrison family huddled near the fireplace with possessions that represented everything they had managed to salvage from a farm that had provided their livelihood for fifteen years—clothes hastily gathered, photographs and documents that connected them to a heritage that transcended material loss, tools that might help them rebuild if they survived circumstances that currently threatened their very existence.

Old Mrs. Hennessy clutched a carpetbag that contained letters from children scattered across the colony, their faces revealed by lantern light that made everyone look like refugees from disasters they had never imagined could reach their carefully protected corner of colonial prosperity. Her usual composure had been replaced by bewilderment that spoke of someone whose understanding of what was possible had been shattered by events that exceeded every previous experience of hardship and loss.

Young Jamie O'Brien sat beside his mother with eyes wide with the particular terror reserved for children who are discovering that the adult world offers no guarantees of safety, no protection against forces that care nothing for innocence or need or the desperate human desire for security that had motivated their families' settlement in territory that had seemed to promise stability in exchange for hard work and patient cultivation.

"How many others made it to safety?" Thomas asked, his question directed toward anyone who might have information about neighbors whose fate remained unknown but whose welfare had become his responsibility through seven years of building relationships that transcended mere commercial interaction to encompass genuine concern for community members whose survival was interconnected with his own family's prospects.

"Henderson's farm is underwater," reported William Morrison, his voice carrying the strain of someone who had lost everything except his family and was trying to calculate whether even they would survive the next few hours. "Saw his barn roof floating past our place just before we abandoned everything and headed for high ground. No sign of the family—hoping they made it to his brother's place in Bathurst before the worst of it hit."

The litany of destruction continued as other refugees shared fragmentary reports about neighbors whose fates remained uncertain, property damage that would require years to repair, livestock lost to waters that had risen faster than anyone had thought possible despite weeks of growing concern about river levels that had already exceeded normal seasonal variations.

But it was Mrs. Patterson's arrival, her German accent thickened by stress that made her normal precise English difficult to maintain, that brought news of immediate crisis requiring response that transcended mere accommodation of flood refugees. "Catherine must not attempt delivery under these conditions," she announced, her midwife experience providing authority that commanded attention from everyone whose circumstances had become dependent upon whatever expertise remained available during an emergency that had overwhelmed normal support systems.

"Labor hasn't started," Catherine called from the bedroom above, her voice carrying clearly through floorboards that had begun to vibrate with sounds that suggested the building's structure was being tested beyond its design limitations. "But the baby's movements suggest arrival could happen soon, regardless of whether timing suits our convenience or current circumstances."

The medical consultation that followed revealed how completely their situation had deteriorated beyond anything community preparation had anticipated. Mrs. Patterson's supplies for managing complicated deliveries had been lost when rising waters forced hasty evacuation from her own home, while transportation to Bathurst—where proper medical assistance might be available—had been rendered impossible by floods that had washed out roads and bridges that connected their district to larger settlements.

"We'll manage with what we have," Mrs. Patterson declared, her determination shaped by frontier experience that had taught adaptation to circumstances that offered no ideal solutions, only choices between inadequate options that might prove sufficient if approached with proper skill and whatever divine assistance circumstances might provide. "Women have been giving birth in difficult conditions since humanity began. The baby wants to arrive safely as much as we want safe arrival."

As morning progressed and water continued its relentless advance toward levels that would make their current refuge untenable, Thomas found himself coordinating evacuation plans that balanced immediate safety requirements with recognition that some decisions would determine not just survival but whether anything they had built together could be preserved for a future that currently seemed doubtful but remained worth planning for if circumstances permitted.

The inn's upper floor offered temporary security for perhaps twenty people, but structural sounds that had been growing more frequent suggested the building itself might not survive pressures that were testing every joint and connection point beyond limits that timber and stone could endure indefinitely. The main support beam that carried weight of the entire upper story showed hairline cracks that expanded visibly while Thomas watched, each surge of water adding stress that brought total failure incrementally closer.

"Building won't last much longer," Thomas announced to the assembled refugees whose survival had become his responsibility through circumstances that admitted no delegation of authority to anyone whose expertise might have been better suited for managing crisis that exceeded his experience or preparation. "Need to move everyone to the roof while there's still time to complete the evacuation safely."

The logistics of moving a pregnant woman, elderly residents, and frightened children to the roof access that required climbing through spaces that had never been designed for emergency evacuation challenged everyone's physical capabilities while testing emotional reserves that had already been depleted by losses that seemed to accumulate faster than human capacity to process their full implications.

But it was Catherine's sudden cry—not of pain but of recognition that their child had decided to make its entrance into the world that seemed determined to test whether new life could establish itself despite circumstances that appeared designed to prevent such optimistic assertion of future possibilities—that transformed evacuation from urgent necessity into a desperate race against time that would determine whether Rivers Staines would inherit parents who had survived to guide her early years or a legacy preserved only through letters that might not survive destruction that threatened everything they had built together.

"The baby's coming," Catherine announced, her voice carrying a mixture of joy and apprehension that reflected an understanding that Rivers had chosen timing that would test everyone's capacity for managing multiple crises simultaneously. "Labor started while we were planning the evacuation. No choice now but to trust that delivery can be completed before circumstances make it impossible."

Mrs. Patterson's response was immediate and professional, her midwife training taking precedence over flood concerns that would have to be addressed after more immediate medical needs had been satisfied. "Move Catherine to the safest location available, gather whatever supplies we can improvise for delivery, and pray that this child inherits its parents' determination to survive whatever trials life presents."

The improvised delivery room that was established in the inn's most structurally sound bedroom reflected colonial society's capacity for adaptation when circumstances demanded innovation rather than adherence to conventional practices that assumed normal conditions and adequate resources. Catherine's labor proceeded with a determination that matched the flood waters' relentless advance, each contraction bringing their daughter closer to a birth that would occur regardless of external circumstances that seemed designed to make such an optimistic act of creation impossible.

Thomas found himself moving between delivery room where his wife labored to bring their child into an uncertain world, and the common room where refugees waited for guidance about an evacuation that might need to happen within hours rather than the days they had hoped would be available for careful planning and adequate preparation.

The building's structural deterioration accelerated throughout the morning, sounds of settling timber becoming more frequent while water pressure against foundation stones created stresses that exceeded design limitations of a construction that had been intended to withstand ordinary challenges rather than catastrophic forces that transformed normal environmental conditions into a survival test that measured human character against circumstances that had destroyed stronger structures than Three Rivers Inn.

"Main beam's failing," Thomas reported to Mrs. Patterson during a brief consultation about whether Catherine could be moved safely if immediate evacuation became necessary to prevent injuries that could prove fatal when medical assistance was unavailable and transportation to proper care had been rendered impossible by flooding that had isolated their district from resources that normal conditions would have made accessible.

"Labor's progressing normally," Mrs. Patterson replied, her assessment delivered with authority that reflected twenty years of frontier midwife experience. "Moving Catherine now would create risks that exceed whatever structural dangers we're facing. Better to complete the delivery in our current location and deal with evacuation afterward, when mother and child can both travel without medical complications that could prove more dangerous than building collapse."

The decision to remain in place while structural failure became increasingly imminent required faith that transcended rational calculation, trust that love could somehow create protection that engineering could not provide, belief that some purposes were important enough to justify risks that prudence would normally counsel against taking.

As afternoon advanced and Catherine's labor intensified, the flood waters reached levels that brought them inside the inn's main floor, their advance marking a countdown toward the moment when structural collapse would become inevitable rather than merely probable. Each contraction that brought Rivers closer to birth was matched by sounds of timber shifting under pressures that had been building throughout the day toward a crisis that would test everyone's character against circumstances that offered no comfortable options.

The community response to their desperate situation revealed colonial society at its most cooperative, neighbors whose own survival was threatened contributing whatever assistance they could provide despite personal circumstances that would have justified focus on individual preservation rather than collective welfare. William Morrison organized evacuation supplies while his wife Sarah coordinated care for children whose terror needed to be managed through activities that provided distraction from realities too frightening for young minds to process adequately.

But it was the Aboriginal workers whose traditional knowledge of flood management provided practical guidance that European experience had not anticipated, their understanding of water behavior offering insights that could mean the difference between successful evacuation and a disaster that claimed lives that careful planning might have preserved.

"Water tells us when building will fall," explained Charlie, whose bilingual abilities made him a valuable interpreter between different approaches to managing crisis that required cooperation rather than competition between knowledge systems that had developed through entirely different relationships with environmental challenges. "Listening to sounds that wood makes when pressure becomes too much, watching how foundation moves when current changes direction."

This cross-cultural consultation provided an early warning system that allowed precise timing of an evacuation that might otherwise have been attempted too early—creating unnecessary exposure to dangers that could have been avoided—or too late, when structural failure made safe departure impossible rather than merely difficult.

The moment of Rivers' birth arrived with the sound of splintering timber that announced the inn's impending collapse, her first cry mixing with sounds of destruction that seemed designed to test whether new life could establish itself despite circumstances that appeared optimized for preventing such optimistic assertion of future possibilities. Mrs. Patterson's experienced hands guided a delivery that proceeded with textbook precision despite conditions that would have challenged the most sophisticated medical facilities.

"Perfect daughter," Mrs. Patterson announced, her voice carrying joy that transcended immediate circumstances to encompass recognition that a successful birth represented victory over forces that had seemed determined to prevent such achievement. "Healthy, strong, ready to inherit whatever legacy her parents can preserve through choices that honor both her welfare and community needs that extend beyond individual family concerns."

Thomas held his daughter for the first time while flood waters rose through the inn's lower level and structural collapse became a matter of minutes rather than hours, her tiny weight in his arms providing a perspective that made every sacrifice seem insignificant compared to the privilege of being called her father. Rivers Staines had entered a world that offered no guarantees except opportunity to shape her own destiny through choices that would be guided by whatever wisdom her parents could transmit through example and instruction that began with this moment of holding her while everything they had built together faced destruction that threatened to claim their lives along with their property.

But as he studied his daughter's face by candlelight that revealed features that combined Catherine's German heritage with characteristics that might have come from his own Scottish bloodline, Thomas felt a peace that transcended immediate circumstances to encompass an understanding that some achievements were valuable enough to justify whatever risks their preservation required. Rivers represented completion of a transformation that had begun with his conviction for theft, continued through seven years of colonial bondage, and reached fulfillment through love that had proven capable of creating new life despite conditions that seemed designed to make such creativity impossible.

The evacuation that followed Rivers' birth required coordination that tested everyone's capacity for managing multiple crises while maintaining focus on objectives that transcended immediate survival to encompass preservation of community relationships that had made their district more than a mere collection of individual homesteads competing for scarce resources.

As neighbors worked together to move Catherine and their newborn daughter to the roof access that would provide safety from structural collapse while leaving them exposed to weather that continued testing human endurance against elements that recognized no distinction between worthy and unworthy recipients of natural forces that operated according to logic that preceded human understanding, Thomas felt gratitude that overwhelmed any fear about personal consequences that might result from choices he would soon need to make.

The inn that had sheltered their happiness might be claimed by flood waters that recognized no human claim to permanence, but the love that had built it would survive to build again, the community that had been shaped by their example would endure whatever destruction claimed physical structures, and the daughter who had chosen this moment to enter the world would inherit wisdom that had been earned through trials that revealed strength rather than destroying it.

Standing on the roof of Three Rivers Inn while Bell River flowed past at levels that transformed the familiar landscape into an alien seascape, holding Rivers while Catherine recovered from a delivery that had tested her strength against circumstances that would have challenged anyone whose character had not been refined through trials that prepared her for whatever difficulties the future might present, Thomas understood that his real test was yet to come.

The inn's main support beam groaned with sounds that announced imminent collapse, while twenty people whose survival had become his responsibility looked to him for leadership that could preserve their lives even if it could not save the building that had provided a focal point for a community that would need to be rebuilt on foundations more solid than timber and stone. The choice between personal safety and others' welfare approached with the same inevitability as flood waters that had been rising throughout the day toward a moment when love would be measured against the ultimate standard that admitted no compromise between service and selfishness.

THE BLACKSMITH'S BEQUEST

Three Rivers Inn, Wellington, New South Wales
27th August, 1852 – Dawn

My Most Beloved Rivers,

I have held you in my arms, my precious daughter, and now I understand what angels must feel when they look upon the face of God Himself. For six hours you have slept against my chest while flood waters rise around the inn that will not survive this dawn, your tiny fingers curled around mine with strength that speaks of determination to thrive despite circumstances that would challenge the bravest spirits.

You are beautiful beyond any dream I dared to dream during the long years when you existed only in my hopes and prayers. Your mother's auburn hair catches the candlelight with copper highlights that speak of German heritage she carries from her father's bakery in Württemberg. Your eyes, when they opened to study my face with solemn attention that marks souls destined for wisdom, are the precise shade of blue that reminded me of Australian skies on the clearest days when hope seemed possible despite circumstances that suggested otherwise.

But it is your hands that have claimed my heart completely—tiny fingers that grip mine with unconscious trust, palm no larger than a shilling but capable of holding all the love a man's heart can contain. When you yawned and stretched against my chest, settling into sleep with the perfect confidence of someone who knows herself beloved, I felt my soul expand beyond boundaries of flesh to encompass possibilities I had never imagined existed.

The waters have reached the inn's main floor now, my darling child, and I can hear the sound of structural timbers shifting under pressures they were never designed to bear. The beam that supports our refuge grows weaker with each moment that passes, its failure imminent and catastrophic unless someone is willing to provide support that might delay collapse until our neighbors can reach safety on roof sections that will survive what cannot be survived below.

I write these final words not in despair but in wonder at the completeness of the gift I have been granted. Six hours to hold you, to study your perfect face, to whisper into your ear words of love that will travel with you throughout whatever years God grants you in this world where your father's presence can no longer provide protection or guidance.

You sleep peacefully while I write, unaware that these may be the last words your father speaks to you in this life, but I am convinced that love strong enough to create such perfect trust will prove strong enough to bridge whatever distances death might impose between us. The Celtic cross I carved aboard the convict ship seventeen years ago now bears your initials alongside your mother's, tiny letters that required steady hand and patient heart to complete in these final hours before dawn brings whatever trials await us.

Should you inherit this cross in years to come, remember that it was shaped by hands that learned through suffering to choose service over selfishness, love over fear, hope over comfortable surrender of limited expectations. Remember that its imperfections speak not of inadequate craftsmanship but of circumstances under which love must sometimes work—in darkness, under pressure, with materials that seem inadequate for creating anything beautiful yet somehow yield treasures that survive whatever trials the future presents.

Live boldly, my darling child, with courage your mother has shown in crossing oceans to find life worthy of her gifts. Love deeply, as I have learned to love through her example of what devotion means when offered without reservation or calculation of return. Serve faithfully, as circumstances provide opportunity for placing others' welfare above your own comfort.

I go now to love that serves rather than demands, that builds rather than protects, that gives everything—including life itself—for the welfare of those whose happiness has become the meaning that makes all sacrifice worthwhile. I go with perfect peace because I have held you in my arms and felt your heartbeat against my chest and whispered into your ear words that will travel with you wherever love can reach across whatever distances circumstances impose.

You are beloved beyond all earthly measure, my precious Rivers. Let that truth sustain you through whatever trials await, let it guide you toward choices that honor the love which created you, let it remind you that death cannot diminish what has been given with sufficient depth and purity and commitment to transcend every limitation that flesh inherits.

Your devoted father, who has learned that love makes even death feel like victory,

Thomas Staines

22 SCOTLAND BOUND

Sydney to Edinburgh — May 2011

The Qantas A380 lifted off from Sydney's runway into pre-dawn darkness that would chase them halfway around the world, carrying Sara and Calvin Wilson toward a Scotland that existed as much in imagination as geography, a homeland neither had seen but both had inherited through bloodlines that stretched back to Kincardineshire's ancient stones and stubborn soil. Sara pressed her face to the small window, watching harbor lights shrink to pinpricks below while understanding that this journey represented more than genealogical tourism—it was a pilgrimage to the source of whatever had made Thomas Staines' transformation possible, the landscape that had shaped people who shaped the people who shaped them.

"Never thought I'd see the day," Calvin said from the seat beside her, his voice carrying the particular satisfaction of someone whose wildest dreams had become a planned itinerary. At seventy-six, he'd assumed that international travel belonged to other people's lives, that his world would remain bounded by Brisbane Water and the familiar rhythms of his workshop routine. But Thomas's letters had changed more than Sara's understanding of family history—they'd changed both their understanding of what was possible when grief stopped dictating the boundaries of hope.

Six months had passed since Sara's discovery in Glen Lena's attic, six months of gradual healing that had transformed careful distance into a genuine partnership in preserving and understanding the wisdom Thomas had left for anyone willing to receive it. The Scotland trip had emerged naturally from their shared research, their growing understanding that some connections required physical pilgrimage to ancestral ground where stories had taken root in soil that still nourished anyone willing to seek guidance from those who'd come before.

Sara pulled out the leather portfolio that had become her constant companion, its contents now expanded far beyond Thomas's original letters to include Rivers' journal, genealogical charts that mapped their family's journey from Scottish parishes to Australian colonies, and the draft chapters of the novel that had become her life's work— her contribution to carrying their story forward to anyone whose heart was ready to receive its wisdom about transformation and redemption.

"Read me the part about Arbuthnott again," Calvin said, settling into his seat with the anticipation of someone who'd learned to find adventure in circumstances he'd never expected to navigate. The man who'd once found comfort only in his workshop's familiar boundaries now carried travel documents and guidebooks with the same careful attention he'd always brought to woodworking projects, understanding that some journeys required similar patience and precision.

Sara opened Rivers' journal to a passage she'd marked with strips of tissue paper, her great-grandmother's careful script as familiar now as her own handwriting: *"Mother told me that Father's people came from Arbuthnott Parish, where the old kirk holds stones that remember our name from centuries before transportation carried him to Australian shores. She said the thistles that bloom wild there are the same ones he carved into his cross, that the land remembers its children even when they're forced to seek their fortunes in distant places."*

"Thistles that still bloom," Calvin repeated, his carpenter's hands gentle on the armrest that separated their seats. "Makes you think about what survives and what doesn't, doesn't it? Houses fall down, people die, but the land keeps growing the same flowers that meant something to someone two hundred years ago."

The observation carried weight that would have been impossible six months earlier, when Calvin's grief had made any reference to survival feel like betrayal of Ellen's memory. But Thomas's example had taught them both something about the difference between loss that destroyed and loss that transformed, between endings that negated what came before and endings that honored it by creating space for something new to grow.

Their relationship had rebuilt itself around a shared purpose that honored Ellen's memory while creating new ground for connection that didn't require her translation services. Calvin had learned to speak more directly about emotions that mattered, while Sara had discovered that her father's silences often contained more wisdom than her own tendency toward immediate verbalization. They'd found common language in research and planning and the gradual recognition that their grief for Ellen had become foundation rather than barrier, shared experience that deepened rather than divided their understanding of what family meant.

The flight to Dubai passed in comfortable conversation punctuated by periods of reading and planning that felt more like anticipation than anxiety. Calvin studied guidebooks with the same methodical approach he brought to furniture projects, making notes about driving routes and accommodation while Sara worked on manuscript pages that wove Thomas's nineteenth-century journey into a contemporary narrative about healing and hope. Their individual obsessions had become a collaborative enterprise, each contribution strengthening the whole rather than competing for attention.

"What do you think he would make of this?" Sara asked as the plane crossed over Southeast Asia, tiny lights below marking cities where millions of people lived stories that probably contained their own versions of exile and redemption, transformation and loss. "Thomas seeing us trace his heritage back to the source he never expected to see again."

Calvin considered the question with the careful attention he'd learned to bring to matters that carried emotional weight beyond their practical dimensions. "Think he'd be amazed that love could travel this far, that letters written to a daughter he held for six hours could inspire people he never met to cross oceans just to understand where he came from. But maybe not surprised—seems like he understood something about how deep connections work, how they survive whatever tries to break them."

The layover in Dubai gave them time to stretch legs and process the surreal reality of being halfway to Scotland, their journey taking them through airports that felt like international space stations—glass and steel and multinational crowds that made the world feel both impossibly large and surprisingly small. Sara found herself thinking about Catherine Krieg making her crossing from Württemberg to Australia in 1843, the courage required to trust that opportunities waited in places that existed more in hope than certainty.

"Catherine would understand this," Sara said as they waited to board their Edinburgh flight. "The faith it takes to believe that seeking connection to heritage you've never experienced directly can teach you something essential about who you are."

Calvin nodded, his own understanding of pilgrimage shaped by decades of creating objects that honored traditions passed down through generations of craftsmen. "She crossed bigger oceans with less certainty about what waited on the other side. We've got GPS and guidebooks and confirmed reservations. She had hope and whatever courage desperation could provide."

The final flight segment carried them over European landscapes that grew increasingly familiar despite being completely foreign—patterns of field and forest that echoed descriptions in Rivers' journal, geography that had shaped the people who shaped the stories that had eventually reached them in an Australian attic waiting for someone ready to claim responsibility for their preservation and transmission.

Edinburgh appeared through morning clouds like a city from fairy tales, its castle perched on volcanic rock above medieval streets that seemed to exhale history with every stone and timber. Sara felt her chest tighten with emotion she hadn't expected—not just excitement or curiosity, but recognition, as if some part of her DNA was responding to a landscape that had existed in her bloodline's cellular memory for generations.

"It looks like home," Calvin said quietly, his face pressed to the window as they circled above Scotland's capital. "Not like anywhere I've ever been, but like somewhere I was always supposed to end up eventually."

Their rental car was a compact Vauxhall that felt toy-like compared to Calvin's reliable Toyota, but it handled the narrow streets and roundabouts with good humor that matched their mood as they navigated out of Edinburgh toward the A90 that would carry them north to Kincardineshire and whatever discoveries waited in Arbuthnott Parish. The countryside that unfolded beyond their windows was green in ways that Australia had never taught them to expect—forty shades of emerald and jade and forest that spoke of climate where rain was a blessing rather than disaster, where growing seasons lasted long enough for beauty to become commonplace rather than miraculous.

"Look at that," Sara said as they passed a stone cottage whose walls probably predated Thomas's birth by centuries, its roof still shedding water that had been falling on Scottish soil since long before anyone thought to call other continents home. "People have been living here continuously for hundreds of years, thousands maybe. Generation after generation choosing to stay, to build, to preserve what matters most."

Calvin slowed the car to study the cottage's construction—dry stone walls that had been fitted without mortar by craftsmen who understood how patience and precision could create structures that outlasted the civilizations that built them. "Makes you think about what lasts and what doesn't. That house has probably sheltered fifty generations while governments rose and fell around it."

They stopped for lunch in a village whose name Sara recognized from genealogical records—Laurencekirk, where William Nicol had been baptized in 1765 before later marrying Margaret Dyce in the Kirkton of Fetteresso in 1794 bringing the Nicol family in her ancestry. The pub that served them shepherd's pie and bitter had probably dispensed similar meals to similar travelers for centuries, its low ceilings and worn floors speaking of continuity that made their own family story feel like a single thread in a tapestry too large and complex for any individual understanding.

"Walter ate here, maybe even his children," Sara said, studying the pub's interior with imagination informed by months of research into nineteenth-century Scottish life. "Maybe not this exact building, but somewhere like this, before one of his children married a Paterson and decided that Australia offered opportunities Scotland couldn't provide."

"Different times," Calvin observed, sampling bitter that carried flavors he'd never encountered in Australian beer. "Young men and women with no land and no prospects, hearing stories about colonies where willing workers could build whatever life they had courage to attempt. Must have felt like choice between slow starvation and dangerous hope."

The afternoon drive north carried them through landscape that grew more recognizable with each mile, despite being completely foreign to their Australian-trained eyes. Rolling hills covered in heather and gorse, stone walls that followed property lines established before written records began, sheep that regarded their passage with the patient attention of creatures whose ancestors had witnessed countless human generations pursuing whatever purposes drove them across terrain that belonged ultimately to weather and seasons rather than any temporary human arrangement.

That night they settled into a little inn, a small and inviting space, one that held memories for so many of the years that its four walls held strong. They dined with other guests, travelers and local folk blending in the benches and cozy chairs that surrounded the bar and kitchen serveries. Talk and chatter blending with laughter and light that glowed from the low-hanging fixtures from the ceilings. As they rested from their travels, both couldn't help but think of Thomas and the Three Rivers Inn and the community he and Catherine had built together. This felt like a little piece of home, amongst history and heritage, a looking glass into the past and the feeling of community.

"We best turn in for the night" Calvin said, "We'll want to make an early start tomorrow".

As they rose and walked to the door leading to the guest quarters, Sara turned and gazed around the room, her heart so full of the joy she felt being here, right now, amongst memories she'll cherish forever.

...

Morning came quickly, birds calling in the distance, chickens brooding in a coop beside the walls of the inn's scullery. It was still, dark, the morning light not yet breaking and a chill held the air like a hand wrapped tight to the skin. Calvin and Sara bundled into the Vauxhall for the short drive to the church yard, a quiet settling between them as they each processed the many thoughts that came to mind as the engine idled and steadily came to life in the cool of dawn.

"There," Sara said as they crested a hill that revealed the Howe of the Mearns spread below them like green carpet dotted with farmsteads and ancient groves. "Arbuthnott Parish. According to the map, the churchyard is just beyond those trees."

Calvin pulled into a car park that served both church and visitors, understanding that they were about to complete a journey that had begun in Glen Lena's attic and carried them across continents and centuries to stand on ground their ancestors had called home before circumstances forced them to seek better opportunities in distant places that promised more than they delivered but somehow proved sufficient for building lives worth remembering.

As a Scottish dawn awakened, Calvin and Sara Wilson stood facing the stones of stories past, two people whose own journey from grief to healing had been guided by wisdom preserved across centuries, proof that some stories were powerful enough to inspire transformation in anyone brave enough to seek it, patient enough to receive it, humble enough to pass it forward to those whose hearts were ready to be changed by love that proved stronger than death itself.

23 THE FINAL CHOICE

Three Rivers Inn, Wellington - August 27th, 1852 - Dawn

The sound that made Thomas Staines' blood run cold was not the crash of timber or the roar of flood waters, but the subtle groan of the main support beam shifting under pressures that had accumulated throughout the night like grief building toward its inevitable expression. He stood on the inn's roof holding his six-hour-old daughter while dawn revealed the full scope of devastation that had transformed their prosperous valley into an inland sea, understanding with the clarity that comes from crisis that the building beneath them was failing in ways that engineering knowledge could predict with mathematical precision.

The beam that carried the weight of the entire upper story—the massive piece of Australian hardwood he had selected and positioned with such care seven years earlier—showed cracks that expanded with each surge of water against foundation stones that could no longer provide adequate support. The split ran nearly half the beam's width now, and Thomas's blacksmith experience with stress patterns in metal provided brutal understanding of what similar failure meant in timber: catastrophic collapse that would crush anyone beneath while opening the building to flood waters that would claim any survivors the falling debris might spare.

Twenty people huddled on roof sections that would survive the inn's destruction, their faces turned toward him with trust that made his throat tighten with emotion too powerful for easy expression. Catherine lay wrapped in blankets hastily gathered during their desperate evacuation, Rivers sleeping peacefully against her chest with the perfect confidence of someone who knew herself beloved. The Morrison family clustered together near the chimney that provided a solid anchor point, their children's frightened faces reflecting trust in adult competence that made every decision feel weighted with significance that extended far beyond immediate circumstances.

Mrs. Patterson moved among the refugees with supplies salvaged from their hasty evacuation, her medical training focused on ensuring Catherine's recovery from delivery that had tested her strength while flood waters rose around them. Old Mrs. Hennessy clutched her carpetbag of memories with hands that trembled not from cold but from recognition that everything familiar was being swept away by forces that recognized no human claim to permanence or security.

"How long do we have?" asked William Morrison, his farmer's understanding of structural engineering sufficient to recognize that their temporary refuge was becoming increasingly temporary with each shift and groan that announced the building's approaching surrender to forces it had never been designed to resist.

Thomas studied the beam's deterioration with attention that revealed both the precision of his technical knowledge and the weight of responsibility that had settled upon him like a mantle he had never expected to wear. The mathematics were brutal in their clarity: perhaps minutes before total failure, certainly less than an hour, probably insufficient time to construct alternative shelter or organize evacuation to ground that might remain above flood levels that continued rising without apparent limit.

But the same calculation that revealed their desperate situation also suggested a solution that would require sacrifice from someone whose death might purchase time for others to reach safety. If human strength could supplement the timber's failing capacity just long enough for evacuation to be completed—if one person was willing to serve as a living support while everyone else escaped the trap that Three Rivers Inn had become—collapse might be delayed until those who depended upon his judgment could find refuge that would outlast whatever destruction the flood imposed upon their carefully built community.

The choice between personal safety and others' welfare crystallized with the same inevitable logic as flood waters that had been building throughout the night toward this moment when love would be measured against the ultimate standard that admitted no compromise between service and selfishness. Thomas felt something settle in his chest that was neither fear nor resignation but something approaching peace—the calm that comes from recognizing the moment when all previous choices have led to a decision that admits no alternatives, when character reveals itself not through dramatic gesture but through quiet acceptance of what must be done regardless of personal preference.

"Catherine," he called softly, his voice carrying across the roof space that separated him from the woman who had taught him what love meant when practiced rather than merely felt, served rather than demanded, given rather than hoarded against an uncertain future that could never be guaranteed regardless of how carefully it was planned.

She looked up from Rivers with an expression that suggested immediate understanding of what his tone implied, recognition that came from seven years of marriage that had taught her to read meanings that words alone could never convey. The love in her eyes was neither surprised nor reproachful—it was the kind of acceptance that comes from knowing someone's character so completely that their final choice feels like inevitable completion of everything they had been building toward rather than an unexpected development that required adjustment of expectations.

"The beam?" Catherine asked, her question requiring no elaboration because her own observation of their circumstances had led to the same conclusion that Thomas's engineering knowledge had reached through a different route.

"Failing faster than I hoped," Thomas replied, understanding that honesty served better than false reassurance when circumstances demanded decisions based on accurate assessment rather than wishful thinking that could prove fatal for everyone whose survival depended upon his judgment. "Minutes rather than hours before complete collapse."

Catherine's nod suggested not just acceptance but something approaching approval—recognition that the man she had married was someone whose character would naturally lead to the choice that placed others' welfare above personal preservation, whose transformation from convicted thief to community leader had prepared him for exactly this kind of test. Her eyes held tears that spoke not of surprise but of pride in loving someone whose final act would be consistent with everything their life together had taught about what made existence meaningful.

"Bring me Rivers," Thomas said, extending his arms toward the daughter he had held for only six hours but loved with an intensity that made a lifetime seem inadequate for expressing feelings that transcended every limitation mortality could impose. "Want to say goodbye properly, make sure she knows she's loved by a father who would choose her welfare over his own survival without hesitation or regret."

The exchange that followed felt both eternal and impossibly brief—moments that contained more meaning than some people discovered in decades of ordinary living, connection that bridged gap between individual existence and universal truth about love that proved stronger than death when measured by proper standards. Rivers settled against his chest with trust that spoke of a bond that transcended rational understanding, her tiny fingers curling around his thumb with strength that belied her size.

"My precious daughter," Thomas whispered into her ear, his words intended for her alone though everyone on the roof could hear the voice that carried love refined to its essential purity. "You've made me immortal in ways I never imagined possible. Everything I learned about redemption, everything your mother taught me about love, everything our community showed me about service—all of it was preparation for this moment when I can prove that some gifts are worth any price love can pay."

He studied her face in the dawn light that revealed features that would develop into beauty that honored both Catherine's German heritage and whatever Scottish characteristics she might inherit from bloodlines that stretched back through generations of people who had chosen persistence over surrender. Her eyes, when they opened to regard him with solemn attention that seemed to acknowledge significance of their conversation, were a precise shade of blue that reminded him of Australian skies on the clearest days when hope seemed possible despite circumstances that might suggest otherwise.

"Your mother will teach you everything you need to know about being strong and kind and brave," Thomas continued, his voice steady despite emotion that threatened to overwhelm speech with feelings too large for words to contain adequately. "But I want you to know that your father loved you enough to choose death over life without you, service over safety, meaning over mere survival when circumstances demanded such choice."

The goodbye that followed required strength that Thomas had been building for seventeen years without knowing what purpose such preparation would eventually serve. Returning Rivers to Catherine's arms felt like surrendering part of his soul, but it was surrender that created rather than destroyed value, sacrifice that built rather than diminished whatever legacy their love had created through patient work and shared commitment to purposes larger than individual advancement.

"Take care of her," Thomas said to Catherine, his words encompassing both immediate instructions about their daughter's welfare and the broader request that she preserve memory of father who had learned to love completely through her example of what devotion meant when offered without reservation or calculation of return.

Catherine's response was immediate and complete: "She'll know her father was a man who learned to love so well that death became his final gift to those he cherished. She'll understand that transformation is possible for anyone willing to choose service over selfishness, hope over fear, love over every limitation that circumstances attempt to impose."

The community's recognition of what Thomas intended to do created an atmosphere of reverence that transformed desperate evacuation into ceremony that honored both individual heroism and collective values that made such sacrifice meaningful rather than merely tragic. William Morrison stepped forward with an expression that combined gratitude with determination to ensure that Thomas's choice would not be forgotten by anyone whose life was preserved through his willingness to pay the ultimate price for others' welfare.

"We'll remember," Morrison said simply, his promise carrying the weight of someone who understood that witness bore responsibility for preserving truth about courage that transcended ordinary human capacity for selflessness. "Our children will know that

Thomas Staines chose love over life, service over safety, meaning over mere existence when crisis demanded everything character could offer."

Mrs. Patterson approached with her medical bag that contained supplies for treating injuries that might result from building collapse, her midwife training unable to prevent disaster but prepared to address its consequences with whatever skill circumstances permitted. "Community will ensure Catherine and Rivers never lack support," she declared, her German accent lending gravity to a promise that reflected immigrant understanding of mutual dependence that made survival possible in circumstances where isolation could prove fatal.

The Aboriginal workers whose traditional knowledge had provided early warning about structural failure contributed their own blessing to a ceremony that honored choice that transcended cultural boundaries to embody a universal truth about love that served rather than demanded. Charlie offered an observation that connected Thomas's sacrifice to the wisdom of traditions that stretched back through countless generations.

"Man who gives life for others becomes part of land itself," Charlie said, his words carrying authority that came from knowledge systems that had sustained communities through trials that tested every assumption about what made an existence meaningful. "Spirit lives in place where love proved stronger than death, teaching anyone willing to learn what courage means when measured by proper standards."

Young Jamie O'Brien, whose terror had been partially calmed by adult reassurance that proved inadequate against realities too frightening for a child's understanding, approached Thomas with an expression that suggested recognition that something sacred was occurring despite circumstances that seemed designed to destroy rather than preserve anything valuable.

"Will you hurt?" Jamie asked, his question carrying an innocence that demanded honest response rather than comfortable evasion that might protect his feelings while failing to honor trust that children placed in adult wisdom during moments when truth mattered more than temporary comfort.

"For a moment," Thomas replied, his honesty tempered by recognition that Jamie needed hope as much as truth, understanding as much as information about realities that would soon affect everyone whose survival depended upon decisions that admitted no delay or second-guessing. "But love makes any pain worthwhile when it serves purposes larger than personal comfort."

The final preparations that preceded Thomas's descent into the inn required coordination that tested everyone's capacity for managing practical necessities while acknowledging emotional significance that transformed necessary action into ceremony that honored both individual courage and community values that made such sacrifice meaningful rather than merely tragic.

"Wait until I'm in position before beginning evacuation," Thomas instructed, his practical knowledge of structural engineering providing guidance for timing that could mean the difference between successful escape and disaster that claimed additional lives through poor coordination of a desperate plan. "When the beam stabilizes—you'll hear a change in the sound it makes—move quickly but carefully toward the eastern roof section where the slope provides safest descent to ground level."

The kiss he shared with Catherine felt like the completion of a conversation that had been developing through seven years of marriage that taught both participants what love meant when practiced consistently rather than merely declared periodically. Their lips met with a tenderness that acknowledged both immediate separation and eternal connection that death could interrupt but never truly sever, understanding that transcended physical circumstances to encompass spiritual reality that made temporary loss acceptable when weighed against permanent meaning.

"Until we meet again," Catherine whispered, her words carrying a faith that stretched beyond the immediate crisis to encompass hope that love this deep could survive whatever trials time and circumstance might impose upon its physical manifestation.

"Until we meet again," Thomas replied, his promise encompassing both his specific commitment to a reunion that death might delay but could not prevent, and broader faith that meaning created through sacrifice would outlast whatever destruction claimed its immediate context.

The descent into a building that groaned with sounds announcing imminent collapse required courage that Thomas had been developing without knowing what test such preparation would eventually need to pass. Each step carried him deeper into the structure that might fail at any moment, closer to a position where his strength could supplement the failing timber just long enough for an evacuation that would preserve lives whose value exceeded any calculation that measured worth according to individual rather than collective standards.

The main support beam that would soon depend upon his assistance for maintaining integrity that kept an entire upper story from crashing down bore weight that exceeded anything human strength could sustain indefinitely. But indefinitely was not required—only minutes that might stretch into a quarter-hour if fortune favored their desperate plan, time that could permit careful evacuation that preserved twenty lives through the sacrifice of one.

The iron bar that would serve as a lever to distribute weight across the broader area than the failing timber could manage alone had been positioned during construction for exactly this kind of emergency, though Thomas had never imagined circumstances that would make such preparation necessary. His blacksmith knowledge of stress distribution provided an understanding of how human strength could be applied most effectively to supplement structural elements that approached their failure threshold.

As he positioned himself beneath the beam that bore responsibility for an entire building's integrity, Thomas felt profound satisfaction that had nothing to do with personal achievement and everything to do with recognition that his life had found a perfect expression in a final choice that honored everything seventeen years of transformation had taught about the difference between existing and truly living, surviving and thriving, taking and giving.

The sound of feet moving across the roof above announced beginning of the evacuation that his sacrifice would make possible, each footstep representing a life that would continue because someone had learned to love completely enough to choose death over survival that required others' destruction. Catherine's voice calling instructions to refugees whose safety depended upon careful coordination reminded him that love found expression through practical service as much as emotional declaration.

The beam shifted again, the crack expanding with a sound like a prayer answered through human willingness to serve purposes larger than individual preservation. Thomas applied pressure that his blacksmith-strengthened arms and shoulders could sustain for precious minutes that would determine whether evacuation succeeded or failed catastrophically.

Above him, voices called coordinates and encouragement as community members whose survival he was purchasing through the ultimate payment worked together to reach safety that his choice had made possible. Mrs. Patterson's medical expertise guided the movement that protected Catherine's recovery while ensuring Rivers' welfare during descent that tested everyone's physical capabilities.

The Aboriginal workers whose traditional knowledge had provided early warning coordinated ground-level preparation that would enable successful completion of an evacuation that European understanding alone might not have managed adequately. Their cooperation represented fusion of knowledge systems that created results neither culture could have achieved independently.

As structural stress transferred from failing timber to human strength that could maintain integrity for the limited time that evacuation required, Thomas felt a completion that transcended immediate circumstances to encompass understanding that redemption had been achieved through choices that proved love stronger than death when measured by standards that honored service rather than mere survival.

The voices above grew more distant as the evacuation proceeded according to a plan that balanced speed with safety, efficiency with care for the most vulnerable members of a community whose welfare had become Thomas's final responsibility. Each person who reached ground level represented victory over forces that had seemed determined to destroy everything their collective effort had built through years of patient cooperation.

When the last voice faded and silence announced successful completion of the evacuation that preserved twenty lives through sacrifice of one, Thomas felt peace that exceeded anything he had experienced during seventeen years of learning what love meant when practiced rather than merely proclaimed. The beam that had been failing for hours stabilized under the pressure that human strength applied with knowledge earned through a lifetime of working metal and understanding how force could be distributed to achieve results that exceeded individual capacity.

The collapse, when it finally came, arrived with sounds like thunder that announced not defeat but victory, not ending but completion of a transformation that had begun with a convicted thief and concluded with a community hero whose final choice proved that redemption was possible for anyone willing to pay its price. Thomas's last conscious thought was gratitude for having been granted the opportunity to love so completely that death felt like a privilege rather than punishment, gift rather than loss, completion rather than interruption of purpose that would continue inspiring anyone whose heart was ready to receive instruction about what made existence meaningful.

The building's destruction created waves that carried debris toward destinations unknown, but also carried something more precious: the story of a man who learned to transform shame into honor through patient service that culminated in sacrifice that preserved community while proving love stronger than any force that threatened to destroy what patient work and mutual commitment had created through faith that some things were worth preserving regardless of personal cost.

24 ARBUTHNOTT STONES

Arbuthnott Parish Churchyard, Kincardineshire — May 2011

The ancient lychgate stood open like an invitation extended across centuries, its weathered timber frame marking the boundary between ordinary Scottish countryside and ground that had been consecrated for the dead since before written records began. Sara Wilson paused at the threshold, her hand resting on stones that bore the accumulated touch of countless mourners, pilgrims, and descendants who had passed through this portal seeking connection to those whose stories had shaped their understanding of what it meant to belong somewhere deeper than geography or citizenship could provide.

"Three hundred years," Calvin said quietly, studying the gate's construction with carpenter's appreciation for joinery that had endured longer than most governments. "Wood and stone fitted together by craftsmen who understood they were building something that needed to last beyond their own lifetimes."

The morning mist that had shrouded the Howe of the Mearns was lifting, revealing a churchyard that seemed to exhale history with every breath of wind that moved through grass grown tall around headstones tilted at angles that spoke of centuries spent settling into soil that remembered every soul committed to its care. Ancient yews cast shadows that shifted with the light, creating patterns of darkness and revelation that made the search for their ancestors feel like a pilgrimage through sacred landscape where each step might reveal treasures hidden for generations.

Sara pulled out the leather portfolio that had become their constant companion, its contents now expanded to include maps of the parish, genealogical charts that traced their bloodline back through centuries of Scottish records, and copies of the documents that had brought them across oceans to stand on ground their ancestors had called home before circumstances forced them to seek opportunities in distant places that existed more in hope than certainty.

"Margaret Nicol should be in the older section," Sara said, consulting notes she'd made during months of correspondence with Scottish genealogical societies. "Born 1722, died in the 1800s I believe. Married to William Nicol in 1794. Mother of seven children, including Jane who's daughter Margaret married a Paterson and became our William's grandmother."

The names felt like incantations, each one connecting them to people who had lived and loved and faced their own choices between hope and despair, endurance and surrender, the kind of patient persistence that could transform harsh circumstances into beauty if approached with sufficient faith and determination. Margaret Nicol—a woman whose existence Sara had discovered through painstaking archival research—was no longer just an entry in parish records but an ancestor whose blood had shaped their capacity for transformation, whose character had contributed to whatever strength Thomas Staines had drawn upon during his seventeen-year journey from convicted thief to community hero.

They moved through the churchyard methodically, reading inscriptions that told stories of lives bounded by seasons and harvests, births and deaths that marked the passage of time in rural Scotland where existence depended more on weather and work than politics or progress. The stones themselves were works of art—some elaborate with carved symbols and Biblical quotations, others simple markers that bore only names and dates but carried equal weight of love carefully preserved for anyone willing to seek it.

"Here," Calvin said, stopping beside a headstone that made Sara's breath catch with recognition. "Margaret Nicol, aged, ahh it's hard to read the years, beloved wife and mother, her memory blessed in the hearts of those who knew her worth."

The stone itself was weathered sandstone, its surface bearing the accumulated patina of centuries of Scottish weather, but the carving remained clear enough to read, the letters cut deep by a mason who understood that some messages needed to survive whatever trials time might present. But it was the symbol at the stone's crown that made Sara's throat close with emotion—a thistle carved with such skill and attention that it seemed to bloom eternally in stone, its thorns and petals rendered with the precision that came from love as much as craftsmanship.

"The thistle," Sara whispered, her fingers tracing the carved flower that was identical to the one Thomas had inscribed on his Celtic cross during the darkest period of his exile. "She's here. Margaret Nicol, 1801 or is that a 4 and then a 1?. The woman whose daughter married a Paterson and carried this bloodline forward to Australia."

Calvin knelt beside the headstone, his carpenter's hands gentle on stone that had endured longer than any structure he'd ever built, understanding that he was touching something that connected him directly to heritage he'd inherited without knowing its source. "Look at the craftsmanship in that carving. Someone took time to make this beautiful, to ensure she was remembered with symbols that meant something to people who understood their significance."

The thistle symbol seemed to glow in the morning light that filtered through ancient yews, proof that some meanings transcended individual understanding and became part of inherited wisdom that shaped character across generations. Thomas's choice of the thistle for his cross hadn't been arbitrary—it had been recognition of heritage that connected him to this place, these people, this understanding that beauty could emerge from harsh circumstances if approached with sufficient patience and faith.

"She would have known about the Jacobite uprisings," Sara said, consulting the historical timeline she'd researched to understand the context that had shaped Margaret's life. "Born during the civil wars, lived through the Restoration, died just a few years after the first failed attempt to restore the Stuarts. Her entire life was shaped by political upheaval, religious persecution, economic hardship that made survival itself an achievement worth celebrating."

The observation placed Margaret's existence in perspective that transformed her from genealogical data point into woman who had faced choices between despair and hope, surrender and persistence, the kind of daily decisions that either built character or destroyed it depending on how they were approached. Her sixty-seven years had encompassed enough hardship to break anyone whose spirit hadn't been refined through trials that revealed strength rather than weakness.

"And she raised seven children in those circumstances," Calvin added, understanding from his own experience of parenting how much love and determination such achievement required. "Kept them alive, taught them whatever skills they needed to build their own lives, passed down whatever wisdom her own trials had provided about survival and meaning."

They found other Nicol headstones scattered throughout the older section of the churchyard, names and dates that documented centuries of people who had chosen this soil for their final resting place, who had lived and died within sight of hills that still sheltered the flowers they'd chosen as their family symbol. James Nicol, 1665. Elizabeth Nicol, 1689. Robert Nicol, 1704. Sarah Nicol, 1734. Generation after generation choosing to stay, to build, to preserve what mattered most about community and character and the kind of love that served others' welfare rather than demanding personal comfort.

"They're all here," Sara said, photographing each inscription with reverence due sacred texts. "The people whose genes shaped Thomas's capacity for transformation, whose blood gave him whatever strength he needed to choose redemption over despair when Australian circumstances tested everything he thought he knew about survival and justice."

But it was when they found the section where Paterson headstones clustered together that Sara felt the full weight of connection to a family story that stretched far beyond Thomas and Catherine's nineteenth-century transformation. Here were the people whose bloodline had carried forward the kind of character that made redemption possible, whose heritage had provided foundation for lives that chose meaning over comfort, service over selfishness, the patient work of building something beautiful from whatever materials circumstances provided.

"William's family," Calvin said, studying stones that bore dates stretching from the seventeenth century through the early 1800s. "The ones who shaped the man Rivers married, who helped her children build Glen Lena and raise children with stories that preserved Thomas's memory for future generations."

The newest Paterson headstone was dated 1822, marking the grave of someone who might have known William's family before emigration carried them to Australia and his eventual marriage to Rivers Staines. The connection felt both ancient and immediate, past and present collapsed into a single moment of recognition that they belonged to something larger than individual existence, that their own choices about love and loss and the courage required to choose hope over fear had been shaped by people whose names they'd never known but whose character they'd inherited through bloodlines that connected them to this sacred ground.

"John Paterson, aged 35 years, faithful servant of God and man, beloved father whose memory lives in the children who carry his name," Sara read aloud. "Died 1822. William's father Robert would have been fourteen then, probably knew his grandfather, learned his trade from him."

Calvin touched the inscription with fingers that bore their own calluses from decades of honest work, understanding that he was connected through generations of craftsmen to traditions that valued skill and character over wealth or status. "Carpenters, probably. Look at the way this stone is fitted into its base—someone who understood how things should be built to last."

The morning progressed as they moved systematically through sections of the churchyard that documented centuries of Scottish life, reading stories carved in stone that spoke of hardship faced with dignity, loss met with faith, the kind of patient endurance that could transform harsh circumstances into wisdom if approached with proper attitude. Each headstone was testimony to someone who had faced their own choices between despair and hope, who had decided that life was worth living despite circumstances that might have defeated anyone whose character had not been refined through trials that revealed strength rather than weakness.

"This one," Calvin said, stopping beside a headstone that was older than the others, its inscription barely legible after centuries of weather but still readable by someone willing to kneel close and trace the letters with patient attention. "Agnes Stewart, 1736. 'Beloved lady whose memory shall not perish while love endures.'"

Sara consulted her genealogical charts, finding the connection that made her pulse quicken with recognition. "Agnes Stewart—this could be a relative of Lady Agnes Schelis, the one family tradition claims as our noble ancestor. The medieval connection that links us to Scottish aristocracy through bloodlines that somehow survived everything that followed."

The discovery felt significant beyond genealogical curiosity, proof that their family's capacity for resilience and transformation had deep roots in soil that had nourished centuries of people who understood that nobility came from character rather than circumstances, from choices that served others' welfare rather than advanced personal interests. Lady Agnes Schelis, if the connection was accurate, had lived during Scotland's most turbulent medieval period, had faced wars and plague and political upheaval that made nineteenth-century transportation seem manageable by comparison.

"Five hundred and fifty years," Calvin said, understanding settling between them like a blessing that connected their present pilgrimage to purposes larger than individual curiosity. "From Lady Agnes to Thomas to Rivers to us. Twenty generations of people who chose to thrive rather than merely survive, who found ways to create beauty from harsh circumstances."

They spent the afternoon exploring every section of the churchyard, documenting connections that wove their individual stories into a tapestry too large and complex for any single understanding but rich enough to provide guidance for anyone willing to seek it. The ancient stones held stories of love and loss, triumph and tragedy, the accumulated wisdom of people who had learned that meaning came from service rather than success, from building rather than acquiring, from the patient work of creating something worthy of preservation through attention and care.

As evening approached and Scottish light took on the golden quality that seemed to emanate from the landscape itself rather than any external source, Sara and Calvin found themselves drawn back to Margaret Nicol's grave, understanding that this stone marked not just one woman's resting place but the source of whatever had made their own journey from grief to healing possible. The thistle carved into its crown seemed to glow with an accumulated significance, a symbol that connected Thomas's understanding of beauty emerging from harsh circumstances to a heritage that stretched back through centuries of people who had embodied such wisdom.

"I want to leave something," Sara said, reaching into her bag for the small bouquet of Scottish heather she'd gathered during their drive through the Highlands. "Something that honors her memory and acknowledges what she gave us, even though she never knew we would exist."

Calvin understood the impulse, recognizing in it the same need he felt to create objects that honored traditions passed down through generations of craftsmen. "She would have liked that. Recognition that her life mattered, that the children she raised carried forward something worth preserving."

Sara arranged the heather beside Margaret's headstone, its purple blooms echoing the thistle carved in stone, creating an offering that connected past to present through symbols that transcended language or nationality or the particular circumstances that had scattered their family across continents and centuries. The flowers would fade, but the connection they represented had proven strong enough to survive whatever trials time had presented.

"We should write something," Calvin suggested, producing the small notebook he'd been using to record their discoveries. "Words that capture what this means, what we've learned about where we come from and who we are because of people like Margaret."

Sara took the notebook and pen, feeling the weight of responsibility that came with attempting to articulate connection that existed beyond words but needed words to preserve it for others who might someday seek similar understanding. She wrote carefully, each sentence building upon previous ones to create testimony that honored both their ancestors' memory and their own recognition of inheritance that transcended material possessions:

"In Arbuthnott churchyard, where thistles still bloom wild among stones that remember our name, we understand finally that some inheritances transcend material possessions. The symbols our ancestors chose—the thistles, the Celtic knots, the careful preservation of stories that shaped understanding—weren't just artistic expression but promises that beauty could survive any hardship, that love could bridge any distance, that transformation was always possible for anyone willing to choose it."

The words flowed like water finding its natural course, connecting their physical presence in this ancient place to the emotional journey that had brought them here, proof that genealogical research could become spiritual pilgrimage when approached with hearts ready to receive whatever wisdom ancestors had preserved for descendants willing to seek it.

Calvin read the words aloud, his voice carrying across the churchyard where evening settled like blessing over stones that held the accumulated weight of centuries spent honoring those whose lives had shaped the understanding of what it meant to belong somewhere deeper than geography or citizenship could provide. The words felt like prayer, like testimony, like a promise that family legacy would continue in lives shaped by ancestors' example of choosing hope over despair.

As Scottish stars emerged in a darkening sky, father and daughter stood together beside their ancestor's grave, their relationship restored through shared recognition that some inheritances were worth any journey required to claim them. The pilgrimage that had begun in Glen Lena's attic with discovery of Thomas's letters had brought them full circle to understanding that heritage lived not in possessions but in character, not in what they owned but in who they chose to become through daily decisions that either honored or betrayed the wisdom their ancestors had preserved through centuries of facing their own trials with dignity and grace.

The thistle carved into Margaret's headstone caught the last light of Scottish evening, its stone petals holding promise that beauty would continue blooming long after individual lives ended, that love carefully tended could survive whatever trials the future presented. Calvin and Sara Wilson stood among their ancestors' graves as night claimed Arbuthnott Parish, two people whose own journey from grief to healing had been guided by wisdom preserved across centuries, proof that some stories were powerful enough to inspire transformation in anyone brave enough to seek it, patient enough to receive it, humble enough to pass it forward to those whose hearts were ready to be changed by love that proved stronger than death itself.

The ancient churchyard held them in its peace, the accumulated blessing of centuries spent honoring those who had chosen to build rather than destroy, to love rather than fear, to preserve rather than waste whatever gifts they had been given for the brief time they were permitted to exercise them. Soon they would return to Australia, carrying with them not just genealogical verification but spiritual confirmation that they belonged to something beautiful, something worth preserving, something that would continue inspiring transformation in anyone willing to learn from the example of people who had faced their own darkness and chosen to become light.

Margaret Nicol's thistle bloomed eternal in stone, and in the hearts of descendants who would ensure that her legacy of love and strength continued flowering in lives dedicated to service, beauty, and the patient work of choosing hope over fear in every circumstance that required such choosing.

Sara's Journal
Edinburgh Hotel
May 15th, 2011 - Late evening

The Thistle's Promise Kept
I'm sitting in this small Edinburgh hotel room, my fingers still dusty from touching Margaret Nicol's headstone, and I feel like I've completed a circuit that began when Thomas carved his Celtic cross in the hold of the *Moffatt* 175 years ago. The thistle symbol that sustained him through exile, that guided Rivers through her preservation work, that Dad carved into the cedar box—it was waiting for us in Arbuthnott kirkyard, as sharp and defiant as the day some forgotten mason shaped it from Scottish stone.

The moment my fingers traced those ancient carvings, I understood why this pilgrimage was necessary. Not just to verify genealogical connections or satisfy historical curiosity, but to complete something larger than individual understanding—to prove that love carefully preserved and thoughtfully transmitted could indeed bridge any distance, heal any separation, restore any connection that seemed lost forever.

Dad stood beside me in that ancient churchyard, his carpenter's hands gentle on my shoulders, and we both wept. Not from sadness, but from recognition. We were home— not in any geographic sense, but in the deeper understanding that we belonged to something larger than our individual lives, something that had been building toward this moment across centuries of people who chose hope over despair, service over selfishness, love over the comfortable numbness of limited expectations.

Glen Nevis, Fort William
May 17th, 2011 - Hiking break

Three days since Arbuthnott, and the Scottish landscape keeps revealing new layers of connection. Yesterday we climbed Ben Nevis—not the whole mountain, but high enough to see the pattern of valleys that had shaped our ancestors' understanding of endurance and beauty and the kind of stubborn resilience that finds ways to thrive in circumstances that seem designed to prevent such thriving.

Calvin surprised me by bringing his woodworking tools on this trip. Not for any practical purpose, but because he wanted to create something here, from Scottish wood, that would carry the essence of this pilgrimage back to Australia. This morning he carved a small thistle from rowan wood we found near Loch Lomond, its details so intricate they seem to hold light even in shadow.

"For your desk," he said, presenting it with the shy pride of someone who had discovered that gifts become more precious when they carry the weight of shared experience. "For remembering that some journeys change you in ways that make return impossible—not because you can't go back, but because you don't want to go back to who you were before you understood what home actually meant."

The rowan thistle sits on the hotel windowsill now, catching Edinburgh's evening light like a promise that some things are worth whatever risks love demands. It will travel back to Sydney with us, but it will carry more than wood and craftsmanship—it will carry proof that pilgrimage completed becomes foundation for whatever work awaits.

Scottish National Gallery
May 18th, 2011 – Afternoon

Spent the morning among portraits of Highland clans and landscapes that captured Scotland's capacity for both harshness and heartbreaking beauty. But it was the contemporary section that stopped me cold—an exhibition about immigration and displacement, about people who left these shores to find better lives in distant places that offered what the homeland couldn't provide.

One piece in particular: a video installation showing letters from emigrants to the families they'd left behind, their words scrolling across screens while Gaelic songs provided soundtrack for stories of loss and hope and the particular courage required to trust that the unknown held more possibility than the known offered security.

Standing there, listening to voices that echoed across centuries of separation, I understood finally what my calling is. Not just preserving Thomas and Catherine's memory, but making their example available to anyone whose heart is ready to receive proof that transformation is possible, that love can triumph over any adversity, that redemption remains available even when circumstances seem designed to prevent it.

I want to write their complete story—not as academic history but as literature that captures the universal truth of what they discovered about choosing hope over despair, service over selfishness, vulnerable love over the safety that isolation promises but never truly provides. Their nineteenth-century wisdom can guide twenty-first-century hearts if transmitted with sufficient care and understanding.

Princes Street, Edinburgh
May 19th, 2011 - Final day

Our last morning in Scotland began with sunrise over Edinburgh Castle, light that seemed to illuminate not just ancient stones but the pattern of connections that had brought us here. Dad and I walked the Royal Mile in comfortable silence, understanding that words weren't necessary when hearts had finally learned to recognize home in each other's presence.

But it was in a small bookshop near the cathedral that I found the final piece of this pilgrimage's puzzle: a collection of letters from Scottish emigrants to Australia, published by someone who understood that personal stories become universal truth when shared with sufficient love and care. The introduction spoke directly to what I've been feeling:

"These letters remind us that distance cannot diminish love willing to transcend every limitation, that separation becomes opportunity for deeper connection when approached with faith sufficient to sustain hope across whatever gaps time and geography impose."

That's what I want to create—not just Thomas and Catherine's story, but proof that their example still has power to heal, still can inspire the kind of vulnerable love that makes any loss worthwhile because of the meaning such connection creates. Their transformation from individual brokenness to shared redemption provides a template that works as well today as it did 160 years ago.

The flight home tonight carries more than genealogical satisfaction or tourist memories. We're returning with understanding that changed us in ways that make impossible any retreat to who we were before we touched those ancient stones, before we stood where our bloodline began, before we proved that love carefully preserved can indeed bridge any distance if transmitted with sufficient courage and determination.

Scotland kept its promise. The thistle's resilience proved real. The connection held across centuries and continents, proving that some inheritances transcend material wealth to offer something far more precious: proof that we belong to each other, that love creates bonds stronger than death, that heritage provides foundation for building whatever the future demands from hands willing to work and hearts brave enough to risk everything for others' welfare.

Tomorrow we return to Sydney, but we return as different people—not just father and daughter who rediscovered each other, but inheritors of wisdom that demands sharing, preservers of legacy that requires transmission, carriers of flame that must not be allowed to die with our generation.

The sacred obligation Rivers identified awaits. The real work begins when we get home.

25 PIECING TOGETHER LEGACY

Kirribilli Apartment, Sydney — June through December 2011

The Scotland trip had changed everything, though Sara Wilson wouldn't fully understand the extent of that transformation until months later when the accumulated weight of discovery finally settled into a coherent understanding of what she'd inherited and what such inheritance demanded. The flight home from Edinburgh had carried more than jet-lagged passengers and Scottish souvenirs—it had transported two people whose relationship had been reconstructed on foundations stronger than what grief had destroyed, built from materials that Thomas Staines' letters had helped them understand could be shaped into something beautiful if approached with sufficient patience and faith.

Calvin had moved into her spare room permanently in July, their arrangement evolving from temporary convenience into genuine partnership that honored Ellen's memory while acknowledging that life continued demanding choices about connection versus isolation. They'd discussed it over morning coffee on his first weekend back at his Gosford workshop, Sara surprising herself by suggesting what had been growing obvious through months of shared research and healing.

"The spare room's just sitting there," she'd said, attempting casualness that didn't quite mask the vulnerability such invitation required. "You're here most weekends anyway, and the commute from Gosford is ridiculous when you're helping with the family research. Makes more sense to have a proper base in the city."

Calvin's acceptance had been characteristically understated, his carpenter's practicality allowing him to recognize structural soundness when partnership was built on foundations that could bear weight without excessive ornamentation. "Been thinking the same thing," he'd replied, his hand finding hers across the table. "Not about convenience, though. About wanting to be where you are, wanting to share this journey properly instead of visiting it on weekends like some kind of genealogical tourist."

The months that followed had established rhythms that felt both entirely new and comfortably familiar, as if they were discovering patterns that had always existed but required Thomas's example to make visible. Morning coffee and the newspaper, evening walks along the harbor, weekend trips to libraries and archives as Sara's research expanded beyond immediate family history into broader patterns that connected their Scottish heritage to Australian settlement in ways that suggested stories far larger than any individual narrative could contain.

But it was Sara's decision to reach out to her extended family that transformed private discovery into a collective understanding of what Rivers Staines and William Paterson had preserved through their descendants. The first call had gone to Michael Paterson, a distant cousin whose genealogical hobby had been mentioned briefly in Ellen's papers but never pursued during the years when Sara had been too consumed by grief to recognize that family meant more than nuclear relationships that death could sever completely.

"Sara Wilson?" Michael's voice had carried surprised delight when she'd explained her connection through Ellen to Helena Jean Paterson, his great-aunt whose stories had shaped his childhood understanding of family history that stretched back through convict transportation to Scottish nobility that seemed almost mythological in its distance from contemporary Australian suburban existence. "Been hoping someone from Helena's line would eventually get curious about the family stories. Your grandmother was the keeper of it all—knew every branch, every connection, every story that made us more than just names on genealogical charts."

The conversation had lasted three hours, Michael's systematic knowledge of the Paterson family tree providing a framework that Sara's research into Thomas Staines could fit within like puzzle pieces discovering their proper arrangement. Rivers and William had seven children, though only five survived to adulthood in an era when infant mortality remained a harsh reality even for families who'd achieved relative prosperity through hard work and community respect that Thomas's sacrifice had helped establish as the family legacy.

"Walter junior was the eldest surviving son," Michael had explained, his voice carrying the particular satisfaction that genealogists feel when complex relationships become clear through patient documentation. "Born 1881, married Hannah Brady in 1907 up in Springwood. They're the ones who built Glen Lena—the house you found Thomas's letters in. Three daughters: Annie, Rivers, and Helena Jean, who was your grandmother."

Sara had felt something shift in her understanding as pieces connected in ways that made Ellen's preservation of the letters feel less like random chance and more like intentional transmission from a woman who understood that some stories were too precious to be lost even when immediate family showed no interest in maintaining connection to heritage that had shaped their character whether they recognized it or not.

"Helena Jean was born in 1912," Michael continued, warming to his subject with enthusiasm that suggested he'd been waiting years for someone to share accumulated knowledge that felt wasted when confined to personal notebooks. "Lived until 1986, spent her whole life in the Blue Mountains and Sydney area. She was the one who kept all the family stories alive—not just facts and dates, but the actual narratives about who people were, what they'd overcome, how they'd contributed to building something meaningful from whatever circumstances they'd faced."

The description matched what Sara remembered of her grandmother from childhood visits that had seemed ordinary at the time but now revealed themselves as precious opportunities to absorb family wisdom that Ellen had tried to preserve despite Sara's youthful indifference to anything that didn't involve immediate gratification. Helena Jean had told stories during those visits—about pioneering ancestors and Scottish heritage and the importance of remembering where you came from even when pursuing where you were going.

"She talked about Thomas Staines?" Sara asked, needing confirmation that the letters weren't just private sentiment but part of a larger tradition of preserving wisdom that had shaped multiple generations.

"Constantly," Michael confirmed with a laugh that suggested fond exasperation. "Thomas the convict who became Thomas the hero. Catherine the German immigrant who had courage to cross oceans alone. The flood of 1852 that engulfed Three Rivers Inn and the sacrifice that made him legend rather than merely an ancestor. Helena Jean understood that those stories weren't just family history but instruction about character and courage and what love meant when you measured it against ultimate standards."

The conversation had led to meeting in person, Michael bringing boxes of family documents that complemented Sara's growing archive with photographs and letters and official records that verified oral tradition while revealing additional layers of complexity that made the family story feel richer than any fiction could capture. Walter and Hannah's wedding photo from 1907 showed a serious young couple whose expressions suggested they understood that marriage meant more than romantic partnership—it meant responsibility for carrying forward the legacy that demanded active preservation rather than passive appreciation.

But it was the photograph of Helena Jean from the 1970s that arrested Sara's attention, her grandmother's face revealing intelligence and determination that had been evident even in an elderly woman's interactions with a young child who hadn't yet learned to recognize wisdom when it spoke through stories that seemed like entertainment rather than education. Helena Jean had been keeper of family lore, and Ellen had inherited that role before cancer silenced her voice too early for completing the transmission to daughter who'd been too absorbed in her own grief to recognize what she was losing.

The months from July through October had become a period of intensive research and writing as Sara attempted to honor what Helena Jean had preserved by transforming family history into a narrative that could reach beyond genealogical interest to inspire anyone seeking evidence that transformation was possible despite circumstances that seemed designed to prevent it. The novel had taken shape gradually, each chapter requiring multiple revisions as Sara learned to balance historical accuracy with emotional truth, respecting living family and fictional storytelling to honor Thomas and Catherine's memory while making their example accessible to contemporary readers who faced different challenges but the same fundamental choice between hope and despair.

Calvin's presence during the writing process had proven essential in ways that transcended practical support. His carpenter's understanding of how structures were built—how the foundation determined everything that followed, how patient attention to detail created strength that could bear weight without obvious reinforcement—provided metaphors that helped Sara understand what a successful narrative required. But more than technical assistance, his daily encouragement during difficult stretches when the writing felt inadequate to capture what Thomas's transformation actually meant had sustained her commitment to completing a work that sometimes seemed impossibly ambitious.

"You're not trying to write the perfect book," Calvin would remind her when she'd read passages aloud with a voice that carried frustration over perceived inadequacy. "You're trying to write a true book. There's a difference. Perfect can't be achieved, but true can be approached through honest effort and willingness to honor what you've discovered about love and courage and the possibility of redemption."

The research had expanded in directions that surprised her, each new discovery connecting to previous findings in ways that suggested patterns too consistent to be merely coincidental. The thistle symbol that appeared on Thomas's Celtic cross and Margaret Nicol's grave in Arbuthnott had led to her investigation of Scottish heraldry that revealed connections and disconnections to Stewart lineage and nobility that seemed almost fantastical in its implications for a family that had experienced transportation, immigration, and frontier hardship that should have severed all connection to aristocratic heritage. Was there truth in the Stewart clan connection from centuries long past?

But the documentation she uncovered was undeniable—birth records and marriage certificates and land grants that traced bloodline back through generations of people whose circumstances had changed dramatically but whose essential character had persisted through centuries of people who chose perseverance over surrender when trials tested everything they thought they knew about themselves and their capacity for rebuilding from whatever materials loss had left them.

Sara had created separate files for what she was beginning to think of as the "Agnes Stewart project"—the trail of breadcrumbs that connected the Paterson family through Margaret Nicol and generation after generation of her kin in the shire going all the way back to Lady Agnes Stewart and Scottish nobility whose heritage extended back to royalty that seemed disconnected from a convict grandfather whose letters had initiated this entire journey of discovery. The research felt important but also premature, something that needed more time and deeper investigation before she could understand what such connections meant for a contemporary family trying to build meaningful lives from inherited wisdom that honored both humble circumstances and aristocratic bloodlines.

Michael Paterson had introduced her to other cousins—descendants of Rivers' other children who'd scattered across Australia pursuing opportunities that distance and different circumstances had created, but who'd maintained sufficient connection to family stories to recognize shared heritage when someone finally took the initiative to gather dispersed threads into a coherent narrative. These conversations had revealed how completely Helena Jean had functioned as the central keeper of family lore, her death in 1986 creating a vacuum that Ellen had partially filled but that Sara was now attempting to honor through more permanent preservation that could survive individual lifetimes.

The Paterson family reunion in November had brought together forty-three people whose connection to Thomas Staines ranged from direct descent to marriage relationships that had grafted them into a family tree that bore fruit across five generations. Sara had shared preliminary findings from her research, copies of Thomas's letters and explaining how their discovery had transformed her understanding of what family meant when approached with curiosity that honored both historical accuracy and emotional truth about human capacity for transformation.

The response had been overwhelming—elderly cousins who remembered Helena Jean and her sisters'stories with tears that suggested grief over wisdom that had nearly been lost, a younger generation whose interest in heritage had been awakened by Sara's demonstration that family history could be more than names and dates if someone was willing to invest effort in understanding what those lives had actually meant to people who'd lived them. Several family members had offered their own documents and photographs, materials that would enrich Sara's novel while suggesting possibilities for future projects that could honor different aspects of a shared heritage.

But it was the conversation with Dorothy Brady, Grandma Hannah's grandniece, that had provided the kind of personal testimony that made historical research feel immediately relevant to contemporary life. At seventy-eight, Dorothy carried memories that connected her directly to people who'd known Rivers personally, who'd heard Thomas's story from a daughter who'd spent sixty-six years ensuring her father's sacrifice wouldn't be forgotten.

"My grandmother Annie used to say that Rivers talked about Thomas like he was still present in their lives," Dorothy explained during their conversation over tea at her Katoomba home that overlooked the same Blue Mountains valleys where Thomas had made his journey West and made choices that shaped multiple generations. "Not as a ghost or memory, but as an example that continued guiding anyone willing to learn what his transformation taught about character and courage and the kind of love that made death feel like privilege when faced in service to others."

The testimony had confirmed what Sara's research suggested—that Thomas's letters weren't merely sentimental keepsakes but love left in letter form as active instruction that Rivers had used to guide her children's moral education, not through formal schooling but through daily application of principles he'd proven through choices that culminated in a sacrifice that preserved a community while demonstrating love is stronger than death itself. Rivers had simply lived according to the wisdom her father had transmitted, allowing her example to inspire a generation of children who understood themselves as inheritors of a legacy that demanded demonstration through their own choices.

Glen Lena having passed from the family property with the sale in 2010 had left Dorothy's saddened to have lost that branch of the Patersons' heritage, though it was close-by and she had witnessed the family home become a home to a new family that now lived and thrived in the property. This seemed like a loving and thoughtful solution to the alternative practicality to justify preservation costs. Sara's discovery of the letters had renewed family interest yet the sense of renewal, of new life and a new family taking on the heritage of their historical family home was a sentiment shared by Dorothy. This put Sara at ease in the decision she'd made that in essence severed the physical family connection yet her work was preserving the most precious of the family gifts—memories—and the courage of redemption from life's choices.

The writing itself had become Sara's primary focus during the final months of 2011, each morning beginning with a coffee at the computer as she attempted to capture Thomas and Catherine's journey in prose that honored both historical accuracy and emotional truth about love that transcended individual circumstances to demonstrate universal principles about redemption and transformation. The novel had grown to sixty thousand words by October, its dual timeline structure allowing her to weave the nineteenth-century narrative with a contemporary story of discovery and healing that made historical events feel relevant to modern readers.

Calvin had begun reading chapters as she completed them, his responses providing guidance about what worked and what needed revision to achieve clarity that served both literary quality and wisdom transmission. His particular attention to scenes between Thomas and Catherine revealed his understanding that their relationship wasn't just a romantic subplot but the central demonstration of how two broken people could create something beautiful together through mutual commitment to serving each other's welfare rather than demanding personal satisfaction.

"This scene where Thomas first tells Catherine about his crime," Calvin said one evening, pointing to a passage that Sara had struggled with for weeks. "You've captured his shame but also his determination to be honest rather than build a relationship on deception. That's not just historical accuracy—that's instruction about what authentic connection requires. Any reader who's ever faced a choice between protecting comfortable illusion and risking a painful truth will recognize themselves in this moment."

The observation had helped Sara understand that her novel's power would come not from dramatic plot developments or surprising revelations, but from honest portrayal of the human struggle with choices that determined whether lives would be defined by the worst moments or by the sustained effort to become worthy of love that had been offered despite inadequacy. Thomas's transformation wasn't one single dramatic conversion but accumulated daily decisions to choose service over selfishness, courage over comfort, vulnerable honesty over protective distance.

By December, the novel had reached eighty thousand words and felt close to completion, though Sara understood that finishing a first draft was only the beginning of the revision process that would refine prose while ensuring that every scene served a larger purposes of demonstrating redemption's availability to anyone willing to undertake its patient work. She'd begun researching publishers, though publication felt less urgent than completing a manuscript that honored Thomas and Catherine's memory while proving their example could still inspire contemporary transformation.

But more important than literary achievement was recognition that the writing process itself had completed her own healing, transforming grief that had threatened to define her permanently into the motivation for creating beauty that honored Ellen's memory while serving purposes larger than personal satisfaction. The novel would be dedicated to her mother, whose preservation of Thomas's letters had made this entire journey possible, but also to Helena Jean, whose role as keeper of family lore had maintained the connection across generations that might otherwise have lost touch with a heritage that shaped their character whether they recognized it or not.

The Christmas tree that Sara and Calvin decorated together in mid-December carried ornaments that reflected their journey—a pressed Scottish thistle from the Edinburgh trip, the miniature anvil that Calvin had carved to represent Thomas's craft, a photograph of Ellen that reminded them why preservation mattered when approached with love rather than mere duty. They'd invited Michael Paterson and several other cousins for Christmas dinner, their celebration becoming a family gathering that honored both immediate relationships and extended connections that research had revealed and strengthened.

"To Thomas and Catherine," Calvin proposed a toast during dinner, his glass raised toward their company that represented five generations of people whose lives had been shaped by choices made during the Wellington flood of 1852. "To their courage in facing what seemed impossible, their faith in building something beautiful from broken materials, their love that proved stronger than any force that threatened to destroy what patient work and mutual commitment had created."

The response around the table confirmed Sara's understanding that she'd accomplished more than historical documentation or literary achievement—she'd helped reconnect family members whose shared heritage had been obscured by distance and different circumstances, creating a community that could support each other while honoring ancestors whose sacrifices had made their existence possible. This was what Rivers had envisioned when she'd written about sacred obligation requiring demonstration through contemporary application of inherited wisdom.

But Sara also understood that her work was incomplete in ways that would require years of additional research and writing to fully honor. The Agnes Stewart connection beckoned from files that contained tantalizing hints about nobility and royal bloodlines that connected her convict grandfather to a heritage that seemed impossibly distant from circumstances that transportation had imposed. That investigation would require Scottish archives and genealogical expertise beyond what she currently possessed, patient work that might eventually produce a second book exploring different aspects of the family story that Thomas's letters had initiated but couldn't fully confirm.

For now, though, it was enough to have completed the immediate journey—from grief to healing, from isolation to connection, from a daughter who'd lost her mother to a woman who understood that family meant more than nuclear relationships death could sever. She'd found her father again through Thomas's example of transformation, discovered her extended family through research that honored Helena Jean's preservation of family lore, created a literary work that proved some stories were powerful enough to inspire change across centuries and continents.

The novel sat on her desk in the manuscript box, awaiting final revisions before submission to publishers, but already serving its primary purpose—demonstration that love carefully preserved and thoughtfully transmitted could heal wounds across generations, bridge gaps that seemed unbridgeable, restore connections that loss and pride and fear had damaged beyond what ordinary effort could repair. Thomas had learned to love so completely that death became the final gift to those he cherished.

Rivers had preserved his memory so that such love wouldn't die with his body. Helena Jean had maintained family stories so that multiple generations could learn from his example. Ellen had kept the letters safe until someone was ready to receive their guidance.

Now Sara was carrying the flame forward, proving that the sacred obligation continued as long as someone was willing to choose service over selfishness, hope over despair, vulnerable love over safety that isolation promised but never truly provided. The river flowed on, carrying their voices into whatever future awaited anyone willing to listen. And she had learned to listen well.

Sara's Journal

Entries — July through December 2011

July 15, 2011

Kirribilli Apartment — Morning

Dad moved in yesterday. Not visiting, not staying over on weekends—actually moved in with his tools and clothes and the particular way he arranges his morning coffee ritual that I've come to recognize as meditation rather than mere habit. We didn't make a big production of it, didn't need to acknowledge what we both understood: that Ellen's death had damaged us badly, but Thomas's example was teaching us how to rebuild from materials that seemed inadequate for creating anything beautiful.

The spare room looks different now—occupied rather than waiting, used rather than preserved as a shrine to absence. His carpentry tools rest in a corner near the window where light's best for detail work. His reading glasses sit on the bedside table next to a book about Scottish castles that we're reading together, planning future trips to explore heritage that research keeps revealing in layers that suggest stories far larger than what Thomas's letters could contain alone.

This feels right in ways I couldn't have imagined six months ago when grief made even breathing feel like betrayal of a mother I'd failed to appreciate while she was alive. We're healing. Not forgetting, not moving on as if Ellen's death was an obstacle to overcome rather than loss to honor—but healing through shared purpose that transforms grief into motivation for building something meaningful from what inheritance has provided.

August 3, 2011
State Library — Afternoon

Michael Paterson brought family photographs today—three generations of Patersons whose faces reveal a mixture of Scottish determination and Australian adaptability that seems to have persisted across a century of people choosing persistence over surrender when circumstances tested their faith in possibilities that couldn't be guaranteed. Walter and Hannah's wedding photo from 1907 shows a young couple whose seriousness suggests they understood marriage meant more than romantic happiness—it meant responsibility for carrying forward a legacy that demanded active preservation.

But it's the photograph of Grandmother Helena Jean from the 1970s that I keep returning to, her face revealing an intelligence that I remember from childhood visits but hadn't recognized as wisdom that came from decades of preserving family stories that shaped her understanding of what really mattered. She looks directly at the camera with an expression that seems to say: "Pay attention. This matters. Don't let it be lost because you're too absorbed in immediate concerns to recognize what you're inheriting."

I failed to pay attention then, too young to understand that her stories weren't just entertainment but instruction about character and courage and the kind of love that made Thomas's sacrifice feel like victory rather than tragedy. But I'm paying attention now, trying to honor what she preserved by transforming family history into a narrative that can reach beyond genealogical curiosity to inspire anyone seeking proof that transformation is possible.

Michael mentioned that Helena Jean used to say that every generation had responsibility to preserve what previous generations had accumulated, but also to add their own contribution through choices that honored inheritance while serving contemporary needs. That's what I'm trying to do with the novel—not just preserve Thomas's story but demonstrate how it can guide modern choices about healing and connection and the vulnerability that genuine love always requires.

September 22, 2011
Circular Quay — Evening

The novel reached fifty thousand words today. Thomas and Catherine have met in the Bathurst market square, their initial conversation revealing two people whose separate journeys through exile and hardship prepared them to recognize in each other the possibility for building something beautiful together. Writing their courtship feels like discovering a template for what a healthy relationship looks like when it's based on mutual service rather than mere personal satisfaction.

But I'm also learning something about my own relationship with Dad through this writing process. The way Thomas chose honesty over comfortable deception when telling Catherine about his crime—that's what Dad and I are learning to practice with each other. The way Catherine accepted Thomas's past without either dismissing its significance or allowing it to define their future—that's what we're learning to do with our shared grief over Ellen's death.

The writing isn't just historical recreation. It's an instruction manual I'm creating for myself, for Dad, for anyone who reads it someday and recognizes their own struggle with choices between safety and connection, between protecting comfortable distance and risking the vulnerability that genuine love demands.

October 31, 2011
Katoomba — Visit with Dorothy Paterson

Dorothy talked today about Rivers with a voice that carried personal connection despite never having met her great-grandmother. "Rivers understood," Dorothy said, "that Thomas's transformation wasn't just an interesting family history but proof that anyone could rebuild character from broken materials if they were willing to choose hope over despair when circumstances tested their faith."

The testimony confirmed what my research suggested—that Rivers didn't need formal educational programs or public recognition to transmit Thomas's wisdom effectively. She simply lived according to principles he'd proven through his choices, allowing her example to inspire children who understood themselves inheritors of a legacy that demanded demonstration through their own lives.

That's what Helena Jean did for her family. That's what Ellen tried to do for me before cancer silenced her voice. That's what I'm attempting to do now through the novel that grows daily on my desk—proving that preservation without transmission is selfish sentimentality, while sharing through story makes wisdom available to anyone whose heart is ready to receive it.

Dorothy wanted to visit, and we took in a glimpse of Glen Lena from the outside—Dorothy recalling visiting there as a child, absorbing family stories, soaking up the memories... it made everything feel more real. More connected. More like responsibility I'm honored to carry rather than burden I'm obligated to bear.

November 20, 2011
Paterson Family Reunion — Springwood Community Hall

Forty-three people gathered today, all descended from or married into Rivers Paterson's family, all carrying fragments of Thomas's story that Helena Jean had worked so hard to preserve before her death in 1986. Watching them respond to Thomas's letters that I'd copied and shared—seeing elderly cousins cry at words their great-great-grandfather had written to a daughter he'd die to protect—I understood completely why Rivers had called this a sacred obligation.

Several younger relatives asked if I'd teach them how to research their own family branches, how to document and preserve stories before the last people who remember them are gone. Michael suggested creating a family website, like on Ancestry.com,where everyone could contribute what they know, building a collective archive that honors Helena Jean's work while adapting it to the digital age where information can reach people who might never attend physical reunions but who need connection to heritage that shaped their character.

This is what transmission looks like in practical terms—not just preserving documents in cedar chests, but actively sharing wisdom with anyone willing to learn from examples that prove transformation is possible. Dad and I are planning a series of workshops for the local historical society, teaching preservation techniques while emphasizing that documentation alone isn't enough. The stories must be told, shared, used to guide contemporary choices about how to love and live and build meaningful connections despite risks such building always requires.

December 15, 2011
Kirribilli Apartment — Late night

The manuscript sits in a box on my desk—eighty thousand words that trace Thomas and Catherine's journey from individual brokenness to shared healing, from exile to belonging, from love that takes to love that gives everything including life itself for others' welfare. It's not finished yet, needs revisions and polishing and probably twenty thousand more words to fully capture what their transformation meant for anyone seeking guidance about redemption and hope.

But it's real now, tangible proof that I've honored the inheritance Ellen left when she preserved Thomas's letters in that cedar chest. More than that, it's evidence that I've completed my own journey from grief-paralyzed daughter to a woman who understands that family means more than nuclear relationships that death can sever. Dad and I have rebuilt something stronger than what we had before, a foundation created from shared purpose rather than mere biological connection.

The research has revealed trails I haven't fully explored yet—connections to Agnes Stewart and Scottish nobility that suggest our family story extends back centuries further than what Thomas's convict transportation might initially suggest. That investigation will require years of additional work, possibly another book that explores different aspects of heritage that shaped the people who faced their various trials with courage that revealed strength rather than weakness.

But that's for future Sara to pursue. Tonight's Sara is content with what's been accomplished—a novel that honors Thomas and Catherine's memory, a relationship with Dad that's been healed through shared discovery, extended family connections that Michael and Dorothy and dozens of cousins represent, an understanding that some loves are indeed strong enough to transcend death itself through legacies they create in hearts willing to receive their guidance.

The river flows on, carrying voices into whatever future awaits anyone brave enough to believe that redemption remains possible, that healing can happen, that transformation is available to those willing to choose it. I've learned to listen to those voices. More importantly, I've learned to add my own voice to the eternal conversation that connects all who choose hope over despair, service over selfishness, vulnerable love over the safety that isolation promises but never truly provides.

Thomas's gift to Rivers has become Rivers' gift to Helena Jean has become Helena Jean's gift to Ellen has become Ellen's gift to me. Now I'm preparing to gift it forward to anyone whose heart is ready to receive proof that the best stories aren't just told—they're lived, shared, and carried forward until they become indistinguishable from the very character of the people they've inspired to love more bravely than fear suggests is possible.

The sacred obligation is fulfilled. The flame carried forward. The story continuing as long as someone believes it's worth preserving, worth sharing, worth living according to the wisdom it contains about what makes life meaningful when measured against ultimate standards that honor both individual dignity and collective welfare.

Tonight I'll sleep well, knowing I've done what Rivers and Helena Jean and Ellen hoped someone would eventually do—prove that their preservation efforts weren't wasted, that Thomas's transformation can still inspire change across centuries, that love this deep never dies but continues healing wounds and bridging gaps and restoring connections for anyone willing to risk everything for the chance of genuine belonging.

The thistle blooms eternal. The promise kept. The river flowing on forever.

26 THE SACRED OBLIGATION

Gleebooks Bookshop, Glebe — October 2012

Sara Wilson stood before forty strangers and friends in the intimate bookshop where floor-to-ceiling shelves and worn wooden floors created the kind of space where stories felt at home. Ten months had passed since she'd finished writing *The Blacksmith's Bequest*, and tonight marked the third public reading since its publication in August. The autumn evening carried the softness of Sydney spring, and through the shop's front windows she could see people passing on Glebe Point Road, unaware that inside, a story about transformation and love was about to be shared.

Calvin sat in the front row beside Margaret Chen from the State Library, whose archival expertise had made the research possible. Michael Paterson had brought several cousins—descendants of Rivers and Walter who'd contributed photographs and memories that enriched the family history Sara had woven into the novel. Dorothy Paterson, at seventy-eight, had traveled from Katoomba to hear how Sara had honored the stories Helena Jean had worked so hard to preserve.

But it was the strangers who moved Sara most—people who'd discovered the book through word of mouth or library browsing, who'd come seeking stories about redemption and second chances, about families healing across distances that grief had imposed. A young woman in the third row clutched a worn copy that suggested multiple readings. An elderly man sat with his daughter, their shared attention suggesting the book had sparked conversations between them. A middle-aged couple held hands, their body language speaking of struggles survived and connections preserved.

"Thank you for coming tonight," Sara began, her voice steady in ways it hadn't been at the first reading back in August when publication had felt both thrilling and terrifying. "This story began with a discovery in my late mother's attic—letters written by my great-great-great-grandfather Thomas Staines, a convicted thief transported to Australia in 1835. What I found in those letters changed everything I thought I knew about family, about redemption, and about the obligation we carry to preserve wisdom earned through suffering."

She had debated what passage to read, eventually choosing the moment when Thomas first meets Catherine in Bathurst market square—two broken people recognizing in each other the possibility for building something beautiful together. The scene captured the novel's heart without revealing its devastating climax, allowing listeners to discover for themselves how Thomas's transformation would be tested by circumstances that demanded everything love could offer.

The reading lasted fifteen minutes, Sara's voice carrying the nineteenth-century dialogue she'd crafted to honor both historical authenticity and emotional truth. When she finished, the silence held weight—recognition that they'd witnessed something more than historical fiction, that Thomas and Catherine's journey connected to their own struggles with choices between fear and faith, isolation and connection.

The questions that followed revealed how deeply the story had resonated. A woman whose mother was battling dementia asked about preserving family memories before they were lost. A man struggling with his adult son's addiction wanted to understand whether Thomas's transformation proved that redemption was possible for people whose choices had damaged everything they'd built. A young teacher asked how to help students understand that mistakes didn't have to define futures if character development was genuine.

Sara answered honestly, sharing what she'd learned during the two years between discovering the letters and publishing the novel. "Thomas spent seventeen years proving through daily choices that his transformation was real. That's what I learned—that redemption isn't an event, it's a process. It requires patience and consistency and the willingness to keep choosing service over selfishness even when no one's watching."

During the break before signing, Calvin joined her beside the display table stacked with copies of *The Blacksmith's Bequest*. Their relationship had found its balance over the past two years—not the careful distance that had characterized the time since Ellen's death, but genuine partnership that honored her memory while acknowledging that life continued.

"Your mother would have loved seeing this," Calvin said quietly, and Sara understood he meant not just the publication success but the way the story was reaching people who needed exactly what Thomas had learned about transformation and hope.

"She kept the letters safe until someone was ready to understand them," Sara replied. "I'm just grateful I finally paid attention."

The signing line moved steadily, each reader bringing their own story of why the book had mattered. A woman who'd left an abusive marriage and was rebuilding her life. A man who'd recently retired and was examining choices he'd made during decades of career focus. A couple whose marriage had survived near-collapse and who saw their own journey reflected in Thomas and Catherine's determination to choose each other despite circumstances that made surrender seem easier.

Margaret Chen waited until the crowd thinned before approaching with the librarian's particular satisfaction at seeing research yield fruit beyond academic documentation. "You've done something remarkable," she said. "Not just preserved a family story, but proved it still has power to change people's understanding of what's possible."

Dorothy Paterson was the last to have her copy signed, her weathered hands trembling slightly as she opened to the dedication page where Sara had honored Ellen, Helena Jean, Rivers, and all the women who had understood that some stories were too precious to be lost through inadequate preservation.

"Helena Jean would be so proud," Dorothy said, her voice thick with emotion. "She spent her whole life keeping Thomas's memory alive, making sure we understood that his sacrifice meant something. You've carried that work forward in ways she could never have imagined."

The bookshop emptied gradually, staff beginning to stack chairs while Sara gathered her reading copy and the flowers several people had brought. Calvin helped collect the remaining promotional materials, their movements synchronized by months of collaboration on projects that honored the past while serving present needs.

Outside, Glebe Point Road bustled with evening foot traffic—students from the university, young families, elderly couples walking dogs. Sara and Calvin joined the flow, heading toward the car park where they'd left Calvin's truck. The October air carried the scent of jasmine from someone's garden, and overhead, stars were beginning to appear in the darkening sky.

"The historical society wants you for their November lecture series," Calvin mentioned as they walked. "And Michael said several cousins are interested in your workshops about preservation techniques."

Sara nodded, understanding that the novel's publication had opened doors to serve the broader purpose Rivers had identified as sacred obligation—not just preserving family wisdom but transmitting it actively, demonstrating through creative work and community education that historical examples could guide contemporary choices about character and courage.

But more important than professional opportunities was the recognition that she had changed through this journey. The woman who'd discovered Thomas's letters in January 2011 had been paralyzed by grief, isolated from her father, uncertain about her capacity to honor what she'd inherited. The woman walking through Glebe tonight had been healed through the process of honoring that inheritance, had rebuilt relationships that grief had damaged, had found purpose that connected personal healing to community service.

They drove home through streets that had once carried convict labor and immigrant hope, crossing the harbor bridge where lights reflected off water that connected all rivers to sea. Sara watched the city lights and thought about the forty people who'd gathered tonight to hear a story about transformation—forty hearts that had been touched by Thomas's example, forty lives that might be changed by understanding that redemption remained available to anyone willing to choose it.

"Thank you," she said to Calvin as they neared Kirribilli, the words carrying weight beyond simple courtesy.

"For what?"

"For believing this mattered. For helping me understand that Mom's preservation of those letters wasn't random but intentional, that we had an obligation to honor what Helena Jean and Rivers and all the women before them had worked to maintain."

Calvin reached across to squeeze her hand briefly before returning his attention to the road. "We honored Ellen by finishing what she started. That's what family does—carries forward what previous generations preserved, adds what they can through their own choices, then passes it on to whoever comes next."

They parked and climbed the stairs to her apartment, their home now in ways that acknowledged their partnership while maintaining respect for the journey that had brought them here. Inside, Sara set down her bag and moved to the window overlooking the harbor, watching ferries cut through dark water, their lights marking passages between shores.

The novel was out in the world now, carrying Thomas and Catherine's story to anyone whose heart was ready to receive wisdom about love that proved stronger than death when transmitted through careful preservation and thoughtful sharing. The sacred obligation had been fulfilled not through explanation or interpretation but through story that honored their memory while trusting readers to discover for themselves what their transformation meant.

Sara thought about Thomas writing his final letter while flood waters rose around Three Rivers Inn, his choice to hold the failing beam so others could escape to safety, his recognition that love meant giving everything when circumstances demanded such giving. She had carried his voice forward across 160 years, proving that some loves were indeed strong enough to transcend time itself when preserved with sufficient care and transmitted with adequate skill.

The river flowed on, carrying their voices into whatever future awaited anyone willing to listen. And she had learned to listen well—learned, too, to add her own voice to the eternal conversation about transformation and hope, about family obligations and personal growth, about the kind of love that made any sacrifice seem small when measured against the privilege of having been trusted with others' welfare.

Tomorrow would bring new projects, new opportunities to honor heritage while serving contemporary needs. But tonight belonged to recognition that she had completed the work—had honored Ellen's preservation, fulfilled Rivers' sacred obligation, proved that Thomas's transformation could still inspire change across centuries.

The story continued. The obligation carried forward. The river flowed forever.

THE BLACKSMITH'S BEQUEST

Three Rivers Inn, Wellington, New South Wales
26th August, 1852 - Final Hour

My Dearest Rivers,

The moment approaches when I must choose between my own life and the lives of twenty souls who depend upon my decision, and I write these final words with hands that tremble not from fear but from the overwhelming power of love too vast for mortal expression. You have given me six hours of perfect happiness, six hours of understanding what it means to hold one's entire world in arms that ache with the knowledge that such holding must soon end.

The structural beam that supports this building fails even as I write, its collapse inevitable within minutes rather than hours. But human strength can supplement its failing capacity just long enough for evacuation to be completed, for those who have become my responsibility to reach safety that will outlast whatever destruction claims our temporary refuge.

I have studied your sleeping face by candlelight that reveals features destined to grow into beauty that honors both your mother's German heritage and whatever Scottish characteristics you inherit from bloodlines that stretch back through generations of people who understood that some things are worth any sacrifice love can make. Your perfect trust as you rest against my chest teaches me that death is a small price to pay for the privilege of being called your father, however briefly.

The choice before me is no choice at all—it is completion of a transformation that began seventeen years ago when pride and desperation led me to steal what belonged to another, continued through seven years of bondage that taught me what character meant when external supports were stripped away, and reaches fulfillment in this moment when love demands everything and I discover that everything feels like insufficient offering for the gift of having held you.

Mrs. Patterson will help your mother through whatever trials lie ahead. The community that has witnessed my journey from shame to honor will extend protection that includes my wife and child. You will inherit not just my letters but the memory of love that proved strong enough to create new life despite circumstances that seemed designed to make such creativity impossible.

I am not dying, my precious daughter—I am completing the work that love began when it taught me to place others' welfare above my own survival. Every choice I have made since learning what redemption meant has prepared me for this final demonstration that some gifts can only be given once but their value lasts forever.

The cross is yours, as is the knowledge that your father's love for you proved strong enough to make any sacrifice seem small compared to the privilege of having been trusted with your care, even for six hours that contained more meaning than most receive in lifetimes measured by decades rather than moments of perfect understanding.

Remember me as the man who learned to live so completely that death became his final gift to those he loved. Remember that transformation is always possible, that redemption waits for anyone brave enough to seek it, that love proves stronger than any adversity when offered with faith sufficient to sustain hope even when hope seems impossible to maintain.

Your devoted father, whose love makes him immortal,

Thomas Staines

I go now to hold the beam that will preserve twenty lives through sacrifice of one. The river gives and takes in the same moment, but love gives forever and takes nothing that matters when measured by proper standards. Until we meet again, my darling child—and we shall meet again, for love this deep creates connections that death can interrupt but never sever.

THE END

ABOUT THE AUTHOR

Joss G. Hamilton writes fiction that bridges the gap between documented fact and emotional truth, specializing in sagas that illuminate universal themes through intimate stories of transformation and redemption. His work emerges from a deep fascination with the ordinary people whose extraordinary choices shape the communities they inhabit.

Born into a family of storytellers, Joss developed an early appreciation for the power of preserved memory and carefully transmitted wisdom. His genealogical research has taken him from Scottish kirkyards to Australian colonial archives, always seeking the human stories that breathe life into historical records and family documents.

The Blacksmith's Bequest represents the culmination of years of research into Scottish and Australian heritage, combined with a novelist's understanding of how past wisdom can guide contemporary choices. The story emerged from a recent pilgrimage to Scotland, where ancient gravestones and family documents revealed connections that spanned centuries and continents.

When not writing, Joss explores people's stories where the past remains vivid enough to inform the present. He believes that family stories, when preserved, can become universal tools for inspiring transformation in anyone willing to receive their guidance. Behind the pen name stands a writer committed to proving that redemption remains possible for anyone brave enough to choose it. Joss lives in Australia with his family, surrounded by trees, birds and kangaroos that continue to inspire new chapters in stories he thought he already knew completely.

www.ingramcontent.com/pod-product-compliance
Lightning Source LLC
Chambersburg PA
CBHW051258250626
47155CB00009B/3340